Disappearances

Disappearances

Howard Frank Mosher

A NONPAREIL BOOK
David R. Godine, Publisher, Inc.
BOSTON

This is a Nonpareil Book
first published in softcover in 1984 by
David R. Godine, Publisher, Inc.
Horticultural Hall
300 Massachusetts Avenue
Boston, Massachusetts 02115

Published in 1987 in a new softcover format
with the original text completely reset
in a clearer, more readable typeface.

First published in hardcover in 1977 by The Viking Press
Copyright © 1977 by Howard Frank Mosher
Cover illustration copyright © 1984 by John Stockwell

Library of Congress Cataloging in Publication Data
Mosher, Howard Frank.
Disappearances.
(A Nonpareil book; 33)
Reprint. Originally published: New York: The Viking Press, 1977.
I. Title. II. Series.
PZ4.M91137Di [PS3563.08844] 813'.8'4 77-22083
ISBN 0-87923-524-1 (pbk.)

First printing
Printed in the United States of America

To Phillis

Disappearances

I

MY father was a man of indefatigable optimism. As a hill farmer during the Depression Quebec Bill Bonhomme had opportunities almost daily to succumb to total despair, but he was impervious to discouragement of every kind. His hopefulness was as inexorable as the northern Vermont weather, and much more dependable. Invariably he predicted a long mellow autumn, a short mild winter and an early spring. It made no difference to him if it was the middle of May and snowing hard with six inches of new snow in the dooryard. He would squint up through the driving flakes and say to me, "Wild Bill, this is the snow that takes the snow. This is the poor man's fertilizer." Then he would predict the earliest spring on record.

I cannot remember such a phenomenon as an early spring in Kingdom County. In late April when the maple trees near Burlington and Rutland and White River Junction were beginning to leaf out, Kingdom County was still getting its best runs of sap. The crocuses around the statue of Ethan Allen on the central green in Kingdom Common blossomed two weeks later than the crocuses forty miles south in St. Johnsbury. My mother's spring flowers were always a week behind those in the Common. Once on the first day of June I measured six feet of snow in a secluded hollow behind our sugar house. Isolated as we were at the end of a dirt road fifteen miles from the Common, every winter seemed interminable to us. By the time mud season arrived even my mother was listening to my father's reckless forecasts while pretending not to.

In his preoccupation with weather, if not in his optimism, my father was no different from most of our neighbors. Up and down Lord Hollow and throughout Kingdom County weather was an infinite source of discourse and speculation. Like farmers everywhere we depended on it for luck with our crops, but weather was intrinsically important to us as well because it provided one of the few external changes in our lives in Kingdom County, which was cut off from the rest of New England by two long mountain ranges, several rings of abrupt wooded hills, poor roads and the seven-month winters themselves.

Talk about weather links me to my youth, so that now when September comes it seems much less than nearly half a century ago that my Uncle Henry Coville drove up the hollow on fall evenings in the white Cadillac he used to run whiskey out of Canada and sat with his feet on the kitchen stove cataloguing signs for the impending winter. Evening after evening Uncle Henry talked on in his speculative and faintly ironic manner, predicting a severe or easy winter according to the scarcity or abundance of beechnuts and butternuts, the thickness of the bears' coats, the date of the first big flock of southbound geese. Sometimes at dusk geese would go over, and we would go out in the dooryard and listen intently until they were out of

4

earshot. If it was a large flock Uncle Henry would resettle his boots on the tarnished ornamental skirt of the stove and say, "It will be a hard snow now within ten days."

Almost always he was right. And almost always snow was still on the ground when the first geese returned, flying high over our hilltop toward the big wild lakes across the border in Canada.

Soon after the geese arrived mud season set in. As the snow slowly melted, the hollow road dissolved into an impassable quagmire. There was no way to get our milk down to the county road for the truck that came out from the creamery in the Common. For two or three weeks every spring we had to feed hundreds of gallons of rich Jersey milk to the hogs. From Monday through Friday my Aunt Cordelia and I walked the five miles to and from the one-room schoolhouse at the foot of the hollow, where she had taught for more than sixty years.

During mud season most hollow families kept their children home from school to help with sugaring. Often I was the only student present. On those days my aunt taught me as rigorously as she ever taught a roomful of scholars, drilling me from early morning until late afternoon in Caesar, Euclid, Shakespeare, Emerson. The spring I was fourteen and preparing to enter the Common Academy in the fall she made me memorize Emerson's poem "Hamatreya" in its entirety, while outside the tall windows with small panes and oval tops the April sun I longed for shone hot and bright for a solid week, drying the muddy hollow road, melting the dark ice on Lake Memphremagog and drawing more sap up the maples than anyone could ever hope to collect.

It was perfect sugaring weather, warm days and clear cold nights, but the previous fall we had cut and sold our maples to buy hay. Now we were out of hay again, with at least two more weeks to go before we could turn our cows out to pasture. I was on edge all day and so was my aunt.

At ninety, Cordelia stood six feet tall. She was gangling and awkward looking, like the blue heron that stood on one leg in our brook in July and August, and she could lash out as fast and accurately with her yardstick as the heron stabbing a brook trout with its long sharp bill. There were many days when she was very free with the yardstick, and this was one of them. For a week I had been her only student. Infuriated by this prolonged absenteeism, she claimed that if she had whipped the parents and grandparents harder and more frequently they would not hold their children out of school now, sugaring or no sugaring. That was an oversight she did not intend to repeat with me. By three o'clock when I finally got through "Hamatreya" without a mistake she had given me at least a dozen whacks on the head.

"Remain standing," Aunt Cordelia said, "and tell me the point of the poem."

It had not occurred to me that "Hamatreya" or any other poem had such a peculiarity as a point. I shared this observation with my aunt, who promptly reached down from her platform and administered a smart crack across my head with the yardstick.

"The point," she said, "is that all land ownership is an illusion. Sometime you will understand that. And sometime you will have sense enough to apply it and leave this forsaken land."

"Why don't you leave it?" I said.

Cordelia gave me a perfunctory whack in case I was being impertinent, as in fact I was, and said, "Because it is also an illusion to believe that anyplace else is much different. But you will have to leave here to find that out for yourself."

I was bewildered. Staying in Kingdom County and owning land was an illusion. Leaving was an illusion too. What was real? Staying and renting? Such paradoxes were typical of Cordelia, who like many outstanding teachers was totally unpredictable. Whether I agreed with her or disagreed with her or simply didn't understand her, I rarely forgot anything she said.

Curiously, her ruthless pedagogical techniques seemed to inspire her students to audacity. "Cordelia, is poetry an illusion?"

She looked at me sharply, her eyes as dark and alert as a heron's. Then she put the yardstick on her desk. "Yes," she said, "poetry is also an illusion. But it is like the Bible. There is sufficient truth in it to merit its study."

She looked past me out the windows. "School is dismissed, William. Your father is coming."

By the time our converted Model A farm truck jolted to a stop outside the schoolhouse, its wheels straddling the deep ruts in the road, I was ready to jump in. My father was whooping over the clattering engine. At first I thought he was shouting about running out of hay, but I should have known better.

"The ice is out of the bay," he hollered. "The ice just went out of the bay, Wild Bill. The run is on."

Twenty minutes later, after an unbroken panegyric to spring, my father whooped again as we turned into the lane between the hotel and the commission barn in the Common. He skidded up beside Uncle Henry's gleaming Cadillac and before I was out of the truck he was sprinting across the vacant lot toward the group of a dozen or so men on the ledge along the Lower Kingdom River just below the falls. By the time I had sauntered over, too conscious of my new height to run in public, my father was standing next to Uncle Henry. His red knitted cap came just even with my uncle's shoulder. Everyone was looking intently down into the rushing milky water below the falls. At the foot of the rapids I saw a single trout flash.

"Here they come, boys," my father shouted. "Thousands of them. The run is on, spring is here."

The trout flashed again. It started up the rapids. At the base of the falls it arched out of the water. For the briefest moment it hung motionless just below the lip of the falls, whipping its tail furiously. Then it was driven tumbling back downriver.

Immediately it surged up through the heavy water again. It leaped, ricocheted across the surface of the falls at a glancing upward angle and was slammed onto the wet rocks at our feet. It thrashed back into the river and was carried helplessly down through the rapids.

Uncle Henry knelt and scooped something off the ledge. He cupped his hand and held it out to show us. Rolling on his palm were several minute saffron eggs.

"Spawn," my father said. "That's gold, boys. Little yellow drops of gold. Hang onto them now, Henry. Them are precious."

Warden R. W. Kinneson was watching us from further down along the ledge, but my father and Uncle Henry paid no attention to him. Uncle Henry pointed downriver, where another trout was coming. It too was smashed back onto the granite shelf as it tried to ascend the near side of the falls. It tailwalked frantically, as though trying to portage out around the falls. Cutting across the broad band of vivid red along its side was a raw gray gash.

At the sight of this wound my father couldn't restrain himself. Quick as an otter he pounced on the flailing trout. In a single motion he caught it behind the gills and heaved it high over the falls. For a second it churned on top of the water; then it was gone upriver. All along the ledge men were laughing and cheering. My father held his dripping hands clasped over his head and shook them.

Out of hay and out of money, with two or three more weeks left before he could turn his cows outside, another man would have been sick with anxiety. My father was performing an intricate French Canadian stepdance, humming a loud jig in a nasal tone, playing an imaginary fiddle. Spring was coming, boys. The trout were running and he was assisting them. He couldn't contain his exuberance and had no intention of trying.

"Here comes Kinneson," Uncle Henry said.

R.W. was coming fast along the ledge. His brown warden's hat jutted out at an officious angle. He planted himself between my father and the river as though to protect the fish from further depredations. My heart began to go faster.

"Don't you know it's against the law to handle those fish?" R.W. said. He made it sound as though handling fish was a heinous and unnatural act. "There's a one-hundred-dollar fine for molesting a spawner."

"We wouldn't want to do that now," my father said, giving his fiddle bow an extra fillip. "We wouldn't want to molest a spawner, would we, boys?"

Some of the men snickered. R.W.'s face was burning. He took a step closer to my father. R.W. was a big man, nearly as big as Uncle Henry, and about my uncle's age, thirty-five or so. My father was just over five feet tall, weighed just over a hundred pounds, and was past fifty.

"The trouble with you overweight outlaws and Frenchmen," R.W. said, "is you don't know how to show proper respect for a white man."

"Certainly we do," my father said, leaping straight up and driving both feet into R.W.'s uniformed chest.

"See him flounder," Uncle Henry said critically, as though there were something slightly indecorous about the manner in which R.W. was swirling down through the rapids.

I was afraid R.W. might drown and my father would have to go to jail, but the warden had an obstreperous self-righteous indestructibility—his inflated opinion of himself kept him afloat. He pulled himself out onto the rocks at the foot of the whitewater and lay there gasping like a stranded trout.

My father was dancing again. He jumped high, laid his body out parallel to the ledge, twisted and landed on his feet to demonstrate his technique.

"Put the boots to him, Quebec Bill," a man called out.

My father ran a short distance down along the ledge, booting imaginary wardens into the river. When I looked downriver again R.W. was gone.

During the next half-hour about twenty fish attempted the ascent. Since our arrival the river had risen several inches, augmented by afternoon snow runoff from high in the hills. The water was opaque as a glacial river. Overnight it would drop a foot. At dawn some of the fish would be able to clear the falls. Now they were too high, too fast, too powerful. Only one other fish was successful, a brilliant male close to a yard long. As it went over in a sparkling parabola of color and motion my father threw his arms skyward and danced furiously on deeply bent knees, as though performing some ancient fertility rite for the trout.

"He don't get excited much, do he?" Uncle Henry said mildly.

Across the Boston and Montreal tracks on the edge of the village the American Heritage Furniture Mill blasted its five o'clock whistle. Gray-faced men in gray cloth caps and gray work clothes appeared along the ledge, holding lunch buckets. The sun went under a heavy bank of clouds over the Green Mountains. The crowd thinned again.

In a week or ten days when most of the snow water was out of the river dozens of trout would go up over the falls every hour. Uncle Henry and my father would fish for them in the deep gravel-bottomed spawning pools in our pasture brook with spawn sewn up in small squares of stocking net while I watched for R.W. Today most of the trout were still finning slowly in the frigid depths of Lake Memphremagog, waiting for that mysterious and infallible urge that would tell them it was time to make the run.

Another large trout was coming. It was driven back onto the rocks. Wriggling like an eel, it managed to work its way into the shallow pocket of water behind the falls, where it lay heaving on its side. My father stood in the spray of the falls, urging the fish onward with French exhortations and empathetic gyrations.

"Them fish have courage, Henry." He roared out the word courage like a Decoration Day elocutionist. "They won't give up. Them Christly trout just refuse to give up."

Saturnine in his sheer bulk, his eyes as inscrutable as a Buddha's, my uncle stared into the water. "The goddamn fools don't know enough to," he said.

As we walked back across the field toward the truck two men with tan overcoats and city hats got out of a Buick with Quebec plates parked near Uncle Henry's Cadillac. "You boys interested in buying a fast car?" Uncle Henry said.

I knew he wasn't serious. The Cadillac was the most powerful car in Kingdom County, a pure white V-16 capable of cruising at ninety miles an hour. With it Uncle Henry earned his livelihood, but it still looked as pristine as it had in 1930 when it had been custom built for him. Soon after it arrived he had named it White Lightning.

One of the strangers said in French, "We're interested in renting it. With the driver."

As my father and I drove down the lane I looked back out the window. The men were still talking with Uncle Henry. I watched them until the corner of the hotel blocked my view.

We turned onto the street paralleling the short north end

of the Common. The sun had not reappeared. Under the bare elms on the Common the statue of Ethan Allen taking Fort Ticonderoga looked forlorn, as though when he had cast it my great-grandfather had not quite believed that Allen's expedition was worth the effort. Momentarily I envied my father, who carried his own good weather with him wherever he went — whom no bleak slants of late afternoon light could oppress or dispirit.

"Now, Wild Bill," he said, "them boys that stopped your uncle by his car was G-men."

I was impressed. "Can you always tell a G-man?"

"Yes, but you can't tell him much."

My father laughed uproariously and pounded the rim of the steering wheel. "We'll have to remember that one for Henry, Wild Bill. Henry loves a good joke. Did you see him smile when I booted Warden down into the whitewater?"

"Dad, do you think those G-men will ever catch Uncle Henry?"

"Not hardly. They never caught Quebec Bill when he was transporting and Henry learnt everything he knows from me. Henry Coville learnt from the old master himself. They'll never catch him. He's too Christly well trained. I showed him mountain roads where nobody could even find him, much less catch him."

"They might pick him up between here and Barre. He could always run into a roadblock."

"He could always go through or around a roadblock. Don't worry about old Henry, Bill. They ain't a-going to land him."

"Do you ever think about getting back into the business?"

My father smiled. "Look at them sugar houses going on that hill, Wild Bill. They'll be boiling all night. Spring is here, boy. Spring is Christly here."

I looked around doubtfully. Steam was billowing out of the Kittredge sugar place, and except for the grimy frozen drifts along the north sides of stone walls and hedgerows most of the snow was gone. The ice was out of Lake Memphremagog. The rainbow run had started; that was usually a sign that winter was nearly over. But the grass in the fields and pastures was frozen flat and brown. The farmhouses that had not been abandoned were still banked high up their stone foundations with spruce and balsam boughs. Far to the east under the gray sky the northern peaks of the Presidential Range of New Hampshire were covered with snow and might be for another month.

Halfway out the county road to the Lord Hollow turnoff we swung into Frog Lamundy's place. Our light truck bounced up the lane. The tires spun in Frog's dooryard, then caught on the frozen dirt under the thin slop of mud as we backed up the high-drive toward the big sliding door of the barn. In accordance with Kingdom County custom we sat in the truck waiting for someone to come out of the house.

Frog's buildings were all weathered gray. Like many of the French Canadian farmhouses across the border the house was banked up to its rotted sills with old manure summer and winter. Across the dooryard, which was cluttered with nondescript pieces of junk, was the small sawmill shed where our maples had been cut into lumber a few months ago.

Frog emerged from the long sagging ell connecting the house and barn. We got out of the truck and he greeted us in French. Frog was a small man, though not so tiny as my father, with quick shifty eyes and a thin mustache. He did a little of everything: cattle trucking, dealing in hay, distilling cedar oil, farming, running the sawmill. Most persons seemed simultaneously to admire and distrust him for his acumen in making a deal. I did not like him at all.

"I can smell rain, Frog," my father said. "A nice warm rain to green things up. Wild Bill here thinks we'll have the cows out in a week. One good load of hay should carry us through."

"I don't have one load to sell, good or bad," Frog said. "I'm out myself. Maybe in a week or so, Bill. You have no idea how Christly scarce hay is this year. Ben Currier had to sell his herd last night for beef. I was there. The best herd in the county is rolling downcountry to some meat packer this minute. Nobody has hay."

I looked at Frog with all the unmitigated hostility of early adolescence. I was humiliated for my father, who knew as well as I did that Frog could always find hay for a man who could pay cash. Uncle Henry said that Frog was receiving hay from Canada by boxcar loads and selling it directly out of the boxcar two or three times every week.

But my father appeared unconcerned. "At least we ain't losing a fortune sugaring this year," he said. "That's one worry I and Wild Bill don't have."

Frog looked down at the idle sawmill. "Nothing chews up a saw like an old sugar spout," he said. He was alluding to the pitifully small price he had paid us for our trees on the pretext that the butt logs were probably full of old metal taps. "I had to buy two new saws to get them cut up. That runs into big money."

I didn't want to hear any more of his lies. I walked down across the dooryard to the shed and looked inside at the saw. It was far from new. I stared back at Frog, but he was looking off at the mountains. Somewhat ruefully, I thought that we would not have lost money sugaring that spring, or any other spring for that matter. We had always made some money sugaring, and the spring of 1932 was the best for sugaring in a decade.

"That old Froggie boy thinks the world of me," my father said as we rattled back down the lane, as light as we had come up.

"I'm sure he does," I said. "He just thinks a little bit more of money."

"No, Wild Bill, Frog would do anything for me. Why, Frog Lamundy is so generous he'd give away his ass and shit through his ribs."

This incredible observation was typical of Quebec Bill Bonhomme, whose analyses of others were invariably more accurate as revelations about himself. He was absolutely incapable of judging persons he liked except in terms of his own personality. My father was generous, and so despite incontrovertible evidence to the contrary, Frog Lamundy, probably the most parsimonious man in the county, must be generous too. He loved a joke, so my Uncle Henry, one of the least risible men I have ever known, also loved jokes. He was sure spring was coming, so I had said the cows would be in the pasture in a week. He was wild and had been wilder in his youth, so his son must be wild too.

Wild Bill: I was proud of this epithet because it had been conferred by my father, but it was as incongruous a misnomer as any he could have devised, reflecting his own personality and accentuating the rather reserved turn of mine. My father was close to forty when I was born, and in our easy amicability we were more like grandfather and grandson than like most fathers and sons I have known. There was no one I liked or admired more. Early in my childhood, however, I began to develop a private tendency toward skepticism as a buffer against the constant disappointments and the ultimate disillusionment that would have resulted from adopting his unqualified optimism. Not that there was anything facile or unauthentic about his positive outlook, but to subscribe to his perennial optimism could have been psychologically disastrous for me. By the time I was fourteen I was cultivating an appreciation of irony for its own sake. Like my father's confidence in the essential fortuity of life, my capacity for enjoying some of its less tragic discrepancies was more a style than a philosophy. In both cases, I think, it was less a way of perceiving the vicissitudes of life in Kingdom County than a stay against being overwhelmed by them.

Now it began to snow. The flakes were gigantic, some as large as the palm of a man's hand. "Sugar snow," my father said, pounding my knee. "The snow that takes the snow. Ain't that right, Wild Bill?"

For a few minutes the snow fell thickly. Then it stopped abruptly. As we climbed higher into the hills, more snow appeared in the fields. The countryside was shaggy with pastures going back to brush and cut-off sugar places growing up to spruce and fir. One by one the farms were disappearing. I noticed a collapsed barn I hadn't seen on the way down to the Common earlier in the afternoon. The heavy snows had built up on the roof, started to melt, frozen again and continued to accumulate until the weight was too great. The barn itself had not been used for years. Broken horse-drawn machinery stood rusting in the scrubby fields.

Yet inherent in the desolation was a latent vitality. Here in the hills of Kingdom County everything superfluous to bare existence had been purified out of the land by the long winter. It was impossible to live in that bleak landscape of fir and granite and cold rushing water and infertile soil without becoming permanently, if ambivalently, a part of it. Particularly in the uneasy hiatus between late winter and early spring, the austere and uncompromised land, now rapidly reclaiming itself, conveyed an intimation of the kind of energy and endurance it exacted of the men

16

and women who still depended on it for their livelihoods.

Ten miles out of the Common we turned north off the county road over a one-lane steel bridge and started up Lord Hollow. The schoolhouse was dark in the twilight. Cordelia had walked home. The road wound steadily up, roughly following the bends of the hollow brook. The wind whipped the snow across the fields. My father switched on his headlights. He had gradually fallen silent, entranced by reveries of spring which remained unbroken until, just as we crossed the plank bridge over the brook at the foot of our hill, we ran out of gas.

So together in the wintery twilight we started the long walk up the lane: past the lower hay meadow; past the ancient straggling apple orchard; through the gigantic snow-covered stumps of the sugar bush; into the dooryard on the crest of the hill, twenty-six hundred feet above sea level. Home.

For a moment we stood in the dooryard. The wind gusted erratically out of the southwest. Wraiths of snow materialized around our knees, ghosted across the frozen mud, vanished. Down the hollow a mile the Royer barn lights flickered through the whirling snow. I felt vaguely unsettled by intimations of the impermanence surrounding our lives — the distant light blinking through the swirling insubstantial snow, the evanescent warmth of the afternoon, the bare dusty hayloft inside the barn.

As though to protect me from the consequences of his own ebullience, my father put his arm around me. With his free hand he pointed to the barn roof. Against the nearly dark sky I could see the white outline of the snow owl that had roosted there for a week. His body was facing south, but his head was turned around to the north. My father squeezed my shoulder. "Look at that rubber-necked son of a bitch, Wild Bill. Ain't he the best sign of spring you ever see?"

I headed for the barn. Like each of the eleven barns built by my great-grandfather ours was round rather than rectangular. It had a central feeding area in the cow stable and above the stable a circular hayloft around the perimeter of which a hay wagon could be driven. By 1932 it was in need of major repairs, listing off on the downhill side like the hulk of a wrecked ship on a reef. But it was still a landmark in Kingdom County and still appeared to be perfectly round when viewed from a distance.

From a distance is how my father usually viewed it. This evening, though, he followed me inside, where my mother and Cordelia were milking by kerosene light. Rat Kinneson, our hired man, was carrying milk to the hogs.

Even in the stanchions at the end of winter my mother's fifteen registered Jerseys were a handsome herd, clean and graceful and red as wild deer. Tonight they were also restive, stamping and shaking their heads at random intervals, unaccustomed to being milked before they were fed.

My mother had not heard us come in. She knelt by a cow, washing its flank with a white cloth. She was wearing a flowered kerchief and her gray barn sweater. My mother was almost twenty years younger than my father. She had very long dark hair and dark eyes, and looked as Indian as her St. Francis grandmother. She was several inches taller than my father and as slim as her brother Henry was stocky. She had been educated in a French convent in Montreal but now spoke only English unless she was angry. She was quite strict with me and quite indulgent with my father. She was the only person I knew who was not afraid of Cordelia.

"Evangeline," my father called. As usual he drew out her name in his best oratorical style, stressing the last syllable. "Spring is here, Evangeline. The trout are jumping the falls. Wild Bill and me had to boot an officer of the law down into the whitewater."

18

"It was Warden Kinneson," I said. "He got out down below. He called Dad a Frenchman."

"What a travesty," Cordelia said.

"I'm sorry he got out," Rat said. "The falls is a good place for a man like Brother R. W."

"Did you find hay?" my mother asked.

"We didn't find any hay, Evangeline." My father made this announcement with as much satisfaction as though we had brought home a truckload of alfalfa. "But we did run out of gas."

"We can't feed fish to the cows," Cordelia said.

"Rat here will figure a way to feed the cows. Ain't that right, Rat?"

Rat stood frowning near Hercule, my father's pet long-horn bull. Hercule was hungry, and was kicking the side-boards of his stall hard.

"Stop that," Rat said. Hercule stopped kicking.

In the lantern light inside the barn Rat looked like a caricature of Ichabod Crane. He was tall and stooped and lean as a bent cedar rail, with a long dissatisfied face and lank colorless hair. Rat was among the last of a certain tradition of hired men which in him seemed to have reached its apotheosis: unreliable, malingering, censorious; per-petually disconsolate, infuriatingly dogmatic; prodigiously talented with crops, animals and machinery. With Rat our farm ran erratically at best. Without him it could not have run at all.

"We'll feed them critters potatoes," he said. "That seems to be the one thing around here we ain't run out of."

"Certainly we will," my father said as though he had thought of the idea himself. "Now what about the truck, Ratty?"

Rat was looking at Hercule. "I always knowed that bull would be good for something," he said.

Twenty minutes later we were all back down by the

bridge. Rat hitched Hercule to the front of the Ford with a long chain. My mother and I pushed. My father sat inside the cab steering. Cordelia walked alongside reciting the following lines from "Hamatreya":

Earth laughs in flowers, to see her boastful boys
Earth-proud, proud of the earth which is not theirs;
Who steer the plough, but cannot steer their feet
Clear of the grave.

"Whoa," my father shouted before we had gone ten feet. "Whoa up there, Rat. Whoa back there. Hark, Aunt. Everyone hark."

We came to an uncertain halt and stood panting in the mud, not knowing what we were supposed to be listening for. Then from high overhead in the dark sky we heard the geese, barking faintly.

"They know," my father said in a hushed cryptic tone.

"Come on," Cordelia said. "Let's get over Donner Pass before the next snowstorm."

"Giddap, Rat, giddap, Hercule," my father called, and our bizarre processional lurched on up the hill.

During supper the wind came up hard, and as always when the wind blew out of the southwest the kitchen was drafty. Despite a good fire in the woodstove cold air seeped in around the porous old window casings, which my mother stuffed with rags every fall. Now she said, "When are we going to replace these windows?"

My father was no more adept at carpentering than farming. To my knowledge he had never repaired anything around the house or barn. Sitting at the table in his wool shirt and wool pants, his back near the stove, sipping hot coffee, he said, "You can't have city conveniences in the country, Evangeline."

"Nor in a mountain fastness," Cordelia said, drawing her shawl closer around her narrow shoulders.

"If by conveniences you mean running water and inside plumbing and electricity, no doubt you are right," my mother said. "I wasn't thinking of such luxuries as those."

"Well, you can't make an old house over into a new house. Can you, Rat?"

I think my father felt that he should not involve me in this debate, but couldn't resist a rhetorical appeal to someone. He had chosen the wrong person in Rat, who as usual was picking at his food as though he expected to find something unpalatable and odious in it at any moment. He turned over a slice of side pork the way he might turn over a rotten plank with his foot and said, "Because if he hadn't gotten out of the whitewater he couldn't go around a-slandering his relations."

"I wasn't thinking of a new house," my mother said, paying no attention to Rat, who was famous throughout the county for his non sequiturs. "I would just like to hope that by next winter we might be warm in our old kitchen."

My father glanced at the windows, crowded with trays of tomato seedlings, broccoli and cauliflower shoots, tiny cabbage plants. The curtains were standing out at a sharp angle in the draft. "You never know what you're going to find when you start fooling with an old house," he said. "Sometimes a stud gives way. Then the wall might buckle and you'd be out an entire wall. Or you might find a sill that needs jacking. If the jack slips the whole house could come down around your ears. No, Evangeline, it's better not to know what's inside an old wall. It's better just to forget about such things."

"I wish I could forget such things."

I noticed Cordelia glancing appraisingly at my mother, of whom even mild recrimination was uncharacteristic.

"Well," my father said, "all you need to do is give the word, Sweet Evangeline. By fall you'll have you a ten-room home with two inside bathrooms and a warm furnace in the cellar and no cracks around the windows. Just like them new houses up to Memphremagog. You say the word, *ma fille,* and you'll have that Christly mansion by September."

He was referring to a number of large houses that had been built during Prohibition in the border town at the south end of the lake. Uncle Henry had told us that like his Cadillac, most of these homes had been financed by whiskey running. They were capacious and stately, with pillared porticoes and secluded second-story porches. Some were surmounted by cupolas or fenced widow's walks overlooking the lake. They were more costly and elegant than any houses built in Kingdom County since the pink brick homes of the sheep boom just before the Civil War. Today they are occupied by doctors, lawyers, a banker, an Episcopalian minister—all of whom owe their educations to money their families made running whiskey during Prohibition.

"William," my mother said, "the cows haven't eaten since morning. You go down cellar now and start putting potatoes in bushel baskets for Mr. Kinneson."

I took one of the extra kerosene lanterns from the woodshed and went through the icy parlor and down the cellar stairs. Along with the circular hayloft, the cellar was one of my favorite retreats on the farm, redolent of cool dry earth and the rich mingled scents of the fruits and vegetables my mother stored there in greater quantities than we could consume if we didn't grow anything for a year. I hung the lantern from a nail driven into one of the eight-by-eight ceiling timbers and looked around. Among the netted hams and sides of bacon a dozen or so cabbages depended from the timbers by their roots, casting grotesque shadows on the stone walls, which were lined with shelves of quart canning jars containing every kind of vegetable that could be grown in Kingdom County. Also there were pint jars of apple butter, wild berry jams and jellies, maple syrup from previous springs. Along one wall were two twenty-gallon crocks of salt pork. There were bushels of old-fashioned varieties of apples, and bushels of pie pumpkins and winter squash — all evocative of a self-sufficiency lost sometime during the past century.

The potato bins were still about a third full. Some of the potatoes had started to sprout soft purple tentacles, a sign of spring that had not passed unnoticed by my father. I got a stack of empty bushel baskets and started to fill one. There was a loud thump, a rush of cold air, and Rat came down the stairs from the outside bulkhead with a wheelbarrow.

If there was a way to do a job slower than necessary, Rat would always find it. I used to think that he did this deliberately to annoy me, but later I realized that he worked just as slowly when I wasn't around. Now he insisted on taking only one bushel of potatoes out to the barn at a time though the wheelbarrow could have easily accommodated two or three. Also he refused to tell me how many bushels he thought he would need. I filled six or eight and left him to finish the job alone.

Upstairs in the kitchen my father had gotten out his fiddle. While my mother and Cordelia washed the supper dishes he sat in his straight-backed chair by the stove and played as blithely as though we were cutting up seed potatoes for spring planting and the cows were eating new green grass in the pasture. He pounded his feet up and down in the clog dancing tradition of French Canadian fiddling. His white hair flew as he nodded his head chivalrously toward my mother. His eyes were an intense blue in the lamplight. His fiddle rang with a pure unquavering wildness reminiscent of the wildness in his past. My mother made a fresh pot of coffee. Cordelia and she and I sat at the table drinking coffee and listening to reels and jigs and waltzes that were hundreds of years old.

Suddenly Rat rushed in through the woodshed shouting my father's name.

"What is it, Rat?" cried my father.

"Oh, Bill, Bill, Bill," Rat shouted. "It's your bull, Bill. Your bull be choking."

My father leaped for the door. He raced across the dooryard and into the stable, where we found him bent over the prostrate bull, driving his fist repeatedly into its neck. He pried Hercule's mouth open and thrust his arm deep inside. Hercule remained motionless. He jumped up and began kicking the animal in the stomach, trying desperately to make him cough. But it was futile. Hercule had choked to death on a potato.

I began to cry. This was terrible, far worse than running out of hay. My father had thought the world of the old bull, and I knew he must be heartbroken.

If he was, though, he didn't show it. "Butcher him," he told Rat. "We'll keep one side and the Royers can have the other. Cheer up, Wild Bill. He was an old fella, he must have been close to twenty."

He put one arm around me and one around my mother and walked us out into the dooryard. It was snowing again. "It's a Christly spring blizzard, Evangeline," he shouted ecstatically. "This is the snow that takes the snow. This is the poor man's fertilizer."

* * *

That night in my loft bedroom over the kitchen I lay awake a long time. Cordelia and Rat had gone to bed, but my mother and father sat up talking at the kitchen table. Since I could remember I had loved to lie under the warm quilts and hear my parents talking, but tonight I tried not to listen. They were speaking French, which meant they were disagreeing. From snatches I overheard I knew my father was trying to persuade my mother to sanction a whiskey-smuggling trip.

There had been a similar argument the previous fall. The summer had been a succession of rainy days interspersed with intervals of hazy sunshine lasting just long enough to seduce us into cutting our hay. As soon as we had a few acres down and drying they would be soaked by another sudden rain, coming out of nowhere. The entire family had abandoned the usual summer rituals of gardening, canning, berrying and getting up a winter woodpile to go to the fields and turn the brown sodden hay between rains. We turned the hay in one field of about ten acres five times before we gave it up as beyond saving. In desperation some farmers put wet hay in their barns, salting it down repeatedly to reduce the risk of fire. Three barns within sight of our farm caught fire spontaneously from damp steaming hay. In September with less than a ton of hay in the barn, my father had almost begged my mother to endorse one whiskey run. She had not given him any kind of ultimatum but neither had she given her blessings to a trip. Ultimately he had cut the maples to buy hay. And as bad as things were with us now, I did not think she would approve a run this time either.

"William, sell part of the herd. Frog would give us enough hay to get through for two good milkers."

"I couldn't do that, Evangeline. I couldn't sell another

living thing off this farm. Not a tree, not an animal. Especially not part of your herd. I could never do that and you know it."

"And you could never run whiskey again and you know that."

After that neither of them spoke again. Except for the wind rattling my window and the fire crackling low in the kitchen stove it was as still as a night in deep winter. I was exhausted but I couldn't sleep. I got out of bed and walked across the cold planks of the loft floor to the small window under the peak of the roof. The snow had stopped again and I could see the owl very plainly. As I watched him I thought once again, as I had frequently during recent months, of certain strange and disturbing events from our family's past that had never been explained to me but that I was somehow aware of anyway.

Suddenly I realized that headlights were coming up the hollow. As the car bounced over the frozen ruts the lights rose and fell crazily. Whoever it was was traveling fast.

2

FROM around a bend ahead of us a loon whooped. Immediately my father called back, and for several minutes he and the loon conversed in plangent warbles that rang out over the cold still cedar swamp like demented laughter. After spending most of the previous night talking and laughing my father was not in the best of voices, but here in our canoe on the river at dawn nothing was going to interfere with his good spirits.

I was still sleepy and somewhat confused. "How did Uncle Henry figure out that they weren't G-men?" I said.

"He wasn't sure they warn't, Bill. That's what he was in hopes the old master could straighten out for him."

"Have you got it straightened out yet?"

"I ain't even going to try. As long as that whiskey is waiting for us it don't matter who them boys be. But that's enough whiskey talk. Sweet Evangeline don't want Quebec Bill filling his boy's head with whiskey talk on such a beautiful morning. See the icicles along them red alders. Ain't they pretty?"

I knew that my father had no intention of changing the subject for very long. Since the previous midnight when White Lightning had come tearing into our dooryard he had talked of nothing but the Canadian whiskey hidden in the abandoned barn near Magog and his incredible plan to get it back across the border. I had been amazed when toward morning my mother agreed to let us go. Even Uncle Henry had strong reservations about the trip.

Surprisingly, it had been Rat Kinneson who had changed their minds. Sitting hunched over the kitchen stove with his gray nightcap trailing down his back he had said, "I ain't telling none of you what to do, but we've got potatoes to last just till the first of the week. That's if we stretch them. Now a thousand dollars split two ways is five hundred dollars apiece, boys. Five hundred dollars still buys quite a little bit of hay. I ain't telling you what to do. If two or three more critters go to choking to death on me we'll have more potatoes to go round for the rest and might make it through."

We had all looked at my mother. It was her herd; she had built it up, nurtured it, kept it going through all the hard times. To her the cows were the farm, and now my father's plan must have seemed like the only way to save either. Perhaps too she may have felt that with staid old Wild Bill along my father would be less apt to take chances or start drinking again. At any rate, she had nodded. I was so excited I nearly fell in the stove; my father whooped and danced and played his imaginary fiddle; Uncle Henry looked thoughtful; Rat smirked; and Cordelia smiled grimly and read aloud a long passage from Sir Thomas Browne's "Urn Burial."

At dawn Uncle Henry and I carried the long birch canoe down the steep hill behind the farm to the river. In places the snow was over our knees. My father sauntered along behind us in the trail we had broken, carrying a pack basket with the barrel of his old eight-gauge shotgun sticking up out of it and humming French reels. From time to time, he called out encouragement to us as we staggered along under the canoe through the frozen drifts and thick softwoods.

We launched the canoe from a wide beaver dam. Below us fringes of ice clung to both edges of the river. Above the dam it was still frozen solid from bank to bank.

"You take the bow, Wild Bill."

I got in and knelt in back of the first thwart. I looked back upriver at the ice, now about at my eye level. "Spring comes a little later down here in the bog than anywhere else," my father said.

"Don't it, though," Uncle Henry said as he shoved us off. "About ten this evening, Bill."

"About ten, Henry."

Just before we went around the first bend I looked over my shoulder. Uncle Henry was still watching us from the dam. Behind him in the clear pink sky over the swamp the sun was coming up. My father glanced back too. "Ain't that a glorious sight, Wild Bill? I hope Evangeline is watching that."

My father and I had canoed together many times on the St. John, which wound down through the cedar swamp and emptied into Lake Memphremagog below the county home. It was a deep slow dark river with a dark gravel bottom. Under the gigantic cedars lining both banks it was almost black. Except for a disused tote road along the north side there was no sign that anyone had ever been there before us.

The cedar swamp was the last big tract of wilderness in Vermont: one hundred thousand acres of wetlands and rivers, beaver flows and low wooded hills enclosed on three sides by the tall Canadian mountains. Most of it was accessible only by canoe. It held an abundance of rare wildlife, including the only remaining moose herd in the state, but now in the early spring it looked empty and barren. The loon had flown off toward the lake, laughing insanely as though it knew something we didn't and might not want to — as all the loons I have ever heard have always laughed. The only other animal we saw was a dark thin otter, which slid off an icy log and swam for a mile or so down the river a short distance ahead of the canoe, sometimes diving, sometimes swimming on its back and watching us.

There was no wind. It was going to be yet another warm and sunny day, though now it was still very cold. I buttoned the top button of my red wool hunting jacket and paddled faster to get warm. Behind me in the stern my father began to sing in French. It was a song hundreds of years old, a paddling song that had been sung by our voyageur ancestors as they moved north in search of furs in the same canoe that was carrying us down the St. John in the spring of 1932:

> *En roulant ma boule roulant*
> *En roulant ma boule.*
> *En roulant ma boule roulant*
> *Rouli, roulant ma boule roulant.*

We ran the six or seven miles from the beaver dam to the lake in less than an hour, with my father singing or talking about the whiskey all the way. Just above the mouth of the river we passed under the railroad trestle and next to it the iron bridge leading out to the county home. There was some mist on the water as we glided onto St. John Bay. Far down across the still blue water through the light mist lay the village of Memphremagog, crowded onto the isthmus between the lake and the big south bay. Creeping north from the village was a yellow tug. It was trailing a flotilla of boomed pulpwood covering at least a hundred acres of water. At its current speed it would arrive at the paper mill in Magog in five or six days.

"Firewood," my father said contemptuously. "That's kindling, Wild Bill. Match sticks. One spring when I was a boy I worked the big drive on the Upper East Branch of the Penobscot. That's up north in the state of Maine. The Penobscot. We drove thirty-two-foot sawlogs down whitewater that would make the Kingdom River look like a millrace. When we come to a big lake we'd haul them across it with a great raft with a capstan on it. A hawser a thousand foot long stretched from the capstan to the booms. We'd walk round and round in the spokes, winding in them Christly booms like a big tired fish. We made a sixth of a mile an hour in calm water. Six hours on, six hours off. We'd lay right down on the raft in snow and sleet and sleep like the logs we was hauling. Sometimes it took ten days or more to cross a big lake. That was bull work, Wild Bill. We was men that did that." He sang:

> They had not rolled off many logs when they
>   heard the foreman say,
> "I'll have you boys be on your guard for the jam
>   will soon give way."
> These words were hardly spoken when the jam did
>   break and go.
> It carried off those six brave boys and their
>   foreman — young Bonho'.

Even when he was hoarse Quebec Bill Bonhomme had a resonant singing voice, with a wild timbre like wind in tall trees and rushing water. He loved to sing and could remember every song he'd ever heard. As we moved up the placid lake in the big dark high-riding canoe, staying near the eastern shore, he sang interminable verses from "The Jam on Gerry's Rock," "*En Roulant,*" "*Sur la Rivière*" and others, making himself the hero of each ballad. He recited pages from William Henry Drummond's French-Canadian dialect poems, including all of "The Voyageur." He composed extravagant extemporaneous odes to our ancestor René St. Laurent Bonhomme—a voyageur of great courage and strength, Wild Bill—and sang paeans in praise of mending fence, plowing, gathering brush for peas to climb on and a dozen other vernal activities he loved to celebrate from a safe distance.

Even the slow northern spring seemed to be conjured into acquiescence by my father's optimism. In places the rocky shoreline was strewn with giant slabs of ice, but further back some of the marshes were already bright with yellow cowslips. Redwing blackbirds clung to last year's cattails along the base of the railway embankment. The lake was perfectly calm but high overhead an osprey soared on the strong upper air currents. "By the Christ, Bill, look at that hawk," my father exclaimed. "If I could do that I'd eat raw fish myself."

A quarter of a mile ahead the county home stood on a knoll near the lake. It was a bleak square-framed wooden building four stories tall that served several purposes: poorhouse, orphanage, jail, old-age home. My father and the superintendent, Dr. Tettinger, were close friends. During good weather my father played his fiddle there every other Sunday night. In the past when the home was crowded some of the residents had stayed for a while on the farm with us.

"Let's pay Tett a short visit," my father said.

We left the canoe at the foot of a narrow meadow sloping down to the lake and headed up toward the dairy barn. Already my legs were stiff from kneeling. It seemed good to stretch them. As we came around the corner of a big manure pile and crossed the railroad tracks we met old Walter Kittredge emerging from the stable with a loaded wheelbarrow.

"Walter K.," my father called. "Spring is here, Walter. What does your fancy turn to?"

"Cow shit," Abiah Kittredge said from the stable door. "Same as any other season. Look at the old fart treeble and tremble. That makes thirteen trips so far this morning. No offense, Quebec Bill, but I told Kittredge just yesterday that if he intended to keep on slaving like a Frenchman he should have hung onto the farm and slaved there."

"Mrs. Kittredge, there wasn't no way in creation to hang onto the farm and you know it," Walter replied. "How be you, Bill? This can't be young Billy? My, how he's growed. Look here, Mrs. Kittredge. Billy's a good foot higher than his pa. I didn't know you had it in you to make a boy like this, Bill. Stand up next to your pa, Billy. You're going to be big as your Uncle Henry, ain't you?"

"He don't need you measuring him like a prize fish," Abiah said. "Don't pay Kittredge no mind, boy. He don't see many new people up here. When he does he don't know enough not to measure them. You look more and more like your ma's side, if I do say so. I call him a Coville clear through, Quebec Bill."

"Yes," my father said, "but he's got the Bonhomme wildness in him."

"He don't look wild to me. Does he look wild to you, Kittredge?"

"No, not a-tall. He don't have Henry's shoulders yet, but they may come later."

I did not much care for this genealogical evaluation, but I liked Walter and Abiah, who had been our nearest neighbors below Royers until they lost their farm to the bank two years before. The entire hollow had turned out for their first mortgage sale. People bid five cents for each head of stock and each implement, ten cents for the buildings, ten cents for the one hundred and fifty acres of land — then returned everything intact to the Kittredges. But they were simply too old to go on and after the first wet summer had to leave anyway. Several of their children had offered Walter and Abiah a home, but they had decided that they would be more independent at the county home, where they could take care of the dairy. Wherever they went, they would go together. They were up in their eighties and as inseparable as Baucis and Philemon. Walter was not much bigger than my father, but he was quite a hale old man. Abiah weighed over three hundred pounds and was afflicted with a brilliant indigo goiter that depended from her chin like a turkey wattle.

Walter looked down the muddy road along the tracks. "Where's your Ford, Bill? I don't see your Ford."

"He don't see period, the cataracted old bat," Abiah said.

"I can see that great long blue necktie you're wearing plain enough," Walter said, winking at my father.

"It's a great deal longer than anything he ever sported," Abiah said.

Walter slapped both his knees. "That's so, boys, and it stands up straighter, too."

"He didn't do that poor," Abiah said. "Give me twelve altogether. Nine gals, one boy and Hank and Harlan. Boy died, the rest thrived."

"I done fair," Walter said. "Just fair. It warn't that difficult. Except for little Kittredge and Hank and Harlan I had the pattern right afore me each time. Where's your truck, I say, Bill?"

34

"We're traveling by water today, Walter. I and Wild Bill are making a trip up Canady way. Might have a small treat for you and Tett and the boys on the way back."

"Well, Bill. That's the trouble. Tett just might not be here when you get back. One day last week a county fella come up from the Common on surprise inspection and found Tett passed out at his desk with an empty bottle beside him. Tett come to and tried to tell that it was witch hazel, but the fella only said if it was, then Tett shouldn't have been drinking it, and went back down the line to write his report. This is three times now since we come here. Tett's down below today answering for it."

"We're afraid the county's going to replace him certain this time," Abiah said.

"Not Tett," my father said, still laughing about the witch hazel. "Tett's fell in the shithouse and come out with a new suit before this. He's too smart for them."

"I hope so," Walter said. "We wouldn't know what to do around here without Tett."

He picked up the wheelbarrow handles and trundled unsteadily toward the manure pile.

"See him treeble," Abiah said proudly. "Oh, Lord preserve me, here come them maphrodites. You'll have to excuse me, boys. They'll pester me all day if I let them. I wouldn't get a tap done."

Two large persons in overalls were shambling down the lane from the main building. "Bon-bon, Bon-bon," they called. It was Hank and Harlan, Walter and Abiah's hermaphrodites.

My father was delighted to see them. He hugged them and gave them each a piece of maple sugar candy from his jacket pocket. It occurred to me that our trip might have been better planned than I thought, since neither my father nor I much liked candy.

While my father was talking to Hank and Harlan, Walter

35

took me aside. "Mrs. Kittredge can't hardly stand to be around Hank and Harlan these days," he said. "She's terrible upset over what's to become of them when we're gone. That's why we need Tett, you see. He'd never send them off."

My father reminded Walter that we would stop back again with a little treat. He said he was very certain Dr. Tettinger would come out with another new suit. He hugged Hank and Harlan once more and called goodbye to Abiah, hiding in the barn from her children.

"Them wonderful people think the world of me," he said.

Out on the lake again he pointed toward a rough obelisk about six feet high along the north boundary of the county home property. "There she is, Wild Bill. That's Canady."

Just beyond the stone marker heavily wooded hills came down close to the lake on both sides. Except for a small Benedictine monastery and the spur line, there was nothing between us and Magog but water and wilderness.

My father was singing again. On the trip a subtle change had come over him. At home he created the illusion that he was in control. It was a marvelous illusion, but ultimately a sleight we all saw through. My mother managed the herd, Rat ran the farm and Cordelia established the tone of the household. Here on the lake my father was not only in control, but at home. He paddled the canoe the way he moved in the woods, as though he belonged there and was part of everything around him—the water, the hills, the sky, the burgeoning spring whose imminent arrival he continued to invoke.

Toward noon he began trolling a small red and silver spoon on a handline. Within five minutes he had hooked a good fish. As it wore itself out my father gained line. Loose coils of slack accumulated in the bottom of the canoe.

A lake trout about twenty inches long came thrashing over the side. My father rapped the back of the trout's head against the canoe thwart and held the fish up in the sun. "Wild Bill's hungry," he said. "Let's eat."

We landed on a densely wooded point, which I explored while my father cooked lunch. From the north side of the point I could look across a bay still partially iced over and see the monastery. It was a large medieval-looking stone building about a third of the way up the slope of the first big lakeside mountain. Surrounding it were walled tiers of apple orchards and meadows. The spur line ran between the big stone building and a low wooden barn, then hooked inland around the east shoulder of the mountain. North of the monastery the lake resembled a mile-wide fjord compressed between twin mountain ranges sheering straight up, gray and leafless, between the blue water and blue sky.

My father fried the trout in bacon grease over a nearly smokeless driftwood fire on a rise overlooking the lake. He tossed a handful of coffee into a pan of boiling water and slowly stirred the grounds to the bottom with the blade of his hunting knife. With our backs against the trunk of a tall black spruce we sat looking down the lake and ate pink trout and thick slices of my mother's homemade bread dipped in bacon grease, and drank steaming hot coffee. After dinner I stretched out on the warm brown needles under the tree and closed my eyes. I could still feel the motion of the canoe under me. Just before I drifted off to sleep it occurred to me that there was no place I would rather be and no one I would rather be with.

"Look up the lake, Bill. Stay low."

I sat up. Through the trees I saw two monks coming across the bay along the edge of the ice in an unpainted rowboat. One of them was holding a short casting rod. The other was rowing and singing:

"*Adoramus te Christe, et benedicimus tibi quia aper sanctam.*"

"Stay down," my father whispered. "I'm going to hide the canoe."

"*Domine, domine, miserere nobis,*" chanted the monk. He pulled harder first on one oar, then on the other, causing the boat to swing erratically from side to side. He was a burly man with a white-fringed tonsure. From behind he looked like the woodcut of Friar Tuck in my Robin Hood book at home.

The fisherman was a lean man with a lugubrious face. As the boat weaved toward the point he said in French, "This is a blasphemous venture, Brother St. Hilaire."

The big monk shipped his oars. He reached into one of several wooden crates in the bottom of the boat and brought out a dark bottle. He tipped back his head and took a long deliberate drink. "Ah," he said, wiping his mouth on the wide loose sleeve of his cassock. "Our Lord Himself was a fisherman, Brother Paul. We will sing His praises to keep up our courage. Let us try the '*Adoramus*' again. That's a fine one for courage. The Holy Ghost will perhaps sing with us."

"Our Lord was not a smuggler," Brother Paul said. "I wouldn't think you'd want to call His attention to this enterprise."

"*Adoramus te Christe,*" sang Brother St. Hilaire loudly.

"They're calling up the devil," my father said in my ear as he crouched back down beside me.

"That's Latin."

"That's mumbo jumbo and they're talking with the devil."

Brother St. Hilaire's voice boomed out over the lake. Brother Paul stared sorrowfully at the wooden crates and did not join in the singing. I noticed that the tip of his casting rod was not bending with the drag of a lure.

Before they had gone fifty feet Brother St. Hilaire stopped again. "Brother Paul, I have a portentous proclamation to issue."

"What is it, Brother? Have you decided to take my counsel and give over this ungodly business?"

"Certainly not. This ungodly business is going to put the monastery on a paying basis. I have to piss in the worst way."

"Surely not in the lake?"

"Where else? You don't want me to besmirch Tettinger's Benedictine, do you? Turn your head aside if you're offended. I've never encountered such delicate sensibilities, Brother Paul. You should have joined a convent. The Holy Ghost needs men in His service, not timid eunuchs."

Brother St. Hilaire got to his feet and hiked up the voluminous skirts of his cassock. He began fumbling with the buttons of his long underwear. Beside me on the ground my father shook with suppressed laughter.

"Take, drink, O Memphremagog, this is holy water," Brother St. Hilaire announced in a solemn pontifical voice, releasing a great arcing jet out over the lake toward shore.

"Here he comes now," my father said.

"Here who comes?"

"The devil, who else?"

He pointed up the lake at a motor launch bearing down on the rowboat. As the launch buzzed past, Brother St. Hilaire lost his footing and nearly pitched overboard. In the process he played a looping stream of holy water over himself and Brother Paul.

The launch had swung around and was returning. In it was the biggest man I had ever seen. He was wearing what appeared to be a blue uniform and a blue cap. His hair, which was totally white, fell out from under the cap over his shoulders and down his back to his waist. Most of his face was concealed by a black beard.

39

As he pulled up alongside the rowboat he said in French, "What would you two men of God be doing out here this early in the year?"

"Trolling for the wily trout, my son," Brother St. Hilaire said as he buttoned his underwear back up.

"That's a strange way to troll," the man said, emitting a prolonged epileptic bellow from deep in behind his beard. "What's in them cases?"

"Clothing for the children at the American county home."

"Pass it over, Father, and I'll deliver it for you. You can't imagine how I love children. That old scow of yours don't look safe anyway. If the slightest breeze come up you might drown."

He made that terrible braying squall again. "Hand over them cases, I say. We'll have no blockade running today."

"Go back to hell, you thieving demon," shouted Brother St. Hilaire, brandishing an oar.

Instantly the man seized the oar out of Brother St. Hilaire's hands and broke it over his head. Holding his head with both hands, Brother St. Hilaire sank into the bottom of the boat. Blood was pouring out from between his fingers and running down his face.

Brother Paul stumbled over Brother St. Hilaire in his haste to transfer the wooden crates to the launch. The hijacker ripped open one of the cases, pulled out a bottle and drained it in three or four long gulps. Trumpeting like an enraged elephant he began to circle the rowboat fast. The churning wash from the launch spilled over the sides of the trembling little boat.

My father ran for his shotgun, but he didn't dare fire until the hijacker headed back up the lake away from the monks. By then he was out of range, braying frightfully over his engine, his white mane flying backwards. The entire episode couldn't have taken two minutes.

"Come on," my father called to me. "Hurry, Bill."

Brother St. Hilaire was thrashing around in the water in the bottom of the rowboat. "Paul," he moaned, "I've been trepanned with my own oar."

"Lie still, Brother. I must administer extreme unction."

"We will omit that exercise. Scull us to shore with the other oar or we'll both need last rites. We're sinking, Paul."

"The other oar fell overboard in the fray. Oh, Brother, here is the wage of our sin. We must compose ourselves. The end is nigh."

"Bullshit. Use your hands. Here, like this."

Brother St. Hilaire took one hand away from his gushing pate and swiped at the lake. Brother Paul promptly slumped over onto his seat.

"Oh, shit," Brother St. Hilaire said. He sounded more exasperated than alarmed. Reaching under his bloody cassock he withdrew a bottle and took a long pull.

Meanwhile my father and I paddled fast toward the foundering rowboat. A minute later we had attached a rope to the bow and were towing the monks to shore. Brother St. Hilaire's head had nearly stopped bleeding; apparently he had sustained the kind of superficial scalp wound that bleeds profusely but isn't serious.

"Wake up, Paul," he said, splashing water into Brother Paul's face. "The Holy Ghost has plucked us from a watery grave. The trouble with Paul, my children, is that he has no faith in the Holy Ghost. Tell me, did you see Him? I'm famished by curiosity. Is He hitched onto the other two like Siamese triplets?"

While we emptied out the rowboat and revived Brother Paul, Brother St. Hilaire talked incessantly. He was the only man I had ever met who talked more than my father. He was highly intrigued by our canoe. He told us that he had written a chapter on the history of birch canoes in his definitive history of the Catholicizing of French Canada. He described how he had been relegated to one obscure monastery after another as punishment for writing the true sordid chronicle of Jesuit fanaticism in Quebec, which had been subsequently distinguished by being listed on the *Index Librorum Prohibitorum*.

"Contain yourself, Brother," cried Brother Paul as we towed them back across the bay toward the monastery. "Your history is a satanic and pernicious document. He lampoons the Holy Fathers mercilessly, my sons."

"Does he now?" my father said, beside himself with delight.

"*Hodie Christus natus est,*" sang Brother St. Hilaire. "*Hodie salvatore aperuit.*"

When Brother St. Hilaire paused for a drink my father struck up a rousing rendition of "*En Roulant.*" "*Derrière chez nous y'a-t'un étang,*" he sang.

Immediately Brother St. Hilaire began to submit the refrain: "*En roulant ma boule.*"

"*Trois beaux canards s'en vont baignant.*"

"*Rouli, roulant MA BOULE.*"

As we approached the shore Brother St. Hilaire had a final drink. He did not appear to be discouraged over losing his shipment of Benedictine. "That warms up *mes boules* all right," he said. "*Avez-vous deux boules*, Paul? *Non?*"

Brother Paul hurriedly crossed himself.

My father declined Brother St. Hilaire's invitation to tour the monastery. It was midafternoon, and we still ad about ten miles to cover. He said we would be back soon for a more leisurely visit.

"If you see Tett before I do tell him we'll be down in a week or so," Brother St. Hilaire said. "Even now the Holy Ghost and I have another batch working."

"You may tell him Brother St. Hilaire may be down in

a week or so," Brother Paul said. "My sailing days are over. I will notify the police immediately about that madman in the launch."

"You'll do no such thing," Brother St. Hilaire said. "We can't have the lake overrun by those dolts if we're to pursue our avocation freely."

Brother Paul looked at us dolefully. The man had a genuinely tragic countenance. "I hope you don't run into him further up the lake, my sons."

"I hope we do," my father said. "Goodbye, monks. Goodbye, Hilarious."

Fifteen minutes later we were paddling between mountains rising thousands of feet on both sides of us. The lake lay deep in the shadow of the mountains, but high overhead the sun still shone brightly on icy granite cliffs. Here in the mountain notch Lake Memphremagog was said to be bottomless. I had heard many persons including my father say that the mountains continued to fall off sharply below the surface to fathomless depths. I did not really believe that the lake plunged down toward black chaos and old night, but the unriffled surface was as still and black as the back of a mirror, and although it was not cold, I shivered and buttoned up my jacket again.

I couldn't stop thinking about that huge hijacker and his wraithlike white hair. I for one agreed with Brother Paul. I had seen all I ever wanted to of that apparition. "Dad," I said, "do you really think that man in the launch was the devil?"

My father laughed. "That's been wearing on you, ain't it, Bill? No. He warn't the devil. There ain't no such critter."

"Who was he then?"

"I'd like to know. If we should run into him again, I intend to slow him down and get a closer look at him. I never see such a looking rig in all my days. That white

43

pelt he was wearing for hair must have hung clear to his ass. I believe he colors his beard. He's an old man. If I'd had a clear shot at him he never would have got no older. A specimen like that ought to be stuffed and set up next to Noël Lord's painter down to the Common Hotel."

"I thought he'd killed Brother St. Hilaire with that oar."

"Yes, that was an awful blow. I hope it don't interfere with his histories. Now there's a real man for you, Bill. Hilarious is a man and a scholar, in that order. Paul, he's a horse of another color. I suspicion that fella is a homocycle. Did you see where he was trying to put his hand to give Hilarious extreme unction? For a minute there I thought he was giving him an extreme enema."

I wasn't sure what a homocycle was, but at fourteen I wasn't going to expose my naiveté by asking. I laughed somewhat uncertainly and turned to look at my father. His paddle was lying across the thwart in front of him and he was smoking his pipe. I had stopped paddling when he began talking about the hijacker. There was no wind, the lake was perfectly still, but we were moving rapidly north through the mountains. My father shrugged and grinned. "Don't ask me, Bill. It's always done this up here. Maybe it's some kind of current."

I was thoroughly spooked by what was happening to us, but I couldn't deny that it was happening. This was no illusion. With no effort on our part we were cutting steadily north through the mountains, leaving a long rippling wake behind us on the dark quiet water. If there was any kind of current, it was imperceptible.

My father smoked his pipe and grinned over his long jaw like a fox. I didn't see how he could be so nonchalant. That was his way, though. He had a boundless sense of wonder, but nothing ever seemed to surprise him. His confidence in life was unshakable. And while I could never

44

attain those rarefield heights of affirmation where he dwelt, so long as we were together nothing could really frighten me either. That is how much I believed in him.

Gradually I relaxed. The bare trees and rocks marched quickly past us. I shut my eyes, then opened them to see how far we had gone. I was mesmerized, nearly unaware of passing time.

"Look there, Bill. Ain't that a grand sight?"

It was late afternoon. Ahead of us the lake opened out wider again. Across an icy bay on the east side was a sweeping escarpment several hundred yards long and at least one hundred feet high, surmounted by a single balsam fir as tall as the Universalist Church steeple in the Common. The upper part of the cliff was entirely glazed over with dazzling frozen springs of every color from deepest blue to light green. Wedged in between its base and the lake was a narrow strip of gravel littered with granite talus and polychromatic chunks of fallen ice, like giant jewels waiting for some Sinbad to come along and pick them up. North of the cliff the jumbled mountains sat further back from the water. Far to the north a rosy pillar of smoke from the paper mill stood motionless in the sky above Magog.

Now my father was paddling again, driving the big canoe along through the floating ice in the bay with short chopping powerful Indian strokes. "Up there," he said, tilting his head toward the tall fir. "That's where we'll be meeting Henry."

I broke a channel through the rotting yellow ice with my paddle blade, and we landed just south of the cliff. This time my legs were so stiff they almost buckled when I stepped out. We carried the canoe up into the woods and turned it upside down out of sight from the lake. I must have been looking at it askance because my father laughed and said, "She won't get up and walk away, Bill. She just plays them tricks on the water."

He slipped into the shoulder straps of the pack basket and started up through the woods, making a wide circuit around the cliff. There was no trail and the slope was very steep. It took us about ten minutes to work our way up and then over to the clearing where the big lone fir stood.

Back on the edge of the clearing a dilapidated cabin sagged into a copse of young beech trees. The cabin had been rough hewn from fir or spruce logs, and no one had lived there for a long time. The door had fallen off its leather hinges into a patch of wild raspberries. Most of the floor had rotted out from snow and rain blown in through the open doorway. Behind the cabin a tote road ran back through the hardwoods toward a cut in the mountains. The road was quite dry, and looked passable.

I got some dead limbs together and my father built a fire a few feet back from the cliffside fir. He made another pan of woodsman's coffee and fried a big steak from Hercule. He didn't seem disconcerted to be eating his pet bull, though he remarked that the steaks would taste better after the beef had hung for a week. Down along the lakeshore a few peeper frogs began to sing, first tentatively, then in a loud unbroken chorus. It was very early in the year for them.

"Hear them go it," my father said. "Them little sleighbell frogs are singing for rain, Wild Bill. In one or two days we'll have a warm rain. Sweet Evangeline will have her herd out in the pasture within a week."

Dusk was settling quickly over the snowy mountains to the northwest. Beyond the peaks lay the St. Lawrence River. Beyond the great river, the enormous Canadian wilderness into which my great-great-great-grandfather had traveled when he was my age, paddling the same canoe,

46

singing with his father the same songs my father had sung all day.

"Dad, tell me about René Bonhomme."

Like many persons with romantic impulses, my father loved to talk about the distant past. While he was almost painfully circumspect about his own past before his marriage, he enjoyed nothing more than eulogizing his ancestors. Now in the lavender mountain twilight he lit his pipe, poured himself more coffee and began again the story of how René St. Laurent Bonhomme had built the birch canoe and come to Kingdom County: the story I had heard from him and Cordelia so many times that I felt I knew it as well as they did, yet always wanted to hear again.

3

IN 1792, when he was fourteen years old, René St. Laurent Bonhomme went into the woods with his father near their home in Trois-Rivières, Quebec, and found a white birch tree seventy feet tall and perfectly straight. It was March, before the sap had started to run, and there was still deep snow where they felled the tree. When the tree was down they stripped off thirty feet of bark, which they laid out on a cleared spot with the outer side facing up. Under his father's close supervision and using only an axe and a crooked knife, René fashioned the gunwales and ribs from a nearby cedar. When the shell was finished he fit in cedar planking and maple thwarts and tapped in the ribs. Before coming out of the woods he etched a fleur-de-lis into the stern and a floating loon on the bow.

During each of the next four years he and his father and two other men of habitant descent paddled the nineteen-foot birch canoe from Trois-Rivières to Lake Athabasca and back, a distance of nearly three thousand miles. They left in April as soon as the ice was out of the St. Lawrence, and from that day until the day in late October when they arrived home they paddled or portaged eighteen hours out of every twenty-four. On the return trip each man carried a one-hundred-and-eighty-pound pack of furs over the portages.

The birch canoe proved durable, but after his father's death of a strangulated hernia on the wild northern shore of Lake Superior in the early fall of 1795, the fabled life of a voyageur no longer appealed to René. In the spring of 1796, the spring he was eighteen, he and his crew of two paddled the canoe south instead of north, traveling up the swollen St. Francis and Magog rivers into Lake Memphremagog. There René's crew disappeared, leaving him to proceed alone up the Lower Kingdom River to the Common Falls, where he used the load of brandy he had stolen from the Northwest Fur Company's warehouse to establish the first tavern in what would later become Kingdom County. It was a strategic spot, catching most of the Indian, trapper and settler traffic between the Upper Connecticut River and what was still generally called French Canada. Even before he finished building the tavern he began to make money.

Today in Kingdom County René Bonhomme is something of a legend. He is regarded as the founder of the village of Kingdom Common, and near the falls is a state historical marker commemorating his exploits as the progenitor of that dubious tradition of whiskey running to which successive generations of our family were to revert so frequently. I admire my great-great-great-grandfather more for being able to build a birch canoe and for having the initiative to break free from a despotic monopoly than for opening the first bar in the area, but as my father pointed out to me in the course of his history, without a reliable local supply of liquor Kingdom County probably couldn't have been settled at all.

Kingdom County — it remains a wonder to me that it

was settled under any conditions. When René first saw it, it was completely covered with a nearly impenetrable forest of pine, fir, spruce and cedar. It was accessible only by water, and much of that was rocky and treacherous and white. Wherever it wasn't mountainous it was swampy. Even the Indians, who could live anywhere, used it only as a trade route. In 1932 Cordelia would call Kingdom County a waste, and like other wastes across the country it attracted many misanthropes and a few genuinely desperate men looking for a sanctuary, including René Bonhomme himself.

Cordelia was his granddaughter and remembered him well. She described him as a tiny man, smaller even than my father, with the same thick white hair and striking combination of Indian features and coloring and shrewd blue eyes. René was nothing if not shrewd, she said. Soon after he arrived it became clear that Kingdom County was going to become part of Vermont and Vermont part of the United States instead of the independent republic many of its citizens still think it should be; so in 1800 he formally changed his name from Bonhomme to Goodman. Later the same year he married the blond-haired daughter of a tall Scottish settler named Calvin Matthews.

René's son Calvin had his Grandfather Matthews' height and his father's dark complexion and vivid blue eyes. From his mother's father Calvin inherited a small library consisting mainly of Wesleyan tracts but including one volume of Scottish history and a complete set of Shakespeare's plays. His mother taught him to read these and accept them all at face value so that later when he was at Yale preparing for the ministry he read widely, if more discriminatingly, in history and literature as well as theology. When he returned to Kingdom County he allocated his time about equally between establishing the first Universalist church in northern Vermont, reading the books he ordered by the thousands from New York and Boston, and drinking with old René, who by then was the second wealthiest man in the county.

René Bonhomme was apparently as generous as my father. In 1845 he gave half his fortune to Calvin to build a library on the west side of the Common across from the court-house and bank. It was a handsome brick structure three stories tall with slender columns of Vermont marble, and throughout the nineteenth century contained one of the finest collections of poetry, drama, history and theology in the state. By the time he built the library Calvin had turned over the church to another minister and was spending all his time reading, hunting and fishing, and drinking with René and his own son, Cordelia's brother.

Like his grandfather before him who built the birch canoe, William Shakespeare Goodman was a born craftsman. By the time he was twelve and drinking in his grandfather's tavern he had constructed intricate scale models of the Parthenon, the Colosseum at Rome, the Temple of Apollo and the Globe Theater. In 1850 when he was sixteen he cast the bronze statue of Ethan Allen for the village Common. The same year he conceived the project that would occupy him for the rest of his life, building the round barns that can still be found in Kingdom County.

Working mainly alone with infinite care and usually half-drunk, he built eleven of these magnificent structures, including one for himself and his bride on our hilltop at the end of Lord Hollow, overlooking much of northern Vermont and New Hampshire and a large sector of southern Quebec. Even Uncle Henry said that William Shakespeare had chosen a homestead with a grand prospect, though my uncle and all the rest of us knew very well that William's objective in building on the hill was not to see Kingdom County but to assure himself that Kingdom County would see his splendid barn — a vanity we paid for all winter when the arctic gales came roaring down across the ice on Lake Memphremagog, funneled between the mountain notch like polar tornadoes, and on over the flat cedar swamp to present us with their full blasting force. If William had not had the foresight to connect the barn to the house with an ell there would have been blizzard days when we simply could not have gotten across the dooryard to the barn to do the chores. Also there was no reliable source of water on the hill, but that problem did not trouble my great-grandfather any more than the winter winds. He was an architect and a builder, not a farmer.

William intended to teach the art of building round barns to his son, but died in Calvin's arms at the first Battle of Bull Run before he had the opportunity, leaving Cordelia and his frail and penniless wife to bring up my grandfather on the hilltop. His name was William too, and in 1869 when he was fourteen he ran away from home and did not return because Cordelia had refused to let him continue drinking after his father and grandfather left for the Civil War.

"They was all rum hounds, Wild Bill." My father pounded my knee. "Rum hounds. Sweet Evangeline wouldn't want me telling you rum tales and whiskey tales.

"Now, Bill. Old René was dead against Calvin and William Shakespeare going off to war. He believed Calvin would be killed the day he returned and William wouldn't return at all. As it turned out he was right about Calvin and nearly right about William, though nobody but your aunt paid much heed to him at the time. He was an old fella up in his eighties, and no doubt they all supposed his mind was wandering."

I listened attentively. This was a part of the story that my father had never mentioned to me.

"So Calvin and William set out like almost every other able man between eighteen and sixty in Kingdom County, as though if Vermont couldn't be sovereign and independent the way they wanted, neither by the caterwauling Christ was the South going to be. René moved up to the farm with Cordelia and William's sick wife and little William, your grandfather that later run off. He had sold the tavern by then, and give the rest of his money to Calvin, who had turned it over to the state war fund, and was poorer than when he'd come to Kingdom County years and years before with the load of brandy. All he had to his name was the canoe and his musket and two sets of clothes. The everyday clothes he'd wore around the tavern, and his old voyageur's clothes. Which Cordelia found him dressed up in early one morning in blueberry time, setting there in the summer kitchen in his mooseskin moccasins and wool leggings and red shirt with the green sash. And his beaver hat, Bill. He was wearing his beaver hat, like it was seventy years ago and he was going back up to Lake Athabasca. He told Cordelia he intended to make one last trip on Lake Memphremagog. He said he wanted her to come along.

"Well, there was a small homemade steamboat on the lake then to carry sightseers up to Magog in the summertime, but old René wouldn't hear of taking that. Nothing would do but they must go by canoe. The only thing a steamboat was good for, so he told Cordelia, was blowing up. Him and her was always very close. She couldn't deny him nothing, so she put up a lunch, and being a rugged gal, she carried the canoe down the back hill to the St. John and off they spun down through the swamp with René in the bow and your aunt in the stern.

"It was a good day, like today, only of course much hotter. By and by he commenced to singing '*En Roulant.*' After Cordelia started keeping track he sung one hundred

53

and twenty-four verses. Every little while in the middle of a verse he would look back and grin at her again and point north with his paddle — like maybe he expected her to transport him clear back to the Northwest Territories. He didn't, though. Because when they got up to the point where we ate lunch today he told her to stop.

"They ate there, too, and after dinner he went to sleep. Or at least he appeared to go to sleep. Your aunt thought he had, and went back up on the ridge where the railway runs now and picked her a hatful of blueberries. She said it was one of them old-time sun hats with a wide brim, and she picked it heaping full in less than an hour. She started back to show the old man, and when she got there he was gone and so was the canoe. She run to the end of the point. All she could see was that little fart-ass steamboat chuffing up the lake about a mile away.

"She waved with her handkerchief but they didn't see her. She turned the berries out of her hat into the water and waved with the hat. Still they didn't see her. They held right on course up the middle of the lake. So being a stronger swimmer than most men she dove in where she'd spilled the blueberries and struck out for the boat. It seems the captain was drunk, and nearly run over her, but she got out of the way at the last minute and clumb up the side like a pirate and told him about René.

"He said they hadn't spied any canoe coming back down the lake, so René must be up in the notch. His name was Kinneson, Bill: he was Warden R.W.'s great-grandfather. The story is that he paid a fella name of Terhune to go to the War of Rebellion in his place. I don't know about that but I know Cordelia made him put on all the steam he had, which warn't that much, and sure enough when they got up in the notch they spotted René's canoe. It was riding high in the water and moving north fast, but the old man warn't nowhere to be seen. They had the devil's own time overtaking it, too, though there warn't no more wind on the lake than there was out there today. They thought maybe René was laying down in the bottom. But when they finally caught up with it all they found was his paddle and musket. René was gone."

"Gone where?"

"I don't know. Nobody ever knew. Gone. He disappeared."

"He couldn't have. René Bonhomme couldn't have disappeared, Dad. He must have drowned and they found his body. Because there's a gravestone with his name and dates on it right in the plot behind mother's garden."

"Cordelia put that stone there. He ain't under it, Bill. He could have set the canoe adrift and then went off in the woods. A man could easy enough get turned around in these big woods even today. Old René wouldn't have though, not unless he meant to. Maybe he meant to. However it happened, they never found a trace."

For a few minutes neither of us spoke. It had been dark for about an hour. The fire had died down to coals. Up to the north I could see the lights of Magog reflected in the sky.

"What about Calvin and William Shakespeare?" I said. "You said René was right about them."

"He was nearly right, Wild Bill. Hark. Listen."

"I am listening. What happened to them? I thought they both died in the war."

"Listen, Bill. There's a car coming down the tote road."

"How was your trip up the lake?" Uncle Henry said, hunkering down by the fire.

"It was uneventful," my father said. "Wild Bill told me stories all day to pass the time. How was your drive up?"

"I'll tell you how it was," Rat said. "It was heathenish

fast. We must have been doing forty miles an hour round them bends. Now you tell him what you told me after we crossed over the line, Henry Coville."

"Well, Bill, I ain't backing out. Neither's Rat. We all need that money in the worst way. But after we went through customs tonight I commenced to thinking again about something that's been bothering me since yesterday."

"What's the matter, Hen, don't you think I and Wild Bill can get it back across for you? You ain't losing faith in the old master?"

"No, Bill, it ain't nothing like that. You could get that whiskey down the lake if the Women's Temperance League was patrolling it."

"Yes, and sell them a case into the bargain," my father said. "But go ahead, Henry, don't let me sidetrack you. What was it you thought of?"

"Here it is. We're going to transport about forty cases. All right. Them two French fellas have agreed to pay us a thousand dollars, flat rate. That's fine. For us that's very fine. Now look at it another way. That comes to twenty-five dollars a case. Where does that leave them? Where's their profit, Quebec Bill?"

"That's easy. What will a case of good Canadian whiskey fetch downcountry these days?"

"A case of Seagram's, which is what we'll be running according to them boys, will go for one hundred dollars."

"Then their profit is seventy-five dollars a case. That's a total of three thousand dollars after paying us."

"Ain't you forgetting something?"

"Spit it out, Henry. What's the trouble?"

"The trouble is they would have to pay seventy-five dollars a case for it right here in Canada to buy it in the first place."

"Henry Coville," my father said, "whatever made you

think they bought that whiskey? They didn't buy no whiskey. They hijacked it. I knowed that much from the minute you started telling me about it. Except for what they pay us, it's all profit. Does that relieve your concern for their financial security?"

"It ain't their financial security I'm concerned about. It's our personal security. I don't like this, Bill. I didn't like it when they first proposed it. I like it less now."

"I won't be a party to common thievery," Rat said. "Transporting spirits is one matter. Common thievery is another. Them spirits don't rightfully belong to them Frenchmen."

"They rightfully belong to the Seagram family in Montreal," my father said. "They're an uncommon family, Rat, so this is uncommon thievery. You don't have a thing to worry about. But if you want to wait here alone in the dark woods for us to get back long after midnight that's fine with me. Hark, what's that?"

"I'm coming," Rat said.

I got my father aside. "Why did he have to horn in?" I whispered. "He'll spoil everything." I was jealous of Rat, whom I regarded as an interloper, a constraint on the adult camaraderie I had planned on enjoying with my father and Uncle Henry.

"Don't pay no attention to him, Bill. He's curious as an old woman; he couldn't stand to sit home and not know what was happening for fear he would be missing something to disapprove of. I knowed all the time he'd come. We'll have some sport with him."

We poured the last of the coffee on the coals of the campfire. My father put the shotgun and the pack basket inside the cabin and we got into White Lightning. Immediately my father began to bounce high up off the back seat. "Bill," Uncle Henry said. "Please."

Uncle Henry was in most respects even less acquisitive than my father, with a contempt for land ownership equal to Cordelia's and Ralph Waldo Emerson's. To him nearly all owned property, if not an outright illusion, was an encumbrance to be eschewed at all costs. He expected only one material object from this code and that was White Lightning. Uncle Henry drove White Lightning hard but with great respect. He spent entire days polishing its alabaster enamel, rubbing esoteric compounds into the white leather upholstery, touching up the white paint on the wheel spokes. It was one of the most luxurious American automobiles ever built, and I didn't blame him for not wanting my father to use the seat for a trampoline.

Even on that rough logging trace the six-thousand-pound car rode as smooth as the canoe on calm water. The myriad dials and gauges recessed into the snowy leather dashboard glowed alluringly. The seats smelled brand new. Under our feet the floors were carpeted with white lamb's skin. I put my head back on the smooth plush seat, took one more deep breath of that heady aromatic leather scent and fell asleep.

When I woke up I imagined for a moment that we were still in the canoe, which was still moving north.

"We're in Magog, Wild Bill," my father was saying. "We'll be stopping here for a short while."

On a Friday night in the early spring Magog was a busy place. The wooden sidewalk along the unpaved and muddy main street was swarming with loggers, truckers and rivermen, going in and out of the taverns across from the long lighted paper mill. The mill whined loudly, permeating the town with its sulphurous acrid stench.

We parked White Lightning in front of a place called Chez Joie de Vivre and went inside. It was a long rectangular dim room reeking of strong Canadian tobacco and crowded with men and a few women. The tables were packed close together. At one end of the room a country band was playing raucously. We got a table near the door and Uncle Henry ordered beers for himself and Rat. My father got out his pocketbook and looked inside. "I'm springing, Bill," Uncle Henry said. "You'll want coffee, and a sarsaparilla for Billy here?"

"You can get me the coffee, Henry. I'm buying Wild Bill a beer."

Rat stared at his beer but didn't pick it up. I thought he was still sulking over running stolen whiskey. "What's the matter, Ratty?" my father said. "You was never a fella to let a head stand long on an ice-cold brew. That's a Molson's, ain't it? You can't get beer like that down to Cousin Whiskeyjack's kitchen. See them little golden beads, boy. See them dance."

"Quebec Bill, you like to talk about drinking as well as any man I ever met liked to drink," Uncle Henry said.

"If you must know," Rat said morosely, "Lord Jesus come to me in the night and said I warn't to drink no beer in Canady."

"Did he give you a reason, Rat?"

"Yes. He said it would give me the dyspepsia."

"What time was this, my boy?"

"I ain't sure except it was afore midnight. Afore Henry arrove. Because I had to get up to go to the privy just afterwards and Henry wasn't here yet."

"Well now, Rat, I've got glad tidings for you. Because along about five A.M. when I was setting in the kitchen loading buckshot into my shells the Lord appeared to me. 'What are you up to now, Quebec Bill?' says He in a stern voice. 'I'm loading buckshot, Lord, in case we run into any hijacking sons of bitches out on the lake.' 'Very good, my son,' He says. 'I ain't telling you what to do, but I would advise a double load. You can never tell what you may run into out there. Now to get down to business. Earlier in the evening I had me a little visit with Muskrat Kinneson and warned him against imbibing of beer up to Canady on account of it causing him discomfort and possibly embarrassing winds. But it seems I neglected to tell Brother Muskrat that he could feel free to have all the hard stuff he wanted. He's sleeping now and I don't want to roust him out again. Would you kindly deliver the message for me when he wakes up?' "

Rat reached out a long arm and snagged a passing waitress. "Fetch me a double shot of straight gin," he said.

I had never drunk beer before. I didn't like the bitter taste, but whenever Uncle Henry took a drink from his glass I sipped from mine. Meanwhile my father was looking keenly around the room. "I know most of these fellas," he said. "We won't have much trouble finding out what we want to find out."

"What do we want to find out?" I said.

"Whatever we can."

In a few minutes the band stopped for a break. My father approached the fiddler and conferred with him. The fiddler nodded his head and handed his instrument to my father, who sat down and began to play. A man in a red-checked shirt and calked boots began to do a Canadian stepdance. Another logger joined him. Soon twenty-five or thirty men were dancing to the medley of jigs and reels my father was playing in his inimitable style compounded of old-time French, western and Cajun techniques. When he stopped the crowd cheered for more. Some of the men called out his name. He played again, smiling, nodding ingratiatingly, doing an intricate clog dance with his feet, shouting out the name of each new song: " 'St. Anne's Reel,' boys; the old 'Devil's Dream'; 'Maple Sugar.' Here's a little bit of the old 'Rubber Dolly.' " He leaped up and

60

held the fiddle triumphantly over his head, still dancing. Slender men with trim mustaches and brightly colored shirts crowded around him to shake hands. He mentioned many of them by name. They all wanted to buy him a drink, but my father laughed and declined; his drinking days were over, he said.

He circulated around the room shaking hands and talking and laughing. My head was starting to spin from the beer and smoke. I leaned over to Uncle Henry. His face looked as though I were observing it through a magnifying glass. "I thought he wanted to get some information," I said.

"He's getting it," Uncle Henry said.

Back in White Lightning my father bounced around in the seat like a jack-in-the-box, clapped Henry and Rat on the shoulder, played his imaginary fiddle. "Did you see them people flock around me, boys? They hadn't heard the violin played like that in years. The whole place was up jigging. I ain't seen jigging like that since I set a crew of drunk lumbermen over Coaticook way to dancing so hard the bunkhouse floor caved in."

"It's past midnight," Uncle Henry said.

"Well, Henry," my father said, putting his hand on my uncle's shoulder, "this keeps getting more and more interesting all the while. It appears that there was two rival gangs of hijackers up here. One was a family of eight brothers named LaChance. They was well known and respected in these parts for years."

"LaChance?"

"Yes. According to what I was told, up until last fall they had a monopoly on all the local moonshining and hijacking. Then Carcajou showed up."

"Carcajou?"

"That's right. He calls himself Carcajou, which is Indian

61

for wolverine, so I'm told. A crazy man that likes to dress up in costumes, with a gang of them white albiner fellas with pink eyes. Carcajou and the albiners, they commenced to hijack whiskey trucks right in broad daylight. He'd pull up alongside a truck dressed like a policeman and signal for the driver to roll down the window. Then he'd lean over and toss a lighted stick of dynamite through the open window and drive off fast. When the cab blowed up them albiners would swarm out of the back of Carcajou's truck and transfer the whiskey."

"What is this that you're telling me?" Uncle Henry said. "They did this in broad daylight? Albiners?"

"Certainly. They seemed to have a sixth sense that told them when a whiskey truck was coming. A couple of times they mined the highways. The Mounties laid for them and the township police laid for them, but nobody could catch them. Nobody knowed where they come from or where they hid out. But them LaChance boys, Henry. Carcajou was cutting into their business. So they set out to hunt him down. They tracked him to a cabin away off up in the Megantic Mountains near the Maine line. All eight of the brothers and their pa and two uncles surrounded the cabin. Just at dawn they fired her. But Carcajou and the albiners wouldn't budge. The roof fell in and then the walls fell in and the LaChances figured the gang had burned up inside. After the fire died down they went up and poked around in the timbers. And Carcajou and his white boys sprung up out of the root cellar where they said no human man could possibly have survived and mowed down five of them on the spot with machine guns, including the father and uncles. The ones that made it to the woods said all the while the machine guns was a-clattering Carcajou was laughing a laugh like they never heard before and never wanted to again. They said the laugh was worse than the machine guns. But not all the ones that got to the woods

62

got away. They split up and Carcajou run four of them down. A deer hunter found one with his throat slit from ear to ear. Just last week a fire warden come across another one hanging by his feet from the top of a lookout tower. It looked like the top of his head had been smashed in, but when they cut him down they see he'd been scalped. The other two they still haven't found. Only two out of the eleven got away."

Uncle Henry started White Lightning. "We're going to get away right now," he said.

My father grabbed his shoulder. "Wait a minute, Henry. There's more you ain't heard."

"I don't want to hear no more. It's off. First thing Monday morning I'll put a lien on White Lightning and we'll buy you hay enough to last a year. This run is off. Canady ain't a safe place no longer. I never heard of such doings. Not over across, not nowhere."

"Shut off that key and hear the rest, Henry Coville. Then go ahead and make up your mind."

"I'll leave the car running. Talk fast."

"All right. When you hear this next I'm sure you'll want to continue. All winter Carcajou laid low. Everybody figured that he'd cleared out. Then last week they found an empty Seagram's truck on a back road between Cowansville and High Water. The cab was blowed completely off it and the driver was splattered all over the field. First they figured it was dynamite again. Then a Mountie found something at the far end of the field that changed their mind. You couldn't guess what in a million years."

"I ain't a-going to try," Uncle Henry said as he shifted into first gear.

"Just take one guess, Henry. I want someone to guess. Look here. It was round and about this big."

Uncle Henry had a subtle sense of irony from which nearly every trace of sarcasm had been refined; but I am

63

positive that it was with mordant sarcasm that he said to my father, "A cannonball."

"Right you are," my father shouted, grasping Uncle Henry's head and wrenching it around so hard I could hear the joints crack like a giant knuckle. "You didn't know I was a chiropractor, did you?" he shouted into Uncle Henry's face. "Ain't you convinced now that this is the run for us?"

"Good Christ, Bill," Uncle Henry said, as close to nonplussed as I had ever seen him. "Did you actually suppose that tale about the cannonball was going to convince me? What can you be thinking of? We don't know who owns that whiskey we're supposed to pick up tonight. We might be walking right into a bear trap. Them albiners and LaChances and Carcajous: if we run onto them they'd as soon shoot Billy here as you or me. And that would be plenty soon. I don't want to be found hanging without no hair from a fire tower. We're going home."

"Right again, Henry. We're going home with four thousand dollars' worth of whiskey."

"It's off, Bill. There's no way in the world you could get me up there near that barn now. I said not to worry about the hay. We'll get the hay if we have to hijack it. But we ain't hijacking no whiskey up here."

"Maybe you ain't, Henry. Maybe Ratty here don't want to go. But I and Wild Bill are going if we have to go alone."

"What do I have to do to make you understand I ain't letting you go? I couldn't ever face my sister again if I let .you go up there."

"Listen to your uncle, Wild Bill. Be there a man in Kingdom County to tell Quebec Bill Bonhomme what he can and cannot do?"

"No," I said doubtfully.

"Then I'm no man," Uncle Henry said equably. "Because I can tell you no and mean it."

64

"Sit tight, Bill," my father said. "A dreadful manhandling is about to take place." He opened his door and got out in the street.

Uncle Henry got out too. I didn't know what to do. I couldn't believe that two men who were closer than most brothers, the two men I loved and respected more than any others, were actually going to fight each other. If they were, I was very worried for my father. As quick and tough as he was, I didn't believe he was any match for Uncle Henry, who despite his lost lung competed in and usually won the annual chain-fighting event at the Kingdom Fair, in which two men linked wrist to wrist by a six-foot log chain fought in a ring with their bare hands and feet and the chain itself until one man succeeded in dragging the other to each of the four corner posts in succession. If my father did beat Uncle Henry he would have to use his feet, in which case he might knock out one of my uncle's eyes or give him a concussion.

They stood close together in the mud. I could see them clearly in the light from the paper mill windows. The car was still running.

"I hate to do this, Henry," my father said.

"I know you do, Bill."

Without any warning Uncle Henry struck my father so hard that he left his feet, slid across White Lightning's hood and landed in the mud on the other side of the car. Later Uncle Henry said that it was as powerful a blow as he had ever delivered — that in fact he had not meant to hit my father so hard, but knew he would have to hit him plenty hard to knock him out.

Uncle Henry went around and bent down by the right front fender. He stayed bent over quite a long time. I was afraid my father was badly hurt. Uncle Henry straightened up and looked around. "That's most curious," he said. "He seems to have disappeared."

Before those words had completely registered with me my father slid up from under the car on the driver's side and scrambled in behind the wheel. He was coated with mud and laughing hysterically. With a terrible rending of gears he gunned White Lightning forward past Uncle Henry, whose face remained solemn and inscrutable.

Under my father's management White Lightning bucked and shook worse than our old Ford. I grabbed Rat from behind to prevent him from flying forward through the windshield. The gears clashed as we shifted into second. I realized that my father's legs were too short to depress the clutch all the way to the floor. Also he was too short to see over the rim of the wheel, and had to peer out between it and the dashboard.

I looked back once. Uncle Henry was standing in the street between the tavern and the paper mill. Again the gears shrieked out. We slued along, throwing mud six feet out to either side. My father was steering with one hand on the bottom of the wheel. We went faster and faster. Frequently he turned back to beam at me, taking his eyes off the road for several seconds at a time.

"Look out," I yelled.

We had driven off into a church lawn containing a lighted manger scene. "These people still think it's Christmas," my father said, sideswiping the crèche. "We'll have to set them straight. Spring is here."

"Stop," I shouted. "What are you doing? We can't steal Uncle Henry's car."

My father turned around again. The red speedometer needle was hovering around one hundred. He began to laugh. "Wild Bill," he yelled with enormous delight, "I think my Christly jaw is broke."

4

ACCORDING to my father the abandoned farm
where we were supposed to pick up the whiskey was
a quarter of a mile off a back road running from Magog
down to the border through the mountains on the west
side of the lake. It was approximately opposite the cliff
where we had eaten supper and waited for Uncle Henry,
and about four miles inland. My father said he had been
there when it was a going farm. He thought that a back
approach leading over a ridge from an old cedar still on
the dirt road might still be open.

The cedar still was gone, but the woods road over the
ridge looked as if it might be negotiable. Moments later
we were jouncing up the steep side of a small mountain.
In places the road had been washed down to bare shelving
ledge where a higher car would probably have tipped over.
Suddenly I saw the long combing drift of a snowbank
directly ahead of us.

As we accelerated toward the drift I held tightly to Rat
and shut my eyes. There was a tremendous crunching

impact. When I looked again we were leveling a new right of way through a stand of small firs. As we mowed down the trees the branches sprang back up and whipped against the underpinning of the car. My father laughed out of his shattered jaw. He said we would put White Lightning through her paces and see what she could do. I only hoped she could get back on the logging road again. My father said he loved a detour. He declared with feeling that more people should get off the beaten path and see the countryside.

We emerged from the ravaged softwoods and careered along at a high speed through some young maples, which played a more peremptory tattoo on White Lightning's underbelly. My father was knocking over small trees. Somehow we got back on the tote road. We were driving close beside a rushing torrent in a deep ravine. Then we were charging down a precipitous incline. "Bridge out," my father announced.

"I have heard the angels and archangels singing my name," Rat said without waking up as we hurtled over the chasm.

We landed with a terrific jar. It was all I could do to hang on to Rat. His head almost hit the dashboard. Before I could pull him back he belched and vomited on the white carpeting.

"There's his drinks," my father said as we tore along. "There's his supper. Good Christ, is he still at it? That must be day before yesterday's breakfast. Henry ain't going to be pleased about this, Wild Bill."

Some minutes later we crossed the height of land, and came down into a sugar bush. My father shut off the engine and headlights. Coasting along under the gigantic trees the battered Cadillac groaned and squeaked on its broken springs. Uncle Henry, I thought with apprehension, was going to have considerably more to be unhappy about than his soiled carpet.

Down through the tall maples I saw a dark cluster of buildings: house, barn, sheds. There was a dim light in one of the back windows. "They ain't expecting nobody from this side," my father said.

"Who is they?"

He stopped the car several hundred yards above the buildings. "You'll see, Wild Bill. You'll see directly. We'll leave Rat here to talk with the archangels and you and me will go down there and have us a look."

I got out and shut the door gently. We started down the lane between the trees. As we approached the buildings I made out a car behind the milk house. From the front of the house it would have been invisible. We moved noiselessly over last fall's leaves. My heart was thumping the way it had the day before when Warden had confronted my father at the falls.

We crossed the dooryard, grown up to burdocks and bull thistles. Close to the back of the house was a very old and gnarled apple tree, unmistakable even in the dark. My father stood behind the tree and looked around into the window. I hung back in the weeds on the pretext of pulling dead burdocks off my legs; actually I was terrified of what I might see inside the house. It was still quite warm but I was shivering all over. The spring frogs were singing from a marsh someplace below the house.

As frightened as I was, I was even more curious about whoever was inside that house. I tiptoed up behind the tree and looked over my father's head into a small rear bedchamber. Five men were sitting around a table playing cards and drinking by lantern light. Each of them was dressed in blue. Each had long white hair, and the man facing the window wore a full black beard.

My father pulled my head down close to his and whispered a single word. He didn't need to, though. I knew already, as he had undoubtedly known back in Magog, that the man with the beard was the hijacker Carcajou, the wolverine who had attacked and tried to drown the monks on the lake and who was now drinking their Benedictine; who with his gang blew people to bits with dynamite, cut them down with machine guns, sliced their throats, scalped them, blasted them to Kingdom Come with cannons; who like the fabled children of Israel had survived an inferno and who had now set this trap for the two men who had hired Uncle Henry to do what they prudently did not dare do themselves.

"Them two Frenchmen with the Buick would be the last two LaChance boys," my father said fifteen minutes later back by the Cadillac. "It all fits, Bill, right down to the Seagram's."

As he explained the situation, he opened Rat's door and began haggling at the reeking lambskin carpet with his hunting knife. "This is good tough material," he said, lifting Rat's feet up and peeling off the entire front floor covering. "There. I doubt Henry will even notice.

"But them LaChance boys. Carcajou must have let it out on purpose to them somehow where the whiskey would be. And they suspicioned that they was being set up. And so they was. But they couldn't know for sure, and they couldn't pass up the opportunity to steal the fella's whiskey that come close to exterminating their family."

"So they set Uncle Henry up to steal the whiskey for them."

"Right, Bill. And that's what lets us off the hook."

"You mean we aren't going to steal the whiskey after all?"

"Certainly we're going to steal it. We just ain't going to deliver it to them LaChance fellas. This run is going to be clear profit, Wild Bill. Come dawn them boys down below there will figure nobody's coming and go to sleep.

70

At the rate they're going tonight they won't wake up till noon or later. By then we'll be back on the other side of the lake with eight thousand dollars' worth of whiskey."

"Eight thousand? I thought it was four before."

"That was before. This is after."

I was so sleepy I didn't really care whether it was eight thousand dollars or eight dollars. All the excitement of the last twenty-four hours had suddenly caught up with me. What I wanted was to go to sleep. I didn't think I could keep my eyes open another sixty seconds if Carcajou and his gang came up through the sugar bush that instant with their entire arsenal of machine guns and cannons and scalping knives.

"What time is it, Dad?"

"A quarter or twenty after one," my father said. "You get in back and lay down, Bill. I'm going to slide on down below and check the lay of the land again. I want to see if there's a guard. I want to see just where the whiskey be, and watch them fellas play cards a while longer. You can tell quite a bit about a man by the way he handles his cards. They seemed to be playing poker. I believe the old man was winning. You're a good whiskey runner, son. I'm most proud of you. I'll wake you up before dawn."

"Be careful, Dad."

"I ain't never nothing else," my father said, heading back down through the trees.

I got in back and stretched out on the beautifully contoured seat. Rat was snoring like a sump pump in low water, but by that time nothing could have kept me awake. I closed my eyes and was asleep.

At dawn we lay on a damp cushion of dead leaves under the maples and waited. When the man appeared I was surprised to see him coming down from the top of the ridge instead of up from the buildings. Although it was still too dark to make out his features, I could see that he was big. Instantly I thought of Carcajou. Maybe he had circled around behind us somehow. But as the big man approached the Cadillac, moving neither fast nor slow and without stealth, I saw that he was unarmed and knew that it was Uncle Henry.

"How did you know he was coming?" I asked my father as we walked down the knoll we had run up five minutes earlier.

"I could hear him huffing and blowing while he was still on his way up the back side of the ridge. Good morning, Henry. I can't tell you how glad I am that you decided to join us. We've got some good news for you. Very good news."

Uncle Henry did not look at us as we came out of the maples into the lane. He was staring at his car. His slightly protuberant eyes traveled slowly over the deep striations along the door and on to the crumpled fenders and the once proud figurine, now twisted and recumbent on the excoriated hood; they took in the hunched and constipated aspect of the body, squatting ignominiously on its broken springs.

Then he looked at my father. His eyes were expressionless, only perhaps bulging a little more than usual. "Whose vehicle would this be?" he said mildly.

"Why, it's yours, Hen," my father replied. "I reckon it got jammed a little. We was breaking it in for you."

As incredible as that remark was, it was not entirely disingenuous. In some ways my father actually admired machines. He enjoyed contemplating their shiny parts and deep inner workings. Without the most rudimentary understanding of basic mechanical principles he enjoyed getting his hands on gears, buttons, levers, switches. He liked to make machines go fast. Best of all he liked to smash them to smithereens, especially when they were careening along at their maximum rate of speed or slightly faster.

Uncle Henry looked blankly at my father, who was beaming over his handiwork. He looked at Rat, now getting back into what was left of the car to go to sleep again. He looked at me. "Is that my vehicle, Billy?"

"Uncle Henry," I said, "look at it this way. You broke Dad's jaw and he broke White Lightning. So you're even."

Uncle Henry gazed at my father's long jaw, which sagged off to the right slightly. "Did I do that, Bill?"

My father nodded proudly and turned his head to give us a profile view. Uncle Henry nodded once and got in behind the wheel.

We got in back and my father put both his hands affectionately on my uncle's shoulders. Every time Uncle Henry leaned forward to get a closer view of the bare metal floor where his carpet had been my father pulled him back in the seat and talked louder, enunciating all his syllables carefully.

"So they're all sound asleep," my father continued, "and the whiskey is waiting in the cow stable. We could steam down there and pick it up in a locomotive and they wouldn't hear us."

"Don't they have a guard?" Uncle Henry said. "Wouldn't there be a guard down below between the house and the road?"

"I checked, and there isn't. That's not all, Henry. That black Packard automobile down there is unlocked. We're going to load that too. We're going to split seven or eight thousand dollars' worth of whiskey, Hen, and you're going to get a backup car for White Lightning."

"Of course I am," Uncle Henry said. By that time I couldn't tell whether he was being sarcastic or ironical or neither, and I doubt that he could either. His eyes were very prominent. I was afraid they might pop right out.

He looked at Rat, slumped into the corner between the seat and the door, wheezing like an asthmatic mule. "What about Brother Kinneson?"

"Brother Kinneson is still choiring with the cherry bins and serry fins. I'm going to wake him from his slumber in a minute. He's got to start the Packard for us."

Uncle Henry sighed. "Bill Bonhomme, this gets worse and worse. Walking up here from Magog I had time to get it all straight. Plenty of time, in fact. This is a setup and you know it. You knowed it last night and I strongly suspected it. Them boys that put us onto this, their name is LaChance. You knowed that last night too. No guards you tell me. I don't like no guards. That ain't right. Why ain't there no guards? Maybe that whiskey is booby-trapped. We don't even have a gun in case something goes wrong. I know that won't stop you, Bill. I know nothing won't stop you. I reckon I can't whup you, neither. Maybe nobody can. But I want you to remember again that I'm against this. I was in three major battles over across. I was shot at and run at with bayonets and finally I was gassed. But I never heard of nothing nowhere to equal this before. I ain't scart. I doubt you was ever scart in your life. If Billy's scart he ain't showing it and not showing it is the better part of any brave man. If Rat was awake he'd be scart and he'd be right to be. I don't know why you're set on doing this. It ain't the money now, I'm certain of that. I don't guess that I want to know what it is. Whatever it is, it ain't worth it. I'll do it because you're going to do it anyway and I couldn't face Vangie if I warn't there to do what I could to help you get out of it. But I don't like it. No guards is the worst part. No guards is very bad."

It was the longest speech I had ever heard Uncle Henry make.

74

"You're a good man, Henry Coville," cried my father. "I and Bill was saying just last night how generous it was of you to lend out your car this way. I don't intend to let you down, neither. There's still the element of surprise. I haven't told you about that yet. Now let off your brake and coast on down behind that Packard. I'll tell you what to do next when we're there."

So just as the sun came up, exactly twenty-four hours after launching the canoe in the cedar swamp behind our hill, we started down through the sugar bush to make our pickup, swaying and bouncing like an old buckboard, un-armed, and trusting to our luck and ingenuity and the element of surprise, which was to be as much of an amaze-ment to Uncle Henry and me as it was to Carcajou. My heart was beating fast again. I was scared all right. I had never been so scared in my life.

The grade was steep enough for us to roll all the way to the barnyard. In daylight the farm looked like any one of hundreds of other abandoned places on both sides of the border. The house sagged, the barn heaved, the fields were growing up to brush. Except for the Packard there was no sign that anyone had been near the place in years.

"Wake up, Rat," my father said. "Rat, wake up. Can you start up a car without no keys and do it quick and not make too much noise?"

"Have you bought another car, Quebec Bill?"

"Yes, Rat. There she is. Here, wake up. There's a bottle for you in this job."

"Say," Rat said, opening his eyes wide, "this don't look like our dooryard."

"The car's right there. Now do this quietly. When I give the word, start her up. Then come back and get in White Lightning with Hen and Wild Bill. We're going to load the Packard right to the gills; there won't be room in it for nobody but me."

As we got out I had a strange and powerful urge to run over to the back bedroom window and look inside. It was not so much that I wanted to assure myself that Carcajou and his albiners were asleep. As frightful as they were to behold, I would rather have seen them doing almost anything than imagine them doing nothing.

Now, though, there was no time for anything but getting the whiskey. We loaded the Packard first while Rat worked on the wires. My father brought the wooden cases out of the milk house three at a time. I carried them singly from the milk house to the Packard, a two-door model with a rumble seat. Uncle Henry stacked the whiskey inside the rumble seat and on the passenger's side of the front seat and the floor in front. In all he managed to pack in thirty cases.

I glanced constantly toward the back of the house. Once I tripped over a discarded harrow tooth and nearly dropped a case. The bottles inside clanked together loudly. I was sure we would be machine-gunned down within seconds. But inside the house nothing stirred.

"Pay attention to what you're doing," Uncle Henry whispered.

Rat seemed to be having trouble with the Packard. Despite all our warnings he grumbled loudly. Uncle Henry began loading the Cadillac. He packed the back from floor to roof. By then White Lightning was right down on her frame, but the springs were already gone so we secured another twelve cases on the wide rear luggage carrier with special straps, which Uncle Henry had ordered with reinforced steel braces for just this purpose. That was as much as she could hold.

My father seemed in no hurry to leave. He strolled leisurely around White Lightning, whose bent fenders were now resting on the ground. He kicked at a tire as though trying to make up his mind whether to buy the car. He did not once look at the house.

After perambulating about the dooryard, surveying the Packard, the apple tree and the back of the house, he motioned for Uncle Henry and me to follow him through the milk house and into the cow stable. As my eyes adjusted to the dimness I saw that there were hundreds and probably thousands of whiskey cases lining the walls. Except for the empty cow stanchions the place looked more like a whiskey warehouse than a barn. But the whiskey was not all my father wanted us to see. At the far end of the stable, directly below a chute from the hayloft, was a large pile of brightly burning loose hay.

"That's the element of surprise," my father said. "A bonfire."

"Christ Jesus," Uncle Henry said, turning for the door. "He's burning down barns."

"Wait a minute, Henry. I want it to be going good when we start up the vehicles. If they know the barn's afire they won't bother with us. Not with all this stock to get out."

There must have been old hay caught in the chute because suddenly the fire was leaping up into it and crackling like mad. Then the entire wall was ablaze.

"That should do it," my father said. "Shag ass, boys."

Uncle Henry and I did not need to be told twice that it was permissible for us to vacate the premises. We bolted for the door. Outside dark smoke was already starting to billow out of holes in the roof.

Rat started the lead car. By the time he was inside White Lightning with us the Packard was moving around the corner of the house. We were so weighted down that we had trouble getting under way, but White Lightning was too much car to buckle under a mere forty cases of whiskey. We came around into the dooryard in front of the house just as a man with a machine gun rushed off the porch, his long white hair flying back over his blue shirt. He began firing at the back of the Packard. He was so intent on what he was doing that I don't think he ever saw us. He went up and over the hood with the gun still hammering. His head struck the windshield, which splintered into a thousand pieces as he went on over the top of the car. Then we were thundering down the lane on the oil pan with our laps full of glass.

The Packard was going at a furious clip and getting well out ahead of us. We were doing better than fifty ourselves, but the dirt road at the bottom of the lane looked forever and a day away. Behind us someone was shooting again. I could hear the bullets ripping into the whiskey cases on the luggage carrier and in the back seat. Uncle Henry pushed my head down. Trying not to get cut on the shards of glass, I held tight to Rat's legs to keep him from jouncing out through the gaping opening where the windshield had been.

There was a tremendous explosion. I thought the whiskey in the burning stable must have gone up all at once. I lifted my head just in time to see the Packard turning end over end through the field beside the lane. At the same time it was coming apart. Wheels and doors, cases of whiskey and fenders flew in every direction, as though bailing out of their own volition. What was left of the car finally flopped into a marshy spot and remained sticking up in the air at about an eighty-degree angle. All that remained intact were the chassis and steering wheel, to which my father still clung, waving to us like a triumphant aviator. We swerved out around the crater in the lane where the land mine had gone off and stopped.

"Stay here," Uncle Henry said. As he got out I heard him say, "I told him I didn't like no guards."

I jumped out of the car anyway and ran after Uncle Henry down through the marsh. My father stood near the skeletal remains of the Packard. "Look at this, boys," he called. "Not a hubcap left on her."

"Oh, Christ," Uncle Henry said, pointing up at the barn. Flames were jumping out through the roof. A man ran up the highdrive and opened the sliding door of the hayloft. Two others emerged from the milk house with whiskey cases. The man we had struck with White Lightning lay unattended in the dooryard.

A large truck rolled backwards down the highdrive from the loft. We began to run back toward White Lightning, which at the same time started off down the lane. Rat was driving off without us. We shouted for him to stop, pounding on the windows as we ran alongside the accelerating Cadillac. Instead of slowing down Rat panicked and drove off the road into the marsh. The hood came unhinged and popped up. Rat got the front wheels back onto the lane, but the rear wheels remained out of sight.

"Oh, Christ," Uncle Henry said again, and if he wasn't exactly praying he wasn't swearing this time either.

There was another explosion. A wicked whizzing whine passed over our heads. Carcajou made his baying insane noise from the dooryard. "LaChances," he bellowed. "Surrender, LaChances."

He was standing in his blue uniform and cap next to the open maw of the truck, from which a long black smoking barrel projected. He lifted his arm and brought it down. "Fire," he roared.

Uncle Henry and my father threw me to the ground. There was that terrible whining noise again, then a metallic shriek. When I looked back in the field I saw that the Packard had been cut completely in two. We jumped up and ran toward the Cadillac.

79

"Steer, Bill," my father shouted.

I got in behind the wheel and pushed Rat over out of the way. He had gotten a whisk broom out of the glove compartment and was busily sweeping broken glass off the seat and singing "What a Friend We Have in Jesus." Over the crazy whinnying laughter from the dooryard the cannon exploded again. The raised hood vanished.

Meanwhile Uncle Henry and my father had their backs up against the whiskey cases tied on the luggage carrier. "Give it to her," my father called. I stepped hard on the gas, and the back wheels spun and dug deeper into the muck. I thought we were going to have to head for the woods to be run down one by one like the unfortunate LaChances, whose name Carcajou continued to bellow between cannonadings.

"Let up," my father shouted to me. "Lift up on your end, Hen. Heave her right on out."

My father and Uncle Henry were probably the two strongest men in Kingdom County, but I was still amazed to look back and see them raise the rear end of that huge overloaded Cadillac entirely out of the mud and over onto the lane. Then Uncle Henry was behind the wheel and my father was sitting on Rat's lap. Rat was singing about a voice calling on his ear; his eyes were shut and his whisk broom was going vigorously over the dash, my father, and me, wedged in the middle looking down through where the windshield had been and into the exposed work-ings of the engine.

"See all them little rods dance," my father said, leaning forward to get a better look. "That's power, Henry. You've got a fine car here."

"Yes," Uncle Henry said. "And well broke in, too."

As we skidded onto the dirt road at the foot of the lane we took a shot broadside. It plowed through the right rear window, the six top cases of whiskey on the back seat and on out through the roof, hurling us sideways across the road, and up on two wheels. Somehow Uncle Henry kept us from turning over and got us back under control again. If all his experience outrunning G-men at high speeds over bad roads ever paid off, it was that early morning in 1932, south of Magog.

At last we were between woods on both sides of the road, and out of range of Carcajou's salvos. Both Rat and my father were in states of exultation, though for very different reasons. Rat appeared to be having an experience of grace, probably induced by shock. He was trembling all over and shouting phrases from a tongue that had not been heard or spoken since the construction of the Tower of Babel. At the same time he was furiously whisking my father, who bounced up and down on his bony quivering knees like a ventriloquist's dummy in the throes of a severe seizure.

"What did I say, boys? Did Quebec Bill say you'd be in for some surprises or not? Did you see them running around up there? See the flames, boys. Look back over the trees, Hen. See the smoke."

Uncle Henry had little leisure for observing barn fires. The impact of the broadside had twisted the body of the car around at approximately a forty-five-degree angle to the frame so that as we sped down the road we seemed perpetually to be veering off into the opposite lane.

The car reeked of whiskey. Rat interrupted his ecstasy long enough to get an unbroken bottle out of one of the damaged cases behind us. He broke the seal, unscrewed the cap and chugged down a third of the contents. Then he looked at my father with just the whites of his eyes showing and shouted, "Abba babba babba. Quinquist, quinquist. Boola boola, Calvin Coola."

81

Uncle Henry was sweating hard and wrestling hard with the wheel. Evidently the rear axle had been bent when Rat drove off the lane. We progressed the way a snake that has been run over drags its paralyzed rear quarters behind it.

"There's where we turned off last night to take that shortcut over the ridge," my father said.

"I know," Uncle Henry said. "It warn't that difficult to follow your trail."

"Wait until Evangeline hears about this," my father said.

"Yes," Uncle Henry said. "Wait until she does."

"Your car's broke in a little more," my father hazarded. Uncle Henry did not reply.

As we approached the church on the outskirts of Magog we met our first car of the morning, a black sedan full of nuns. We must have appeared to be coming directly toward them because they pulled far over on their side of the road, then swerved off onto the church lawn into the damaged crèche. Shepherds and wise men, kine and asses were scattered in every direction. The members of the holy family were maimed nearly beyond recognition. A crude wooden image of Mary, which resembled a heavy-limbed cretin more than the virgin mother, flew out of the manger and landed in a salacious position on top of the radiator cap of the sedan. As we pulled away from this scene of desecration Rat reared up through the windshield shaking my father off his lap onto me. He brandished his whiskey bottle and shouted back at the nuns, " 'Thou shalt not make unto thee any graven image, or any likeness of any thing that is in heaven above, or that is in the earth beneath, or that is in the water under the earth.' Exodus twenty: four."

There was not much traffic on the long street between the taverns and the paper mill. By the time we reached the other end there was even less. Two cars and a horse-drawn milk wagon had run up onto the wooden sidewalk. A third car took refuge down a side street.

"How far is it to that log trace?" Uncle Henry said between clenched teeth.

"Not far," my father said.

Uncle Henry peered over the wheel at the smoking engine. "That's too far," he said.

He was right. Just as we turned off the gravel road onto the trace leading down to the lake we threw a rod. We had to keep going, though; now the lake was our only way out. Clattering, knocking, smoking like a chimney fire, smelling like a bombed distillery, White Lightning ran out her last five miles like the noble creation she was.

"Take her right up under the big fir, Hen," my father said.

Uncle Henry did, and I have never been sure whether he shut off the key when we got there or White Lightning just died. As we sat looking out over the lake in the heavy silence that often follows the conclusion of long or difficult trips, I didn't dare ask.

Rat, who by this time had finished his bottle, opened his eyes and looked at the burned-out engine. "How are Henry and me going to get back home?" he said.

"By canoe, the same as I and Wild Bill," my father said.

Rat shut his eyes and did not open them again until late afternoon.

My father and Uncle Henry and I got out and looked at White Lightning, which was no longer white, or any other recognizable color. The hood was gone, the windshield was gone, the springs and engine were shot, the back seat and rug were soaked with whiskey. "She looks like she was struck by lightning all right," my father said.

Uncle Henry was examining the gaping holes where the cannonball had bashed in the rear door windows and curled up part of the roof like a piece of bent tin. "See there, Wild Bill," my father cried, "I've doubled him over laughing."

"I don't think Uncle Henry is laughing," I said.

83

My father ran over and looked up into Uncle Henry's face.

"He's laughing inside, Bill. You don't know how Henry laughs inside."

Uncle Henry looked at my father. "What time do you figure on setting out again?"

"At dusk, Hen."

Uncle Henry nodded. "Well, boys, if you don't have any objections I reckon I'll lay down and sleep for a while. And maybe when I wake up this will all be a dream and I'll be back in the hotel. Maybe White Lightning will be down in the lot behind the hotel as shiny as ever. But I doubt it."

"Henry," my father said, "you are the best brother a man ever had. Do you know what I'm going to do for you? I'm going to get you a brand new Cadillac. See the haze on the lake this morning. It's going to rain. We may not have to buy any hay at all. A ton or two at the most will carry us through. The rest of the money belongs to you, Hen. We've still got twenty-five full cases. That's at least two thousand dollars profit after buying hay if we need to. That's a new Cadillac, Henry. That's Quebec Bill's gift to Henry Coville."

"Bill," Uncle Henry said, "that used to be a nine-thousand-dollar automobile. I ain't going to tell you how many runs in my old Ford I had to make to buy it. I ain't trying to lay the blame on you neither. I was the one that come to see you about this run, not the other way around. But I want you to understand one thing. You don't always listen too good but you listen to this. I don't want another Cadillac. I want White Lightning. And if it takes four thousand dollars or eight thousand dollars or twelve thousand dollars, I aim to put her back on the road again. Somehow. As good as ever. Do you understand that?"

Without waiting for a reply he lay down close beside White Lightning with his head on his arm and shut his eyes.

My father was so moved he was speechless — briefly. He ran back to the cabin and got our blanket out of the pack basket and covered up Uncle Henry. "We'll do it, too, Hen," he said. "You and Bill and me. We'll do it."

"No," Uncle Henry said without opening his eyes, "we won't. I will."

It was only about nine o'clock, though so much had happened since dawn that it seemed much later. While my father built a fire and shaved with his hunting knife I unloaded the whiskey. There were twenty-five full cases left, including three cases of loose bottles. I asked whether I should start carrying them down to the canoe.

"No, Bill, we'll tend to that later. I feel like a swim now. Quebec Bill and Wild Bill are going swimming."

Fifteen minutes later we were diving into the lake, out of which I immediately jumped again. But the cold didn't bother my father. He was a superb swimmer, as agile and quick in the water as an otter. He dived and frolicked in the icy lake like a laughing white-headed seal. Once he stayed under for the better part of a minute. When he came up he was holding a rainbow trout nearly as long as his arm.

Rat and Henry continued to sleep while we cooked the trout. After breakfast we left the last of our bread and some fish for them, which my father assured me Rat could get his friend to multiply, and went for a walk back through the woods.

The sun was shining through the haze, and it was warm enough to leave our hunting jackets by the pack basket inside the cabin. Behind the cabin the beeches were beginning to put out fuzzy green buds. Further back in the hardwoods spring beauties and trillium were up. A few trout lilies were in blossom, bright yellow against the brown leaves on the floor of the woods. Off in the mountains a male partridge began to drum. A snowshoe rabbit, still mostly white, bounded out of a brush pile. "He don't know it's spring, Bill," my father said. "If he don't change clothes pretty soon he's going to make a tasty dinner for some smart red fox."

After a long climb we came out into a clearing full of blueberry bushes. From here the view was spectacular. Everywhere we looked there were lakes, rivers, forests and small farms. Far down the lake I could just distinguish the yellow tug, still well south of the notch. Back in the hills across the lake smoke was still rising from Carcajou's barn. Beyond that the Laurentian Mountains lay scattered under the hazy blue sky.

My father put his arm around me. With his other hand he pointed off across the mountains. "Wild Bill," he shouted as loudly as his broken jaw would permit, "ain't that a Christly wonderful sight to see?"

In the middle of the field sat a giant boulder. It was not an outcropping but a glacial erratic picked up by the ice sheet in northern Canada and later dropped here on the ridge. My father walked over to this house-sized anomaly and sat down on a patch of moss under the side facing the lake. As I sat down next to him he got out his pipe and began to fill it.

Looking down the lake through the notch, I thought again of René St. Laurent Bonhomme, who had disappeared near here seventy years before. I wondered why my father had chosen the previous evening to tell me about René's disappearance. I had also been surprised to hear him refer to his father, whose life, like my father's own past before his marriage, had always been one of those taboo subjects my family refused to discuss. Even Cordelia, that

86

most irreverent of all iconoclasts, never mentioned my Grandfather Goodman.

Now it occurred to me that my father might actually want to tell me something about those times in his own life he had never to my knowledge discussed with anyone. Even if he didn't, I might be able to get him to; a taboo, I suddenly realized, was at the least a two-way agreement, a contract that one person alone could not enforce.

"Dad," I said quickly so that I wouldn't have time to change my mind, "tell me what happened to Grampa Goodman after he ran away."

"Wild Bill wants to hear about his grandfather," my father said to his ever-present gallery. Then in his lilting narrative voice he began to talk about his father and that three-quarters of his own life that he had not mentioned half a dozen times to me since I could remember.

5

SOON after running away from Cordelia in 1869 my Grandfather William Goodman apprenticed himself to a gunsmith. He was talented at the work, but after two or three years he left with the eight-gauge shotgun that he had made himself and went to work for a professional smuggler. One night my grandfather and the smuggler drank more than usual. They began to argue, my father didn't know what over, and the gun went off. After that my grandfather ran the business himself.

He specialized in transporting whiskey across the Canadian line, and covered up his clandestine operations by ostensibly dealing in timber lots. During the spring and early summer he traveled through southern Quebec and New Brunswick and northern New England, cruising played-out border farmland for marketable stands of timber, on which he then leased stumpage rights for the following winter. He would locate two or three wood lots, not too large, within an hour's traveling distance of one another and the border and always near or in a dry county or township. Later in the summer he would move his wife and ten children, of whom my father was the eldest, to a centrally located farmhouse, invariably run down and invariably a long way from any settlement. Then he would begin cutting.

From the time he was six until he was sixteen and left home for the first and last time my father worked in the woods with my grandfather. For the first year or so he piled brush. Then he learned to use a small bucksaw to cut the upper limbs and tops of down trees into kindling. By the time he was ten he was driving my grandfather's team of big woods horses, hauling tree-length logs out to roadside landing yards during the day and by night driving those same horses back and forth across remote unwatched border crossings in front of a wagon or sleigh loaded with whiskey. My grandfather would make one run with him to show him the route. After that my father went alone, often driving twenty-five or thirty miles over roads that were little more than log traces through heavy forests, sometimes in temperatures of thirty and forty below zero. He told me he first began drinking in order to keep warm on those night runs.

My grandfather's rationale in sending a boy of ten out alone at night in winter through wilderness country was that if he happened to be stopped and questioned he could always say that his folks were sick and he was going for help or the house had burned down or a tree had fallen on his father. My grandfather had enormous faith in my father's resourcefulness. Very early on their relationship developed into a professional partnership based on mutual respect for one another's competence. They worked together in the woods. They smuggled whiskey together, and by the time my father was twelve they were drinking together, and between them consuming at least two bottles of white mule moonshine whiskey every day.

If there were schools my father and his brothers and

sisters never went to any of them. Apparently my father taught himself to read and write sometime after leaving home. As is often the case with persons who learn to read later than usual, he rarely forgot anything he heard or observed. He learned how to speak English and French with equal facility and how to discern from looking once quickly at a stranger which language to address him in. He could walk through a section of spruce or fir or mixed hardwood and softwood and estimate with the precision of a professional cruiser how many cords of pulp or feet of logs could be cut on it and how long the work would take. He was an expert trapper; by the time he was ten he was making enough money on the pelts of the muskrat and mink and otter and beaver he trapped to buy his own clothes and ammunition—my grandfather furnished his whiskey free in exchange for making the runs. From moving so frequently and from his night whiskey runs he developed a preternatural sense of direction, like a wild animal's. He often told me that I could take him blindfolded to any spot within twenty-five miles of the Canadian border from eastern New Brunswick to western Quebec and he could remove the blindfold and walk directly to the nearest town.

He did not walk to many towns while he was growing up. Without exception the farms where my grandfather bivouacked his family were as far from town as it was possible to be. Home for my father was a succession of incredibly isolated, barely habitable houses where they never stayed for more than a year and to which they never returned. This nomadic existence was especially hard for my grandmother, whom my father described as trying at first to make a home of the falling-down shanties, planting a kitchen garden, harvesting a few early table vegetables, having to leave the rest for the coons and deer and bears, and finally giving up gardening altogether—finally giving up everything but the daily routine of caring for the children and the house and her husband. My father did not know where she originally came from or who her people were, except that they were French.

My father said my grandfather was not abusive to my grandmother or to him and the other children, but regarded them all as accoutrements to his two trades and valued them in accordance with their respective abilities to handle an axe, a peavey or a loaded whiskey wagon. As my father described him to me he was a big man, well over six feet, with a dark beard and a bluff, shrewd, not unkind manner, who seemed to enjoy teaching his sons how to play the fiddle Canadian style, shoot a spruce grouse on the wing, sing the old voyageur paddling songs, tell time and direction from the sun and stars, fight like a wildcat and drink a quart of whiskey a day without falling down or getting sick. Like my father, my grandfather did not talk much about his past, though he once said that he began drinking with his father and grandfather and great-grandfather — that would have been René Bonhomme — as soon as he started walking, and that since running away from Cordelia when he was fourteen he had drunk at least a quart of whiskey a day himself.

"I run away over whiskey too," my father said after a short pause, his voice casual and anecdotal. "Only it was under different circumstances. We was living near here then, in a cabin right where that one down below sets, though it warn't that cabin, and Pa, he had a big load he wanted to send over the line. It was early April, and still winter. I drove north of here a mile to a spot where I could get down to the lake. Then I drove back over the ice through the notch and on to where the county home is now. From there I picked up the Memphremagog road. Back then the county home was a summer place that belonged to Dr. Tett's folks and warn't used at all in the winter but there was two, three farms on the road and so they kept it rolled pretty good in the winter, and it was passable.

"I had clear coasting from there down to the covered bridge over the St. John, where the iron bridge and trestle are today. It was a great long bridge, the longest in the county, and it was there until the flood of twenty-seven. During the winter they had to shovel snow onto the floor so the sleighs could get across. At the south end they had a little toll building that was open in the summer. Winters they didn't bother.

"Well, Bill, I was sixteen at the time. I'd made hundreds of runs and never come up against anything I couldn't handle. It was a clear night, though way down below zero, but I was bundled up good with a buffalo robe over my legs and a bottle to keep me from minding the wind. I didn't pay much attention when the horses shied as we started over the bridge. I thought that was just because it was dark and narrow, or maybe that they heard the water running free in the middle of the river where it had started to thaw and they wanted a drink. I was halfway over before I saw the lantern at the other end. For a second or two I still thought it was all right — that the lantern was my pickup and they had mistook where they was supposed to meet me by a mile or so. Then there was a loud thumping, and the sleigh was scraping and bumping along over the bare boards of the bridge where the hijackers had shoveled off the snow to slow me down. I reined in just at the other end with the sleigh still partly inside. There was two of them. One was holding my off horse's bridle and the other was up ahead fifty feet or so by the empty toll shed. The near fella had a horse pistol aimed right square at my head.

" 'Climb down, boy, this is where you unload,' the fella with the pistol says.

" 'Don old me hup, meester,' says I. 'Papa, ees cut him foot most hoff wit de haxe and lay pass out on de cabin floor. Mama, she don know how long he las. Me, I ave to get de doctor, hor papa, she be gone.' "

My father laughed. "That part about Pa laying passed out on the floor was true enough. Earlier that evening he'd got up a full head of steam and commenced to fighting the War of Rebellion with William Shakespeare and Calvin again. He'd put on a foolish blue cap he kept a-purpose for such occasions and set my little brothers and sisters to mounting a charge on the hog pen. Just before I left he clumb over into the pen himself and picked up a four-hundred-pound sow by the ears. Picked her right up off the ground, Wild Bill, and hollered at her, 'You, sir, Robert E. Lee, sir. Will you surrender, General?' It was a rare sight to see and a fine moving speech to hear with the little uns standing at attention and saluting, and me laughing so hard I couldn't hardly harness the team. 'You, sir, Robert E. Lee, sir. Will you surrender, General?' And the poor hog squealing and hanging up there in front of Pa helpless as a small piglet. You and Pa would have taken to one another, Bill. The wilder a boy was the higher Pa prized him. He prized me very highly, and would have you.

"Well, I knowed by the time I got to the bridge that Pa was laying like a stone on the floor, and for a minute I thought the fella with the lantern believed me, because he says, 'We won't hold you up long, boy. We wouldn't want your Pa to bleed to death after cutting off his foot with that haxe.'

"Then the other fella shouts out, 'No, not after sending us all that whiskey you've got loaded in the back of that cutter.'

" 'Climb down now directly,' the first fella says. 'No more of your tricks. This gun shoots smart-mouth French boys just as quick as white men.'

" 'This one shoots thieves and sons of bitches just as quick as rabbits and pa'tridges,' says I, and blasted a great hole clean through the buffalo robe with the shotgun I had pointed at the fella the whole time. He jumped like a Christly deer when the buckshot hit him, and flinged that lantern ten foot in the air. But I didn't have time to admire the fireworks. I got the other fella with the second barrel before the first one landed on the snow down below by the river.

"I clumb fast out of the sleigh and went up to where the second fella was laying dead across his rifle by the toll shed. I taken his feet and started to drag him down the bank to the river. But his head was half blowed off at the neck and I was afraid it would come clean off, so I had to go around and take holt of his shoulders and skid him down to the ice with the head lolling off to one side, hanging there by just a cord or two. Next I went up in the woods and found a pole, and I wasn't long about it neither. I pushed them two bodies out over the ice with the pole, one at a time, being careful not to catch that fella's head under him and shear it off. I shoved the carcasses off the ice into the open water, and throwed their lanterns and guns and the pole in after them. I never did find their team. They must have bolted when they heard my shotgun let go.

"Well, Bill, your father had a decision to make, and there was never a man who could make up his mind any faster than Quebec Bill Bonhomme — which was my second decision, to change my name back to Bonhomme. The first was to whup up the team and drive straight to the drop point to pick up my money. Then on at a dead gallop through the main street of Memphremagog and out past the lower river to the Common and along the county road and up the hollow to Cordelia's, where I'd never been before in my life and only heard about once or twice when

Pa was drunk and recollecting how he and my grandfather that built barns had gotten drunk together. But I knowed right where to go. And Cordelia, who had never seen me afore or had any way to know I even existed, come to the door and held her lantern up to my face and knowed me too. 'You look like my Grandfather René,' she said. 'You smell like him too. You're young William's boy and you've been drinking.'

" 'That's not all I've been doing,' I says. 'Let me in, Aunt Cordelia. I just shot and kilt two hijackers.' "

My father asked Cordelia to deliver the team and sleigh and part of the whiskey money to my grandfather and to explain what had happened. She agreed to do this and to put him on the morning train for Boston. She told him that it was near the St. John River where the men René St. Laurent Bonhomme brought to Kingdom County with him had vanished. She talked to my father about time, its cyclical and illusory nature, and the recurrence of themes and events down through the generations. Her speaking of René Bonhomme may have inspired his decision to assume the old French surname as an alias. They sat up talking all night, with Cordelia doing most of the talking. At dawn she took him to the train.

From Boston my father decided to go west. By 1896 most of the east was used up, but he had heard about the vast forests and plains of Wyoming and Montana and Oregon and Washington, so he bought a ticket for Seattle and headed out. He told me that he was drunk most of the way, though not quite so drunk as the drummers who paid for his whiskey and from whom he won hundreds of dollars at poker believed.

My father liked Washington. He said he didn't miss home because he'd never been in one place long enough to have a home to miss. Undoubtedly he missed his parents and brothers and sisters, but thinking about what he left behind in the St. John River that April night must have tempered his loneliness. He accepted the fact that for some time he would have to remain a fugitive.

From Seattle he went north to work in the tall coastal forests. He began as a bull cook, assistant to the head cook in a lumber camp. Soon he was climbing up giant Douglas firs with an axe and a safety belt and hacking off the top thirty or forty feet of the trees to prevent them from hanging up on smaller trees as they fell. When the crown snapped off, the upper trunk to which he was belted whipped and jumped like a bucking horse. He said he liked that, twanging back and forth two hundred feet up in the air. He also liked to gaze out from the treetops over the Pacific Ocean, but he never looked too long at a time because he sensed that if he did he would be a sailor the rest of his life. He tried to stay within sight of the Canadian border from the top of a tree.

When he grew tired of lumbering he moved over to northern Montana and worked on a ranch. From there he crossed the border to a wheat farm in southern Saskatchewan. He drifted back into whiskey running because it was an easy way for him to make money. He drank every day.

One night in a backroom gambling parlor in some nameless border fourcorners in northern Idaho a self-styled promoter of quick money-making schemes watched my father beat into insensibility a man more than a foot taller and a hundred and fifty pounds heavier than himself. A week later they were in Denver, where my father was fighting barefisted matches for purses of several hundred dollars against some of the toughest men in the Rocky Mountains. Denver was still a wide-open settlement then, and such activities were apparently regarded as principal attractions of the city. Men congregated there from New Orleans and

Chicago, San Francisco and St. Louis and Portland to bet on the fights, promote them or participate in them. Every night bouts were held on back street corners, in makeshift rings inside warehouses, in abandoned mining camps on the outskirts of the city. The only regulation was that no weapons were permitted, so if he got into trouble with his fists my father could and did use his feet, against which even the biggest men were helpless. He told me that before Uncle Henry broke his jaw he had never lost a fight or sustained a lasting mark on his head or body. Then just as the promoter was talking about arranging for him to turn professional and fight as a lightweight, he left Denver to visit his family, departing as suddenly and with as little forethought as he had gone west originally. This time, though, he was not running away from anything. He said that April night on the covered bridge was the only time in his life he had ever had to do that.

It was April again. He had been away five years. Possibly it was the time of year that stirred that desire in him to leave Denver, to begin the pilgrimage which he had no way of knowing would become a quest that would last more than fifteen years. Not that he expected to find his family in the cabin on Lake Memphremagog where they had been living the night he ran away—he knew they would have left there years ago. A farmer who lived a few miles from the abandoned cabin said that the Goodmans had left in the spring after that first winter. He thought they had headed over toward Megantic, near the Maine border. My father didn't expect to find them in Megantic either, or in Chateauguay in upstate New York where he heard they had gone next. But as the summer wore on into fall and the first snow found him back in Memphremagog with no money and no idea where his parents and brothers and sisters might be, he thought of Cordelia. It was possible, he supposed, that his family had maintained some contact with her. She was in the barn when he arrived, and she knew who he was without even looking up from the cow she was milking. "Is the sky the same color out there?" she said.

Cordelia hadn't heard of William Goodman or his family since the day she returned the team five years before. She said she hadn't thought about them. She had spent the time since my father had left milking her cow, feeding her chickens, carrying water from the well to the barn and house, and when the well was dry carrying it from the brook a quarter of a mile away; scything enough hay off the meadows to get her cow through the winter; making a little maple sugar; teaching Milton and Aristotle and Pope and Virgil to children who if they spoke English at all often did not know their letters; immersing herself in the isolation of the hilltop farm, her profession and her conviction that all human endeavor, including her own, was illusory though not necessarily futile.

"Where do you think they might be?" my father said.

"Anywhere," Cordelia said. "Nowhere."

Then she had told my father how René Bonhomme had disappeared.

"You mean they just disappeared like Grampa René?" I said. "Twelve people disappeared off the face of the earth?"

"Eleven, Bill. I was the twelfth, and I ain't disappeared yet."

"They must have gone somewhere."

"You'd think so, wouldn't you? I thought so at the time. I couldn't see what some old man drownding on the lake or walking off to die in the woods had to do with my folks. Just like you, I figured they had to be someplace. So I set off in earnest to find them."

He persuaded Cordelia to outfit him with a team and

98

sleigh, and spent that winter traveling along the border inquiring for his family and taking orders for a seed company out of Montreal. In the spring the seed company branched off into farm implements, which he sold that summer and fall to subsidize his search. By the following winter he had built up a sizable clientele and was beginning to be well known along the Canadian line: a small man, not old, with white hair and sharp blue eyes who sold more seeds and machinery than most of the other men who worked for the company precisely because he didn't seem to care whether he sold any seeds or machinery at all; the selling was incidental to the search.

"Goodman? I believe there's a Goodman over near Edmunston, across the line. I think he works at the depot. I don't know whether he has a family. May be. Now that corn planter in your book there. Where would I have to go to see one of them in operation? You come in and have a bite, mister. I want to show that book of yours to Marie. She might be able to tell you more about that Goodman fella."

My father's search was gradually becoming a way of life. He learned not to raise his expectations as one after another he met dozens of wrong Goodmans: lumberers and tenant farmers; railroad clerks and teamsters; mill workers, blacksmiths, a bank president and even a few whiskey smugglers. He realized after two or three years that he was probably not going to find his family, though like those mythological knights who devoted their lives to searching for mythological chalices he remained as optimistic as ever. He stayed on with the company because he liked the work.

He made money fast and spent it and gave it away faster, trusting farmers who while they were perfectly trustworthy had no money and no expectations of getting any.

99

Often he exchanged a harrow or hay rake for a woods horse or a couple of Jersey heifers, which he hitched behind his wagon and traded or sold in the next town or next county. He never seemed to be in a hurry. He spent hours drinking coffee in kitchens, tea in lumber camps, liquor at the schoolhouse parties and dances where he played his fiddle almost nightly. He often visited five or six farms a day, played half the night at a dance, traveled all the following day and fiddled again that night. Regular customers who knew his route and approximate schedule arranged weddings and other family celebrations to coincide with his arrival. He was well liked by everyone for his vitality, his generosity and his keen disinterested curiosity about people — who they were, what they did, where they came from. He was an entertaining talker and a good listener and never forgot anything his customers told him about themselves or their families.

Everywhere he went he was deluged with invitations to eat meals, stay overnight, stay for a week. With the men he spoke knowledgeably about crops, stock, hunting, fishing, local politics. He was equally conversant with effective ways of canning applesauce, putting up wild blackberry jelly, appliquéing quilts. He made a good deal of the children and was much made of by them and by their older sisters, but he was not ready to settle down. There was always a hamlet twenty miles to the south that he hadn't visited; a Goodman who worked a farm or leased a section of softwoods on the back side of a mountain ten miles to the north; a man in the next county who could tell him who was running whiskey locally. Even after he knew that his family was gone for good he acted as though he would discover them next week or next month or by fall at the latest. Everything else was secondary to that epic hunt. It structured his life as a family or profession or religion or driving personal ambition structures the lives of other men and women.

Once every year he visited Cordelia. He found her unchanged, uncompromised by time, which she refused to acknowledge anyway. In contrast the cabin on Lake Memphremagog where he had last seen his family and which he also visited annually was progressively ravaged by the years, sinking fast into the encroaching woods, a windowless shell hidden by fireweed and paintbrush and beech saplings, the song of a white-throated sparrow high in some distant pine or the laughter of a loon on the lake the only sound. But even after it was only a cellar hole of charred timbers he continued to return, as to a family burying place. He tried to find some sign of his family's brief habitation — a horse hame in the fallen shed, a whiskey bottle, anything at all that would be tangible proof that the family of which he had been dispossessed had actually been there at all. Maybe at those times more than any other he was aware of that longing for permanence, for a home, which Cordelia once told me has haunted every born wanderer since Odysseus.

He carried his fly rod and shotgun with him everywhere, the same gun his father had made, which he had used that night on the covered bridge and then given to Cordelia to store for him while he was west, the old eight-gauge he later taught me to shoot with and that we had brought with us on our trip in 1932. When he had temporarily had a surfeit of the selling and talking and parties and dances he would leave his team and wagon at some farm at the end of a dirt road and walk miles back into the mountains to hunt or fish for a few days. He was equally at home performing for a large group of people and completely alone in the woods.

He began to run a little whiskey again, carrying a case

or two at a time under the boxes of sample seeds and catalogues. He continued drinking. Somewhere in his travels he acquired the name Quebec Bill, pronounced with the hard French k. He ran an impromptu delivery service, carrying notes, invitations, packages, covered dishes, word-of-mouth messages. Sometimes he crossed the border several times a day. He was never more than twenty-five or thirty miles north or south of the forty-fifth parallel, that arbitrary demarcation that had stretched through five generations of our family like a five-thousand-mile umbilical cord to the past, along which he had sojourned all his life and which existed only on paper but represented all the geographical and historical continuity he had ever known.

He loved just to travel through the countryside, as he later enjoyed driving around in our Ford. Often he was up before the family he had stayed overnight with, especially if there was a daughter of eighteen or twenty with an even better reason than she had the night before to want him to stay. He drove out of dooryards in the chill dawn, sometimes catching half a dozen speckled trout and cooking them for breakfast along some misty wild stretch of the St. Croix or Allagash or St. John; sometimes stopping between farms at noon and eating cheese and crackers, sitting with his back against a sugar maple and looking down over the variegated patchwork landscape of corn and standing hay and cut hay and buckwheat and oats and clover grown from the seeds he sold, so that he was able to enjoy a sense of accomplishment and belonging without being tied down to one piece of land. He worked hard, played hard, drank hard, measuring time by the seasons that governed his comings and goings and by his yearly visits to Cordelia and to the cabin site on Lake Memphremagog.

Years passed.

"William Goodman? I knowed some Goodmans over Sherbrooke way. Not those? I can't call to mind no others. My boy might know. He's traveled all over these parts girling it, but he's over across in France just now. That would be Henry. He's a great big fella, like his pa you might say. That's most likely why they taken him. I've got a picture of him inside. You say your name is Bonhomme? I'd like to see that book you've got there. I work in the woods mainly but I've got ten, twelve acres of hay up on the ridge that I'd like to cut off for the horses. Do you rent out equipment? Just me and the girl here now that Henry's over beyond whupping Kaiser Bill. Stay around a day or so. It gets downright lonely. Girl's down from Montreal on holiday this month. She goes to nun school up there. Studying to be a sister, she be. One of them black praying kind. I'd like to change her mind, but she promised her ma just before she passed away . . ."

It was July, the time of year my father usually visited the overgrown clearing on the lake where his parents had lived twenty years before. Now the garrulous man who already at eleven in the morning was quite drunk was leading him into a cabin almost identical to the one he had left for good on the same site two decades before, except that it was so new that pitch was still oozing out of the logs, some of which were still encased in bark. It was the sort of crude tight cabin René Bonhomme might have thrown together, working hurriedly so he could get on to something more important. To this huge verbose hearty intoxicated woodsman, clearing the land and drinking were more important, so my father couldn't avoid connecting him with his own father and feeling that he had finally through sheer perseverance found something like the home he had spent half his life searching for.

On and on the big man talked. He told how cheaply he

had bought the land and how he had put up the cabin in less than two weeks. He had great hopes for the place. He would cut the woods off, root out the stumps, make a farm of it if it killed him. He and Henry would run the farm together after Henry finished whupping the Kaiser. The farm was not all he intended to run with Henry. With the lake and the border so near there were other ways of making money besides farming. If my father, whom he had not known for five minutes, wanted to stay on for a few days he might tell him how. He looked at my father with amused eyes and poured him a drink. "You might be just the man to save Vangie from the praying nuns," he said.

"By that time, Bill, I was thinking exactly the same thing," my father said. "As soon as I laid eyes on that slim dark-haired gal setting an extra place at the table I knowed that if I had anything to do with it she was never going to be a praying nun or any other kind."

I think that my father's resolution may have been inspired more by his discovering a family, or part of a family, where he had left his own than by my mother's good looks. As Aunt Cordelia once said, my mother was a woman of considerable pulchritude, but my father had seen hundreds of good-looking girls in his travels, many of whom would have liked to marry him and some of whom undoubtedly had good reason to wish they had. Psychologically, the impact of discovering anyone at all on this haunted spot by the lake must have been so overpowering that he had no choice other than to stay and help Hercule Coville.

It is impossible to know what attracted my mother to my father. Sometimes, growing up on the farm, I thought she loved him most for his laughter, especially since like her brother, Henry, she was a rather grave person herself. Since she was five she had spent eleven months of every year at a convent school, where there could not have been much levity of any kind. She had just turned eighteen the summer she met my father, and had one month to decide whether to become a cloistered nun. Until the day my father appeared in the dooryard of the cabin she had never considered any other course than joining the convent. As my Grandfather Coville told my father during the first two minutes of their acquaintance, she had made a vow to her dying mother.

There was nothing sacred about this vow to my father or old Hercule. Immediately they entered into a conspiracy to change my mother's vocation. This did not prove difficult. Except for his white hair, Quebec Bill Bonhomme never looked or acted any older than my mother. She later implied to my father that their unsubtle machinations were all unnecessary — she had fallen in love with him almost as quickly as he fell in love with her. Evenings after he had worked in the woods and drunk whiskey and plotted all day with her father, he and my mother canoed on the lake, picked blackberries and blueberries, sat talking around the bug-swirled lantern while Hercule smirked in the background or conspicuously absented himself to go drink in the woods. Sometimes they went riding in my father's wagon. Sometimes they walked to the clearing on the ridge to sit under the boulder and look down the long blue sweep of the lake. I have often wondered whether I might have been conceived in that spot, with Hercule rubbing his whiskey-numbed hands together down at the cabin or lurking like a satyr in some nearby copse, delighted to have reduced the risk of an isolated old age by having acted the part of a procurer for his own daughter, the erstwhile novitiate.

My mother told my father that that summer was the happiest time in her life since her own mother had died.

It was marred by only two considerations, neither involving her vow to enter the convent—she had apparently decided not to do that so suddenly and unequivocally that there had never been any period of uncertainty at all. One day she implicitly accepted the inevitability of the nunnery; the next she realized that she had renounced it forever without even having to decide to do so. Her main concern was for Uncle Henry's safety in France, which must have secretly worried my grandfather as well, quite possibly contributing to his uninterrupted drinking. That, the drinking, was my mother's second anxiety. Hercule and my father were drinking together every day, all day, as my father had drunk with his own father before going west. They drank whiskey like water from the time they got up in the morning until they went to bed at night. It did not seem to affect my father, but over the years my mother had seen its effect on my grandfather, that bemused scheming giant who like my Grandfather Goodman had saturated himself in alcohol all his life.

Uncle Henry made it safely home from France, surviving both the loss of a lung in a gas attack and the subsequent medical treatment at an army hospital. But as a result of one of those unaccountable and tragic ironies to which both sides of my family have been susceptible, Hercule Coville never had the opportunity to rejoice in either his son's safe return or the formal consummation of that deliverance from the convent he had spent so much time intriguing to obtain for his daughter. The day in August my parents drove up to Magog to be married, planning to surprise the old man with the news on their return, a bull spruce he was cutting swiveled on its half-severed base, kicked off at a diabolical angle and crushed him to death. Late that afternoon they found him by the alcohol reek, potent and unmistakable over the evergreen scent of the tree that had killed him.

My mother apparently believed that Hercule's death would sober my father up if anything could. But he continued to drink, consuming a quart of whiskey while he dug his father-in-law's grave on a knoll above the cabin. He laughed at my mother's objections and began transporting Canadian whiskey by boat down to Memphremagog. He laughed with delight when she told him she was pregnant, and he continued drinking and smuggling and laughing until one morning in October after the leaves were down he returned from a whiskey run to discover that she had disappeared, vanished as inexplicably as his parents and brothers and sisters.

When he first discovered my mother's disappearance he believed that she might have wandered into the woods and gotten lost. Sometimes, so he had heard, pregnant women isolated from other persons did strange things. He spent days and nights combing the wild ridges above the lake and found nothing. A horrible possibility occurred to him: she might be in the lake itself. He began to dive, going down sixty and seventy and eighty feet where the water was so dark he had to grope along the bottom feeling for her body with his hands. He continued diving on into November, but found nothing.

When the lake froze over he drank himself into a raving frenzy and found the convent where my mother had studied in Montreal. He threatened to kill the mother superior if she didn't tell him where his bride was. A priest rushed in. My father promptly kicked him through a stained-glass window. He ran through the inner sanctum of the convent, flinging open cell doors and blaspheming like old Karamazov. He told me that during this privileged if hurried tour he hoped to expose priests and nuns in lewd embraces. He did not, he said, expect to find my mother. Before the police arrived he got out through a back door and scrambled over a tall stone wall.

Again it was April. He was standing in Cordelia's dooryard without being able to remember how he had gotten there or why he had come. It was twilight and snowing. Cordelia was chopping wood, bent cronelike over the big maple block on which she was hacking up slabs for the kitchen stove.

"Ah," she said. "They're gone."

Full of whiskey, malnourished, having spent the winter raging through border towns in search of my mother, my father thought that his great-aunt was succumbing at last to senescence. He thought that in her conviction that the passage of time was illusory and events only repeated themselves infinitely she was confusing his appearance with that other abrupt appearance nearly twenty years before when he had announced that his parents had disappeared. Then almost as quickly as that thought entered his mind he knew he was wrong. He knew that Cordelia was referring to my mother and me.

My father had not yet told Cordelia he was married. He did not know how she could be aware of our existence at all, any more than she could have been aware of his existence when she first saw him. Yet she not only knew about us, she knew where and how to find us and was determined to do so and bring us back to Kingdom County. She did not even wait for my father to sober up. Two hours after he rode into her dooryard they were sitting in the station in Kingdom Common waiting for the next train to Montreal, which left at dawn. They had to sit on a bench near the tall coal stove all night, a bent woman with a relentless almost prehistoric aspect, to whom the perpetuation of her grandfather's family against all odds had suddenly become an end in itself, and a tiny white-haired man who might except for time, which she refused to acknowledge, have been that grandfather. My father told me that once during the night she looked at him and said calmly, "Your canoe is still safe in the barn. It will be there when you need it." So maybe it was the perpetuation of René St. Laurent Bonhomme and the past itself that Cordelia was trying to ensure, as though to persuade herself that the past at least was real.

It was dawn, and they were riding north, headed back toward the city from which René Bonhomme had departed for good more than a century before. Cordelia had never been in Montreal. She had never been in any city. But she walked straight from the train station to her destination a mile away in the old part of the city, my father skipping to keep up as she led the way through the narrow cobbled slushy streets. She veered sharply without breaking stride and swung open a black iron gate. She had never before failed to close a gate in her life and would have rather misquoted Dryden than left a gate open. Now she did not even swing it to behind them. Nor did she shut the massive black door of the convent. She walked straight past the astonished nuns, past the new stained-glass window, up two winding flights of stairs my father had overlooked in his rampage and directly to the room where I had been born three days before and where now the mother superior and the priest were filling out the papers that would relegate me unnamed and fatherless to a Catholic orphanage. My mother was holding me for what she thought was the last time and crying.

Cordelia went straight to the bed. "Get dressed and get your son ready," she said. "Your husband is here to take you home."

The priest started to object.

"I'll brook no priestcraft," Cordelia said. "They are man and wife."

"We'll brook no priestcraft," shouted my father, who

was still somewhat hung over, as he rushed by the priest to embrace my mother.

The priest must have thought my father was going to kick him through another window. He leaped back, struck his head against the wall and collapsed unconscious on the floor. The mother superior pulled a great wooden crucifix off the wall. She held it extended toward my father. "I cast you out," she said.

"Good luck to you," Cordelia said. "They've been part of the family for generations."

Hours later, as we rode south together toward Vermont, he was almost sober again. Great flakes of sugar snow began to fall on the flat black fields of the St. Lawrence Valley. My father took me in his arms. He held me close to the window. "This is the snow that takes the snow," he told me. "This is the poor man's fertilizer, Wild Bill."

6

WE lay under the fir tree on the edge of the cliff and watched the launch come around the tip of the point. Uncle Henry and Rat were both still asleep, though it was already the middle of the afternoon. We had spotted the launch from the ridge, going along through the notch on the west side of the lake. By the time we had raced down to the cliff it was coming back up our side, moving quite rapidly. The man standing beside the driver was sweeping a machine gun back and forth along the shoreline. Both men were dressed in blue, and both had long white hair.

Now we could see that neither of the two was Carcajou. But if Carcajou was the devil, these dead-faced white-haired mutants were the devil's spawn, zombies devoid of all human or demon vitality including the vitality of madness. My father cocked back both hammers of the shotgun. They were within easy range now, but apparently he was going to let them pass by unless they noticed the canoe or got a glimpse of White Lightning.

Suddenly the one standing with the machine gun lifted his head and sniffed like a hunting dog. He slung the gun over his back, stepped onto the covered bow of the launch and leaped to the shore. Without breaking stride he started directly up the icy mountainside, running just inside a ragged line of stunted spruce trees where I would have said it was impossible for a mountain goat to go.

"Christ," my father said, "the son of a bitch smelt us. Us or the whiskey."

"Shoot him," I said. "For God's sake shoot him."

"I want them both."

My father dipped his head toward the water. The boat was out of range up the lake and just starting to turn back.

Through the little spruce trees I could see the blue movement of the man with the gun, ascending the escarpment in great vaulting bounds. Once on the edge of the cedar swamp behind our hill my father and I had watched a wild dog pursue a doe along a low ridge. We were bird hunting with shotguns and had to stand helplessly and hope the doe could escape. The dog, which must have weighed at least one hundred pounds, moved in a long primitive lupine gait, swinging its heavy dark head from side to side. More frightening than its size or speed or darkness was its silence. Steadily gaining on the deer, it made no sound at all. That is how the man with the machine gun came bounding up that cliff—in total silence.

He had only thirty or forty feet to go to reach the top. My father was on his feet, bringing the long heavy double barrel up into position and firing. The blue man collapsed in midleap. He hit the sheer face of the cliff, bounced once and plummeted toward the water. Weighted down by the machine gun, he sank like a stone.

As quickly as he had shot the second hijacker on the covered bridge more than thirty-five years ago my father swung around and fired down on the boat, which was heading back our way. Splinters flew up from the stern. It turned sharply and headed out into the lake.

By the time my father had reloaded, the launch was out of range again. As it sped away the driver looked back over his shoulder like the snow owl on our barn. Uncle Henry was standing beside us, watching the retreating boat. His face was expressionless.

"That boat ain't going to make it, boys," my father said. "I put a hole as big as your fist through the bottom back near the engine. She won't get halfway over before she goes down."

He was right, the boat was already foundering. It took another minute to sink but before it did the owl-man was out of it and swimming fast toward the opposite cliffs.

"What I wouldn't give for my deer rifle," Uncle Henry said.

"You don't need it, Hen. That water's ice cold. There's still ice floating around in it. That albiner ain't no polar bear. Likely he won't make it."

Uncle Henry looked out across the lake at the white speck that was the man's head. His face showed no emotion at all. "Likely he will," he said.

Uncle Henry said he was going for a short walk in the woods. My father and I remained on the edge of the cliff, watching the swimmer out of sight. There was no way to tell whether he had made the crossing safely, but I was inclined to agree with Uncle Henry; that was how our luck had been running.

There was a breeze now. A few scattered riffles began to appear on the water. My father put his arm around me. "She's starting to come up," he said happily. "We might just have an old-fashioned sleigh ride out there tonight, Wild Bill. Ratty won't much like that, will he?"

I shook my head, but I wasn't thinking about Rat. I was thinking again about my father's past. "Dad, what about your people? Grampa and Gramma Goodman and your brothers and sisters. Did you ever find them?"

My father squeezed my shoulder hard. "I stopped looking, Bill. When I found Sweet Evangeline and Wild Bill, I stopped looking."

He reached up and ruffled the hair on the back of my head. "I'm going to get the coffee on. It's time to sober Rat up. It'll be dark in two hours. It'll be time to start out on Lake Memphremagog, Wild Bill. We're going to have a sleigh ride all right. See them dark clouds a-coming."

For a few minutes I stayed there, watching the lake rise. Out in the middle small whitecaps were beginning to show up here and there. I knew my father was right. It was going to be a rough trip back, and not just for Rat. Now the bay between the cliff and the point was growing choppy. Far under that dark crawling surface a dead warlock twisted and bobbed, pulling against the drag of his machine gun, his long hair waving like seaweed. I shuddered.

I sensed that my father had not told me everything he knew about our family. There were black holes in our history, dense with mystery, maybe ultimately impenetrable: René Bonhomme's fate; Calvin's fate, and William Shakespeare's; my own grandfather's disappearance along with his entire family except my father. At the time I did not know what to think, but I believe now that in that troubled spring of 1932 my father needed to come to terms with the collective past of our family, including his own secret past, by transmitting it to me so that we could confront it together. This, I think, was his main purpose in making the whiskey-running trip and taking me along.

My father's spirits seemed to be rising with the wind, but Rat woke up bilious as an old buck goat.

114

"Have some fresh-caught rainbow trout, Ratty. Ain't this fish savory and sweet, though, boys?"

"It's tasty," Uncle Henry admitted. He seemed to feel better himself now that he had gotten some sleep and had his walk in the woods, though I noticed him look with an interrogatory expression at White Lightning once or twice, as if maybe he still wasn't completely sure that it was his car.

"I don't want no trout," Rat said. "I don't eat nothing that don't walk on four legs like a man. I've got the headache from all that touring around. I wish I had a sup of something."

"You'll have all the sups you ever dreamed of as soon as we get that whiskey safely down the lake, Rat. For now have a sup of coffee or you'll be walking on all four legs yourself."

My father handed Rat a boiling hot cup of coffee. Rat looked at it as though it might be strychnine and then gulped it down.

"Didn't that taste good, now? What goes better outside in the woods than a hot cup of coffee, Mr. Muskrat Kinneson?"

Rat was looking steadily at the stack of whiskey cases near White Lightning. "A sup of something," he said.

"Rat, if you help us load the canoe and unload later and don't beshit yourself in between whilst we're rolling around in them great cresting breakers, I'll give you an entire full case. How's that now?"

"I ruther have a sup now and be sure of getting it. Great cresting breakers, is it? I ain't setting foot in that canoe, Quebec Bill. I wouldn't trust myself to a canoe on a millpond, and certainly not in no great cresting breakers."

"You'll just have to walk home in the dark, then, my boy. Maybe that kindly old gentleman with the white hair will happen along and give you a lift."

"The canoe might be all right if I had a sup just before I got in."

"One sup, Rat. That's fair enough. Now how about a bite of mountain trout fried to a golden turn?"

"I like it better baked," Rat said as he helped himself to a large chunk of fish. "Fried foods give me gas."

"Hear the wind in that fir tree," Uncle Henry said. "It's going to be a rough night on that lake, Bill. Best we be heading out now if we're going at all. She'll be dark by the time we lug this whiskey down to the canoe."

"We ain't going to lug this whiskey nowhere," my father said.

"How's that, Bill?"

"What do you think I brung along that rope for? I'm going to lower them cases down to you. Wild Bill, you take Henry and Rat down to the canoe and paddle up to that little strip of gravel directly below us. Stack the cases so the weight is evened out. Leave room for Henry in the stern and me in the bow and yourself and Rat in between. Go very easy with the cases. If you drop one it'll smash clean through the bottom of the canoe. Take the gun and pack basket down with you."

Uncle Henry walked up to White Lightning. "I reckon we ought to remove the plates," he said. "Just in case anybody blunders down here before I get back."

My father came over and reached down and wrenched the back plate right out of the standard, screws and all. He went around in front and repeated the process and flung the twisted plates out over the cliff. The wind caught one and it sailed back and landed on a projecting ledge.

"I'll be back," Uncle Henry said to White Lightning. "Don't never doubt it. It may be one day, it may be two or three, but I'll be back." He put out his hand to pat the crumpled fender and cut it quite severely on a sharp ridge of torn metal. As the blood dripped onto the ground he looked in turn at his hand, the car and my father.

"What happened, Hen, did you scratch yourself? Well, when them LaChance boys see you come home without your car and hear what happened to her they won't never think to question what become of the whiskey. That's all clear profit, boys."

"I think," Uncle Henry said, his hand bleeding steadily, "that you had better bandage this up. If you intend for me to do any paddling, that is. And I think that if I run into the LaChance boys the LaChance boys had better worry about what is going to become of them. Because it will not be their jaws I will break. It will be their necks."

"About that sup," Rat said, repairing to the whiskey cases.

I got the shotgun and pack basket while my father tied his red handkerchief around Uncle Henry's injured hand and Rat had his sup. Then I led the way out around the cliff and down the slope to the canoe. Rat scrabbled along behind on his rear end, holding his bottle high over his head. When we got to the bottom, he refused to ride over to the cliff in the canoe.

"He's going to get hot again," I said to Uncle Henry as we paddled across the bay. "He won't be any good to us at all."

"That's so, Bill, but then he's less apt to be in the way if he's hot. Leave him go ahead and have his sup. See him stumble along over them rocks. Graceful cuss, ain't he?"

"Why did he decide to come? I wish he hadn't come."

"He said he's always wanted to see foreign lands. Maybe I shouldn't have brung him, Bill. If I'd knowned half of what was in store for us I wouldn't have. But then if I'd knowned half of what was in store I wouldn't have come myself."

117

"Uncle Henry, I'm sorry about White Lightning. Dad is too. I know he'll help you fix her up."

"Billy," Uncle Henry said, "you don't ever have to make excuses for your father. But that is one thing he won't do. I'll take care of White Lightning myself."

When we got to the base of the cliff I got out in about a foot of water and held the canoe for Uncle Henry. I remained standing in the lake to steady the canoe. The water was still only a degree or two above freezing. I didn't see how anyone could survive such cold for long.

High above us my father stood on the edge of the cliff paying out rope. In a loose hammock fashioned from one end were four cases of whiskey, which he began to swing like a pendulum to clear the projecting shelf about twenty feet below him. Gradually he increased the arc, a maneuver that required all his extraordinary strength and balance. When the cases were clearing the edge of the shelf he let several feet of rope slide through his hands. I was surprised the rope held. It was no bigger around than a clothesline, but a few moments later Uncle Henry was easing the cases down onto the gravel.

While my father retrieved the rope and secured the second load Uncle Henry carried the cases across the thin strip of shore to the canoe. Two cases fit neatly side by side in the bottom with room for two more to be stacked on top of them.

"Lake cold enough for you?"

I nodded. Before the next load reached the bottom I was shivering all over. My feet were beginning to get numb, but I couldn't come ashore. Here directly under the cliff the bay was quite exposed to the big south wind coming up the lake. Despite my efforts the canoe rocked like a cradle. Further out the lake was running in long swells. The evening sky over the western mountains was an ugly dark blue, the color of the outlaws' uniforms. I was shivering harder. We were in for it, I thought. We were really in for it.

The second load banged against the edge of the rock shelf. The next cleared the edge with a foot to spare but glanced sharply off the cliff below. My father was almost yanked off his feet, and I heard the sound of glass breaking.

"Send down two cases instead of four," Uncle Henry called up. "We ain't in that much hurry."

Rat was picking his way along over the talus like some ancient aquatic denizen coming ashore for the first time and not much liking it. He looked up at the descending whiskey and quickly sat down and covered his eyes. Then he uncovered them and looked straight up at my father. "Quebec Bill," he shouted, "you be careful of my case. Don't you bang my case like that."

Six cases were now descending from the top of the cliff, and now lodging, as anyone but my father would know they would, on the shelf. With the sudden release of pressure he staggered back out of view, jerking one corner of the rope sling off the cases. A case tottered on the edge of the shelf.

"Look out," I yelled.

Uncle Henry flattened himself against the base of the cliff. The falling case smashed to bits on the rocks at his feet. His face remained quite calm as he wiped the whiskey off it.

"I hope that warn't mine," Rat called up.

"No, Rat," my father said. "Yours is hung up on the ledge. Just climb up like that albiner fella did and tie the rope back on again if you will."

Rat looked up at the smooth beetling granite. In spots below the ledge exfoliation had actually cut the cliff back toward its base at an obtuse angle. "What albiner?" he said.

"Leave them go," Uncle Henry called up to my father,

who had tied the free end of the rope around the fir tree and was unraveling the slack down onto the shelf beside the stranded whiskey.

"Leave them go, for Christ's sake," Uncle Henry shouted.

Paying no attention to us, my father hopped down the face of the cliff on the taut rope. He knelt on the ledge and readjusted the sling. Then he stood up and lowered the remaining five cases to the bottom. He walked back up the cliff on the rope and successfully lowered the last seven cases — all at once.

"Are you going to climb down the rope?" I called up hopefully.

"No, we may need it." He snapped his wrist and the rope came down in a long undulating wave and coiled up like a snake at the foot of the cliff.

"Paddle back to where you put in," my father said. "I'll meet you there in five minutes."

Uncle Henry got into the stern. "Come on, Rat," I said.

Rat sat on a rock back near the base of the cliff, working on his bottle. "I can't do it," he said. "I've got the lumbago too bad to risk it. My whole spine is numb."

"Both my feet are numb," I shouted. "Get in this canoe."

"Have another sup and get in," Uncle Henry said.

Rat had another sup. "I still can't do it," he said philosophically. "Seasickness runs in the family. You don't know how deathly sick us Kinnesons get when we leave dry land."

"Fine," Uncle Henry said. "You can stay behind on dry land and greet General Grant for us. Something tells me he'll be along sooner or later. Get in, Billy."

"I believe it'll be sooner," my father called down. "Get in that canoe like the devil was after you, Rat Kinneson. Because I think he is. Quick now, boys. Beat for the point. There's a vehicle coming down the tote road."

Rat nearly swamped us in his haste to get into the canoe. I thought my father was playing a trick to get Rat in gear, but he shouted again for us to head for the point as quickly as we could.

"What are you going to do?" I yelled.

"Join you directly. Paddle now. Paddle, boys."

Uncle Henry and I began to paddle fast. The canoe was stable, but we were moving directly into the waves angling in off the lake. I looked back over my shoulder and saw my father's red hunting jacket moving through the dark branches of the fir. "Paddle like hell," he shouted. "It's that cannon truck and it's backing up."

A moment later we heard fiendish bellowing followed closely by a cannon blast and the clangorous rending of metal. White Lightning plunged over the edge of the cliff. It bounced off its nose on the rock shelf, exploded and fell flaming like a meteor into the lake.

"No," Uncle Henry said.

"Did you see that, boys?" my father shouted from the fir tree.

I didn't dare look at Uncle Henry's face, but Rat's was uplifted and had assumed a beatific mien.

"Zacchaeus," a voice rumbled, "come down out of that tree."

The top of the fir tree was shaking. It began to sway in long rhythmic dips. My father's body came catapulting out of the spire in a compact tumbler's ball just before the next blast. Halfway up its trunk the fir split in two. The upper half dropped onto the ledge. Meanwhile my father shot through the air a hundred and fifty feet above the lake.

"Hallelujah," yelled Rat. "He has been taken up." He threw both his arms over his head, and for the second time nearly capsized us. "Whup. Here he comes back down again. See there, Henry, they won't have him. Look out. There he goes. He's under. He's gone. I warned him. That's the end. Goodbye, Quebec Bill."

We had nearly reached the point by then. The cannon truck appeared under the splintered fir. Standing beside the projecting muzzle was Carcajou. He was wearing a black suit, with his beard tucked inside a clerical collar, small and white against the dark suit and the dark sky. His white hair was flying back away from his head in the gale. His arms were outstretched in a parody of a benediction. He looked like a crazed old Elijah, a storybook wizard rocking up a storm to drown us, an enraged and blinded Cyclops preparing to hurl boulders at fleeing Odysseus. He did not look like any man I had ever seen. I was overpowered by a dreamlike helplessness, as though I were entering a realm of myth and illusion over which I had no control.

Rat evidently had a similar impression. "There were giants in the earth," he informed Uncle Henry and me with great piety before fainting away on the whiskey cases.

My father emerged in the middle of the bay. He rolled onto his back and swam with only his head out of the water, looking back up at Carcajou, bracing himself against the wind.

"Fire," Carcajou roared.

The cannon went off. A waterspout geysered up near my father's head. Instantly he sounded.

"Fetch him, Gabriel. Bring that soul to Christ."

Out of the dark interior of the cannon truck sprang one of the two remaining members of Carcajou's gang. He ran straight off the edge of the cliff like a water spaniel and hit the water swimming.

My father surfaced again.

"Look out," Uncle Henry and I shouted together.

We were having trouble keeping the canoe off the ice chunks and rocks at the end of the point but Uncle Henry was going to have to handle that job by himself. I reached for the shotgun. "Swing the bow around," I shouted at Henry.

My father and Gabriel had both gone under while still a hundred yards or so apart. While we waited for them to come up I kept expecting to be blasted to bits by the cannon. But Carcajou evidently didn't care about us, it was my father he wanted. A white head appeared fifty feet away: Gabriel's. I pulled up, fired and missed. The head turned inquiringly in my direction, reminding me again of a spaniel searching the water for a dead duck. I fired the second barrel. The canoe pitched. Another miss.

I fumbled in the pack basket for shells, stuffed two more in the gun and swung it up. A fraction of a second before I fired Gabriel vanished like a duckling pulled under by a turtle.

"Look," Uncle Henry said. "Deliverance is at hand."

A boat was speeding across the bay out of the north. As it drew closer I could see the RCMP insignia on its prow. An officer in a crimson coat and a black hat stood up behind the wheel. His gun was out and pointed in our direction. I quickly lowered the shotgun. Uncle Henry gestured with his paddle toward the cliff. The cannon thundered again just as the officer started to turn his head, which simply disappeared from his shoulders. For a second or two the decapitated Mountie continued to stand behind the wheel while a fountain of blood spurted out of his torso and sprayed back over the lake on the wind. Then he toppled overboard and the boat veered in toward shore. I watched in amazement, horror, disbelief. It was like watching a matinee at the Common picture show, with myself as one of the actors. I couldn't accept the fact that this was happening to me, even though I was training the shotgun over the bay again, waiting for Gabriel to come up, determined this time to blast off his head like the Mountie's.

My father surfaced close to the canoe. He pulled himself over the side and grabbed the bow paddle. The last sound we heard as we rounded the point was a simultaneous baying, whinnying, crowing, bleating, the frenzied ululations of an entire deranged barnyard.

I kept turning back, expecting to see Gabriel pursue us in the Mountie's launch.

"Don't worry about him," my father said. "He's down below keeping his brother company."

Ahead in the dusk the looming notch resembled nothing so much as the gates of hell. Whoever or whatever Carcajou might be, that wild dark lake was no myth.

"Dad," I yelled, "the whiskey isn't worth it. The farm isn't worth it."

"You're right, Wild Bill, they ain't. There's only one thing now that's worth staying here for one more minute. That is killing that son of a bitch Carcajou. I intend to kill him."

7

THE lake was running in long high rolling oceanic swells coming directly up through the notch from the south, so that we seemed to be trying to paddle against the current of a large and powerful river that over the eons had cut its own dark canyon into the mountains. The indistinct gleaming of the cliffs above us enhanced this riverine illusion. When I looked up at the whitish clouds scudding north across the face of the moon we seemed to be moving very fast. This too was an illusion; it was the clouds that were making good time, not us. I tried to gauge our progress through the notch by taking a sighting on a particular cliff. Then the moon would go under the racing clouds. When it reappeared I couldn't tell whether the cliff we had seemed to gain on was the same one. My father was in the bow again and I was kneeling close behind him to offset Uncle Henry's weight in the stern. Rat was still stretched out on the whiskey, dead to the world. That, I thought, was the one thing in our favor.

The water between those mountains was more like a

tidal bore than a lake. The waves were so close together that as they broke one after another onto the rocks to our left the spray rose six or eight feet into the air in a continuous line.

"Them are real breakers," my father shouted. "Hear them thunder, boys. Hear that old wind howl. I told you we'd have us a sleigh ride."

I was badly frightened. René Bonhomme had built his canoe to move heavy loads over heavy water, but anything that floated, from an outrigger to a battleship, would have had trouble on the lake that night. Uncle Henry said later that he would have run for shore despite my father's objections if there had been any way to make it safely through those breakers.

I was also afraid that we had not seen the last of Carcajou. I couldn't believe that anyone but my father would enjoy being out on any part of Lake Memphremagog in that storm, much less caught in the middle of the notch, but as Uncle Henry had said, Carcajou was crazy. Now he had a boat again, and a good one. He might do anything. He might come at us at any moment from any direction, baying and howling like the wind.

I still cannot understand how I managed to go to sleep in the midst of all that fury. Rat was drunk, but I wasn't. Some persons have the marvelous faculty of dropping off to sleep in seconds when they are worried or afraid. I have never been able to do this. Motion can be lulling, but the wild heaving of our canoe on Lake Memphremagog that night could not be described as soporific. I must have been terrifically fatigued, physically and mentally, but too excited to know it until I woke up and realized that I had been asleep, and for some time, since the moon was now noticeably lower in the sky.

Over the wind and waves I could hear the faint steady

rapping of the launch engine. We were still in the notch and there was no place to land. The noise of the engine seemed to fade. Then it grew louder. A light appeared several hundred yards behind us. It swept over the shoreline, illuminating the spray on the dark cliffs. It traveled methodically out toward the middle of the lake. It swung back toward shore. The launch did not appear to be moving fast. It was barely possible, I supposed, that it was another police boat, searching for the missing officer.

My father turned around. "Load the shotgun, Bill."

"It is."

"Good. Change places with me. You come up here."

He inserted the paddle under the bow, and we crawled past each other. He handed the shotgun up to me. "Hold it over the side like it was a paddle, Bill. Now listen. There will be two of them. The albiner will have the gun. I'll tend to him. Then I'll holler. When I holler you fling up and let loose for Carcajou. Don't aim. Just point and cut loose. Bag yourself a wolverine, Wild Bill."

So Wild Bill Bonhomme was going to get a trophy for himself. That was my father's incredible plan. He had brought us out on that wild night so that I could shoot my first man. Squeeze the trigger, Bill, don't jerk it. When them birds go up from under that apple tree point the gun, don't aim. You won't have time to aim. Whiskey running warn't all I learned him, Evangeline. Wild Bill shot his first wolverine out there on that lake. We was going to set up the head on the wall down to the hotel, only Bill here blowed it clean off. Rat dressed off the carcass; it's hanging in the Canada plum tree outside Cordelia's window. Wild Bill bagged him. Our boy. How was it, Bill? Did it give you satisfaction? Did you feel like you felt when you got your first buck. Look out in the plum tree, Aunt. See Bill's wolverine. What's left of it.

Yes, and if I had my way there was not going to be

127

much left of it. I knew now how my father had felt back on the covered bridge over the St. John when he was not much older than I was. I knew that I wanted to shoot Carcajou more than I had ever wanted anything in my life. And although I was vaguely aware that as bad as they were our circumstances did not justify my wanting so much to do it, I knew also that if we were going to get off that lake with our lives, I was going to have to.

Behind us the light moved unhurriedly over the water. We were only a hundred yards or so beyond its range when I heard the strains of singing over the rapping engine. First I couldn't make out the words. Then I could hardly believe what I was hearing. Carcajou was singing *"En Roulant,"* the voyageur's song. For a moment I was afraid my father was going to join in.

The moon appeared from under a galloping wrack of mares' tails, and the searchlight and *"En Roulant"* cut out at the same time. My father put his hunting knife between his teeth and slipped over the side of the canoe. I looked back and made out the tossing outline of the launch. I knew Carcajou had seen us.

"Bon soir, voyageurs."

Deep bestial laughter came over the water, followed closely by a bright orange burst of machine-gun fire.

"Arrêtez," Carcajou shouted. He did not waste any time circling us but gunned the launch up to within a few yards of our bow. In the moonlight I saw that he was dressed in a voyageur's costume, including the sash and plumed hat. The remaining member of his gang was dressed similarly. As my father had predicted, he was the one with the machine gun. Carcajou was steering, and lashed into the seat between them was the uniformed corpse of the headless Mountie.

"Où est le petit LaChance?"

"He drowned," Uncle Henry said, keeping the bow of the canoe angled slightly away from the launch so they would not see my shotgun. "His name ain't LaChance."

"*Je ne crois pas. Où est-il?*"

"Right here," my father said behind him, raising himself partway over the side of the launch and lifting his arm.

The gunman whirled. My father's arm drove forward. The machine gun clattered wildly, but my father was already out of sight, and the gleaming point of his hunting knife was jutting out of the back of the falling outlaw's neck.

The launch was starting to turn. I brought up the shotgun as I had brought it up dozens of times before when my father and I walked slowly through the old apple orchard below the maples, cider-fragrant, October-still, waiting for the hard sudden burr of wings, the flash of pastel gray and soft brown, the gun swinging up almost independently, leading, leading, point don't aim, point, lead, the roar — you got him, Bill, you got him.

Still in the water, my father was shouting about dead wolverines and albiners. Carcajou had bellowed when the buckshot struck him, but he had not fallen. Now the launch was heading straight toward the cliffs. Just before cracking into the rocks it flipped over. My father was back in the canoe congratulating and hugging me and doing his best to tip us over. The lake was as wild as ever.

"Paddle," Uncle Henry said. "Paddle, by Jesus Christ."

We were emerging from the notch into the open lake, which if possible was rougher still. Here the waves were at least three feet high. The surface was unbroken whitewater. But my father insisted that we forge on down the lake while there was no possibility that anyone would spot us. He said that by morning the lake would be crawling with police searching for the Mountie. Now was the time to move, boys.

High on the mountainside over the lake the darkened monastery resembled a ruined gothic stronghold. A single light flickered from a lower chamber: Brother St. Hilaire's laboratory, no doubt, where now in the dead of night he and the Holy Ghost were pursuing their avocation.

My father was paddling the bow again. Kneeling behind him, I wondered whether I could get to shore when we capsized. Now that I had done it, I did not have any strong feeling at all about shooting Carcajou. Not satisfaction, certainly not remorse, only uneasiness because I had not seen him dead. My father assured me that half of Carcajou's face had been blasted away. But the hijacker he had shot from about the same distance long ago on the covered bridge had been lifted completely off his feet. Carcajou had just turned away. I should have fired the second barrel. I didn't understand why I hadn't pulled the second trigger.

"What's that?" Uncle Henry said. "You hear that, Bill? Can that be thunder?"

"Yes," my father said. "No. I don't know. Yes I do too. Head for shore, Hen."

Ahead of us I heard a low steady grumbling. Ten years later I would be reminded of that sound when I heard the convoys rumbling endlessly over the thick-slabbed concrete highways by night. At the time I too thought of thunder, distant summer thunder that growls on and on over the Green Mountains on a sweltering July night when the hay is down in the fields and drying.

We turned toward shore, but it was too late. All around us in the waves were heavy moving objects. There were dozens of them, hundreds of them, as long and cylindrical as torpedoes, grinding together, growling and pounding into the canoe.

"Christ," Uncle Henry shouted. "The pulp."

He was right. As I started to fend off the logs with the stock of the shotgun I realized that the booms behind the tugboat had separated in the storm; we were canoeing in a melee of pulpwood.

René Bonhomme's canoe had been built tough. You could drive your fist hard into the side with no effect. You could run over a submerged cedar stump and put a crease an inch deep in the bottom without opening it up. It had safely logged thousands and maybe tens of thousands of miles through parts of three centuries over some of the wildest water in the world. But no canoe, no small craft of any type, could have survived long in that pulp. It would have been literally ground to pulp itself.

"We've got to sink her," my father shouted. "Stay close to Henry, Wild Bill. Swim underwater. I'll bring Rat."

Without giving us time to object he seized the right side of the canoe and threw himself hard to the left, turning us out into the water. I couldn't catch my breath. Nothing could have prepared me for that stunning cold. We were quite near shore but my first thought was that if I ever did get my breath back I couldn't live sixty seconds in that arctic element, which was entirely unlike any water I had ever been in. A pulp log crashed into my shoulder. That gave me something else to think about. I dived.

That day and night had contained many marvels and revelations, but I did not expect to experience two more during the next ten seconds. First, I noticed with absurd detachment how contrastingly calm the water remained just a few feet below the surface: a fine lesson in the principles of fluidics for Young Lycidas. At the same time I sensed the briefest intimation of that mysterious allure drowning is said to hold, that seductive promise of a surcease of all travail, a psychological phenomenon I would

131

never have believed if it had not happened to me. Then I was swimming underwater beside Uncle Henry, as bulky and deliberate as an old grampus.

Each time we surfaced to breathe and get our bearings we had to ward off the pulp, which seemed much denser toward shore. Under the water I had yet another vision. My life did not pass before me, but I vividly imagined the stretch of rapids in the Upper Kingdom where I had learned to swim. It was July, and I was very small and riding on my father's back like a young muskrat as he swam up through the whitewater. My mother and Cordelia were blackberrying along the woods edge of a nearby meadow. My mother waved. "Evangeline," my father shouted as he swam. "See Wild Bill swim, Evangeline." Cordelia said something to my mother. My mother waved again. Cordelia did not wave.

I stood in water about to my waist, trying to push my way through a solid mat of shifting pulp. It was tearing my clothes, bruising my legs and back. I staggered and fell. I tried to force my way up through the pulp but couldn't. My strength was gone. It occurred to me that I was going to drown in four feet of water. I made a last futile effort to bull up through that heaving layer of wood. Just as I began to swallow the lake Uncle Henry picked me up and carried me onto the rocks.

I coughed and sputtered. I shook uncontrollably and vomited. There wasn't much in my stomach but water, but everything there was came up. Uncle Henry held my head. I couldn't stop shaking. Finally I got myself under control enough to speak. "Uncle Henry," I said, "thank you."

"Oh," Uncle Henry said mildly, "don't thank me, Billy. Thank your father."

He turned and started back into the lake complacent as

Proteus himself. Suddenly he stopped short. "Well," he said. "Well. Look there, will you, Billy."

I raised myself to my elbows and looked out at the lake. Running toward shore over the grinding chaos of wood and water was my father, with Rat in his arms. How he did it will always remain a mystery to me. He may have been inspired to that superhuman attempt by the dreadful possibility that if Rat should drown he would have to run the farm again by himself—but that doesn't explain how he accomplished it.

As soon as he reached shore my father set Rat upright and delivered a ferocious blow to his midsection. A quart or more of watered-down whiskey spewed out of Rat's mouth and he began to cough. My father shoved him down onto his stomach and proceeded to jump up and down on his back. Rat coughed some more. He lifted his head and croaked, "I have been down to the sea and been baptized by great fishes and small fishes."

He choked and spewed more water. "Leviathan has sung to me sweetly," he said.

He passed out again, but my father apparently did not feel that further resuscitation was necessary. "Rat's all right," he said with great relief. "He thinks he's been to Sunday school with the whales."

He rubbed his hands and played a bar on his imaginary fiddle. "What do you say, boys? Ain't this the trip to end all trips?"

Uncle Henry looked at me. He looked at Rat. He looked at the lake, absolutely primeval in its moonlit tumult. He looked at my father. Just loudly enough so that we both heard him he said, "Quite possibly."

With that reply my father seemed to attain a true epiphany. Failure of any kind had always inspired his finest moments, but we had gone far beyond mere failure. We had lost every bottle of whiskey. White Lightning had been totally demolished. We had been shot at and nearly drowned. The blood of five men, outlaws or not, was on our hands. We would have to sell our cows or watch them starve. Very probably we would lose the farm, yet my father was leaning into the screaming wind, his white hair flying like mad Lear's, and laughing and whooping and laughing at the sublimity of his own ultimate hopefulness in the face of ultimate futility.

"That's wonderful," he screamed. "Ain't it all wonderful, Wild Bill?"

8

M Y father had not been whooping and laughing the previous October when he and Uncle Henry had cut our maples. He had loved those trees, which that provident Scotchman Calvin Matthews had planted to replace those he cut and burned for potash. With a cleared hillside and a southern exposure the trees had grown rapidly as they passed down through the family. William Shakespeare Goodman cut a few off the top of the hill to make room for the round barn and the house. When she moved up to the farm during the Civil War Cordelia tapped a few near the barn for table sweetening. But my father was the first member of our family to make a commercial enterprise of sugaring.

Unlike every other commercial enterprise he attempted after leaving the seed and farm equipment business the sugaring venture was quite successful, maybe because it demanded an enormous amount of energy over a relatively short time rather than long endurance or any particular agrarian skill. My mother later told me that tapping the trees was my father's first project when he and Cordelia brought us back home to Kingdom County from Montreal in the spring of 1918. That first week it continued to snow, so he spent his days cutting a supply of firewood and his evenings whittling out beech taps. He borrowed a dozen buckets here and half a dozen there, and when the first thaw set in he tapped fifty maples, hanging three or four buckets on each tree. For several days he worked eighteen and twenty hours out of every twenty-four, rushing over the snow from the trees to the potash kettle where he was sugaring off, carrying two sloshing sap buckets on a wooden yoke across his shoulders. He made enough money from the maple sugar Cordelia and my mother finished off on the kitchen stove to buy two good registered Jerseys from Ben Currier.

That summer he cleared the encroaching cedar and beech and fir trees out of the maples. He built a sugar house and cut ten cords of wood for the coming spring, selling the potash kettle to an antique dealer and buying a boiling pan. He made a wooden vat for collecting sap and carved out runners for it. In his initial burst of enthusiasm for farming he scythed enough hay off the lower meadow to get the two cows through the winter. He got up a big woodpile for the house stoves, and banked the foundation with fir and spruce brush. He and my mother were happy. While Cordelia read *The Aeneid* to me in Latin in the kitchen, they went blueberrying on the north slope of the hill above the cedar swamp, picked up bruised apples in the orchard for cider, sat on the back stoop and husked sweet corn from the kitchen garden. In September Uncle Henry came home, missing one lung but otherwise healthy. He and my father became friends instantly. On fall evenings Uncle Henry held me and talked to me about the weather and the woods while my father played his fiddle and my mother canned tomatoes and corn and apple sauce and Cordelia read Sophocles and Aeschylus and Euripides.

Cordelia was attracted to themes of revenge, incest and patricide with a horrible compulsion that I later realized she did not understand herself. She had terrible nightmares and woke shrieking in Greek and in Elizabethan English. Sometimes she shouted out in the night in habitant French, the language of René Bonhomme. She openly mocked my father, whipped me for confusing ablatives with datives, refused to talk to Uncle Henry except in Greek or Latin. Yet this haunted woman who saw too much and could not stand what she saw never spoke a harsh word to my mother, whom, when she began to have her miscarriages and then the two stillborn girls who would have been my sisters, Cordelia nursed and loved like a daughter. Once she called my mother Queedabaum, correcting herself quickly. I was about ten at the time, and did not encounter that outlandish name again for thirty years, when I came across it in one of Calvin Goodman's journals in the Common library. He was writing about René Bonhomme's early history, and mentioned that he thought his father's mother, a St. Francis Indian, was named Kwee de Baum. Cordelia was a strange woman, even to herself, but it is to her that I owe not only my education but my deliverance from the cold gray existence of children without a past.

She gave my father a free rein to do whatever he pleased with the farm. He bought my mother three more registered Jerseys the second spring with the maple sugar money, but except for the sugaring, which he loved doing up until the year he cut the trees, his interest in farming began to wane. He did not return to whiskey running or drinking, but he counseled Uncle Henry in the business and found many excuses to neglect the routine work of mending fence, haying, spreading manure. While my mother and

Cordelia worked the farm he hunted and fished and rode around the country in his wagon, purporting to look for stock to buy or trade. Before I was old enough to walk he carried me out to the barn several times a week to see the prizes he brought home from his daily peregrinations. Sometimes it was a horse with chronic heaves or an old cow gone dry. Sometimes it was an animal he had found hurt by the side of the road: a hawk with a broken wing; a three-legged mink that had escaped from a trap by chewing off its own foot; a baby lynx separated from its mother.

His greatest prize of all was Rat Kinneson, whom he discovered late in the spring of our second year on the farm, about the time his fervor for living off the land had started to cool. He was walking down the north end of the Common, undoubtedly on some spurious mission he had invented to give himself a chance to ride the roads or talk to Uncle Henry, when he noticed a group of jeering children standing in a circle in the commission sales barn- yard. Thinking that they might have found some strange animal he could add to his collection, he hurried over and discovered instead a man sprawled out in the mud. My father was quite alarmed. He rushed up to the man and lifted up his head. "Are you all right?" he said.

"Certainly," the man said indignantly. Reeking of whis- key, he raised himself up on one elbow. He opened one yellowish eye and stared at my father. "I'm just showing these boys and girls how to set mushrat traps."

Nothing pleased my father more than that kind of pres- ence. "You better come home with me," he said. "I can use a man like you."

That turned out to be a monumental understatement, probably the only one of my father's career. Without com- promising his obstinate recalcitrance a single degree, Rat took over the farm, liberating my father to ride about the countryside like a squire, hunt and fish with Uncle Henry, play his fiddle, take long walks with my mother, tell me stories and for two or three weeks in the spring run his frenzied sugaring operation.

Every day the road was passable he took the milk cans down to the county road and dropped Cordelia and me off at school. Then he usually went to see a man about a hog or a goat or a woodlot. Often he did not return until late afternoon, picking up the empty milk cans and us at the same time. Taking the milk down to the county road every day instead of every second day was an inspired ruse. It permitted my father to lead approximately the same kind of picaresque existence he had always enjoyed, circumscribed now only by the boundaries to which he could travel and still return by late afternoon.

The rest of his work could be divided into two distinct but interdependent categories. The first consisted of a difficult and time-consuming process called getting Rat started. Getting Rat started always began about the same way. "Rat, come look at something most curious down in the barn." Or, "I'd like to show you something I can't for the life of me figure out, Ratty. You'll know what it is, all right." These standard overtures never amounted to anything more than futile exercises in the rhetoric of chicanery. They might work with men of lesser sophistication, men like Warden R. W., for example, but never with Rat. Next my father resorted to cajoling. Then threatening. When these tactics proved inefficacious he would have Uncle Henry bring up a bottle from the Common and ply Rat with whiskey until he would stagger down to the pasture that needed ditching or the stone wall in need of repair. Rat, who knew more about farming when he was so drunk he could hardly stand up than most professors of agriculture, would tell my father how to begin. My father would hurl himself into the job with all his characteristic ardor. He would work furiously for twenty minutes or half an hour, but never longer, because no matter how drunk he was, Rat could never stand to see another man do a job he could do better. Despite all his better judgment, he would take the shovel or scythe or axe or post maul away from my father and continue the job himself. My father would watch admiringly for a few minutes, then concoct a reason to go to the barn or better yet the Common, knowing that Rat could not leave a job unfinished once he had started it.

After he had gotten Rat started, my father could devote himself to his projects. I cannot remember a time when he didn't have at least one elaborate project under way for making money. As the years went by these schemes became progressively more grandiose and impractical, finally culminating in the whiskey run of 1932, but the first one was easily the most absurd. "By the Great Roaring Christ, Evangeline," he said one spring day when I was five, "let's start us a game farm."

With his obsession for collecting the halt, infirm and unfit of almost every species of domestic and wild animal found in northern New England, my father had a fairly good start already. Our barnyard was crowded with featherless turkeys, hideously goitered ducks and geese and other fowl absolutely indistinguishable by virtue of their esoteric handicaps. At first he had combed the country in search of these blue ribbon grotesqueries; but by the time he decided to formalize his pursuit by opening up the game farm, people were bringing their freak offcasts to him. At least once a week a wagon or truck would appear in the dooryard carrying a six-legged mule, an albino fawn or some other rare and useless mutant.

My father decided to specialize in what he called crosses,

and began to interbreed different species. He tried to mate cats and rabbits, and when this failed he caught some gray squirrels on the Common and attempted to breed them with barn rats. He always had to report his most trivial activity to my mother, and was forever running into the kitchen to announce the birth of some surpassingly bizarre hybrid. The large population of wild coydogs in Kingdom County is said to have evolved from the litter of pups he bred from my mother's cow dog and a female coyote someone brought us from New Hampshire.

My father took ads in little country newspapers all along the border. "Visit Bonhomme's Game Farm. See Rarities of the Animal Kingdom." He lettered out garish signs. "Bonhomme's Wonder Place and Zoological Gardens, Five Miles Ahead at the End of the Road." City people in Reos and Franklins and Landovers drove up our hill. They took one look at the unholy congregation of anomalies clucking and neighing and hissing and bellowing in our dooryard and sped back down the hollow without even getting out of their cars. An incredulous biologist from the University of Vermont spent a week with us. He shook his head every time a new monstrosity hove into sight around the corner of the house or crawled out from under the barn. At one time during the heyday of the game farm we took an inventory and counted two hundred and thirty-four animals of every kind, coloration and disability. My father paired these off with all the vigor of Noah. Under his unflagging nurturing they thrived and multiplied, bringing forth their own kind and preserving their grossest discrepancies. He refused to cage any of them. The obtaining principle seemed to be the survival of the most outrageous. Our entire farm was overrun by freaks, flouting with impunity their huge vestigial claws and limbs, bunches and distentions, superfluous organs and double sets of teeth. A team of evolutionists from Harvard came to visit. The second night they made a pact not to write a word of what they had seen and went back to Cambridge under the cover of darkness.

Finally our family began to come apart under the strain. Rat went off with the fair, vowing not to return until every last cross was gone. My mother, who for three years had not been able to grow anything in her kitchen garden or walk across the dooryard to the barn without stepping on or being stepped on by some squawking unidentifiable renegade from the bird or mammal phylum, delivered an ultimatum: either they went or she did. My father temporized, promising to give away some of the more fecund individuals in his flocks. No one would take any off his hands, so he transported scores in crates deep into the cedar swamp, releasing them miles from our farm. They all returned, hitching up the north hill singly, by pairs and in droves. When she saw them reappearing my mother began to pack. My father rushed off to the Common to seek Uncle Henry's advice.

As soon as he was a mile down the road Cordelia said, "This is a sufficiency."

She got his shotgun and hatchet and dispatched more than two hundred of the most egregious aberrations in less than two hours. Working methodically and dispassionately, she piled the dead in a huge cancerous heap in the upper pasture across the lane from the sugar place. She drenched them with kerosene and ignited them. My father and Uncle Henry saw the billows from the county road and thought the barn was on fire. They whipped up my father's team of Siamese mules and came sluing up the hill, my father standing and lashing the mules with the reins, Uncle Henry sitting complacently beside him.

"What are you doing?" my father shouted to Cordelia,

who was standing near the blackened remains of his game farm and reciting "The Cremation of Sam McGee." Periodically she poked a partially immolated corpse over onto the glowing part of the pile with a long stick.

"Your blasphemous menagerie is gone," she said when she finished the poem. "Go cleave unto your wife. I'm not up to another excursion to Montreal."

With the population of the game farm diminished to a scant twenty or so of the hardiest and least deformed prodigies, Rat returned. My mother planted her garden again. My father remained an easy mark for a farmer who wanted to get rid of a superannuated cow dog or woods horse, but he stopped bringing home freaks and launched into his second project. This was the establishment of a private and most assuredly nonprofit asylum for unwanted and homeless persons. Beginning with Rat Kinneson, his clients burgeoned into an eclectic group of unfortunates of every description. Over the next few years our farm was a sanctuary for dozens of derelicts from the human race. There never seemed to be a time when an old man in the latter stages of delirium tremens or an opium addict or a homeless boy or girl was not staying with us. They slept everywhere: on the parlor couch, in the hayloft, across kitchen chairs, in my bed. For years we hosted a man whose name was Clyde or Floyd, he wasn't sure which, whose chief function was to rush out of the backhouse, where he spent most of his time, and open the barnyard gate when the cows came up from the pasture to be milked, affording my father the distinction of employing the only full-time gatekeeper in the county and probably in Vermont.

Nothing pleased my father more than seeing one of his protégés performing some token task around the place. "Look at old Obadiah weed that lettuce, Evangeline. There's a man that earns his keep." Obadiah had cataracts over both bleary eyes and earned his keep by groping up and down the neat rows of my mother's garden on his knees and systematically rooting up everything in his way. The lettuce came up with the witch grass, the carrots with the pigweed. My mother didn't have the heart to interfere.

Some of my father's clients required only short-term crisis intervention — detoxification, two or three hot meals and a ride down to the freight yards behind the American Heritage Mill. Others settled in for a longer regimen of more intense therapy. My father provided superb counseling in the arts of whiskey running, poaching and warden-baiting. Cordelia conducted all her therapy sessions in Greek. Rat, who regarded the clients as interlopers and rivals, handled the encounter sessions for us. In addition to Clyde or Floyd there were six or seven other long-term residents who stayed a year or more. One was an escapee from Windsor State Prison, an aged counterfeiter my father harbored in the attic, who for exercise walked the woods by night reciting serial numbers from his confiscated five-hundred-dollar bills. Another, a laudanum-crazed anile woman from the county home whose name was Mary Magdalen, spent the last months of her life in the parlor rocking chair talking to the children she never had. She mistook my father for Arthur, her youngest boy, and Lake Memphremagog for the ocean. There was an emaciated fifteen-year-old girl named Little Gretchen who had run away from the septuagenarian farmer to whom her father had sold her two years before. To my father's amusement, Little Gretchen crawled into my bed and tried unsuccessfully to seduce me when I was nine. I had just lost a molar and supposed that she was the tooth fairy, and was disappointed that I couldn't oblige her. My mother was neither amused nor disappointed. The next week she found another home for Little Gretchen, who I think may have had designs on my father also.

Where did these sad, lost persons come from? Some were farmed out from the county home. Others just seemed to materialize. They were all attracted to my father, whom they worshipped like a saint. My mother, too, was loved by pariahs, mad persons and runaways of every description. But while she could live happily enough in a halfway house environment, she could live just as happily without it. My father could not; he depended upon his coterie of hangers-on as much as they depended on him. They gave him an opportunity to be generous while simultaneously aggrandizing his ego. Also, I think he derived enormous satisfaction from providing for rootless persons the home and family he never found himself during that fifteen-year search along the border.

My father had a passion for reading through catalogues that almost equaled his interest in road maps and atlases, which he would pore over for hours. One winter night when we were all assembled in the kitchen he began to read aloud to us from a fruit and berry catalogue sent out by a nursery in Minnesota. According to this bulletin, a brilliant Scandinavian immigrant had developed superhardy northern varieties of pears, peaches, plums, cherries and apricots that had been tested to survive temperatures of forty below zero. No feat of endurance was too much for these miraculous trees. "Listen to this, Evangeline. 'Guaranteed to resist every known blight and rust, bear abundantly the first year, withstand fierce arctic temperatures.' "

The counterfeiter was staying with us at the time, and my father told me to go up in the attic and get him out of bed to come down and hear about the fruit trees. I went up the stairs off the hall and knocked on the attic door. "Don't attempt to lay hands on me, Warder," the old reprobate shouted. "Ned's a desperate man and danger's his middle name." I had every reason to believe this statement, so I retreated to the kitchen.

My father then went up himself. "I know your tricks," I heard Ned yell. "You've got Ned's bright green money and now you want him. Good enough. Quebec Bill Bonhomme and I stand ready for you."

"This is Quebec Bill Bonhomme," my father said through the door. "I want to read you something."

"Bill Bonhomme stands here by Ned's side, ready to defend him with life and limb. Open the door if you dare."

My father prudently came back down to the kitchen.

"Is Father after scourging you again, Arthur?" Mary Magdalen said to him as he passed her rocker. "Don't fret, lad. He'll soon be rolling at the bottom of Northumberland Strait, with the blue whales and great sea fishes nibbling his white bones."

"Do you like fresh peaches, Mother?" my father said.

"I don't know, Arthur. I never had them. Can I smoke them in me pipe?"

"You can do that as soon as you can eat any he'll grow up here," Cordelia said.

Despite this inauspicious beginning, Bonhomme's Fruit and Berry Farm was already a reality in my father's mind. He spent the rest of the winter compiling his order, studying the glossy catalogue evening after evening. In the spring he sugared feverishly, dragooning Rat and my mother and me and Clyde or Floyd and old Ned out to the sugar bush and marshaling our dubious talents in a brilliant demonstration of field generalship. He even carried Mary Magdalen out in her rocker for part of each day so she could warn us if she smelled a storm coming off the Grand Banks. She thought the sap buckets were full of cod and mistook Rat for a giant squid. "I bore twelve children," she told my father. "Ten was boys, and my continual prayer to God was that not a one would go to sea." She looked up at the maples, not yet leafed out. "The fleet's coming in off the Banks, Arthur. What lovely tall masts they have. See the white waves break on the keels." To Mary the snow was surf, the blue sky the distant sea. Meanwhile, old Ned scampered like a red squirrel under the trees, writing the serial numbers of his bills in the snow with a stick. Clyde or Floyd tried to urinate in the boiling pan. Somehow my father managed to make several hundred pounds of sugar, enough to order a thousand fruit trees from Minnesota.

The order arrived in May. It filled the back of our wagon. It was a glorious sight, hundreds of little budded whips, limber twigs jutting proudly out of compact moist balls of peat moss wrapped in burlap. Multicolored tags bearing extravagant illustrations of lush fruits were wired to the tiny stalks above the grafts. The Scandinavian horticulturist had outdone himself. My father danced in the street in front of the railway station.

He had plowed up part of the upper pasture across from the maples. Now he threw himself into digging and planting, pacing off rows, making esoteric measurements and calculations. Assisted by his Barnum and Bailey gallery, he watered and mulched and cultivated and sprayed all summer. In the evenings he projected bumper crops of golden peaches, succulent rose-tinged pears, juicy plums — "as big as baseballs, Wild Bill" — a profuse Keatsian harvest of grapes, nectarines, berries of every variety. It rained frequently that summer. The hay rotted in the fields, but my father didn't care. His trees and bushes were thriving. In the fall he banked them high with straw and manure, neglecting in the process to bank our house or get Rat started with the banking. He swaddled his trees securely with roofing paper to protect them from

147

rabbits and mice and deer. "Sleep tight, my darlings," he said.

Winter came early. The first spitting flurries fell on the last day of August. By the end of September the frost was deep in the ground. October was a month of heavy pelting snows. The wind came whipping down over the vast frozen expanse of Lake Memphremagog. In January the temperature dropped to fifty below zero. The big maples cracked in the cold like rifle shots. The old square nails in the walls of the house snapped like firecrackers. We burned a cord of wood every week and still couldn't keep warm. One night in February Clyde or Floyd went out to the backhouse without letting anyone know he was going. The next morning we found him sitting frozen on the four-holer, the Montgomery Ward mail-order catalogue open to the ladies' underwear section in his rigid hands. My father's capacity for affirmation was unshaken. He called all of us out to the backhouse and delivered a short elegy. "Grieve not, friends," he shouted into the frosty air. "A good shit was all Clyde or Floyd had in this world and probably the next to look forward to." When we dug the poor man's corpse out of the sawdust pit behind the barn where my father had wintered him over until spring burial, a hideous grin was still frozen on his face. "He died happy" was the epitaph my father carved into his slate marker.

It was a winter of death. Mary Magdalen died in her rocker in March, though we did not know it immediately because the chair continued to rock for several hours after she was cold. The ground was still frozen four feet deep, so down she went into the sawdust pit with Clyde or Floyd, tied into the rocker, in which my father buried her in May when the ground finally thawed. He got Rat to build a large square box resembling a packing crate, and when we put her inside and nailed down the top the chair began to rock again. My father put his mouth up to the crate. "It's Arthur, Mother," he said soothingly. "You can rest quiet now. Your sons are all on dry land." Immediately the creaking stopped.

Cordelia, who had informed us that Mary Magdalen was dead without even looking up from her book, said that there would be a third death soon and she hoped it would be hers, she could not endure much more of my father's lunacy. A week after Mary Magdalen died in the rocker old Ned failed to return from one of his night walks in the woods. It had snowed the day before and my father and I were able to trace his path down the north side of our hill and across the beaver dam into the cedar swamp. He had walked in a straight line, stopping now and then to scratch into the snow numbers from plates melted down twenty years ago. A mile into the swamp the tracks stopped. We spiraled out in widening concentric circles but could not pick up the trail. Ned was canny in a crazed way. Maybe he had backtracked somehow. We checked, but found nothing. His tracks simply stopped, like the tracks of a snowshoe rabbit picked out of its stride by an owl. It was as though he had been translated, like Elijah. Cordelia said this was undoubtedly the case; some benign power had swooped him up to spare him from the fate of the sawdust pit.

Long after the rest of us gave Ned up as lost, my father went to the swamp to search for him. Several times he walked the ten miles to the Canadian line. Once he followed the old tote road along the river all the way to the lake. I was eight at the time and had seen enough death to know that Ned was gone. I did not understand what drove my father day after day to fight his way through blowdowns and over beaver dams and up frozen streams, treacherous with spring holes, in search of someone who had obviously disappeared. I asked Cordelia and my mother why he persisted. They looked at each other, but said nothing.

With the first thaws the cedar swamp became a morass of flowing water and quaking bogs, and my father had to abandon his hunt.

I have always suspected that Ned, master counterfeiter that he was, walked backwards in his own tracks, maybe a long ways, then climbed an overhanging cedar without stepping out of his original footprints. I think he then worked his way high into the tight branches, wedged himself in and went to sleep. Of course this possibility occurred to us at the time. We actually climbed and searched several trees. But there was no way we could investigate them all, and in spots they were so dense that spry old Ned in his frenetic and gleeful self-satisfaction over at last eluding his imaginary pursuers might have scrambled for another half-mile from tree to tree above the swamp before curling up for one last night's sleep.

The spring of 1926 was a busy time for my father. He had to tap the maples, bury Clyde or Floyd and Mary Magdalen, and visit his orchard a dozen times a day to see whether his trees had survived the harsh winter. Early in May when we had our usual week of false spring a few scattered plum and pear trees started to show green buds and he danced all over the farm. Then the weather froze up again and it snowed steadily for two days. The snow did not go that year until the end of May, leaving hundreds of black sapless rigid sticks where my father's Eden had been. He was charmed, and averred that with proper management the lifeless stocks would put up even hardier shoots from their roots. He hitched the team to the great wooden sap vat and brought up water from the brook all summer.

By fall not a single tree had put up any shoots. "Well, Bill," he said cheerfully, surveying that blasted chiaroscuro of leafless switches, "we can use any with a fork in them for divining rods."

My father was an expert at witching water. He knew just how to handle a wand so that it would pull down in his strong hands like a striking trout. His own optimism seemed to flow into the wand. Everywhere he went he found water. Everywhere, that is, except our hilltop. Water was a perennial problem for us. The lower meadow was full of good springs and the brook itself rose halfway up our maple orchard, but the only supply for the house and barn was a hand-dug well that ran dry every two or three years. Sometimes it would go dry in the winter, and we would have to bring up water in milk cans from the brook until spring, chopping a fresh hole through the ice every day.

Just behind our house on the northern brow of the hill was a low granite outcropping that was always covered with a dark gleam of cold water, even in drought time. For his own amusement my father occasionally cut a witching wand and had it nearly jerked out of his hands over this ledge. The fall he gave up on the orchard he decided to dynamite the hairline fissure out of which that cold water seeped and reveal the spring he was sure lay just below the rock.

Now my father loved to blow things up. Detonations of all kinds excited him, and he was always looking for an excuse to dynamite something. The previous year he had dynamited the beaver dam across the St. John, which he claimed was backing water up so he couldn't get near his favorite brook trout hole. A week later the beavers had replaced it under the supervision of a large chocolate-colored male with huge yellow incisors. This time my father placed three charges, one at each end of the dam and one in the middle. Sticks and mud flew a hundred feet into the air. Whiskeyjack and Two Bottles Kinneson, Rat's cousins from down the hollow, came galloping up with their shotguns, riding double on Two Bottles' mule, thinking a G-man had blown up a still. For several weeks there was no beaver activity in or near the river. Then one afternoon late in August when my father and I decided to go fishing we discovered the entire colony working feverishly on a new dam. This one was wide enough to drive a team across, the biggest dam we had ever seen. The chocolate beaver with big teeth was working alongside the others. Sitting on the dam directing the emplacement of the last sticks was a black beaver that must have weighed close to a hundred pounds. "I should have knowed they'd do that," my father said. "Wild Bill, they've went up to Canady and gotten theirselves a French engineer to build that dam so she'll stay built. I've heard beaver will do that. This is the proof. Just look at that great black Frenchman. He ain't a bit afraid of us. Well, he don't have to be. We'll save the rest of our dynamite for another project."

So equipped with three sticks of dynamite and a dead Bartlett pear sapling my father went out to that outcropping to blast for water. My mother and Cordelia and Rat and I stood back by the Canada plum tree at the corner of the house. We were all quite apprehensive. My mother did not say so, but I could tell that she didn't want my father fooling around with explosives. Cordelia was afraid he would blow up the house along with the ledge. When Rat saw my father pretend to be yanked off his feet by the nonexistent attraction of that dead forked stick to the water he was outraged. He said blasphemy was walking abroad up and down in the land and that my father was making a mockery of Moses' striking the rock with his rod to bring forth water. My father overheard part of this. He began to laugh uncontrollably and flail the ledge with his pear switch. He held each stick of dynamite in his teeth to light it, then walked casually off to observe the blast from a short distance away. There was a fearsome explosion. A shower of rock fragments fell all over the dooryard and rained down on the house roof. We ran toward the ledge. My father stood in a sulphurous cloud of smoke and dust pouring out of a jagged aperture about three feet long and two feet wide. When the air cleared we looked into the crevice and saw water rising up its sides. My father began to caper all around the edge of the hole. He ran into Cordelia and nearly knocked her down in. She smiled grimly and went back to the house. Rat followed her, muttering about the devil's work. In his ecstasy my father leaped back and forth across the gaping hole like a puppet. The water continued to rise steadily. It was almost to the top. My father stooped and reached out his hand.

Instantly the water started to recede. Like a disappearing mirage, it retreated leisurely down the smooth granite sides of the opening until it was out of sight. My father looked at his dry hand, still extended. He ran it over the dark high-water mark inside the hole and brought it away damp. He sniffed his fingers and touched them to his tongue. "It's water," he said. "It's water, all right. It has to be down there still. Somewhere."

My mother knelt beside him and put her hand on his shoulder. "William," she said, "who else but you could have done this? You are a true miracle worker, and I love you."

"I love you too, Dad," I said. "Can we go down in the hole?"

"Evangeline," my father shouted, putting an arm around each of us, "Wild Bill here has just give me another brilliant idea. Fetch my paintbrush, Bill. We're going into business."

This time we put signs at every crossroads in the county.

"Visit Bonhomme's Sinkhole — See Subterranean Geological Phenomena." Under the lettering my father painted a crude picture of four goggle-eyed sightseers being lowered into a hole in the ground in a bucket. After getting Rat drunk three times, my father finally got him to construct a windlass over the crevice. He secured the tub from our old cider press to the end of the windlass rope and while Rat and I turned the crank made the maiden descent himself. We ran out of rope at sixty feet.

Many persons drove up to our farm to view the hole, but after seeing the windlass few cared to go down. Those who did invariably demanded to be pulled back up again before they had been lowered ten feet in the swaying cider tub. I can still hear their panicked cries echoing up the sides of the crevice as Rat and my father and I cranked like demons. One day four of our sheep fell in, disappearing one after another like lemmings leaping into the sea. We added another forty feet of rope to the windlass and sent the cider tub down empty, but we never did hit bottom. Nor did we detect any smell indicating that the sheep had either. Finally Cordelia went out and broke up the windlass and boarded the hole over. We didn't need any more disappearances in our family, she said. At the time I thought she was talking about Ned and the sheep.

For years afterwards that arid and fathomless fissure that was to have supplied us so bountifully with water was a haven to my father in times of trouble. When it rained for two days on cut hay or a sow had a litter of thirteen dead piglets; when a fetus petrified inside a cow or it did not rain for two months; when the sugar house caught fire and burned down; when Rat deserted us in haying time; when the minister from the Common came calling after my mother's stillbirths; when my father got shingles — whenever a minor or major tragedy struck, my father returned to the ledge. He would remove one of the boards over the hole and stare down into the exposed bowels of our hill with an expression simultaneously puzzled and hopeful, as though half expecting a limpid geyser to gush forth at any moment.

"I reckon I'll slide down to the spring in the ledge, Evangeline. Would you like to go along?"

My mother was always morose at these times. Sometimes I went, but after the first ten minutes I was bored.

"I know it's still down there," my father said, not unhopefully. "It's down there somewhere." Though there was no water there, he was drawn to the crevice as Melville and Thoreau say men are drawn to water, and always came away refreshed and optimistic. "It's not every farm that's blessed with a mystery hole," he told us.

There were many other projects over the years, whose successive failures inspired my father to new proclamations of faith. His spirits flourished under each adversity. Mine did not. As I grew older, my ambivalence toward the farm deepened. I was not lonely. I couldn't have been lonely if I had tried. But I was isolated from friends my own age, from town sports, from neighbors. When I read Robert Frost's "Birches" years later I knew that boy too far from town to learn baseball. We did not get a newspaper. We didn't have a radio or the electricity to operate one. Under Cordelia's pedagogy I learned much about the Anglo-Saxon heptarchy but little about the government of the United States since the Civil War. My entire family was apolitical. Sometimes we saw a ball game or a movie in the Common, but except for Uncle Henry we had no social connections there. Once when I was eight or nine we went to Montpelier on the train to watch my father win the New England Oldtime Fiddling Championship. The main event of our year was the Kingdom Fair.

Yet I don't think that we were a provincial family, except in a very narrow literal sense. Cordelia's awesome knowledge of the seen and unseen worlds was matched only by my father's faith in both. My mother's tolerance and endurance were equally remarkable. There were other places I would have chosen to grow up than on that remote hilltop, but there was no family anywhere I would rather have belonged to.

Some of my father's projects almost worked. These he quickly lost interest in. He had Rat plow up the orchard and in the spring he planted several thousand cabbages. He harvested a good crop and kept the cabbages down cellar until just before Christmas when the market had always been favorable. Just before Christmas the bottom fell out of the market. That spring he planted the cabbage field to field pumpkins. His slogan was a one-hundred-pound pumpkin for every boy and girl in Kingdom County. In July he started force-feeding the pumpkins milk through a thin glass tube. They attained monstrous and obscene proportions, frightening all the children who saw them. We couldn't give them away.

Over Warden Kinneson's strenuous protests my father got a license to guide hunters and fishermen. A bumptious cigar-smoking judge from Boston hired him for the first day of deer season. He put the judge on a good runway halfway down the north side of our hill. "You'll have to put out that cee-gar," my father told him. "A buck deer will scent that a mile upwind from you."

"I'll worry about the cee-gar, my little man. You worry about getting me the buck, and I'm not talking about any puny underweight little six-pointer. Is this where you propose for me to stand?"

"Yes, sir," my father said. "Just be kind enough to turn around and face downhill."

When the judge turned around my father booted him all the way to the cedar swamp.

The judge took him up in front of Justice Bullpout Kinneson. Bullpout listened attentively to the judge's account, nodding sympathetically. "How many points would you like on that buck of yourn, Jedge?" Bullpout asked.

"Well, Justice," the judge said condescendingly, "ten would be all right."

"Ten is just what I'm a-going to fine you," Bullpout roared. "Ten dollars or ten days in jail, I don't care which. Any man that would smoke a cee-gar on a deer stand ought to consider hisself fortunate to get off that easy. Court dismissed."

My father impaled his guide's license on a nail in the woodshed and decided to try another cash crop. This time it was oats. He used his sugaring income to buy the seed and a steam-driven threshing machine so antiquated even Rat couldn't seem to figure out how to repair it. The oats grew well, as the cabbages and pumpkins had; despairing of the threshing machine, my father bought some antique flails for winnowing out grain by hand. Before we had an opportunity to use them five marauding black bears descended on the oatfield and ravaged the crop. They knocked the heads off the stalks with long raking powerful swipes and gorged themselves. Then they regurgitated and repeated the process. My father horsewhipped all five of them out of the field but they returned at night, gluttonous as banqueting Romans, and devastated the entire field. My father shot the two biggest.

"This bear roast is Christly tasty, Evangeline. It puts me in the mind of good western beef. I wonder why a man couldn't make a dollar up here raising a herd of beef cattle."

His eyes acquired the visionary luminosity we had all

come to dread. With my father there was rarely any lapse between the conception of an idea and the first steps of its execution. He was off and running again, this time with the most quixotic scheme of all. Several local farmers had tried to raise Herefords for beef, but without much success. The cost of hay and grain over the long winters ate up any profit. My father's solution to this dilemma was to introduce a tougher breed of cattle, one that could stay out all winter and forage most of their own food. After considerable research, he decided on the Texas longhorn.

He wrote for information to state agricultural departments and colleges, private ranches, local historical societies. He received hundreds of letters, all of which he insisted on reading aloud. Everything about longhorns interested him intensely — their history, their physiognomy, their adaptability and toughness and speed. Everyone who wrote advised him against the project. For one thing, longhorns were almost extinct. They had all but disappeared from Texas, if there were any left at all. Their scarcity reinforced my father's determination to own a herd. He began to perceive himself as the chosen savior of a noble and endangered species, for which Kingdom County was to be the promised land. He read about a lost longhorn herd in a paperback western of the type specializing in lost silver mines and lost Aztec tribes. He resolved to travel to Texas, find this wandering herd and bring it back to Lord Hollow.

That spring he sugared with unprecedented energy. He gathered sap until the last week of May when the trees yielded only a crude low grade which he boiled down into a thick dark blackstrap used to sweeten chewing tobacco. Somehow he persuaded Uncle Henry to agree to accompany him. Then the day before they were scheduled to leave for El Paso to find the lost herd he came down with shingles. For the next several months he was in agony.

The pain was excruciating. He screamed imprecations against doctors, who he was convinced were responsible for all human disease. He grew worse instead of better. He lay on a pallet on top of the kitchen woodbox, lapsing into deliriums in which he roared out cowboy songs, deployed the ghosts of old Ned and Mary Magdalen and Clyde or Floyd up and down dusty arroyos in pursuit of the elusive lost herd. He delivered impassioned defenses of buffalo, eagles, whooping cranes and other threatened species. He was haunted by disappearances and the possibility of disappearances. He reverted to this theme each time his fever returned. I was afraid he would die. Rat was so distressed he began working around the clock on the threshing machine. My father raved on. "I looked fifteen years for you," he shouted. "Now I've found you here in El Paso. I ought to put the boots to you, you old son of a bitch, running off on me like that. What is it you run across this border?" I had no idea whom he was talking to. He stopped eating and lost weight. He lost more weight. He couldn't have weighed sixty pounds. When he went into a coma my mother got old Doctor Rupp to come up from the Common.

By the time Doctor Rupp arrived my father hardly seemed to be breathing. His legs were thinner than mine. "This man needs a physic," Doctor Rupp said.

Doctor Rupp was a notorious alcoholic. A physic was his panacea for every illness. He extracted a huge purging apparatus from his bag and asked for warm water. I stood at the foot of the woodbox, frightened and weak from weeping, but also angry. I knew my father would not want this old drunken quack to touch him. Rupp mumbled about purgatives as he prepared the massive enema. He said a dose of salts in time would have prevented my father's shingles.

My father opened one feverish red eye. He looked straight

159

at me and winked. Doctor Rupp called for a chamberpot. When it was in position he bent over to turn his victim. Instantly my father leaped up and seized the astonished physician by the windpipe. There was a brief and furious struggle. Doctor Rupp lay pinned on his back on the woodbox, my emaciated father astride his chest in his nightshirt. My father thrust the long rubber tube of the enema down Doctor Rupp's throat, simultaneously pumping the red ball full of water. He began to bounce up and down on his shriveled knees on Doctor Rupp's taut distended stomach. The effects of this procedure were worthy of the medical journals. The doctor gagged briefly, then produced a copious double evacuation which he later admitted surpassed the most violent discharges of his most responsive patients. With a hand clapped over the source of each eruption, Doctor Rupp rushed out to his Ford.

Nothing could have been more salubrious for my father than this diverting masque. That night he sat up and ate supper with us. His fever subsided and did not return. He was able to concentrate again on planning the Texas trip with Uncle Henry.

They left the Common on New Year's Day, 1929. I wanted to go and my father wanted to take me but that time my mother said no and wouldn't change her mind, so I stood outside the station between her and Cordelia, waving sadly, while my father danced on the platform of the caboose, shaking his clasped hands over his head, until Uncle Henry pulled him back inside out of the cold. One of the most senseless cross-country misadventures of all times was under way.

In order to save his money to get the lost herd back to Kingdom County my father worked out impromptu arrangements with the conductors of several lines to earn his fare and Uncle Henry's by entertaining in the lounge cars.

160

Uncle Henry played the banjo, rocking with the rhythm of the train, his huge fingers flying, his slightly protruding eyes watching my fiddling father, whooping and nodding and cakewalking.

"We're cattlemen," my father told every salesman and pregnant woman and concessionaire and porter and conductor and waiter between shows. "I and this big fella are cattlemen from Kingdom County, Vermont."

Texas, 1929. In one respect it resembled Vermont, since the Depression that was about to rock the rest of the country would be largely unfelt in both states. Texas was too rich to notice, Vermont too poor. It was vast even beyond the Canadian wilderness our farm overlooked. Uncle Henry said that it made him uneasy. It was so full of anomalies — cities soaring out of desert wastelands, oil where there wasn't even water — and except for the anomalies so flat and expressionless. Maybe the flatness was what unsettled Uncle Henry, as though his own expressionlessness needed contrast to be effective. My father on the other hand could not have been more at home. As soon as they got off the train in El Paso he produced a forked stick he had broken off one of our red astrachans before leaving and announced that he would witch an oil well for anyone who could tell him where to find the lost herd. Uncle Henry said they hadn't been on the station platform two minutes before my father had a crowd around him, laughing and hanging on every word he said.

No one seemed to be able to tell him anything about the lost herd, but with his affinity for discovering grotesqueries he quickly learned about a woman rancher named Yellow Rose who was said to know about longhorns and possibly own some. She lived a short two hundred miles from El Paso, and was also said to discourage visitors of all kinds by conspicuously displaying two forty-five pistols holstered in bandoleers crossed over her abundant bosom. Everyone advised my father against attempting to make her acquaintance, much less offer to buy one of her sacred longhorns. Of course he was all the more determined to meet this flower of the desert, and set out for her ranch by rented car. The driver refused to go beyond the ranch gate, so he and Uncle Henry had to walk the last twenty miles to the house, where Yellow Rose was busy barbecuing a beef in celebration of their arrival, which she had been anticipating for several hours. "That cowardly El Paso driver dropped you off at the wrong gate," she roared. "I've had a car waiting for you by the main entrance since sunup. Break out the whiskey, boys. The Varmintors have arrove at last."

My father was a great success on Yellow Rose's ranch. He fiddled all night and rode with the hands all day. Uncle Henry said they were amazed at his ability with a lariat, which he had picked up during his year in Montana and never forgotten. He challenged a Mexican knife thrower to a contest and won easily. He won a free-style wrestling contest. The second day on the ranch he found three new oil wells with his divining rod. Yellow Rose offered him a thousand dollars a well, but he turned it down, telling Uncle Henry that he would lose the gift to divine if he accepted money for it. She offered him a salary of five hundred dollars a week to bring my mother and me to Texas and stay on the ranch as foreman. This offer, too, he turned down. He wanted only to get his longhorns and get them back to Vermont.

Yellow Rose finally admitted that she had only one true longhorn, an old bull that ran wild on her rangelands impregnating her whiteface heifers and goring her other bulls and any horse that he could run down. She did not want to do away with this obstreperous animal, but was more than willing for my father to take him home to Vermont if he could catch him. Meanwhile, Yellow Rose was doing her best to catch Uncle Henry. Although she did not wear two pistols, or even one, she was a giant of a woman, as tall as my uncle and fifty pounds heavier, with long golden hair and a face the color of the half-raw beefsteaks she devoured three or four times a day. She was good-natured if she liked you, and a millionaire many times over, but Uncle Henry was not about to relinquish his bachelorhood.

Later Uncle Henry told me that on one occasion during the visit he was actually afraid for his reputation as a man. It was late at night. Yellow Rose was eating a three-pound uncooked steak alone in the kitchen for a bedtime snack. Uncle Henry saw the light and wandered out, unable to sleep in the heat. "It's you, is it?" Yellow Rose said, tearing off a large chunk of meat with her teeth and offering it to him. He stood with his back to the kitchen table, holding the raw slab of steak, his face no doubt expressionless and inscrutable. That is the time Yellow Rose chose to make her declaration. "I've took a strong liking to you, Henry Coville," she said. "I don't care if you don't have but one lung. You've got a great big red heart and that's what counts."

Uncle Henry was still wondering what to do with the beefsteak when she grabbed him. "She taken me completely off guard," he said. "So when she threw that bear hug on me I was pretty helpless. My arms was pinned right to my sides, and it warn't that hard for her to bend me back over that round kitchen table and begin kissing me. It was like being kissed by a lively side of beef. Mister man, I was overpowered. The table was on casters and presently we begun to roll along across the kitchen floor. We come up short against the cast-iron stove. I give a lurch and by Jesus if we didn't start back the other way, table and all. I guess by that time Rose believed I was being affectionate. The more I thrashed about and struggled to get loose the harder she squoze. She was right up on top of me on that rolling table. They was a great wide entranceway from the kitchen into the dining room, and a downhill ramp, and we sailed right on through. We got by the end of the long eating table and from there on it was clear coasting, out the archway onto the patio, where the table finally tipped over. I got free in the crackup, and a good thing for me I did. 'That's the best ride this old gal ever had,' Rose shouts. 'Let's lug this old wooden rolycoaster back in the kitchen and go again nekkid.' Well, sir, she commenced to peeling off her clothes. I don't know what all would have happened if just then we hadn't heard a commotion from out toward the corral. 'What's that?' says I. 'What's what?' Rose says, ripping at her shirt. My, Bill, warn't she doublebreasted under that Texas moon. I was almost tempted to make another run with her. But not quite. 'Out by the corral,' I says.

" 'Rustlers, is it?' she shouts, and tears off across the dooryard without even stopping to button her shirt back up.

"Well, much to Rose's disappointment it warn't rustlers. It was your father and the knife thrower and two, three others your father had roped into helping him round up that bull. Your father was riding the bull into the corral. It was tame as a cow pony. He had evidently let the bull chase him into a box canyon, and once they was inside he jumped on its back and rode it until it fell down or rammed into the canyon wall or just give up. He never said, and them other boys was afraid to go inside and see. The knife thrower says it was a case of pure sorcery. Which for all I know it may have been."

I was only twelve when Uncle Henry told me this story the first time, and probably would have believed him if he said my father whistled once to the wild bull and it followed him home. I had seen him climb up into the massive antlers of the bull moose that grazed with our cows one summer and ride it all over our farm. He could call birds out of the woods to eat from his hands like St. Francis; converse for hours with owls; pick up a baby wildcat while the mother watched purring. Later Uncle Henry and I would both see him ride the bull bareback from Lord Hollow to the Common. So I believed the story and still do, but I don't know how my father caught the bull.

By the time he did he had apparently given up hope of locating the entire lost herd, and was ready to start home. Uncle Henry was ready to go anywhere at all to escape the powerful blandishments of Yellow Rose, but he was not enthusiastic about my father's plan to accompany the longhorn back to Vermont in a cattle car. The only compromise my father would make was to substitute a boxcar for the slatted cattle car he had picked out. They left El Paso late in January, with Yellow Rose crying on the patform and the bull placidly munching hay in a corner of the boxcar.

The next two weeks, Uncle Henry said, were among the very worst in his life, almost as bad as the trenches and worse than the army hospital. The bull was docile enough, though he made it plain that he preferred my father to Uncle Henry, but the ride itself was hellish. They were stranded for three days on a siding in Kansas City. Two yard detectives mistook them for hoboes and my father, impatient of explanations, carried the misunderstanding to a violent conclusion. There was a routing mistake in Chicago that my father, with his built-in compass, detected as soon as the train was out of the city limits but could do nothing about until they arrived in Milwaukee. Between Cleveland and Buffalo they were delayed thirty hours by a blizzard bringing three feet of snow and gale winds in off Lake Erie. Uncle Henry said the one advantage of the storm was that their hands were too cold to play High, Low, Jack and the Game. He said they must have played a thousand hands between El Paso and Cleveland. It wouldn't have been quite so bad if the bull could have sat in, but he was content to watch with his chin on my father's shoulder. I never saw my uncle play a single hand of cards again. Until it got too cold, he told me, my father would climb up on the roof and run along on top of the moving cars for exercise, leaping from one car to the next while the train swayed across the deserts and prairies at sixty and seventy and eighty miles an hour. Occasionally he would go all the way up to visit the engineer.

They arrived in the Common on February 12 at a little after midnight. Uncle Henry wanted only to take the bull over to the commission sales barn and fall asleep in a bed again. My father had other ideas. He looked up at the sky, which was perfectly clear, and said he wanted to see how his longhorn stood up under brisk weather, and so would ride him home. It was about forty below zero, and Uncle Henry said that while he had no doubts about the longhorn's endurance he himself had stood up under all the brisk weather he intended to. But of course he couldn't let my father ride out the county road and up the hollow alone; he might fall off and freeze to death, and he supposed that having seen things through this far he could see them the rest of the way. They hitched the bull to the statue of Ethan Allen and woke up Armand St. Onge, who loaned Uncle Henry a big woods horse to ride. My father grasped the bull by his horns and somersaulted over onto his back.

"Giddap," he said, and the bull trotted up the Common and on out the county road as though he knew exactly where he was going. Uncle Henry said the bull knew that there was only one place in all New England outlandish enough to accommodate him and that place was our hilltop.

I was sleeping with my window open, and as they came up the lane below the barn my father's voice woke me up. His song rang out clearly on the cold night air.

> Come a ti yi yay
> Git along little doggies,
> It's your good fortune and also my own.
> Come a ti yi yay
> Giddap my fine longhorns,
> You know that Lord Hollow will be your new
>   home.

"Wild Bill," my father shouted. "Evangeline, Cordelia, Rat. Here's Quebec Bill Bonhomme home from Texas with the lost herd."

I rushed downstairs and outside in my nightshirt. I jumped up to hug my father, who wrapped his sheep coat around me and rode me across the dooryard and back. Rat put his head out his lower chamber window. He was wearing his long nightcap. "Did you ride all the way from Texas?" he said.

"Yes, Rat my boy," my father said. "Didn't we, Henry?"

"I feel as if we must have," Uncle Henry said.

My mother was standing in the woodshed door. "Evangeline," my father shouted, jumping off the bull and running to her, "I've brung you the lost herd, Evangeline."

He set me down and stood up on his tiptoes to hug and kiss her. He was wearing riding boots with high heels. The crown of his ten-gallon hat came almost even with my mother's nose. He looked like a small boy in a cowboy suit running to kiss his mother. "I've named him Hercule," he shouted. "In honor of your father."

"He would be pleased," my mother said. "Nothing would have pleased him more."

That was the beginning of the great Vermont longhorn saga, which would end as absurdly as it began, but not before Hercule became famous beyond even my father's expectations. Before leaving for Texas my father had gotten Rat started on a cedar-pole lean-to in the upper pasture, into which he now drove Hercule and out of which Hercule immediately bolted, galloping back down the lane and across the lower pasture and frozen brook to a deer yard in the softwoods. There he spent the rest of the winter. It was as if our hill brought out in him the wildness of his Spanish progenitors. For the next three months we had to take his hay and grain down to the deer yard by hand sledge. When he and the deer smelled us coming they tore off through the woods, returning to eat only after we were gone. Except for his tracks we wouldn't have known he was there. When spring came he abandoned the deer and went berserk. He ran wild through the county, tearing up gardens, rampaging through hayfields and impregnating dozens of Jerseys and Holsteins and Guernseys and Ayrshires, so that in time a new breed of milking cows with long wickedly curved horns began to emerge in Kingdom County.

We spent all spring and summer hunting him. Sometimes at dawn we would start him out of a cedar brake deep in some swamp. For a moment he would stare at us with red malicious eyes before snorting furiously and charging off to wreak new havoc. Enraged farmers fired at him with rifles, shotguns, Civil War pistols. They filled him with buckshot and slugs and birdshot and even one musket ball, none of which penetrated beyond his hide. He never trampled or gored anyone or really did much damage, but there was no way farmers could secure the chastity of their heifers against his onslaughts. He was as devious and crafty as the conquistadors who had brought his ancestors to this hemisphere. When a direct assault was impracticable, and this was increasingly the case as farmers began confining their heifers, he bellowed to them at night from the woods until they broke down barn doors and joined him.

In the fall when the foliage was at its peak and the hills were solid banks of red and yellow my father convened more than one hundred farmers and organized the largest drive ever put on in Kingdom County. His strategy was to array beaters in an elliptical loop high on the ridges above Lord Hollow and at a prearranged signal have them move down toward the narrow valley, enclosing Hercule in a tightening ring of men. Equipped with his lariat, he stationed himself and Uncle Henry in the road just below Whiskeyjack Kinneson's and fired off his shotgun. The roundup was on. The farmers were armed with noise-makers of every kind. They beat sticks against dishpans and whaled triangular gongs with short metal rods. They rang dinner bells, honked on duck and goose calls, blasted cavalry charges on bugles handed down from ancestors who had participated in the wars against the Indians. Those without wind or percussion instruments augmented the clamor by hooting like bears, blatting like goats and roaring like rutting bull moose. My mother and Cordelia and I watched from our hilltop. Cordelia said there hadn't been such a devilish tumult since the convocation of fallen angels in *Paradise Lost*.

As the drive contracted the din intensified. A dark animal burst out of the woods behind Whiskeyjack's place. At

169

first I thought it was Two Bottles' black dog that he kept for running deer. When it stood up on its hind feet and looked around I realized it was a bear. A smaller tawny animal was racing along the edge of the woods on the other side of the road. This I identified immediately as a wildcat. Several deer appeared. Then several more. Suddenly Hercule was thundering straight down the road toward my father and Uncle Henry, who seemed to be engaged in some acrobatic maneuver. Uncle Henry was bent over. When he straightened up my father was standing on his shoulders, twirling his lariat. As Hercule charged by my father lassoed him around the horns and at the same time leaped onto his back.

This time Hercule did not intend to be so quickly subdued. He began to plunge up and down in long humping leaps. My father held on. Somehow he got the lasso down around Hercule's thick powerful neck. Men appeared in the fields, which were swarming with frantic deer, rabbits, bears, porcupines, wildcats, fishers, skunks. Uncle Henry seemed to be watching it all impassively. Hercule began to run down the road. He was running flat out like a race horse. The closing ring of men broke apart in panic. Hercule disappeared around the bend, my father still aboard.

"The Ford," my mother cried. "Get the Ford, William."

I started the Ford and with my mother and Cordelia beside me we went fast down the hollow. Uncle Henry and Whiskey-jack and Two Bottles and Orie Royer and Justice Bullpout Kinneson and two or three others jumped in the back as we went by. Along the way people who hadn't participated in the roundup pointed toward the Common to indicate the way my father and Hercule had gone. Whiskeyjack and Two Bottles fired their guns in the air from time to time. Cordelia declaimed from *Paradise Lost* and my mother held my arm tightly. When we reached the Common Hercule was grazing serenely on the grass under the statue of Ethan Allen, and my father was doing lariat tricks for a group of small children.

Hercule never ran away again. He was not young when my father brought him home from Texas, and he apparently exhausted his passionate capacities forever on that one last amorous rampage lasting five months. Periodically I still notice a Jersey or Guernsey with a wide-shouldered and rangy aspect or a peculiar outward sweep of its horns, but Hercule lost all interest in procreation after that first summer. He developed a lachrymose expression as though he missed Texas or perhaps sensed that he was one of the last of his race, doomed to grow old in a foreign land, an avatar of a time that had passed long ago and that he could not quite recall and certainly not revive and perpetuate. Only people, very unusual people like Cordelia and my father, could do that.

9

W E had been lying on our bed of fir boughs remin-
iscing over my father's projects for about an hour
when he declared that he intended to salvage the whiskey.

"I was afraid you'd say that," Uncle Henry said. "I ain't
going to inquire how you propose to do it. Don't you tell
me neither. I want a few hours peaceful sleep tonight.
Damn few at that, Quebec Bill. It must be long after midnight already. Will you pipe down now and leave us get
twenty minutes rest?"

The next thing I remember is waking up in a quiet
drizzling dawn and looking out at my father roasting some
kind of animal over a fire and Uncle Henry standing nearby.

"What's that you're cooking?" I said.

"Good morning, Wild Bill," my father said, "and a
beautiful spring morning at that. Feel that rain, boy, smell
it, taste it. Here's spring's warm rain to green the grass."

He held out a slice of meat on Uncle Henry's hunting
knife. "Don't burn your tongue. This is a young roebuck
that was sleeping a mite too heavy this morning. Ain't

that tasty? See how still the lake is. There's hardly a stick of pulp on her. What wasn't thrown up on shore was driven north. I wonder if the tug made it. Maybe I'll find it down there with the whiskey. Quebec Bill's going diving today, boys. Diving down where the sturgeons live. I want in the worst way to see a sturgeon."

"Bill," Uncle Henry said, "I'm going to tell you something. You listen, too. You listen good. It's raining, as you've already pointed out. If it don't freeze back up you can get your cows out in a day or two. If it does freeze, I'll furnish the hay. You have my word on that.

"Now I want you to stop all this. You're overreaching yourself. Splashing around in that ice water and being shot at and setting barn fires. You're losing your grip. I see it happen over across more than once. First they stop sleeping. Then they stop eating. He ain't et a bit, Billy. Not a bite. Then they start in trying to get theirselves killed. And unless they get stove up first they usually succeed. Sometimes the other fella gets kilt trying to keep it from happening, too."

"What other fella? Is that you? Are you that other fella, Hen?"

"Don't provoke me, Quebec Bill Bonhomme. I've had all a man can stand and I won't be provoked. You'll hear me out. They was a city boy name of Kelly. He somehow come to be put to driving artillery mules with me. Now you know and I know that a mule above every other animal is independent-minded. Trying to get a mule to do what it don't want to will drive a man plumb crazy. And that's just what happened to Kelly. It was bad enough for me that had been around horses all my life but Kelly, he'd never seen a mule or horse either until a month before. Watching that man try to drive mules was one of the saddest sights I ever hope to see. He'd gee and they'd haw.

He'd whoa and they'd go. The harder he tried the worse it got. Kelly stopped sleeping and set up nights thinking of new ways to drive mules. He stopped eating. He most likely could have got himself transferred but he wouldn't ask. He said he was going to drive them mules if it kilt him. And then we hit Château-Thierry, and that, by Jesus, is just what happened.

"I've never told this next to nobody, but I'm going to tell it now. It come time to go up closer behind the trenches with the artillery. So we started in. Kelly was right beside me with his team and for once they was doing somewhere near what he wanted them to. Then somebody hollers out gas. Sure enough, creeping along through the bob wire we see what looked like fog. We'd been instructed beforehand what to do if that happened. We was to mask first the mules, then ourselves. Out come the mule masks and you can wager it didn't take me long to clap them on and lower my own. Then I see Kelly, a-fighting and struggling to mask his mules. And the mules raring and plunging, and that fog a-creeping closer and closer on the morning breeze. I said to myself, the hell with that man, Henry Coville. Any man that will lose sleep over mules deserves what he gets. But I knowed he didn't deserve to be gassed. Nobody deserved that. So I shouted to him to forget the mules and lower his mask. By then the gas was very near, no further than from here to the lake. It was the most fearsome sight I ever see — until recently. But no, Kelly had his orders and he was going to mask them mules or die trying. And they warn't about to be masked, and the mule that was doing most of the raring, he reached out and bit that raised gas mask off the top of Kelly's head and chomped the end right out of it. And Kelly, he continued trying to force on the mule's mask until the gas was lapping around his knees.

174

"Well, I hollered for a spare mask. And while I was doing that I was knocking Kelly down and getting my mask over his head, and holding my own breath, as though that was going to do any good. He fit like a wildcat to get me off him, but I held his arms and strapped on my mask. Somebody come up quick with a spare mask and got it on me, but you know the rest as well as I do."

"What about Kelly?" my father said.

"He died right there under his mules. He'd took too much of it. Now, Bill, I can't whup you. You've proved that. I can't tell you what to do. Nobody can. But I can beg you again to stop all this. Don't go back on that lake. Don't try to mask no more mules. You go on home. Go on home to Kingdom County and Vangie. You'll have your hay. You'll have enough hay to start up the game farm again. Plant you a big pineapple grove and mulch it with hay. I'll go back to Texas myself and bring you home a herd of sidewinders packed in hay. But stop this mule business here, now and forever. I can't stand no more."

With tears in his eyes my father ran up to Uncle Henry and embraced him. "Brother," he said, "you're right. It's time to go home. As soon as we finish breakfast I'll run down to the lake and fetch up the whiskey and we'll head straight home by the quickest way. We won't even go back to get that cannon truck with the whiskey in it."

"Good Christ, was that what you was planning? Why, that cliff will be swarming over with Mounties by now. So will the lake for that matter as soon as they get the pulp cleared away. They're likely dragging the upper end right now. Sufficient unto the day is the evil thereof, Bill. Don't go looking for no more."

"Right again, Henry. All we're going to do is get our whiskey and go home. A rattlesnake farm you say? There's money to be made in training poison serpents. Big money.

Cadillac money. People will come hundreds of miles to see vipers perform. What's more, I've always had a way with them."

My father rushed over to the lean-to and began tickling Rat's neck with a fir bough. "Snakes," he shouted. "The snakes are coming, Ratty."

Rat screamed and leaped to his feet, knocking down the lean-to. My father clung to his neck like a weasel. Rat charged into the woods with my father dangling from his neck.

Uncle Henry stared after him. "We could bind him in his sleep," he said. "If he ever slept, that is."

Now Rat was pursuing my father with a big stick. My father leaped over the spitted deer and ran toward the lake. Rat stopped to catch his breath. "What's that?" he said. "Roast deer meat?"

"Yes," Uncle Henry said. "You better have a bite, Rat. It may be a long morning."

"I have to have it well done," Rat said. "I can't stand the sight of pink. Clyde or Floyd once catched a case of worms from eating pink. Great long slender white fellas, they was. He put up a dozen or so in a quart mason jar."

"Didn't they put you in the mind of snakes?"

"Yes they did. He liked to get the jar out and look at them now and again. They was looped up in there like tripe. Bill buried them with him, jar and all."

That was too much for me. I followed my father down to the lake, where I found him getting ready to embark in Brother St. Hilaire's small blue rowboat.

"When did you get that?"

"After you and Henry went to sleep, Wild Bill. I come across the deer on the way over to the monastery."

"Dad, I can't stand that Rat Kinneson. He's up there telling Uncle Henry about Clyde or Floyd's pet worms."

176

"Rat's a good enough fella, Bill. When you get to know him the way I do, he's the best."

"You think everybody's a good fella. You probably think Carcajou's a good fella."

"Not no more, Bill. Carcajou's a dead fella. Wild Bill Bonhomme blasted a great hole in the side of his head last night. Just like his father back on that covered bridge when he blasted them two hijackers."

Uncle Henry came down through the wet bushes. "Rat's still running on about tapeworms," he said. "He ain't doing a bad job on what's left of the deer neither, though he says to tell you he prefers it parboiled and fried with a side dish of turnip greens and a glass of something.

"Bill, I can't say I ain't curious. Was you actually proposing to go back to that whiskey truck? Not that I want to, you understand. I just would like to know if that was truly your intention."

"Certainly, Hen. I was thinking I would keep the cannon and you could use the truck for your runs. Think what you could lug over the line in that."

"It boggles the mind. What was you going to do with the cannon?"

"I thought I might fire it out over the swamp from time to time. Maybe first thing in the morning and then at noon and again in the evening. It might come in handy in other ways too. Keep the wardens away if nothing else."

"Where do you suppose Carcajou got it?"

"That's just what I've been wondering. Maybe he drug it up off the bottom of the St. Lawrence. It's full of them, they say. Maybe he stoled it from an old fort. He might have made it too."

"Here's another one for you. Wherever would a fella like Carcajou and his gang come from? He just seemed to appear from nowhere."

"Henry Coville," my father said, "a fella like that always comes from nowhere. The first time I see him, back here off this very point two days ago, I told Wild Bill he was the devil. I was wrong, though. Because even the devil comes from someplace. That fella didn't. He didn't come from nowhere, and he didn't know who he was neither. That's why he called himself a wolverine: part bear, part skunk, part wolf. All of them and none of them. I am sorry I didn't get a closer look at him. You know, boys, there's a sadness about a thing like that. A thing that don't belong nowhere. I wanted to look in its eyes and see if they was sad."

"Bill Bonhomme, next you'll wish you'd took him home and tamed him. I never see a man like you in all my life. That fella called himself Carcajou because the wolverine was the fiercest animal he could think of. Sad? Fierce, Bill. Fierce and cunning and cold-blooded as a wolverine."

"Not no more he ain't," my father said, winking at me. "He ain't sad or fierce or nothing else no more. He ain't nothing but dead. Wild Bill here properly seen to that last night. Wild William Bonhomme, Henry. What do you think, Bill? Was he man or beast, fierce or sad?"

By that time I didn't know what I thought about Carcajou. For one thing, I couldn't believe I had killed a man. As I looked out across that gray still water the entire experience of the past night, the past two days, seemed illusory. I could no longer be sure what was real and what was imaginary. But I was certain that if we ever did find out who or what Carcajou was, we would not like the answer. I said so, and neither my father nor Uncle Henry disagreed with me.

"But," my father said, "I'd still like to know. I'd still like one good close look at its eyes."

178

"A man ought always to be careful about what he wishes for," Uncle Henry said gravely.

"Why's that, Hen?"

"Because he might just get what he thinks he wants."

"Well," my father said, "here hath been dawning another blue day. On a morning like this it's just good to be alive."

The morning was wet and chilly and gray, but Uncle Henry and I both agreed with him fervently.

"I wish you wouldn't go down in that freezing water again, though," Uncle Henry said. "I ain't even sure where that whiskey is now."

"You row then, Henry. I'll tell you where to go. Bill, you set up in the bow. Head straight out off the end of the point."

About one hundred feet offshore my father told Uncle Henry to stop. I started to lower the anchor.

"Don't bother, Bill. That rope ain't near long enough."

"There must be forty feet of it."

"That ain't half enough. We're riding over ninety or a hundred foot of water here."

"You can't go down there," Uncle Henry said. "It's as dark as night down there."

"I see good in the dark."

"Not that good. Nobody sees that good. Nobody can dive that deep in ice water neither."

Remembering what my father had told me about his search for my mother, I didn't say anything. I didn't want him to dive, but I didn't doubt that he could do it. I suppose that I didn't believe any remotely possible feat of strength or endurance was beyond him. He took off his work shoes and vanished over the side.

Uncle Henry sighed. "He's still trying to mask them mules," he said.

After a long minute my father's arm emerged holding the shotgun. Rat's slouch hat appeared with my father's head inside it. He swam over to the boat and handed me the gun and hat.

When he dived again I tried to hold my breath until he surfaced. I held it three times before he appeared with the end of the rope he'd used to lower the whiskey down the cliff. "It just reaches," he said. "Haul it up."

Uncle Henry hauled the rope up hand over hand. Tied to the other end was a case of whiskey. My father took the free end of the rope between his teeth and sounded.

I started to hold my breath again.

"Don't do that," Uncle Henry said.

In all my father recovered ten cases of whiskey, the shotgun and the pack basket with his hatchet still inside. His skin was blue when he finally got back in the boat but he was in excellent spirits. When he got to shore Rat demanded to know which case belonged to him.

"You wait till we get home and I'll show you," my father said. He wiped away a thread of blood trickling out of the corner of one nostril. "You should have heard the singing down there, Ratty. It was like a whole choir of angels."

"They was choiring, you say?"

"My, yes. They was asking about you, what's more. They said they needed a good falsetto. The choir master was a great strapping fella along in years with long white hair like Moses."

"Moses?"

"Moses with a black beard."

"Bill," Uncle Henry said, "stop guying Mr. Kinneson for a minute and tell me how we're going to get the whiskey down the lake. That little boat won't hold us four and the whiskey. Even if it would, we'd surely be stopped. I'm surprised the police ain't out already."

"Just what I was thinking myself, Henry. Now here's what we'll do. I'll row this old tub across the bay to the monastery and get Brother Hilarious to stash the whiskey where it won't soon be found. You boys wait an hour. Then go up to the tracks and head north. I'll meet you before you get to the monastery. Leave me do all the talking."

"Don't worry about that," Uncle Henry said.

"Hand me my hat," Rat said.

By the time we came out of the woods the monastery bell was ringing. As we started up the tracks we heard voices calling in French. Over them my father was shouting our names. Cassocked figures appeared. The bell continued to peal. My father had organized a search party for us.

"There they are, brothers," he shouted in French. "They have been lost and now they are found. My prayers have been answered."

Shouting nonsense, he came prancing down over the ties and embraced us all.

"They have prevailed over Beelzebub," yelled Brother St. Hilaire, waving an empty whiskey bottle. "They have triumphed over Moloch. Belial has been bested, monks."

"Only through the intercession of the Benedictines," Brother Paul said.

"Yes, yes, the good Benedictines," my father said, producing another bottle. "Here, brothers, here's more stimulant for the Benedictines. Here, Hilarious."

"I think Brother St. Hilaire has had ample stimulant," Brother Paul said.

"I think he hasn't," Brother St. Hilaire said, taking a hearty pull from the bottle. "A drop now and then wouldn't hurt you either, Paul. You don't always have to put yourself up on a pedestal like Simeon Stylites, you know.

"So here are the wandering Jews at last. You've been out here thrashing around for two nights, have you? How would you like to try forty days? How would you like to try forty years, my children?"

He passed the bottle to Rat. "Stimulant for the infidels," he cried. He drove his elbow hard into Paul's lean ribs and said, "Laugh, Paul, laugh. William, my son, Paul here would rather fart loudly at Christmas mass than laugh. Laugh, Paul. There is a season for laughter. In fact there are four seasons. Don't you know laughter is good for the soul?"

"So is stimulant," my father said, taking the bottle away from Rat and giving it back to Brother St. Hilaire.

"Stimulant all around for the Benedictines," cried Brother St. Hilaire. "Quaff, monks, I enjoin you to quaff of the stimulant."

"I enjoin you to abstain from all stimulants," Brother Paul said. "A demon has possessed Brother St. Hilaire. A small demon with white hair."

"All demons are stunted, Paul, you know that. Dwarfed little fellows that hardly come up to your knees. Drink, monks. It is the sacred elixir." Brother St. Hilaire staggered about proffering the bottle to other monks in the party.

"I forbid you to listen to Brother St. Hilaire. All spirits are proscribed."

"By whom? By what authority?"

"By all that is holy."

"All that is holy is immanent in these sacred waters. I maintain that you will quaff."

Some of the monks took a small drink from the bottle. Brother Paul was beside himself with anxiety for their souls. Meanwhile Brother St. Hilaire had struck up a booming Gregorian chant. Others joined in as we headed up the tracks. Bottles were passing up and down the procession of chanting monks. Brother Paul raced along trying to intercept them. The monks laughed and tossed the bottles back and forth just out of his reach. The tower bells continued to peal. Rat began to chant too. "Ooma looma booma puma," he intoned.

"Lustily, monks," roared Brother St. Hilaire. "The '*Adoramus.*'"

"'*Adoramus* Number One' or '*Adoramus* Number Two'?" a red-faced young monk inquired.

"'Number Two,' most certainly," Brother St. Hilaire said. "Come in with the burden, monks."

"*Adoramus* Number Two" turned out to be the "Mademoiselle from Armentières" World War One song. It seemed to have as many verses as "*En Roulant.*" As we trooped into the monastery courtyard Brother St. Hilaire and the monks roared:

> Tony the Wop went over the top
> *Parlez-vous.*
> Tony the Wop went over the top
> *Parlez-vous.*
> Tony the Wop went over the top,
> And he got more than the Frenchman got.
> Hinky dinky
> *PARLEZ-VOUS.*"

On this divine crescendo Brother St. Hilaire reared back and hurled one of the empty whiskey bottles high into the air. It shattered against the bells high in the open tower, producing one final inspired peal. Up from the reeling column of monks went a mighty cheer.

"I hope them ain't from my case," Rat said to my father.

Uncle Henry looked at me, his face expressionless.

At lunch the decorum and order of the monastery continued to deteriorate. We learned that the abbot had been ill and bedridden for a week and that Brother St. Hilaire had appointed himself to fill this august office. There was nothing covert about his usurpation. He had forcefully occupied and converted into a still the laboratory where Paul toiled for mankind and the glory of God to discover a cure for gout. In the refectory he had supplanted the religious tome read at mealtimes with a copy of his infamous *History,* and moved onto the abbot's dais to take his meals. For several days he had been issuing liberal rations of his home-brewed cordial at each of the canonical hours.

Now he provided us with sandals and white linen choir surplices to wear while our clothes dried in front of the huge stone fireplace. We had an opportunity to wash, and were warm and dry for the first time in nearly twenty-four hours.

The food was hot and abundant. We had homemade vegetable soup, pot roast with potatoes and gravy, cider, three different kinds of cheese and a French torte. The monks seemed to be living very well under Brother St. Hilaire's tenure. During the meal Brother St. Hilaire punctuated the reading of the *History* with flatulent reports. He called out jovial remarks to my father and attentive inquiries to Rat, who looked especially ascetic and devout in his surplice and slouch hat. On the dais beside Brother St. Hilaire's plate sat another whiskey bottle.

Flushed and corpulent, in the mad heyday of his saturnalian reign, Brother St. Hilaire lurched to his feet and began beating on his drinking mug with his knife. A chunk of the heavy crockery broke off and sailed across the room, lacerating the reader's nose and causing him to cry out in pain. This accident did not curb Brother St. Hilaire's exuberance. "I used to be quite the Don Juan myself back in my day," he announced, apropos of nothing. "Oh no, I wasn't one to be shy around the little girls."

"I imagine you wasn't," my father said, shoving back his chair and cocking his sandaled feet on the white table-cloth. "Tell us about your first time, Brother."

Some of the other monks smiled and nudged each other.

"Brother," Paul said, "I must remonstrate with you. Put an end to this bacchanal, I beg you."

"Silence, Onan," shouted Brother St. Hilaire. "Monks will maintain strict silence at table."

While calling for silence he broke wind explosively, occasioning an outburst of laughter from my father and several of the monks. I looked at Uncle Henry, who seemed to be smiling slightly.

"I went to a tiny parochial school out on the Gaspé between Metane and Rimouski," Brother St. Hilaire said reminiscently. "The teacher was a nun. Her name was Sister Francine. Francine of the Codfish, we boys called her, as she rather resembled one, particularly about the mouth and eyes. Francine boarded with a different family each term. The term I was about young William's age, Sister Francine boarded at my father's house. And all through the long dark winter evenings when the wind off the river roared in my father's chimney she taught me Latin — and I taught her French."

Raucous laughter broke out. Brother Paul rose and left the refectory.

"Was it old Francine of the Codpiece that got you interested in the brotherhood?" my father inquired.

"She did indeed, William. Throughout her French lessons she said repeatedly, 'But who will give me absolution, dearest one?' And I would say, 'I shall, my little sister. My father will send me to the monastery soon, and after I take my orders I shall return and give absolution to both of us.' "

"Did you, Brother?"

"Oh, yes, William, many times. And to many sisters. No one ever accused me of being the cloistered capon.

185

Where's that gelding Paul, brothers? Off in his cell spilling his seed on the ground again, no doubt. Let's go see if we can catch him at it."

Brother St. Hilaire and several young monks rushed out of the refectory to search for Brother Paul. As soon as they left a middle-aged monk asked us to accompany him. He led us through the cloister along the enclosed inner court-yard. The floor of the cloister was covered with bright mosaic tiles. The mortar between the granite blocks of the wall had been tinted in black, yellow and red patterns. We looked into a small candlelit chapel. Our guide told us that twelve different kinds of wood had been used to finish the interior of the chapel. The cloister and chapel were imbued with a serenity that appealed to me deeply after the tumult of the past two days.

Uncle Henry seemed impressed too, but Rat got my father aside and muttered something about dungeons and inquisitions. As we continued down the beautiful arcade Rat looked at the walls as though the remains of dozens of fundamentalists were immured within them. He was still wearing his hat.

My father was chafing. Inaction of any kind had become intolerable to him. "You got a nice place here," he kept saying. "But it's easy to see how Hilarious would get bored, it ain't lively enough."

The monk took us through a passageway off the cloister and stopped in front of a plain dark door. He knocked and stepped inside, signaling us to wait. After a minute he opened the door and beckoned for us to come in. It was a very small room containing a washstand, a desk and chair and a low narrow bed on which an elderly man was lying. Brother Paul was sitting next to the bed in the single chair. "My sons," he said, his face infinitely sorrowful, "you have been granted an audience with our abbot."

The abbot looked more frustrated than sick. As it turned

out he was recovering from an attack of gout and expected to be on his feet again within a day or two. He was very concerned about Brother St. Hilaire's conduct, but also seemed quite sympathetic with him. He explained that about a year ago Brother St. Hilaire had pretended to recant his heretical views on the history of the Church in Canada. He had traveled to the hallowed site of the old Benedictine monastery at Fécamp in northern France and publicly repudiated his *History,* then stolen the formula for the famous liqueur manufactured there and brought it back to the small monastery on Lake Memphremagog. Since his triumphant return he had also written a brilliant renunciation of his repudiation. The abbot was at his wit's end to know what to do with him.

"We might be able to help you out, your Holiness," my father said. "I was thinking that Hilarious might like to come up to my place for a while. Say in about a week. My wife's a devout believer. She was training to be a black nun herself before I come along and changed her mind. Also I've got an old woman up there that he could talk Latin to when he felt lonesome. I believe he'd be inspired to write more histories and renunciations too. It's a lively place. Wouldn't he be right to home up there, Hen?"

"Yes," Uncle Henry said. "He'd fit right in."

"Do you think he would consider coming?" the abbot asked.

"I know he would. We've already discussed it. He'll be ready as soon as this batch him and the Holy Ghost have working now is done. He don't like to leave a job half finished."

Brother Paul looked slightly less dejected. The abbot was smiling. "I commend you for your hospitality, my son. I believe I feel well enough to go out and discuss the proposal with Brother St. Hilaire myself."

"I commend all of you," my father nearly shouted. "Now

I have a little proposal I want to discuss with you, your Holiness. In private."

The abbot nodded, and the rest of us went outside. About five minutes passed. My father opened the door and called Brother Paul back in. When the door opened again the abbot was up and dressed in a cassock. Leaning on two canes, with my father at one elbow and Paul at the other, he accompanied us back through the cloister.

Before we had progressed far a door at the far end flew open and Brother St. Hilaire appeared astride the red-faced monk, who was down on all fours making loud horse noises. Brother St. Hilaire had removed the surcingle from his cassock and made a loop in the end, which he was trying to twirl around his head. Without spotting us he spurred his steed off down a side passageway. "He's down in the laboratory, no doubt," we heard him shout. "Giddap, Brother Theophile."

"What was that commotion?" the abbot said. "I've come away without my spectacles. Has Brother St. Hilaire brought a horse into the cloister again?"

"They're up to more unseemly antics," Brother Paul said. "I told you it was getting worse and worse."

"They shouldn't bring horses into the cloister," the abbot said. "I suppose I should have dealt more severely with his infractions in the past. But he has great faith in the Holy Ghost, Brother Paul. You can't disparage his faith in the Holy Ghost. You go along with William, now. I can negotiate quite well with Brother Dominic's assistance. I will try to be very severe with Brother St. Hilaire this time. Don't forget, my son, you will come back for our friend one week from today. Goodbye, my children. Goodbye, Brother Muskrat."

While the abbot and Brother Dominic went off to the laboratory to expostulate with Brother St. Hilaire we went back to the refectory and put on our dry clothes. Our work shoes had shrunk, and Rat's wouldn't go on at all so he had to continue to wear the sandals.

"That gives me another fine idea," my father said. "Put them white smocks back on over your clothes, boys. Paul here don't mind if we borrow four smocks for a few days, do you, Paul?"

"Not if they help speed you on your way," Brother Paul said. "Follow me now. We will have to work quickly before the train arrives."

Twenty minutes later we were standing in the rain in our surplices on a wooden platform between the dairy barn and the spur line. We could hear the train coming down the grade from around the shoulder of the mountain. On the platform beside us were twenty milk cans. Fourteen of them contained milk. Packed in straw inside the others were our whiskey bottles.

10

"I DON'T like this business one bit, Quebec Bill," Rat said. "I don't like this white smock and I don't like this heathenish place and I don't like trains."

"Fear not, Brother Kinneson. You're going to love this ride. So are you, Wild Bill. I'm going to see if I can get the engineer to let you and me ride up in the cab. There she is. There she is, boys. There's Old Ninety-seven. Just look at that, will you."

I was as interested in trains as any boy, but my father was obsessed by them. He spent hours sitting on the hotel porch in the Common with Uncle Henry watching them go by and announcing for the delectation of anyone within two hundred yards the names on the sides of the cars. "Wabash, boys. There's the old Wabash. Great Northern. Hi, there's the Pine Tree State; that's the State of Maine, gentlemen. Canadian National, Canadian National, Canadian National — that's all newsprint from them big paper mills up on the Gaspé. There we go, there she is, that's the one I and Henry took: Santa Fe. Ain't that a glorious name for you? Northern Pacific, Northern Pacific, Central

Vermont. Pine Tree State; that's the State of Maine, boys. I come down on the rods from Houlton to Portland once and this railroad detective thought he'd play a trick on me . . ."

Or we would be at home playing High, Low, Jack and the Game and listening to Cordelia read to us around the kitchen table on a winter evening when the wind was right, and we would hear the whistle of the evening freight from Montreal on the downgrade outside the Common, faint and faraway and unmistakable. My father would raise his head like a hunting dog and say in the mystical voice he reserved for the passing of trains and geese, "Hark. There she is, Wild Bill. There she goes. Don't that sound send shivers up and down your back."

The milk train from Magog to Memphremagog and the Common was no less exotic to my father than the glorious Santa Fe. He was infatuated by trains, any train at all, even a super-annuated local laboring to pull a milk car, two flatbeds piled high with hardwood logs for the American Heritage Mill, two closed boxcars and a caboose.

The engineer was a heavy man named Compton with a red face and a red bandanna. While Brother Paul and Henry and Rat loaded the milk cans Compton checked the logs by pulling on them with a hooked pike at least eight feet long. When he was satisfied that they were secure he replaced the pike in its vertical slot at the end of one of the log cars and started to climb back into the engine.

"Excuse me, Captain," my father said. "I and these other clergymens was wondering if we could ride along down to—"

"Nope," Compton said with satisfaction, continuing up the ladder into the engine. "No riders. Company policy."

A moment later he leaned out the engine window. "Watch out for that steam. That'll scald your legs."

"Who runs the company, Captain?"

191

Compton stared at my father. "Who runs the company? Judas Priest, I don't know who runs the company. They do. The company."

"Does the company run your engine for you too?"

"I run my engine."

"Good, then you wouldn't mind if I and this young brother here had a look at her, would you? Climb up, Brother William."

I climbed up the short ladder into the cab, followed by my father.

"Here now," Compton said.

"What's this?" my father said, pulling down sharply on an overhead lever.

The whistle emitted a screeching blast. I jumped about a foot. "Here," Compton said.

"Here yourself," my father said, handing him a whiskey bottle. "Company don't say nothing about not drinking Seagram's, does it?"

"Well. No. Not so long as I don't drink at the throttle, no, they don't. Thanks, Father."

"I can tell by one look that you ain't the sort of man that drinks at the throttle, Captain. Company don't have no worries on that score. You got a fine engine here and a fine train. All we wanted was a peek. It's most unfortunate that you have to work for an outfit that don't let you determine who's to ride on your own train. We just hoped to ride down to the county home. Rules are rules, though, I always say. Especially company rules. You're Catholic, Captain?"

"Judas, no. I'm English."

"I suspicioned as much. That's actually the reason I wanted to have a word with you. We're Anglican priests in disguise, my son. We're trying to spread the re-formation a bit further. A wedge here, a wedge there, you know; po-

pery will fall before you know it. They give us the bottle
so's we wouldn't report what we see in there. Last night
they had a party of women of the night down from Montreal. I never see such goings ons."

"Hoors, you say? I always suspected it. How many of
you are there? Four, five?"

"Just four. Them other two could ride right in the milk
car. But I don't blame you for not wanting to go against
the company. That's your bread and butter."

"You wait a minute, Pastor. I don't hold with popery
myself. I wouldn't stop to get their milk if the company
didn't make me. Hoors, is it? The boys up to the Legion
should be interested in this piece of news. Just last fall we
was saying we ought to bring a cross down here and burn
it. I want to hear more about that hoor business. You and
your 'prentice wait right here."

Compton stepped back to have a word with his fireman.
When he returned a minute later his bottle was not quite
full. "What the company don't know won't hurt them,"
he said. "Tell your two friends to get in the milk car."

"This must be a grand job," my father said to Compton
as we pulled away from the platform, waving to Brother
Paul, who watched us as though we were close relatives
being deported.

"It used to be," Compton said. "Back before they started
hiring Frenchmen on the section gang. Now we never
know whether we're going to make Memphremagog or
not. They've let the track go all to ruin. Loose rails, rotted-
out ties, spikes laying all over every which way. It's enough
to make an old railroad man cry, Pastor. You can't get
one of them Canuck fellas to do an honest day's work to
save your life."

"They're a shiftless lot, all right," my father said.

Compton warmed to his subject. "You can say that

193

again. I went to work walking the line from St. Hyacinth to Drummondville when I was twelve years old. Nothing escaped my eye. By the time I was sixteen I was head flagman in the freight yards up to Granby. I engineered my first run for Canadian National on my twenty-first birthday. I had the Portland to Montreal for thirty-two years. Until they commenced hiring Frenchmen. That was the end of the line for me. 'I won't engineer with a frog crew,' I says. 'Then you won't engineer for Canadian National,' they says. 'Suit yourselves,' I says, and walked out. It was the high monky-monk from the head office. 'Suit yourselves,' I told him and walked out on thirty-two years and a good pension. I come home to Magog, and when the boys to the Legion heard about it they made me an honorary member and helped me get this job. That was back before this company started taking on Frenchmen. The sight of them little dark frogs smoking their black pipes by the side of the tracks makes me sick, Pastor. It's gotten so they act just as lordly as a white man."

"They're a bad bunch, Captain. We don't let them in the church. They ought to be kept down in their place. I've always said so."

"They ought all to be sent back."

"Sent back?"

"Back over across. Where they come from in the first place. That or cut, so's they can't have no more. There's your main social problem in a nutshell, Pastor: the French, going about dropping litters of ten and twelve like the Pope tells them to. Just last night we had a meeting down to the Legion on it. We don't just set around and guzzle up beer the way some seem to think; we try to deal with real social problems. Like the French. I stood right up on my hind legs and said send them back or cut them. We don't need them babbling little darkies slaughtering the

King's English and taking jobs away from white men. Not when jobs are scarce as they are now. Not any time. You should have heard the boys holler and stomp. Commander said he'd put that about the babbling darkies in next month's newsletter. We send a copy to every post in Quebec. Every English post, that is. It ain't them being little that I mind, Pastor. You ain't that big a chap yourself. It's the dark part I can't go.

"It wasn't no French gang that killed that Mountie and cut off his head last night out on the lake, though. You hear about it, did you? They was big doings last night. It's been two big days in fact. First thing yesterday morning the boys down to the fire hall got a call on a barn fire over the other side of the lake. They skun right out and going up the lane they hit some kind of crater and turned the hook and ladder over onto its side. It was my day off and I was there. I try to go to all the fires on my day off. I've got a blue light on the Ford and a hand si-reen that the wife cranks. Sometimes we'll see where the smoke is and beat the hook and ladder."

"Anybody hurt?"

"No. Frenchman named Gagne got throwed off of the truck but he landed on his head so he was all right. Eula and I was further behind than usual. She was in church at the time and I had to pull her out. That's the Anglican church, Pastor. Time we arrived the shooting had started. We thought it was shooting. From the stable, loud pops like a twenty-two might make. Talk about confusion. Commander down to the Legion's also the fire chief. He took right charge and ordered the boys and me and Eula to retreat into the swamp and lay low. 'We'll smoke them jerries out of there,' Commander says, just as though he'd set the fire for that purpose. We was all very proud of him.

"Then Gagne had to go and spoil it all by saying he didn't think it was jerries or nobody else up there shooting. He said his wife's mother's cousin's place over to Stanstead burnt down this winter and the mason jars exploding in the cellar sounded just like them pops. 'Get down, you fool,' Commander says and shoved Gagne into some bushes but the Frenchman gets away from him and runs up the lane to the barn. When he see that Gagne wasn't getting shot Commander explained to the rest of us that he always sent the frogs in first over across too, and now it was safe for us to go along up. But as it turned out it wasn't mason jars that was exploding at all, but whiskey bottles. That shipment that was stolen here four, five days ago when the driver got his head blowed off by the cannon. We had run into that Carcajou's hideout. All of which goes to show you how much a Frenchman knows. Mason jars indeed."

"You've had a busy time of it," my father said. "Getting shot at by whiskey bottles and making a patriotic speech to the Legion and such."

"That's not all by any means. Along toward evening somebody reported shooting from down the lake. Loud shooting, maybe cannon fire. So Sergeant MacPhearson from the local barracks went down in his launch to investigate. By dark he hadn't come back. The wind was blowing up a hurricane out over that water. We'd never seen the lake so high. There wasn't much we could do. Chaplain Burroughs down to the Legion said a prayer for him before we got onto the French element, but I fancy it didn't take. Because sometime during the night the pulp coming up to the mill broke loose in the storm and this morning they found MacPhearson stripped and without no head throwed up on the village beach with several hundred cords of pulpwood. Eula and I had to hurry to get there before they took away the remains. Eula got her claxon horn going that I gave her last Christmas, and with that and the si-reen they got out of our way quick enough. Most gruesome sight I hope to see. There wasn't a square inch of skin left on that man's body. It had all been ground off by the pulp. The only way they could identify it for certain was by a ring that had gotten smashed down over the finger bone. It was the third finger on the right hand."

"Did he have a family?"

"No. It's too bad he didn't, because the Mounties have wonderful benefits for the families of those killed in action. He had a sister. We got up to her place just in time to hear Chaplain Burroughs break the news."

"Did they find Carcajou?"

"Not yet that I know of. Just before I left for my run they found his cannon truck. It was on the opposite side of the lake from the hideout so he must have driven right through Magog yesterday. We've got the biggest manhunt in the history of the townships going. We'll find him all right."

"You're going to lose your voice," my father said. "You'd better have a short one."

"A short one wouldn't hurt. There. Look up there on that siding. That's exactly what I mean. Not a one of them doing a single thing. Judas, that burns me. Every time we have a little shower they get off onto a siding or hole up around a warm stove in a shanty and smoke them black pipes and play cards."

"Not cards?" my father said in a shocked voice. "Cards are the devil's picture book, my son. His prime work for idle hands."

"They're idle all right," Compton said. "Look at that, will you."

Ahead on the siding several men in work clothes were sitting on a long handcar, waiting for us to pass. Compton gave them a salutatory blast on the whistle and waved. He smiled and called effusive greetings out the window. My father winked at me.

"I have to keep on their good side," Compton said. "Otherwise they might pull up a rail on me."

"I don't know as I'd put it past them. Except they might not be smart enough."

"It don't take a lot of brains to prize up a rail."

"That's so. I like that word prize too. I mean to work that into my next sermon. Here's a man that knows how to use the King's English, Brother William."

"The boys down to the Legion seem to think so."

"You ain't no slouch at handling Old Ninety-seven neither. See all them dials and needles. See them levers and switches. This must be the throttle."

"Yes," Compton said. "I leave it right here on this notch all the way up the next ridge. Oh, it ain't such a hard job as you might suppose. It requires sound judgment more than anything else."

"Sound judgment and an open mind," my father said. "Do you think you could show a young boy how to drive her?"

"As long as he didn't have no French in him I could. Step up here, boy. Duck your head. I can see he's no Frenchman. Put your hand right here on the throttle. Feel her throb? That's seventy tons of steel under your hand."

"I don't know but what I'd like to try it myself," my father said.

"Why not? Here, put on my gloves, Pastor. Let's see how you look in my cap. Now the bandanna. Say, ain't that a caution? I wish the boys at the Legion could see this."

"Caution's my middle name, Captain. Have another sup, why don't you? Old Ninety-seven's in good hands."

Compton took a long drink. He stepped back to survey my father and began to expel his reeking breath in a long hissing wheeze which I interpreted as laughter.

In order to prevent the cap from coming down over his eyes my father had to balance it on the back of his head and keep his head tipped back. The grimy bandanna came halfway down the front of his surplice. The gauntlets on his gloves extended well above his elbows. Pretending to adjust the gloves, he pushed the throttle forward a notch.

I leaned out the window. Ahead was a steep incline through two rock walls. It looked like a long sloping roofless tunnel.

I heard my father saying, "Do you like to go fast, Captain?"

"Fast?" Compton's eyes were getting red.

"How fast will Old Ninety-seven do?"

"Old Ninety-seven?" Compton said as though he had never heard of the engine. "Oh, Old Ninety-seven. At first I thought you meant did Eula and I go fast. She'll do about eighty on a downgrade, Ninety-seven will. Not down the other side of this ridge, though. There's a hairpin curve at the bottom. Twenty's the limit around there."

"What if she ever got out of the traces going down the mountain. Would you jump?"

"Abandon Old Ninety-seven? Never. I'd almost as soon turn her over to a Frenchman."

"Couldn't prize you loose, eh? True for you, Captain. Have another short one."

Compton took a drink. He looked out the window at the wall of the cut. "How them rocks do rush by," he said. "I never noticed when I was behind the controls."

"It always seems faster to a passenger," my father said, pushing the throttle up as far as it would go. "What's in them shut boxcars, Captain? Newsprint?"

"No, that's hay from Ontario. Alfalfa hay."

"Alfalfa hay. That's a valuable commodity in these times. Alfalfa hay he says, Brother William."

Compton was quite drunk now, but he couldn't help noticing how fast we were going. "Here," he said, "I'd better take back over."

My father glanced back out the window. "Who's that dark curly-headed fella?" he said.

"What?"

"They's a little fella looks like a section hand hanging onto your ladder, Captain."

"Judas Priest, one of them dirty little French darkies hitching a ride," Compton said. "Keep the controls another minute."

"Certainly. What are you going to do with him? Make him pay a fare?"

"How big did you say he was?"

"He's only a pitiful little fella. Not much bigger than a boy. He looked scared."

"He better look scared. This is the last straw. See this big boot, Pastor? I'm going to put it to him."

In the best style of an honorary Legionnaire, red-faced Compton came bulling back through the cab. As he went by I noticed that he did not seem to have any neck at all. His head was clamped down tightly between his shoulders like something round and hard and ugly in a vise.

My father was close behind him. As Compton drew back his foot and lunged toward the open entranceway above the ladder my father drew back his foot and lunged toward Compton's barrel of a rear end. *"Bon voyage,"* he said as Compton disappeared through the opening.

Somehow Compton managed to catch hold of a rung of the ladder with one hand. Dangling with his short legs just out of reach of the driving cams, he shouted for his fireman. The fireman rushed up into the cab. He knelt in the entranceway and extended his arm.

An interesting exhibition ensued. Compton flailed out with his free hand and caught the fireman's wrist. The fireman heaved up, but without much success. At the same time Compton seemed to be trying to pull his would-be rescuer off his perch and down on top of him. The fireman was no match for his engineer in this tug of war. With some slight assistance from my father, he steadily lost ground. Suddenly he was sailing through the air over Compton, who had less than a second to enjoy his triumph before being yanked off the ladder over the flying fireman. Clasping one another's wrists like trapeze artists they rolled in tandem to the base of the rock cut.

Meanwhile my father had discovered Compton's long-spouted oilcan and was diligently lubricating the gears and levers on the instrument panel. Weighed down by all of his engineering accoutrements, he grinned his manic grin at me. "Wild Bill," he said, "we have just become the proud new owners of two carloads of alfalfa."

"We can't steal that hay," I said. "That's going too far. Uncle Henry wouldn't like this at all."

"Uncle Henry's back in the milk car. He don't need to know nothing about it."

"How are you going to keep him from finding out?"

"I wonder where the brakes are," my father said.

"You can't just hijack a train, Dad. We're going to be in a lot of trouble."

"So's Compton," my father said, as though Compton's difficulties would solve all of ours. "He won't be burning no crosses or attending no more beheadings for a while. The company ain't going to like this."

"Dad. Listen to me, Dad. What are we going to do with a train?"

"I'll figure out something. Where do you suppose the brakes are, Wild Bill?"

"Pull this back first."

I pulled back the throttle, but we had already crested the ridge and started down the long grade on the other side. Far ahead through the light rain I could see the lake. It did not look inviting.

We were entering another short cut. For some reason I looked back over the tops of the cars. "Oh no," I said.

"It ain't that bad, Bill. I think this is them '

I grabbed my father's arm. "A Mountie just jumped onto the train."

My father swung around fast just as the policeman disappeared over the side of the caboose. "I saw him," I said. "He dropped down from the top of those rocks. I'm positive I saw him."

"All right, my boy. You stay here and see if you can find the brakes. I don't want to lose that alfalfa. I'll go back and tend to the Mountie. Compton don't want unauthorized riders on his train. It's against company policy."

He scrambled over the coal gondola and leaped up onto the top of the first boxcar. I looked out the window and down the track. About halfway down the ridge to the lake I could see a trestle built into the grade. I hunted frantically for the brakes.

"You're under arrest in the name of the King," said a voice behind me in a thick Scottish accent.

My most immediate feeling was relief. We might be carried off to jail, but at least we weren't going to be killed in a train wreck. "The brakes," I shouted, spinning around. "Where are the brakes?"

I was staring up into the face of a monster. Huge chunks of flesh had been torn away from it. The right ear was hanging by a few shreds of cartilage. Part of his right nostril was gone. The right eye socket was a leaking gelatinous pulp. His beard was stiff with dried blood. I could see a row of stubby dark side teeth through a hole in his cheek. When he opened his mouth to laugh I realized that he had no cheek at all.

"Where's the wee mun, lad? It's the wee mun the King wants. Do na say he drouned this time. Sergeant MacPhearson kens better."

I couldn't stop staring into that creature's ruined eye. "She is na pretty, lad, but I think she's nathing to what you'll resemble if you do na tell me. Look ahead."

I looked out. We were close to the trestle and going much faster.

He gestured with his pistol. "She's a great ways doun, eh, laddie? Unless you tell Sergeant where he can find the wee mun you'll be lepping into the teeny wee burn that chuckles along below."

Carcajou trilled his r's and drew out certain words in an insane parody of a Highland accent. He was so big that he had not been able to button the Mountie's jacket across his chest, which was covered by a thick mat of blood-soaked white hair. As we moved out onto the trestle he reached up and casually plucked off his wounded ear, which he lofted out over the chasm. His good blue eye seemed quite calm, quite amused.

He motioned with the pistol. "Step out, lad."

I had no choice. I had to do what he said. As I passed him I was nearly overpowered by the reek of blood. If I could just stall until we were off that long trestle I would have a chance. I made up my mind that regardless of what happened I was not going to jump into that gulf. Anything would be better than that.

Now Carcajou was facing me with his back to the instrument panel. I stood on the edge of the entranceway.

He gestured with his pistol for me to jump. I shook my head. He raised the pistol to a height level with my eyes and fired.

Carcajou staggered back into the panel and fired again. He was shooting wildly. Both shots had gone through the roof of the cab.

"Jump, Wild Bill," my father shouted from the top of the boxcar behind the gondola.

We were off the trestle, but I didn't know whether I had strength enough in my legs to jump clear of the train. I looked at Carcajou once more. He was bent over, struggling to raise the gun with both hands. As he started to straighten up I saw the long wooden handle projecting from his red coat. My father had skewered him with the pike pole.

The gun went off again just as I turned and leaped. I hit on my hands and knees and rolled down the embankment. Cinders and gravel cut into my palms and face. The earth seemed to rotate under me.

I got to my feet but everything was tipping. The whole ridge was tilting. I fell and got up again. This time I stayed upright.

The train was really rolling. I saw my father swing down through the open door of the milk car. Immediately milk cans began to fly out, followed closely by Rat, Henry and my father. Still dressed in their surplices, they rolled down the embankment like three big white rabbits, and had the same trouble getting to their feet. I waved and shouted that I was all right.

Old Ninety-seven was breaking all her speed records. Near the bottom of the ridge the whistle began to scream. It continued blasting as the engine derailed itself and plunged over the embankment into the lake. The six cars were whipped off the track behind the engine. They came uncoupled and flipped lazily through the air end over end, descending into the lake beyond the engine, which lay on its side in shallow water, still puffing, like some stranded and dying behemoth surrounded by its offspring. The whistle continued to shriek for another half-minute or so. From where I stood the derailment had resembled the wreck of a little boy's toy train.

My father had hobbled back up on the track and was sitting with his right leg spraddled out at a curious angle. "That was a dandy," he said. "It warn't what I'd call spectacular, but it was better than adequate. Did you see that spout go up when she hit? I wish Compton could have been here to see that. Don't she looked like a beached whale, though, boys? Our alfalfa got wet, I reckon. We seem fated to have our hay get wet, Bill."

"Are you all right?"

"Certainly. Look at Rat down there in the bushes seeing if he can recover his case. I would give that wreck an eight out of a possible ten, Henry. How would you rate her?"

Uncle Henry had cut a long slit up my father's right pant leg with his hunting knife. Now he was ripping his surplice into bandages. He squatted by my father's leg and began to wrap it above the knee.

I leaned over his shoulder. "I thought you said you were all right?"

"I am. I'm fine, Bill. It's just my leg here that's got a hole in it. I don't know how he did it with that pick pole through his chest. Jesus, boys, the Christly hook on the end is ten inches long and I swear it went clear through him and out the other side. He fell back too. But then he just commenced to bringing that pistol up and up, a-holding it in both hands. There, boys, is one tough hombre. You should have seen his face, Hen. What was left of it. It didn't look like a human man's. It was blowed all to pieces.

That man just won't kill. Or wouldn't until now. I reckon we don't have to worry about him no more. Not with seventy tons of steel on top of him."

Uncle Henry tightened the tourniquet. He stood up and looked down through the rain at the wreck. "I reckon we do," he said. "I reckon if I seen him laid out in state and buried I would still worry about him at least once a day for the rest of my life."

Without another word he went down to help Rat recover what was left of the whiskey. Some of the covers had been jarred off the milk cans, and many of the bottles were smashed. When we had packed those that remained into two cans, we had only fifty-two bottles.

"Plus the joker," Rat said, holding up the fifty-third, which was about three-quarters full. He took a drink and smacked his lips loudly. "You know, boys," he said, "I don't so much mind trains after all."

"How do you like railroad detectives?" Uncle Henry said. "Because in about an hour this stretch of track is going to be crawling with them. Them and Mounties and border patrol and sheriffs and deputies and G-men."

"See the fog rolling in, boys" my father said. "They may not even spot her until morning."

"Are we going to wait for them to arrive so's we can assist with the investigation?" Uncle Henry said.

"Listen," my father said. From up the track I heard a regular clicking, like the telegraph at the railroad station in the Common. It grew louder. The section handcar appeared on the trestle. It was Compton, pumping like a madman.

My father lay back on the cinders beside the tracks. He crossed his hands over his breast. He was still wearing Compton's engineer gloves and the surplice. Nothing I had ever seen looked more ludicrous. As wretched as our circumstances were, I had to laugh.

The handcar was slowing down. Compton leaped off. "Where is he?" he shouted. "Where's that bastard dwarf that stole my train?"

"Easy, my son," Uncle Henry said, his face expressionless. "Can't you see he was kilt jumping off the train? Have respect for the dead."

"Respect for the dead? What about respect for my train? Where's Ninety-seven?"

"She's all right," Uncle Henry said. "After we got scart and jumped she just went on down the line. She'll run out of steam shortly and we'll overtake her. Now let's get the deceased aboard. Be careful, boys. They'll probably want to martyr him. He was a most uncommon priest."

"I don't care what you do with the carcass. I want my train back."

"The milk must go through," Uncle Henry said as he and Rat set the two cans on the platform of the handcar. "Where's your fireman? I hope he ain't hurt."

"He's walking back up the line to Magog. He said he'd had enough train rides for one day."

"That's why he's still a fireman and you're an engineer," Uncle Henry said. He and I picked up my father, who held himself stiff as a board, and laid him on the opposite side of the platform from the milk cans.

"Are you sure he's dead?" Compton said. "I thought I seen a tremor."

"No doubt. Sometimes priests and monks will jerk like that for hours. It's the spirit departing."

"I thought he said you were Church of England?"

"The same is true of them."

"See him jerk. He must have a lot of spirit. Jumpy as a dead snake, ain't he?"

Compton bent down over my father. "I wish Eula could see this."

"I wish she could see this," my father said, raising his

207

good leg and booting Compton down over the embankment for the second time in half an hour. "That will learn you some respect for the dead."

Simultaneously Uncle Henry and I began to pump. Rat sat between the milk cans, hugging them close. Compton was on his feet again, giving pursuit and shouting maledictions.

"Plucky fella, ain't he?" my father observed.

"Pump," Uncle Henry said.

He seemed anxious to get home.

I I

YEARS later, when my own son was growing up, I was struck time and again by his physical resemblance to my father. Young Henry had the same tiny frame, light hair and vivid blue eyes, the same extraordinary strength and agility.

There were striking differences too, which may have made their external similarity more remarkable to me. Henry did not, for example, have the slightest interest in trains, cars, live animals, music or games of any kind, though he once remarked to me that when he played baseball at school he could see the individual seams on the ball as it came spinning up to the plate. He liked the woods but did not care for hunting or fishing. He was not unpopular with other children, but he had none of my father's intense feelings about people. He had little of my father's capacity for affirmation, but was not cynical. He possessed the most remarkable powers of divination in a family noted for this gift.

These first came to our attention when he was about

four. For a year he had talked in his sleep, but whatever he was saying was unintelligible to us. Shortly after his fourth birthday my wife, whose family spoke only French, began to pick out certain habitant expressions. When I listened carefully I too recognized old French words and phrases. Henry would sit upright in his bed with his blue eyes wide open and talk or shout in an archaic dialect until we woke him. Sometimes he seemed to be conversing pleasantly. At other times he pleaded or railed. Remembering Cordelia's terror-filled nights, her shrieks in Greek and sixteenth-century English, I was not reassured. In desperation we decided to consult a psychiatrist.

Dr. Weinstein was a vague amiable low-keyed man who, I supposed at first, had been mellowed by much contact with the profoundly and irremediably mad. Two hours after he arrived I realized my error. Dr. Weinstein, I discovered, had been mellowed by the astonishing variety of pills and shots which he administered to himself at frequent intervals and which kept him dazed or euphoric throughout his three-day visit. By night he took handfuls of amphetamines to stay awake for his vigils at Henry's bedside. In the morning he descended from his nocturnal flights with massive doses of narcotics.

Henry put on several memorable evening performances. Twice he tried to choke Dr. Weinstein to death, mistaking him for a seventeenth-century sergeant-major named Davignon who had raped his sister. During his waking hours he refused to take either Dr. Weinstein or his questions seriously.

"Henry," Dr. Weinstein said in what I came to suspect was an affected accent, "it makes Toctor sad when you von't talk sincerely to him. Vouldn't you like to make Toctor happy?"

"No," Henry said.

"Vouldn't you like to be happier little boy, Henry?"

"I like the way I am."

"Henry, do you know vat you shout out in night?"

"Certainly. Do you think I'm deaf?"

"Vat is it you shout?"

"You've been sitting there listening for the past two nights. You ought to know."

Dr. Weinstein unscrewed a bottle with shaking hands and popped two large bright green pills into the back of his mouth. "Henry," he said, "do you know you talk in French? Dat last night you said in French you slit two men's throats?"

"Be grateful it wasn't three."

It was September. From our dooryard we could look out over hundreds of square miles of lovely mountain country. "Vermont is so beautiful," Dr. Weinstein said. "See all the beautiful colors. I feel so free here. It's so good to talk to you, Henry."

"You're an old fake," Henry said, going into the house.

"Dat vill be twelve hundred and fifty dollars," Dr. Weinstein said to me the next day.

"What?" I said. "What are you talking about? You haven't even given us a diagnosis."

"Oh, dat is most simple. You see, Mr. Bonhomme, young Henry is having linguistic identity crisis. Ve have to remember dat he is undoubtedly very sensitive about being Franco-American."

I was furious. "He isn't a Franco-American," I shouted, "he's a four-year-old child. Put that syringe away and listen to me, Weinstein. You haven't done a goddamn thing for us."

Dr. Weinstein was engrossed in hunting for a vein. "I never do," he said abstractedly. "I know I'm a charlatan. Charlatan, mountebank, what have you. Have one of these tablets, Mr. Bonhomme. It'll calm you down."

I grabbed Dr. Weinstein by his shirt front. "I'm not

going to pay you twelve hundred dollars. I wouldn't pay you twelve cents."

"I didn't really suppose you would," he said mildly. "It was worth a try. After all, I paid Henry."

"You paid Henry?"

"Of course. I paid him fifty dollars for talking to me."

"You gave fifty dollars to a child?"

"Ah, but what an unusual child. It really did make me feel much better to talk to him. After our little chat I almost decided to cut down on my medication. You have a fine family, Mr. Bonhomme. What nationality is the old woman? I couldn't understand her at all."

"What old woman?"

"That woman who keeps coming into Henry's room at night. She's very tall."

"There isn't any old woman. What nationality are you, if I might inquire? Where the hell has that accent of yours gone?"

"Gone with my fee," Dr. Weinstein said cheerfully. "You've heard of Brooklyn? I'm from Brooklyn. The accent is phony as a three-dollar bill. Things aren't always what they appear to be, you know. Could I tell you another little secret? You seem like the sort of person I can confide in."

"No," I shouted. "No, no. I don't want to know any more of your secrets. Don't tell me another word."

"I'm not even a real psychiatrist, Mr. Bonhomme. Henry was right. I'm a fake. My diploma is from the Queens School of Chiropody. You don't need my help for Henry and you don't need a real psychiatrist. Are you religious?"

I was dumbfounded.

"It doesn't matter whether you are or not. Take Henry to a rabbi. If you can't find a rabbi, take him to a priest. There are different charlatans for different occasions. You need a religious charlatan. I really do have to go now. I'm running low on medication."

That night my wife and I sat in the kitchen drinking beer with Uncle Henry and looking out the window and down the hollow at the few remaining farm lights. The crickets were singing loudly. As Uncle Henry talked on about the fall it could have been 1932 again. Up in the loft where I had spent so many hours listening to my parents when I was a boy Henry was conversing heatedly with a presence named Robertshaw about the French and Indian Wars. I found myself drinking more than usual and actually missing the addicted Dr. Weinstein. Just before driving off in his Lincoln Continental he had repeated his remark about my having a fine family. He had tried to give me fifty dollars for talking to him. How my father would have relished him, I thought. He would have kept the man around for years.

After a while my wife mentioned that it wouldn't hurt to consult a priest. I thought about that for some time. Why not? The times were out of joint again. The falcon could not hear the falconer. Maybe Weinstein was right. Maybe we needed a different kind of shaman. If so, I knew just the one.

Brother St. Hilaire was up in his sixties and still going strong. When we arrived at the monastery, this time by car on a paved road through the woods from the county home, he was in Brother Paul's laboratory developing prints for his *Pictorial History of Convents in French Canada*. He told us that he was journeying to Montreal several times a month to recruit prostitutes to simulate the licentious activities of early Canadian nuns. He showed us some blown-up black and white prints of gaunt tired-looking women in various stages of dishabille in front of a tawdry backdrop depicting the interior of a stone chapel.

"A representative progression of doxies and trulls wantoning at Our Lady of the Laurentians, my children. Late eighteenth century probably. This sequence is provisionally entitled *Preparing for the Arrival of the Fathers*. What do you think?"

"I think," said Brother Paul from the corner to which he and his retorts and petri dishes had been relegated, "that you had better come over here and look at this."

Brother St. Hilaire squinted down into Paul's microscope. "Look here, William," he said. "Paul's done it again."

Brother St. Hilaire thrust my head close over the eyepiece. Racing to and fro on the slide were richly caparisoned homunculi. Some were jousting on tiny horses. Some were hunting with miniature bows and arrows. In the distance others stormed a castle on a windswept crag.

I straightened up and looked at Brother Paul. I had never seen him more lugubrious. He shook his head. "Every day a new deception," he said. Before my wife had more than a glimpse of his medieval tableau he snatched up the slide and dashed it into a metal waste can.

"I wish I could persuade Paul to take his peepshows on the road," Brother St. Hilaire said. "He could make a fortune. Some are quite instructive. You should see the Roman Saturnalia on agar-agar. It quite outdoes my *History* for sheer Rabelaisian vigor. Like his namesake, Paul is a true illusionist.

"Your father, William, Quebec William I mean, was the grandest illusionist of them all. Sometimes I think he was an illusion himself. I can't stop marveling over young Henry's resemblance to him."

My wife's eyes were standing out almost as far as Uncle Henry's. She clutched our son's small hand and started backing toward the laboratory door. "I think, William, that we had better go home now."

"But you've just arrived," cried Brother St. Hilaire. "Wait, my children. We haven't even begun the exorcism. The Holy Ghost and I haven't exorcised a true demon since Brother Theophile caught one in the form of a retired railroad engineer planting a charge of dynamite in the dairy. I scourged him halfway to Magog before he stopped babbling about his legions. Here, open your mouth, my young son. Sometimes they roll up in a ball at the base of the tongue."

My wife was running down the cloister with Henry in tow. Her high heels clacked on the tile floor. The old abbot, who had been dead ten years, put his head out of a passageway. "Has Brother St. Hilaire brought a horse into the cloister again?" he said.

On the way home my wife sat between Uncle Henry and me with our sleeping son on her lap. "Maybe he needs some more pets," she said.

"He doesn't like pets," I said.

"Well," she said, "maybe we should try some different kinds."

Uncle Henry looked straight ahead and said nothing.

We were keeping a few animals on the farm at the time: a milk cow, some chickens and hogs, my bird dogs and any number of barn cats. Before we could augment this assortment with a pony, Henry became interested in animals of a very different type. He began making sightings over the cedar swamp of gigantic airborne reptiles with long bills full of sharp teeth and wide leather wings bristling with claws. He saw icthyosaurs diving in the upper reaches of the St. John, and pointed out herds of triceratops cropping grass by moonlight in our upper meadow. He decided to specialize in the study of ice-age mammals, and through his mother and me initiated correspondences with three Pleistocene paleontologists. He drove imaginary herds of extinct longhorn bison around tarpits and glacial fissures in our dooryard, tethered prides of American lions in the cow stable, developed an obsession to breed short-faced bears. His night screaming abated. By the time he was five it had stopped altogether.

Remembering my father's menagerie, I wondered whether Cordelia had been right. Perhaps time and events repeated themselves endlessly; illusion and reality might after all be interchangeable; extinctions and disappearances, like beginnings and endings, were matters of human perception. Late at night my wife and I began to hear the thundering of bison and screaming of mammoths from Henry's loft. We looked at each other in terror. My life was becoming more fantastical and inexplicable as I grew older. I felt a desperate need to talk to Cordelia or my father. We stopped sleeping. Uncle Henry shook his head and looked very grave.

One afternoon Dr. Weinstein reappeared. He was on foot and clad in a pink negligee. He had stopped taking drugs. He had shaved his head and no longer ate meat. With him he carried a worn copy of the *Bhagavad-Gita*. He had adopted a new name. We were to call him Swami Poomdakhuba.

Swami Poomdakhuba had walked barefoot over the mountains from a carnival in Maine to undertake the salvation of our family. He had been shot at twice, and on several occasions nearly run over. He told us that bringing people to an awareness of the godhead was even more challenging than ministering to their psychoses.

"Henry," he said kindly, "these pets of yours no longer exist. They did not strive to attain a higher consciousness and so were superfluous. There is no glyptodont in the hayloft. I want you to chant with me now."

"There are two glyptodonts in the hayloft and I intend to breed them," Henry said.

The swami had fashioned a crude pair of extra arms from papier-mâché and attached them to his sides with glue. He now contrived to extend these appendages toward Henry in a supplicant gesture. "Show me," he said.

That night as Uncle Henry and my wife and I sat in the kitchen Swami Poomdakhuba chanted by Henry's bedside. The whole house shook with the stampeding of creatures that had vanished eons ago. The trumpeting and snarling and bellowing drowned out the swami's chants. Finally I couldn't stand any more. I rushed up to the room and pulled on the light. I found my son sitting up in bed holding a grayish creature somewhat larger than a cat. He was thrusting it toward the swami. "Here, Doubting Thomas," he said in Cordelia's voice, his eyes wide open, his forehead lined with intense concentration. "Does this satisfy you?"

I grabbed the thing by the scruff of its neck and held it out in front of me. It was ice cold. "Put it in the root cellar," Henry said. "I've prepared a box there for it."

Henry fed his new pet raw hamburger. It grew fast, but never warmed up. The root cellar had become as cold as an ice house. I asked Henry where he got it. "Up in the cedar swamp," he said.

"Don't you think it would like to go back there?"

"No. I want to get it a mate."

One day I started down cellar to get some salt pork. The creature was crouching at the foot of the rickety wooden stairs. It was now nearly as big as my springer spaniels. When I switched on the light I saw the glint of two fangs protruding an inch below its lower lip.

I shut and locked the cellar door and went up into Henry's loft. He and his mother had gone blueberrying. On the bookshelves along the wall near his bed technical works on the ice age had supplanted my sets of Dickens, Scott and Stevenson. For a while I looked out the window over the ell at the roof of the barn, where years ago I had watched the snow owl.

I went back downstairs and out into the dooryard. It was a wonderful day in August. Perfect blueberry weather. I walked across the dooryard to the granite outcropping, and looked out over the swamp and up the great lake into the distant notch where René Bonhomme had disappeared almost a century before. It was 1953, and the lake and swamp were still unspoiled, undeveloped. From Cordelia's old back bedroom by the plum tree I could hear the chanting of Swami Poomdakhuba droning on and on, persistent as a locust.

Often in difficult times I would think of some advice Cordelia had given me: "Determine as best you can what your father would do in your situation, William. Then do exactly the opposite."

As I stood on the ledge looking north I had no difficulty determining what my father would do in this situation. He would keep the cat and help Henry find a mate. Maybe he would even tame it. I couldn't tame it, and sooner or later it would tear one of us to pieces. I believed I might be jeopardizing my relationship with my son, but I had no choice. I couldn't let the thing live another day.

I returned to the kitchen, opened the gun cabinet and without any hesitation took out the old eight-gauge shotgun that I had used back in 1932 to shoot Carcajou. I inserted two shells loaded with buckshot into the chambers. Then I went back to the head of the cellar stairs, turned on the light and blasted that creature back into the oblivion out of which Henry had retrieved it.

"You done the only thing you could," Uncle Henry said to me that night in the kitchen as we listened to the slow

218

grinding retreat of the glacier from the loft. "Even your father wouldn't have kept that thing around to devour his family. You done just right."

"Yes, William," my wife said, putting her hand on mine, looking at me with her level brown eyes. "I know Henry will understand when he's older. We'll get him the pony tomorrow."

A downdraft of arctic air came sweeping out of the loft. The rumbling receded. Swami Poomdakhuba chanted urgently.

Henry dutifully rode the pony a few times around the dooryard. The next morning the cellar door was open and I found his pet on the earth floor with a visceral banner of blue and red trailing behind it down the steps. It was still kicking, and I had to dispatch it with the eight-gauge. Henry viewed the remains dispassionately.

That night we were awakened by screams from Cordelia's room. I rushed in to find Swami Poomdakhuba thrashing on his bed. He seemed to be struggling with a large invisible creature. I grabbed him by the shoulders and brought my hands away wet. His throat had been torn open from one side to the other.

"Poor swami," Henry said in the morning. "I'll miss him. Now we must burn the remains."

"What?" I shouted. "Burn the remains?"

"Certainly. He left instructions with me in case something like this happened. We have to build a pyre and burn him. The remains are to be immolated."

My son built a cunning rectangular crib of firewood in the meadow near where Cordelia had burned the remains of my father's deformed flocks. He filled the hollow center with hay, which he soaked with gasoline. In a daze I stuffed the swami's remains into a large feed sack, which I carried down to Henry's impromptu crematorium. Twenty min-

219

utes later there was nothing left of the protean chiropodist from Brooklyn but his two papier-mâché arms, which lay on the pile of ashes upraised and unsinged.

"There, Wild Bill," my son said with an air of satisfaction. "That should propitiate the smilodon."

He did not bring home any more pets, and there were no more sanguinary deaths on our hill. The estrangement between us that I had feared didn't materialize. The ice age gradually came to an end. Henry proceeded to an interest that would preoccupy him for years: the study of man's evolution.

When he was about ten Henry began to spend whole days at a time alone in the cedar swamp. By the time he was twelve he was camping there for three or four nights in succession. One June evening after he had been away camping two days I walked down the hill behind the house with Uncle Henry to fish off the beaver dam for the evening rise. As we approached the dam we saw Henry standing on it and talking with a tall stooped woman. Their backs were to us and the woman was pointing upriver. Suddenly a hirsute creature about Henry's size dropped out of a cedar tree a hundred yards or so beyond them. It landed with great agility on its hind feet on a rock sticking out of the still water. It looked incuriously at them, its legs bent, its knuckles loosely brushing the rock. The sinking sun shone directly on it. I saw very plainly that its features were neither simian nor human, nor anything in between. Casually it reached up and swung into the cedar. Henry started up through the swamp after it. The old woman disappeared just as I opened my mouth to call out to her.

I looked at Uncle Henry with astonishment.

"I saw it," he said. "But I ruther I hadn't."

The flat water above the dam was dimpled with rising brook trout, but already Uncle Henry was walking back

220

up the trail. It was the first time in my life that I had seen him pass up an opportunity to fish.

I think that Uncle Henry would rather not have seen a great many things during his life, but it seemed to be his inescapable fate to be subjected by our family to the outrageous and impossible, as it seems to have been my fate to spend most of my life in the shadow of either my father or my son. Their personalities were not only indomitable but overwhelming, and throughout my adult life I have had to pause repeatedly and remind myself who I am, apart from a son and a father: first a young country lawyer practicing out of a room in the hotel next to Uncle Henry's; then a middle-aged lawyer with an office in the courthouse, who would rather sit on the hotel porch talking with Uncle Henry and a few broken-down poachers and retired brakemen than practice law; then a county judge and weekend farmer who would still rather sit on the hotel porch and talk, or fish in the few remaining spots where a trout can be caught, than sit at the head of a courtroom.

Now as I look back over my life and ask that question once more it seems that if I have been or done anything important it was to transmit life from one remarkable person to another and to endure and love them both, without really understanding either of them. Of the two, I believe I understood my father better, perhaps because his sense of humor made him more approachable. But at the core of both there remains a mystery as unfathomable as the mystery of man himself, which Henry pursued so relentlessly and with such an unexpected result that I still find his conclusion as unacceptable and irrefutable as the sabertooth tiger he brought home from the ice age when he was five years old.

12

"How's your leg?" I asked my father as we spun down the tracks in the rain.

"It never felt no better, Wild Bill."

"I never felt better," Rat said, taking another drink. He looked at me cannily. "Your father's been shot, boy. How his leg must throb and burn. You'd think he'd take a sup to ease his great travail."

"Keep your thoughts to yourself," I said. "He doesn't need a sup."

It was dusk, and much colder. The temperature had dropped at least twenty degrees since morning. Across the lake clouds were settling in over the dark mountains. I was afraid it was getting ready to snow.

I was also afraid that we had not seen the last of Carcajou, that we would go to jail for wrecking Compton's train and that my father would succumb to the temptation to take a sup to ease his great travail. I was so angry with Rat I could have shoved him off the handcar. Just a few moments ago he had announced that he had had a vision the previous night in which fifteen lean cows came out of the cedar swamp and devoured our fifteen Jerseys.

My father was as cheerful as ever. He assured us that he had never felt better. He said he doubted that there would be anybody to stop us at the American line, and he was right. The big stone border marker above the lake was as lonely as an ancient and forgotten cenotaph. It would be two or three hours before Compton could get to a telephone to report the theft of his train, my father said.

Walter Kittredge was standing on the platform between the county home barn and the track. He was very surprised to see us pull up on the handcar. "Why, Quebec Bill Bonhomme," he said. "You ain't the milk train."

"See them cans Ratty's hugging, Walter? That ain't milk in there."

"I could use a sup," Walter said. "If ever I could use a sup this is the time. Hello, Henry. I warn't sure who you was in the dark. Who's that? Rat Kinneson? How do, Rat."

"Give Walter K. a sup out of your bottle, Rat. What's the matter, Walter? Surely you ain't that upset over the train being late."

Walter took a long drink from the bottle Rat reluctantly handed him. "My, my, my," he said. "That warn't squeezed out of no Vermont-growed corn. Now if I could just figure a way to sneak into Abiah's room tonight things would be looking up all over."

"What do you mean sneak into Abiah's room? Do you have to sneak into her room after being married to her for sixty years? What's going on here? Is Abiah sick?"

"Abiah was never sick a day in her life. What we was afraid of has happened, Quebec Bill. Tett's been fired right out. The new superintendent give him his walking papers and told him to go down the road yesterday. Said if he showed up on the premises again he'd put him away for good. Since then things have changed drastically. The women was all made to sleep on the second floor last night. Men on the third."

"Husbands and wives?"

"Husband and wife don't make no never mind. We've been put asunder, Bill. I and Abiah have been put asunder after sixty years. I didn't sleep a wink and neither did she. First night we spent apart since the night before our wedding. I'm going crazy here with worry. They don't let us set together to eat neither. Men on one side of the table, women on the other. They're all in eating now but I couldn't stand it no more. I had to get some air or go crazy."

"Who is they? Who's making up all these new rules?"

"Kinneson."

"Kinneson?"

"None other. Warden R. W. Kinneson, Rat's brother. The county figured he done such a good job as warden they appointed him in Tett's place. Or maybe they figured he such a poor job as warden they wanted somebody else in his place and didn't know how else to rid theirselves of him. Whichever. It don't matter, because now he's more warden than ever. I tell you, Quebec Bill, I truly am going to go crazy if I don't sleep next to Abiah tonight. This just ain't natural."

"Walter," my father said, "do you still have your grandfather's violin?"

"Quebec Bill," Uncle Henry said.

"I've got it."

"You wouldn't have no objection to me using it tonight?"

"None at all. But I misdoubt Kinneson will allow any music."

"Never mind Kinneson. I'll deal with him. You bring me your fiddle, Walter. If you can find one bring a stretcher. I hurt my leg a little up the line."

"That leg commencing to stiffen up?" Uncle Henry said as Walter went off to get his fiddle and the stretcher. "I maybe could loosen the bandage a turn. We shouldn't fool around here, Bill. We've got to get you to a doctor."

"I don't know when it's felt so good," my father said. "If I had a pair of tongs I could reach in and yank that slug right out of there and make it feel better yet."

"You mean the bullet's still in there?" I said.

"Maybe that's what makes it feel so good," Uncle Henry said.

"He won't take a sup," Rat said.

A few minutes later Uncle Henry and I were carrying my father up the long drive to the front door of the county home. He was sitting up on the stretcher playing "*Joyeux de Quebec*" on Walter Kittredge's grandfather's fiddle.

"What's this uproar?" said Warden, stepping out onto the porch. "Oh, a new cripple? Stop that unholy racket and come this way."

He led us into a long dim foyer. My father continued to play loudly. "I said, stop that," Warden began to say. Then he recognized my father. "Oh, no," he said.

My father stopped playing. "What sort of welcome is this?" he said. "Do you want us to go round in back where the coalman comes in? The least you could do is invite us in for a feed, seeing as we're going to play for you tonight."

"Do you usually play sitting on a stretcher?"

"He's broke his leg," Uncle Henry said.

"You haven't come here to convalesce, have you?"

"No, rest easy, Superintendent. Evidently in all the to-do of the changeover to your administration nobody told you. Me and my band here are on tap to play for the folks after dinner tonight. We'll be coming twice a month now that spring's here."

"Well, that's all off."

"Spring is off?"

"Good Lord, you Frenchmen are thickheaded. Your show is off. The new curfew is eight o'clock. We don't have time for traveling minstrel performances. These old folks and unfortunates have to get their proper rest. Who's that back there by the door? Is that my shiftless brother? What instrument does he play?"

"The spoons."

"Spoons?"

"Yes, ain't you never heard of spoons? He's a virtuoso on them."

"What do you mean shiftless?" Rat said. "Now you've moved up in the world you seem to be too high and mighty for your own kin."

"Has this man been drinking?"

"You're goddamned right I've been drinking," Rat said. "Jesus give me the say-so. Ain't that right, Bill?"

"This man is intoxicated. Remove him immediately or I'm going to call the authorities."

"Easy, Superintendent. Easy now, Rat. Superintendent here is a man of grave responsibilities. He's right. These people shouldn't be excited by no show. Get them all heated up and they don't sleep good, they're up and down all night. Tettinger never understood about that. He had me come up here for years but I could never see that it did the least good. Them that was old never got no younger. The feebleminded never got no smarter. Speaking of feebleminded, how do you like Hank and Harlan, Superintendent?"

"They are not feebleminded, they are retarded. Profoundly retarded. Alternative provisions have been made for their care."

"Tett used to send the worst ones up to my place. We'd be happy to have Hank and Harlan come up. Wouldn't take a cent for it."

226

"They need professional care. Provisions are being made."

"Where's Tett? I thought he might take a look at my leg."

"Tettinger is where he won't do any more mischief. I must say your leg looks pretty bad. What did you do to it? Stab it by mistake trying to spear pickerel?"

"Are provisions being made for Tett too?"

"Indeed they are. Now if you will kindly return to your vehicle and take that inebriate with you, I will call on your services if I ever need any music. Perhaps at Christmas."

"Well, that's the trouble, Superintendent. You see we didn't know nothing about the shakeup so we had Orie Royer drop us off. He's went on to Memphremagog to visit friends and won't be back for two, three hours."

"Oh, no. Not tonight of all nights."

"I'm afraid so. I reckon you got us on your hands all right. You've got my word we won't be no bother, though. Your brother there ain't really drunk, he's been having dizzy spells. We thought Tett might take a look at him too."

R.W. looked at us. "All right," he said. "It's soup and coffee tonight. Just remember: no music."

"Except for Christmas," my father said.

"Maybe on Christmas. I said maybe. I won't be held to any promises."

"We wouldn't want to hold Superintendent to any promises," my father said.

As we carried him into the long dimly lighted dining room he played the shave-and-a-haircut, two bits ending to a hoedown. Warden rounded on him, puffing out his cheeks like an outraged adder and extending a fat and threatening forefinger. My father made a placating gesture and frowned reprovingly at the fiddle as though it had committed a serious indiscretion.

There were about forty persons at the table, most of

227

whom called out greetings to my father. As Walter Kittredge had reported, the men and women were sitting opposite each other. Next to R.W.'s seat at the head of the table were several empty place settings. My father jumped off the stretcher and hopped along on one leg to Warden's chair. Uncle Henry propped my father's leg up on another chair and sat down beside him. Rat and I sat across from Uncle Henry. Warden had to sit on my uncle's left next to old Prof Elihu Corbitt and across from Abiah Kittredge. Warden shot my father another Gorgon look, but said nothing.

Everyone wanted to know what had happened to my father's leg. He laughed and said that he broke it dancing.

"What happened to your jaw, Quebec Bill?" Mason Cobb inquired. "Did you break that dancing too?"

"No, I broke that calling dances."

"This soup is watery," Rat said.

"Turnip soup is very nutritious," Warden said.

"Where's the sandwiches?" my father said. "Tett always had sandwiches with soup. Leftovers from noon dinner."

Abiah Kittredge leaned out around Rat, immersing her dewlap in her soup. "What noon dinner?" she said loudly.

"Don't you remember?" Prof Corbitt said. "That marvelous gruel that Beadle Kinneson served us this noon." He turned to his elderly son, sitting on the other side of him, and shouted, "Wasn't that gruel we had for lunch delicious, Areopagitica?"

"Eh?" Areopagitica said.

"We don't encourage talking at mealtime," Warden said.

"Yes, Beadle," Prof Corbitt said. "No talking at mealtime. No sandwiches with the soup. No conjugal correspondence. Beadle has initiated some fine new regulations, gentlemen. As you know I have been accustomed to giving

228

a symposium every year on my birthday. Corbitt's Chautauqua, we called it. I have been informed that this practice also will be discontinued."

Prof Corbitt was one hundred and six years old. He had been Cordelia's mentor at the Common Academy back before the Civil War and was an outstanding classicist. His birthday symposia were attended by ex-students from all over New England, many of whom, like Areopagitica, appeared to be much older than Prof himself and had to be wheeled or carried into the county home. He began speaking at daybreak and continued without interruption until midnight. The lecture itself was different each year, but always included at least one abstruse explication of the *Aeneid*. According to Cordelia, Prof Corbitt had gained strength with the passage of the decades. He conducted his symposia in both the peripatetic and Socratic traditions, rushing from the vegetable garden to the barn to the dining hall, firing difficult questions at the bevy of devotees hobbling after him or being carried in his frenzied wake on pallets by their children and grandchildren, themselves gray and old.

All year Prof Corbitt prepared for his birthday symposium by going from room to room at the county home trying out his lectures on shut-ins. Sometimes he took off his suspenders and threatened to flog the bedridden elderly. All the sick residents greatly looked forward to Prof Corbitt's daily visit, but he informed us that this diversion too had been discontinued under Superintendent Kinneson's administration.

Throughout this tirade Prof was winking and grinning at a thin girl sitting diagonally across from him. I suddenly realized that this was Little Gretchen, my would-be seductress. Tonight she paid no attention to anyone but Prof, at whom she gazed with great moon eyes.

"This soup is filling at least, Quebec Bill," old Mason Cobb called up from the other end of the table.

"How's that, Mason?"

"You ain't heard nobody ask for seconds, have you?"

Warden stared down at Mason. Meanwhile Uncle Henry was doing something under the table with the coffeepot. He turned toward Warden. "Let me help you to more java, Superintendent," he said.

Further down on my side of the table Hank and Harlan were looking at my father with reverence. He winked at them and made a fiddling gesture with his hands. They laughed and nudged each other.

"No, no," Warden said. "No touching, boys."

"Boys?" my father said. "They're forty-five Christly years old."

His eyes were very blue. He had laid Walter's fiddle conspicuously on the table in front of him, and I knew he was working himself up to something Warden would not soon forget.

"You've got a quiet well-run place here, Superintendent."

"It was being badly mismanaged," Warden said, pouring himself more coffee. "Extravagant grocery expenditures. Gross fiscal unaccountability. Consumption of alcohol on the premises."

"What, drinking on the premises? Did you hear that, Rat? No wonder they brung in your brother."

My father raised his voice to address the table. "He'll straighten affairs out for you, folks. He used to be the best warden in Vermont, you know. There wasn't a poacher alive that could put nothing over on him. Was there, Henry?"

"It's getting close to lights out," Warden said.

"Lights out? They ain't even gone on yet as near as I can see. How's about just one little tune for the people?"

"No exciting music," Warden said.

"That's true, I keep forgetting. Say, folks, did you hear how Superintendent swum over the falls down to the Common as his last official act as warden?"

"One song might not hurt," Warden said. "Make it a slow one. A nice slow waltz or something."

"True for you," my father shouted. "True for Superintendent Kinneson. You're a white man through and through. What'll she be, ladies and gents?"

"None of your fast ragtime now," Warden said. He was pouring more coffee. His face was quite flushed.

" 'Turkey in the Straw,' " Mason Cobb said. "They don't come much slower than that, Bill."

While my father tuned Walter's fiddle other people called out suggestions. " 'Under the Golden Eagle,' Bill. The 'Frenchman's Breakdown.' 'The Grumbling Old Man and the Cackling Old Woman.' 'The Devil's Dream.' "

" 'The Devil's Dream'?" my father cried out incredulously. "That'll put you to sleep in your chairs. Not 'The Devil's Dream.' "

"That's the one," Warden said. " 'The Devil's Dream' or nothing, Bonhomme."

"Are you sure?"

"Positive. Hurry up now and get it over with."

"The old 'Devil's Dream,' " my father shouted. He was off and fiddling. I had never heard the song played slowly before and suspected that the pace would soon increase. White heads nodded time. My father nodded at Warden. Uncle Henry had the coffeepot under the table again. This time I knew what he was doing with it. Walter Kittredge appeared and slid in beside Abiah. Warden didn't seem to notice this infraction. He was very busy with his coffee.

After five minutes my father was still playing. He knew many variations of the old "Devil's Dream," and went through each one in several different keys. Ten minutes went by. Fifteen. Warden's thick finger began drumming on the tabletop. Uncle Henry poured him more coffee. Up and down the table people sighed and relaxed. Rat began clacking two spoons together. Warden's heavy hog jowls wrinkled. He was smiling.

Hank and Harlan stood up and clasped their right hands together, like two persons shaking hands. They began to shuffle around in a strange simulation of a stepdance. Mason Cobb did a brisk jig. Prof Corbitt snapped his suspenders and looked at Warden as though sizing him up for a flogging. Warden nodded with approval as Uncle Henry poured a generous shot of straight Seagram's into his cup.

I got up and went out to use the bathroom. There was a men's latrine somewhere back by the kitchen but I also remembered a small water closet off the superintendent's office next to the dining room. The office door was ajar, and the green-shaded desk lamp was on. I stepped inside.

The room was a shambles. One corner was heaped with empty bottles. Papers were strewn all over the floor around the desk. Dr. Tettinger's framed oil paintings of ducks and trout had been piled carelessly on the leather couch.

The door to the water closet was locked. I had supposed everyone was in the dining room. Then I remembered that Dr. Tettinger always locked the water closet himself when he had beer cooling inside the stool. Probably Warden hadn't found the key yet.

Just as I started to leave, the office door opened and Little Gretchen stepped inside. Wild fantasies raced through my mind. Here was an opportunity to redeem myself in her opinion and my own. This was too good to be true.

Little Gretchen shut the door, put a bony finger to her lips and walked past me to the desk. She opened the top drawer and reached up under the bottom panel of the desk

232

top and brought out a piece of adhesive tape to which a key was stuck. Without saying a word she handed me the key and pointed at the water closet. Well, I thought, at least we wouldn't be interrupted.

I unlocked the door, and discovered that I had been right about the closet being occupied. Tied to the stool in a straitjacket with a large white bandage over his mouth was Dr. Tettinger.

My disappointment was sharp but short-lived. An assignation with Little Gretchen could be arranged any time. I was so angry I could barely unlace the thongs of the straitjacket. I wanted to kill Kinneson, and thought my father probably would when he found out what had happened.

"Thank Christ," Dr. Tett gasped when I yanked off the gag. "He was going to send me to the lunatic asylum. I came back to get my paintings this afternoon and he hit me from behind. He's going to send Hank and Harlan too, Billy. They're coming tonight for us. I need a drink."

"Wait here," I said. "Dad's getting Kinneson drunk. I'm going to tell him. Don't you worry, Dr. Tett. We'll fix Kinneson."

Back in the dining room pandemonium reigned. Everyone who could stand up was dancing. Someone had built up the niggardly little fire in the fireplace into a fine manorial blaze. As good as his word, my father was still playing "The Devil's Dream." Warden was leaning back in his chair, leering and drinking out of the Seagram's bottle.

"He had Dr. Tett tied up in the toilet," I whispered into my father's ear. "Little Gretchen gave me the key. They're coming tonight to take Dr. Tett and Hank and Harlan to the lunatic asylum."

My father nodded and smiled. He inclined his fiddle toward Warden, who was looking at us suspiciously, and played a rapid series of ingratiating syncopations. "Tell

233

Henry to come over here," he said to me. "This couldn't be working out better."

His leg was swollen nearly twice its normal size and pulsing visibly, perhaps in time with the music, but I had never seen him happier.

The next hour was full of unexpected events. First my father instructed Uncle Henry to go into Tett's office and call the LaChance brothers at the Common Hotel. "Tell them to get right up here if they want their whiskey," he said. "Remember now, we ain't supposed to know their name. Just ask for the two Frenchmen that own the big Buick. Tell them to leave their vehicle down by the barn and come up to the front door."

"They're on their way," Uncle Henry reported five minutes later.

"Good," my father said, smiling at Warden, who was trying to learn how to play the spoons. He said something else I didn't catch, and Uncle Henry left the room again and motioned for me to follow him. When we were out in the hall he told me to return and tell Warden two men were waiting in his office to see him.

"What?" Warden said, dropping his spoons on the floor again. "Already? Well, that's all right if they are. This will be a good example for the others. Tell them I'll be right in, boy."

I ran into the office and warned Uncle Henry and Dr. Tettinger that Warden was on his way. As he lurched into the room Uncle Henry pinned his arms to his side. "It's chilly in here, Superintendent," he said.

"Just slip this jacket on," Dr. Tettinger said.

A minute later Warden was locked in the water closet and Dr. Tettinger was making his triumphal entry into the dining room. Everyone cheered. Hank and Harlan fell over each other to be the first to hug him. "I'll flog you until you can't stand up if you ever desert us again," shouted Prof Corbitt. To demonstrate that he meant business he began unfastening his suspenders. His pants collapsed around his ankles, and he joined the general laughter. "Attention, scholars," he roared. "Aeneas has returned from the underworld." It was a supreme compliment, which Dr. Tett graciously acknowledged after draining the last of the Seagram's from the bottle by Warden's place.

"Rat," my father called out, "fetch us up some more good cheer from the handcar. Take Mason along to help."

"Not mine?" Rat said.

"No, no, yours won't be touched. Where's R.W., boys?"

"Out of harm's way," Uncle Henry said.

"We bundled him up tight," Dr. Tettinger said. "He won't catch cold. Good heavens, Quebec Bill. That's a terrible wound. I didn't see that at first. What on earth happened?"

"Just a scratch, Tett. I think there's still a sliver in it. You might bring your tongs when you have a free minute."

The party gained momentum. Rat and Mason Cobb brought in one of the two milk cans from the handcar. Walter Kittredge got a huge tin washtub and he and Mason and Rat began filling it with whiskey. "Eureka," shouted Prof Corbitt, stepping out of his trousers and into the tub.

A short while later Uncle Henry ushered in the LaChance brothers. They were wearing their tan coats over double-breasted suits with pronounced bulges under their coats. They stood uncertainly on the edge of the crowd around the table and watched Dr. Tettinger work on my father's leg.

My father continued fiddling throughout the operation. From time to time he shouted lay advice into Dr. Tettinger's ear. "Probe deeper, Tett. You ain't through the hide into the meat yet."

235

When Dr. Tettinger finally extracted the slug my father grabbed Prof Corbitt's flogging suspenders off the table beside him and fired the hunk of lead out of them into the pine mantel above the fireplace, where it imbedded itself half an inch deep, having just missed the head of one of the LaChances. The bootlegger turned to his brother and said in French, "This is a most curious place, eh, André?"

"I do not like this place at all, Origène. I hope that is not our whiskey in the tub with the old man."

Two stocky men in white uniforms appeared in the doorway. "I'll handle this for you," my father said to Dr. Tettinger, who was trying to stanch the flow of blood from the wound. He handed his fiddle to Mason Cobb, who began to scrape away at "The Devil's Dream." "Wild Bill, you and Henry lug me over there to greet our newest arrivals."

"We're Croggins and Hathaway," the younger of the two men said. "We're looking for the superintendent."

"How do you do?" my father said. "I am Superintendent Kinneson."

"I'm Croggins, Superintendent. This is Hathaway. We're from the lunatic asylum. I see what you meant on the phone. Things seem to be a little out of hand here. What happened to your leg?"

"Old Tettinger put the fire poker through it in one of his drunken rampages," my father said. "He's tied up in his office now; he won't be any trouble to you. It's the other two you'll have to watch out for. Don't look straight at them or they'll know something's afoot. They're the two in overcoats standing back by the fireplace. Them are very dangerous, them two."

"What?" Croggins said. "Them two re-tards you told us about? Don't worry about them. Show them your bottle, Hathaway. See that little blue bottle of Hathaway's? That's chloroform. We'll slip up behind them and they'll be out like a light. Then into the restraints and off we go in the van. By midnight they'll be in their own padded cell."

Hathaway tapped his bottle. "Great little equalizer, Superintendent. You ought to keep a supply on hand for times like this."

"Where are the restraints?" my father said.

"Just outside in the hallway," Hathaway said. "Can you get them out there?"

"That shouldn't be difficult."

"Good," Hathaway said. "Let's get on with it."

"That Hathaway," Croggins said admiringly to my father as his partner stepped into the hall. "He loves a chloroforming more than anything. He'd arrange for his own mother to be committed if he could be the one to put her under. Hathaway studied for years to be an anesthetist, you know. He'd get them to go to sleep pretty good, but they didn't always wake up."

Hathaway suddenly reappeared. "Do you have to tell that every time we go out on a call?" he said angrily. "There's not a grain of truth to that, Superintendent. This is merely the quickest and cleanest way to do a nasty job."

"Let's not argue about it, Hathaway," Croggins said. "If you weren't damn good at your job you wouldn't be on the squad to begin with."

Rat and I carried my father over to the LaChance brothers. Their guns were quite prominent under their coats. "Let's go get the whiskey," my father said to them in French.

They looked at Uncle Henry, who nodded.

"Who are those two men?" André said.

"They're orderlies that work here," my father said. "They help with the more high-spirited folks. Give them their medicine and put them to sleep and so forth."

"I like this place less and less," Origène said.

"You'll soon be out of it all," my father said. "Lead on, boys. We'll be right behind you."

The LaChances led the way into the hall. Before they had gone five steps Hathaway leaped out from behind a clothes tree, armed with a cloth in each hand. He slammed their heads together with a loud crack and held his cloths over their faces until long after their struggling subsided. Meanwhile Croggins got the straitjackets on them.

"Do you want any help lugging them out to your van?" Uncle Henry said.

"No," Croggins said. "It's just like carrying a sack of feed. We'll meet you in the office." He slung one of the LaChances over his shoulder and headed down the hall toward the front door. Hathaway followed close behind him with the older brother.

"Dad," I said, "we can't send Warden off with them. They're crazy. There's no telling what they'll do to him."

"There's no telling what they would have done to Tett and Hank and Harlan," my father said. "Hen, fetch R.W. out of the toilet and set him up in Tett's chair."

Warden Kinneson proved to be less tractable than the LaChance brothers. As soon as he saw Croggins and Hathaway he began to scream that they were committing the wrong man. "I'm the new superintendent," he shouted.

"I'm Calvin Coolidge," Hathaway said. "You think we better give this cuckoo a whiff of the sleepy-sleep, Superintendent?"

"I don't believe it would hurt," my father said. "He's apt to rave all the way down the line if you don't. Next thing you know he'll be telling you he used to be a game warden."

"I was," Warden screamed. "I was a game warden for

seven years before being appointed superintendent. That man on the stretcher is an impostor. He's nothing but a filthy Canuck poacher."

"Was it after you was King of the Jews that you got to be a warden, or before?" Hathaway inquired, dousing his cloth generously. "The only appointment you've got is on the locked ward, Tettinger. Here now. Stop thrashing. Take it like a man."

Warden went under reluctantly. "He's a big fleshy one," Croggins said. "Best we lug him out together, Hathaway."

My father and Rat and Henry and I accompanied them out to the van and watched them strap Warden in between the LaChance brothers. Hathaway and Croggins kept saying that they had never bagged three at once before. I was beginning to realize that my father, while incapable of a mean or petty thought, could be extremely ruthless on occasion. I despised Warden; my father seemed actually to like him, but had no scruples about sending him to a lunatic asylum that employed lunatics. In part his attitude could be explained by that frontier hardness he preserved to the end, or perhaps it was his sense of humor that led him to such excesses. I don't know, and maybe I don't really want to.

It was very cold now, but before we could get my father back inside another opportunity for him to display his ingenuity presented itself. Just as Croggins and Hathaway were getting into the van a man came running up the lane from the barn. "Help," he shouted while still some distance away. "I've been robbed. My train's been stolen and wrecked."

"Who on earth is that?" Croggins said.

"That's Ebenezer Trucott," my father said. "He was a brakeman on the old St. Johnsbury and Lamoille for years before the big wreck back in twenty-one. After that he

239

come here. Every once in a while he gets the idea his train has been wrecked again."

Compton rushed up to us. "Get the police," he panted. "They drove it right into the lake. Hurry, men."

Suddenly he recognized my father. "You," he said. "It's you."

"Of course it's me, Ebenezer. Has your train been derailed again? We'll get it back on the tracks first thing in the morning. Run inside now, your soup's getting cold."

Compton sprang for my father with his hands outstretched. There wasn't anything Uncle Henry and I could do without dropping the stretcher, but Croggins and Hathaway were both accustomed to acting quickly. Croggins grabbed the infuriated engineer, whom Hathaway proceeded to anesthetize with great expedition.

"What should we do with this one, Superintendent?" Croggins said. "We don't have any more room inside the van. Not unless we stack them up like cordwood."

"We don't have papers for him either," Hathaway said. "We can't take him without papers."

"This is an emergency," my father said. "You saw him try to throttle me. We'll tie him to the roof. Wouldn't you like to bring in four all to once? That would be a record that would stand for a good while."

"Tie him to the roof?"

"Certainly. Like a deer. Heist him right up there, Croggins, before he wakes up."

"I don't think he'll be waking up for some time," Hathaway said. "I used up the rest of the bottle on him. We'd be heroes, Croggins. Let's do it. Four to one haul ain't nothing to sneeze at."

"Papers be damned," Croggins said, lifting Compton onto the van roof. "Have you got some rope, Superintendent?"

"I think we can spare a few lengths," my father said. He turned to Rat. "Orderly, fetch up a piece of that rope from the pack basket, if you will. Bring back a small token of our esteem from the milk can for these fine gentlemen."

After Compton had been secured on the van roof, spread-eagled like a dead bear, my father presented Croggins and Hathaway with two bottles of Seagram's.

"Very nice to meet you," Croggins said, shaking his hand.

"Yes," my father said. "I hope we can get together again under more pleasant circumstances."

"I can't imagine any more pleasant circumstances," Hathaway said, shaking hands.

"You don't know what a service you've done me," my father said.

Hathaway held up the empty blue bottle and tapped it.

"That Hathaway," Croggins said.

As they drove off I said, "Won't Compton get cold up there when he wakes up?"

"I expect he will," Uncle Henry said.

Back in the dining room everyone seemed to be thriving under the restoration of Dr. Tettinger. Fred Stillwater was accompanying Mason Cobb on the concertina and many people were still dancing. Someone had gotten Prof Corbitt's doctoral robe and hood. Attired in all his academic resplendence, he sat in the washtub and presided over the distribution of the whiskey. Little Gretchen got up on the table and began taking off her clothes. Undressed she looked incredibly wanton and emaciated.

"Come, Dido, my inamorata," cried Prof Corbitt, divesting himself of his robe as Little Gretchen tumbled off the table into the tub.

Toward dawn Dr. Tettinger passed out in front of the fireplace. Prof Corbitt and Little Gretchen were asleep in

241

one another's arms in the washtub, exhausted from a night of Olympian calisthenics. Everyone else except Walter and Abiah Kittredge had gone to bed. Now they said good night and slipped off hand in hand.

"I reckon we can go home now, boys," my father said.

"Bill," Uncle Henry said, "somehow I have the notion that it just ain't going to be quite that simple."

13

"THE first reason I'm against this," Uncle Henry said, "is that you're the one that ought to ride in the Buick. We can put the whiskey in the boot and stretch you out on the back seat and Billy and Rat and me can set up front. That leg ain't nothing to fool with. You heard what Tett said before he passed out. You freeze it up and you'll surely lose it. Besides that, they're bound to be patrolling them tracks with Compton's train twelve hours overdue. They'll pick you up before you get to Memphremagog, much less the Common. Your ideas get wilder and wilder, Quebec Bill. We'll all go together in a nice warm car."

We were standing beside the handcar in the first light of the morning. It was still at least an hour before sunrise, and bitterly cold. I agreed with Uncle Henry. If we all went in the Buick and kept to the back roads, I doubted that we would be picked up. Also I dreaded the idea of pumping that handcar all the way down to the Common in the cold. The temperature couldn't have been much above twenty degrees, and the air smelled like snow. I kept thinking about poor Compton, lying roped to the top of the van. He would freeze to death for certain, I thought. He was probably stiff already.

"I'll think about it," my father said. He was sitting up on the seat of the handcar and twirling the chambers of the revolver Uncle Henry had gotten away from one of the LaChance brothers just before Croggins slapped the straitjacket on him. Beside him sat the one remaining milk can and the pack basket containing the rest of our rope, the hatchet and twelve bottles of Seagram's Rat had apparently transferred before taking the other milk can up for the party.

"You go fetch Rat down, Hen. I and Bill will think on what you said."

"You'll run off on me is what you'll do. I know you better than that."

"No, I promise we won't do that. Just look at that Roadmaster, Henry. See it begin to take shape in the light. That's a fine automobile you've got there."

"It ain't White Lightning."

"You could paint her white and pretend she was."

"I'll go get Rat," Uncle Henry said.

After Uncle Henry left I said to my father, "We'd better go in the Buick, Dad. It's too cold to fool around out here. Uncle Henry's right."

I know what my father's answer to that would have been, but before he could reply we were illuminated in a bright swath of headlights.

"What's Henry doing with that Buick?" my father said.

The car started up with a roar and came straight down the lane for us. Berserk laughter erupted into the dawn.

"Christ," my father shouted. "That ain't Henry. Pump, Bill."

I leaped onto the back of the handcar and began pumping. The Buick missed us by inches and rammed into Walter Kittredge's prize manure pile.

"There goes Henry's bumper," my father said. "Pump for your life, Bill."

The big car backed fast out of the manure pile, spun around and started after us down the tracks.

"This is too bad," my father said. "I'll have to bust Henry's windscreen."

Encircling the last milk can and the pack basket with his left arm, he held the LaChance brother's pistol out in his right hand at arm's length and took careful aim. He fired and the windshield shattered. I kept pumping. The Buick kept coming.

"Damn that man," my father said with admiration. "He's indestructible."

He fired again. Still the Buick came on. Over the engine and the pounding of the tires on the ties we could hear that baying laughter. I had a terrible vision of Carcajou driving with the pike pole still in his chest.

"There goes a tire," my father said. "There's another. That'll slow him down, Wild Bill."

The handcar was going very fast now on the long downhill grade toward the trestle over the St. John. All kinds of impossible expediences occurred to me. Maybe we could jump off and run into the cedar swamp; but my father couldn't run, he couldn't even walk. Periodically Carcajou emitted a long uncanny imitation of a train whistle. The tire rims thundered over the ties. My father fired three more shots, but mad Rasputin was gaining on us. My arms were tiring fast. We were all through, I thought. He had us.

"Pump, Wild Bill," my father shouted.

He was trying to stand up. As we sped out onto the trestle with the Buick only a few feet behind us, blinding me with its lights, my father did stand. He fired his last bullet directly into the driver's seat at point-blank range. More laughter. I pumped furiously. Once again my only objective was to get off a trestle, as though it wouldn't be so bad to be crushed to death on dry land.

"Pump, Bill."

"Pump," shouted Carcajou as the Buick bore down on us. He began to laugh again, and was still laughing when my father, standing on his swollen wounded leg, lifted the last milk can high above his head and hurled it through the broken windshield and into the front seat.

"There goes Henry's Roadmaster," my father shouted as the Buick plunged into the river.

We stopped to reconnoiter just the other side of the trestle, where many years before my father had shot the two hijackers. Over in the east above the cedar swamp the sky was pink again. Three days ago we had looked at the same sky with hope in our hearts. Since then we had lost the canoe and Henry's Cadillac. We had lost eight thousand dollars' worth of whiskey and been instrumental in the wreck of a freight train and a new Roadmaster Buick. We had killed five men, including Carcajou, seen another man decapitated and sent four men to a lunatic asylum. Back home our cows were starving and my mother was doubtless sick with concern for us. My father had a fractured jaw and a leg that he might never walk on and that was now beginning to bleed again, the blood soaking through the bandages onto the platform of the handcar. Besides the clothes on our backs, we had nothing left but the pack basket, some rope, a hatchet and twelve bottles of whiskey. Already I was beginning to get cold again.

My father pointed to the east. "Wild Bill," he said, his voice quavering with wonder, "here hath been dawning another blue day. Ain't that sky just about the grandest sight you ever hope to see?"

The grandest sight I ever hoped to see was our farm-house, but I didn't say this to my father. What I said was, "Your leg is bleeding. We've got to stop that bleeding."

"That's just the wound cleaning itself out. Wounds will do that, you know. Hark. What's that buzzing?"

I ran back to the trestle to see what Carcajou was doing now. The dark surface of the river was still; there was no sign of the Buick. The buzzing seemed to be coming from out over the lake. A small gray float plane appeared out of the mist. It was coming in above the bay and heading up the river. All that occurred to me was that here was a way to get my father to a doctor before he bled to death. I ran out on the trestle, took off my hunting jacket and waved it over my head.

The plane banked and landed in the bay. It turned and taxied up into the mouth of the river. Two men were inside. Both were wearing uniforms. I thought they might be wardens.

The pilot brought the plane up under the iron bridge to the trestle. His partner got out on a pontoon and fastened a rope to one of the trestle pilings. On the side of the plane and the wings were the letters U.S.B.P. I realized that we were being rescued by the border patrol.

"Hurry, Officers," my father called as the two men climbed up on top of the trestle. "Thank Christ you've arrove at last. He tried to run us down with a locomotive. He's murdered my brother-in-law and hired man."

"Who has?"

"The outlaw Carcajou. He stole a train and wrecked it trying to mash us. I got shot up in the fracas."

"We know all about the train. Carcajou did that, did he? Say, I guess you got shot up all right. We better get you to the hospital right away. Get his legs, Stu."

While the border patrol officers carried my father to the trestle and lowered him down to the plane he talked constantly. He told them that he and I had been spearing pickerel in one of the slangs up north of the border when he had been shot and captured. He said that Carcajou had tied him and his brother-in-law and hired man to the tracks; that I had been able to cut him free just in time but the other two had been sliced off at the neck and knees. Then Carcajou had wrecked the train and we had found the handcar and gotten as far as the trestle with it, where his leg had started bleeding badly. I don't know whether the officers believed any of this or not.

I brought along the pack basket and helped get my father inside the float plane. It was a two-seater with just room enough for him and the pilot and the pack basket. "The boy and I'll go on down to Memphremagog on the handcar and meet you at the hospital, Stu," the pilot's partner said.

"Wait a minute, Officer," my father said as the pilot started to get in. "I'm in bad shape. No doubt we'll get there in time but I've lost several gallons of blood already. I'd like a last word alone with my boy if you don't mind. Just in case, you know."

"All right, but for God's sake, hurry," the pilot said.

I scrambled inside, trying not to cry, but my father was grinning at me. "Pull that door to," he said. "Wild Bill and his father need a little privacy. This leg is perfectly fine. So long as I don't run no foot races on her she won't leak no more. She's stopped already."

The engine sputtered and caught as the pilot yanked down on the propeller. He started back along the outside pontoon, motioning for me to get out. His partner had untied the rope and was holding onto the piling with one arm. The nose of the plane started to swing around with the current.

My father reached across me and pulled down on the door latch, locking us in.

248

"Switch places with me, Wild Bill," he said.

My father was even more obsessed by planes than by trains. About once a year one would go over our hill, and he would rush into the dooryard and gaze after it in silent awe, like Moses looking upon the promised land. He always took me up for the dollar scenic tour when the air show came to Kingdom County. Once he signed up for flying lessons from a bush pilot out of Memphremagog, but after the second lesson the pilot refused to go up with him again.

Now as we taxied down the river and into the bay with the border patrol officers clinging to the pontoon struts my father said he would show me some real flying. Stu beat on the door. "No riders," my father said sternly, shaking his head.

The other officer got to his feet, pulled out his revolver and shot off the door handle on my side. The door remained locked. The officer lost his foothold and fell into the bay. Stu remained crouching on the other pontoon as we lifted off the water. My father was pulling on a leather aviator's cap which he had found on the seat beside him. He looked like a flying gnome with a two-days' beard and a misshapen jaw. "I wish Henry was here," he said. "Henry would love this."

We were climbing at an alarming angle. Before ascending very high we rolled over and flew along upside down for some distance. We flipped back over and Stu hung from the strut by one hand with his legs dangling several feet above the water.

With his free hand Stu got out his pistol and fired into the air. My father began dipping the big double wings from side to side. This was too much for the tenacious pilot, who disembarked not far from the shore.

Now we were able to gain some altitude. As we headed

249

up toward the low ceiling my father remarked that this was the only way to run whiskey. He said that first we would have a little ride and then we would land in the St. John just below the beaver dam at the foot of our hill.

His leg had stopped bleeding. As we banked around to the southeast I could see our buildings, bare and gray on the hill above the swamp. We were over the county home and banking again. "Let's see what Hilarious is doing this fine morning," my father said.

On the way up the lake we passed a small engine pulling a crane car south on the railroad track. A dozen or so men were gathered around the scene of the wreck. A plane similar to ours floated near the engine. The men waved and my father dipped his wings. "Henry would have loved seeing me do that, Wild Bill. Wouldn't Henry have appreciated that?"

From the air the secluded monastery looked even more serene and medieval. The cows were filing out into the barnyard but no monks were in sight. It didn't look like the same place we had visited the day before. From up here nothing seemed the same. It was as though we were looking at a vast panoramic scale model of Canada and Vermont. Even the flat cedar swamp looked more like a watercolor than a real swamp.

I knew we were in more trouble than even my father was apt to get us out of, but as we soared over the mountain notch where we had recently come so close to being killed, I didn't care. I felt completely secure, as I had felt traveling up the lake with my father in the canoe three days before. I still felt that so long as he and I were together nothing could ever harm either one of us.

Off to the west the charred remains of Carcajou's barn looked like the blackened circle of an old campfire. Further north the booms behind the smoking paper mill were only about half full. The beach was still heaped high with pulp. There was no sign anywhere of the yellow tug. I tried to get a glimpse of the St. Lawrence River through the northern mountains, but the clouds were too low.

Looking down at the gray-toned landscape north and south of the short stretch of border where so much of our history had transpired, I knew much that I had not known a week ago. I knew that the country below us was not only a hard place to live in, but a treacherous place as well, full of unexpected and unavoidable horrors, including some that had nothing to do with furious winds and deep cold water and swamps and mountains. Yet despite my first clear vision of the darkness in which the human heart is enshrouded, I knew that my father was right when he put his hand on my shoulder and said, "Bill, ain't all that down there the most wonderful thing you ever see?"

I must have been very tired because I found myself fighting back tears again; but I was not going to deny the truth of my vision, the truth on which my father had based his life, just because I was tired or scared or too proud to be seen crying.

"Ain't it wonderful, Wild Bill?"

"Yes," I said, crying. "It is."

At three other times in my life I was to experience this heightened vision of wonderment. Each experience also involved a perception of horror. Each time I came away convinced that my vision had been strengthened, as a religious faith is said to be strengthened by some arduous test, though it had little to do with religion:

It is the night of June 3, 1967. Along the marshy shore of Lake Memphremagog the small frogs are singing loudly, nearly drowning out the low putter of Uncle Henry's three-horse motor. Once again I am headed north, this time with my son and uncle, knowing that this will be the last time, because Uncle Henry is an old man with his single lung going bad and my son is defecting from the United States and going home to the country of our ancestors, the country of his great-great-great-great-grandfather, René Bonhomme. I keep thinking, who is rejecting whom? Is Henry rejecting his country or is his country rejecting him? He sits motionless in the bow of the boat with my father's eight-gauge shotgun across his lap. In the starlight his profile exactly resembles my father's. Canada, I conclude, is where my son belongs. Like my father, he needs space and wild country to be happy, and like my father and old René, he acknowledges no allegiance to any particular country.

As we approach the county home, which has now been transformed into a luxury resort with a long lighted dock for pleasure boats and a long pipe discharging kitchen waste and human waste directly into the lake, time seems to repeat itself. With no warning at all we are blinded by a powerful searchlight. A voice through a loudspeaker commands us to stop. My first thought is of the F.B.I. agent who personally delivered Henry's draft papers this afternoon, after Henry had sent them back unopened twice.

"Easy," I say. "Easy, Henry."

And I seem to be talking to my own father.

"Easy, boy," Uncle Henry says softly.

The patrol boat approaches, blinding us with its light. The amplified voice tells Henry to put down the shotgun. Strangely, I am as aware of the outrageous stench of effluvia from the resort as I am of the boat intercepting us. "You shut out your light," Henry says in that abrasive voice so like Cordelia's. "Then maybe I'll put down this gun."

The launch is now directly across our bow, and directly in line with Henry's shotgun, which he holds easily and surely, he who never shot anything but a clay pigeon in his life and is the best shot I have ever seen with the possible exception of his grandfather. Time is repeating itself, I think.

"Put the gun down, Henry," I say.

"Shut out your light, Captain," Henry says, his voice rasping.

The stench is really overpowering.

The voice crackles out again. "Drop the gun."

It sounds familiar but I can't quite place it.

"Who are you?" my son says.

"Border Patrol R. W. Kinneson," the voice says, and my son laughs out loud, a short harsh barking sound such as Cordelia might have made if she had ever laughed.

"Border Patrol Kinneson," Henry says with delight. "Shut out your light, Border Patrol Kinneson, or I'll blow you to Kingdom Come."

Silence.

The light goes out.

"Now, Border Patrol Kinneson," Henry says, "you have a choice. You can go on about your border peregrinations or you can pull that trigger and get yourself blasted to Kingdom Come. I don't care which."

I can see Warden's bulky outline and the shape of the pistol he holds pointed at my son. Warden too is an old man now, almost ready to retire. Too old to risk being killed by a disaffected boy with a shotgun. "What the hell," he says. "Go on back where you come from. I wish all of you frogs would disappear off the face of the earth."

"Yes," Henry says, holding the shotgun pointed directly at Warden's chest, "I'm sure you do."

A few minutes later we drop Henry off at his own request just north of the stone border marker. He says he wants to walk up the tracks to Magog alone. He wants to be alone and think. He shakes hands with his uncle and me and stands looking up at us with a calculating half-amused expression like his grandfather's. Then he hugs and kisses us both and begins walking north.

Somewhere off on the lake a loon whoops — maybe the last loon on Memphremagog. Henry whoops back. They continue talking to each other for a long time while Uncle Henry and I stand on the shore and listen. Once again I think that time is repeating itself, or maybe running backwards now, and Henry is not only walking north along the abandoned railway but heading back into the past, as my father and I did in 1932, with the difference that he will stay there, where he belongs.

Uncle Henry begins to cough. I don't have to ask if it is the lung that bothers him. I know it is. I know that he too has seen his last full cycle of seasons in Kingdom County and that next year at this time he will not be here, or anywhere where I can talk to him. Everything, it seems, is disappearing.

Out on the lake there is a solid splash. Uncle Henry returns to the boat and begins assembling his fly rod, though it is well after midnight. "A small white coachman would be right," he says.

And the world again seems full of terror and wonder.

It is a week later. A letter has arrived from Henry, written in the crabbed hand he inherited from Cordelia:

Dear Wild Bill and Mother,

I have given a considerable amount of thought to Border Patrol Kinneson's parting words to us on the lake, and decided that without knowing it he was accurately prophesying not only the fate of us Canucks but of the entire human race. This observation sheds some new light on the disappearances in our own family, which can be seen as emblematic of the unalterable destiny of the species. In our tendency to vanish we are only a little closer than most others to our collective annihilation, which, I am certain, cannot be far away. A generation or two at the most, I suspect.

I have read that the northern Cree understand this and do not burden themselves with unnecessary possessions or cumbersome technologies. They know their tenure is brief, and rounded by a dreadful bang. I hope to visit them soon, following the same route Grampa René took in 1792. I am saving to buy a canoe out of my earnings at the Magog paper mill. I know you would gladly pay for the trip but I want to remember always why I went, and working here will assure me of that; paper mills, Wild Bill, are the best arguments against newspapers.

On Sunday I visited Brother St. Hilaire and Brother Paul at the Benedictine monastery. When I arrived they were playing a fast game of rugby in the cow pasture with the old abbot you keep wondering about, who, it turns out, is not really the abbot at all, but a clone. Paul tried to shut him up, but Brother St. Hilaire was determined to tell me that one afternoon back in the mid-1940s Brother Paul accidentally cloned the abbot from a cell taken from a scraping of his swollen foot. When the abbot died the clone lived on. It is a benign creation, like its progenitor, and seems greatly amused by Brother St. Hilaire, who is somewhat senile now and persisted in calling me William, my son. All three of them asked about you and mother and hoped you would both get up to see them soon. Brother St. Hilaire is keeping the monastery going by writing for the Montreal sex tabloids. He said he has some choice passages to read you. He also has a new girlfriend, a Gretchen somebody, whom I met briefly. She is a burned-out old lady who claims to remember you and who goes around all day with a tape cassette blaring Hank Williams' songs plastered to her ear.

This weekend I will visit Grandmother Evangeline in Montreal. Of course I will see her again before I head north.

Take care of yourself, Bill. Last week when you and Uncle Henry dropped me off at the border I thought you seemed somehow withdrawn from this world. You ought to stay around a while longer. It's full of wonders, you know.

My love to you, Wild Bill, and to Mother.

Your expatriated son,
Henry Bonhomme

p.s. If that sneaking F.B.I. agent comes around asking for me again, give him a Christly good kick in the ass.

This afternoon the F.B.I. agent returns. I show him the letter, which he squats in the dooryard, country style, to read. He is a big man with quiet eyes and a slight southern accent. He reads the letter impassively.

"Yes, sir," he says, handing the letter back.

After a while he says, "My name's Weed. Waylon Weed."

A little later he says, "I've got two boys in Canada myself. Waylon defected last spring. Beauregard Benedict defected a month later."

He stands up and shakes his head. We shake hands. "Tell your boy not to come back, Mr. Bonhomme. If he does I'll catch him. Same as I would my own. Tell him good luck. Tell him you kicked my ass."

As Waylon Weed drives back down the dusty hollow road I look out over the cedar swamp. It is vast and wild and shimmering a little in the heat of the young summer. It is a place of mirages and illusions. A place of horrors and wonders. It is a vestigial corner of the primeval world, waiting patiently for us to disappear.

I cannot stop thinking about the sentence in Henry's letter: "It's full of wonders, you know." And for one brief moment I believe I know how Saul felt on the road to Damascus.

And I felt that intensity of wonderment once again, almost a decade later, when I stepped out into the dooryard just as the sun came up and realized that Kingdom County had disappeared:

It is July 4, 1976, the Bicentennial of my country, and like Saul's my eyes have been opened again. I hadn't seen it coming because it didn't happen the way Henry predicted and I expected, with a bang. No rough beast came slouching from the primordial cedar swamp. No wind blew Kingdom County away. No fire rained down on it from the sky. It was not that way at all, but much more dreadful. And I had watched it happen without knowing what I was watching.

This is what I see from our hilltop at sunrise on the two hundredth birthday of America:

To the south the hollow road is quiet. Orie Royer's place has been bought by a young couple who keep some goats and chickens and a milk cow and like us cut their own firewood and raise their own vegetables. Between the old Royer place and the county road there is not a single working farm left, though three big flags hang limply in the morning stillness above the three farmhouses that have been renovated as summer homes. There is no flag in our dooryard. My wife and I have decided that the day Henry comes home will be the day we will fly our flag.

To the north and northeast the cedar bog is gone, inundated by one hundred thousand acres of warm brackish still water backed up behind a so-called flood control dam built by the Army Corps of Engineers in 1972. With the swamp went the last herd of moose; the beaver and otters and mink; the pink swamp orchids and the gigantic white cedars; the speckled trout Uncle Henry loved to catch on his delicate flies; and five miles of the Upper Kingdom River, the last wild stretch of whitewater in Vermont.

To the northwest Lake Memphremagog is lined with resorts, campgrounds, trailer parks, marinas and three new industries. The monastery folded in 1970 when Brother St. Hilaire died, and has been converted into a laboratory for a rocket research corporation that uses the mountains on both sides of the lake for its testing grounds.

Although I cannot see it, the Common too has changed. There are a few healthy isolated elms on some of the side streets but the trees on the central green have all died of the Dutch elm disease. The Academy where Prof Corbitt taught Cordelia and where I went to high school has been razed, replaced by a large regional high school built on the site of Frog Lamundy's old place along the county road. The statue of Ethan Allen still stands at the south end of the village, but Calvin Goodman's church and library have both been taken down and an absurd shopping mall catering mainly to tourists now runs along the west side of the green. With the big dam across the river, the rainbow trout have stopped coming up over the falls in the spring.

I think too on this lovely Bicentennial morning when I would like to be celebrating my country's birthday, maybe even putting on my old uniform and marching in the Common and giving the address I had to decline making because of my loyalty to Henry, of the people who have disappeared and without whom Kingdom County cannot exist, for me anyway.

258

I think of my mother, who died in 1969 in the convent in Montreal where she grew up, and in a sense died the day she reentered the convent in the summer of 1936, the day after I graduated from high school.

I think of Cordelia, who disappeared in the spring of 1932 at the age of ninety and reappeared twenty years later to counsel my son on the origin of man.

And of Henry, living with his Cree wife in a cabin on the northern shore of Lake Athabasca.

And Brother St. Hilaire and Brother Paul, buried side by side in the small cemetery above the rocket research corporation, where the cloned abbot still has a cell with a cot and desk and still wanders through the nonrestricted areas.

Of Uncle Henry, who in the fall of 1967, with his lung disintegrating into little bloody shreds that he coughed up by the hour, took his fly rod and deer rifle and disappeared into the cedar swamp, where nearly a year later I found and did not disturb his body, inside a large beaver house not far from the Canadian line.

And of my father. And thinking of my father, I decide to see if there is still time to make the speech. There is, we'd be delighted, Judge, so I go down to the Common in my uniform and get up and try to tell about the wonders and the horrors of Kingdom County and America, to the absolute astonishment and growing outrage of the local citizenry, but I keep right on, telling how René Bonhomme settled Kingdom County with a canoeload of brandy and a long knife, and Calvin preached and drank and went off to the Civil War with his son; about my son's flight into Canada, and the disappearance of Kingdom County, gone the way of Melville's Nantucket and Hawthorne's Salem, Thoreau's Concord and Frost's New Hampshire. Listen to this, someone says, the judge is losing his marbles. No, friends and fellow celebrants, I shout, you listen to me because all I mean to say is that even though it has disappeared, Kingdom County is still a place of wonders, and even though it is disappearing, America is still a place of wonders.

And even though I was a good judge, at election time a petition was circulated and I lost my judgeship by two votes and considered going off to live with the Cree myself. I didn't, though. I went back to my law practice in the dim musty office on the third floor of the courthouse overlooking the Green Mountains, which hadn't changed at all, and where I have had much time to think about time and my family, Kingdom County and America, wonders and horrors and illusions, and my father and the spring of 1932.

"I wonder what kind of plane this is," my father said.
"I think they're called flying boats."
"I wonder how high they'll go."
I was still wondering at the country below us, musing over all that had taken place down there, no longer bothering to differentiate between past and present.
"I don't know," I said. "I don't think they're built to go very high."
This observation was a mistake on my part. Immediately we were climbing. When the engine started to stall out we began to circle, moving upward through layer after layer of clouds. We ascended in great spiraling loops. Nothing was visible but clouds. Still we climbed. I lost all track of time and place. He's doing it, I thought. He's finally doing it. Soon we would soar into that forbidden ethereal bourn from which we would be hurled headlong toward the earth.
My father began to sing "*En Roulant.*" This is it, I thought. The ultimate voyage of the voyageurs. Those magnificent frogs in their flying machine. Daedalus and Icarus, sunbound and hellbent.

I didn't see how my father could sing at all. The air was so thin and cold I could hardly breathe. I thought I was going to black out. Then I did.

In recent years this incredible flight has been incorporated into a recurrent nightmare. Again I am entrapped with my father inside that lumbering purloined float plane, laboring ponderously up into the clouds. Again I start to black out. When I come to we are still climbing, with Aunt Cordelia sitting on the upper port wing.

"*Ad astra*," she says grimly, pointing up with her yardstick.

Croggins and Hathaway from the lunatic asylum are leering in through my window at me. Hathaway's reeking chloroform cloth comes closer. It covers my window. I struggle. Darkness.

"Hail to thee, blithe Baron von Bonhomme," Cordelia says. She is wearing an astronaut's suit and is tethered by a long cord to the port wing strut, against a background of stars as dazzling as the ceiling of a planetarium. She quotes:

> Higher still and higher
> From the earth thou springest,
> Like a cloud of fire;
> The blue deep thou wingest,
> And singing "*En Roulant*" dost soar,
> And soaring ever singest.

Then she deliberately casts off her lifeline and without looking back floats off into the universe. It is very quiet. The dream ends.

"We can't go no higher, Wild Bill," my father said. "We're out of gas."

I have never dreamed about our noiseless descent through the clouds and back into the present and the real world,

261

though there was a distinctly dreamlike and surreal quality about it. My father handled the plane so well we almost wafted to the ground, circling again, but this time the way a glider circles, using only air currents.

I had no idea how long we had been up there or where we were going to come down. I hoped that if we were over the lake we could land near shore. Then we were out of the clouds and dropping toward thick flat green woods, cedar woods, stretching for miles in every direction and interrupted only by the threads of frozen beaver flows and the irregular white expanses of frozen backwaters.

"Stay low and hang tight," my father said as we swooped down over the treetops.

The silence of our fall was terrible. Any amount of thundering would have been preferable to that premonitory noiselessness. Again my expectations had been reversed. Death was not supposed to be so quiet. When something gave beneath us with a sound like a buzz saw splitting a big log I was relieved. The pontoons, I thought. The pontoons had been ripped off by the treetops.

The pontoons were of no use to us anyway with the watercourses still frozen solid. It was undoubtedly the cedars that saved us by breaking our fall and cushioning our impact. We would not have blown up. There wasn't any gas left to explode. But if we had ever hit that ice and frozen snow head-on, we would have been dashed into more pieces than the Packard demolished by Carcajou's land mine. As it was the trees tore off part of the starboard wing as well as the pontoons. We flipped over and the pack basket flew through the air. Bottles shattered. It was raining Seagram's and glass.

My father and I lay on the roof of the cockpit. My hands and face were cut in several places, but otherwise I seemed to be all right. My father was jubilant. "Warn't that the best crash landing you ever see executed?" he shouted.

The plane was caught by its tail in the cedars twenty feet above the ground. Through the shattered window I could see the detached piece of the wing sticking out of the snow. Part of the government insignia was visible. "What's the border patrol going to say, Dad?"

"They ain't going to say nothing for a while. We're back in Canady again. Welcome back to Canady, Wild Bill."

14

AGAIN my father and I were alone in the cedar swamp, this time miles from any help. Every time we moved, the fuselage swayed in the branches. Both doors were jammed, and I wondered how either of us was ever going to get out.

My father was fumbling in the bottom of the pack basket. He pulled out an unbroken whiskey bottle, which he put in his jacket pocket. He rummaged around again and brought out the hatchet. With a short hard blow he smashed out his window. He reached out and yanked the door handle down hard. The door opened stiffly.

"Stick this in your belt, Wild Bill," he said, handing me the hatchet.

Next he found an end of the rope and tied it around a brace under his seat. He dropped the slack through the door, picked up his smashed leg, and lifted it over the edge of the doorway. Turning over on his stomach, he began to ease himself off the seat and down the rope, moving with great deliberation.

"You come along when I give the word," he said.

I waited for what seemed like a long time before my father called to me. As I descended through the limber interlocking ends of the cedar branches, I felt the tail start to slide. The entire fuselage was tipping sharply. I yelled and let go. I dropped the last ten or twelve feet, hit the frozen snow and began rolling, expecting the plane to come crashing down on top of me.

It didn't, though; it remained hanging in the dense branches at an almost impossible angle. My father was sitting on the snow with his back against the broken wing. He was grinning through the sweat running down his face, trickling through his whiskers and off the end of his long twisted chin. I had never seen him in need of a shave before, and was surprised to notice how dark his beard looked under the glistening sweat.

"Bill, does it look to you like that Christly plane can be seen from the air?"

I looked up through the cedar branches, thick as a rain forest, and shook my head.

"Good," my father said. "Now take your hatchet over there to that clump of small trees and cut two poles about twelve foot long. Get them about three inches through at the base."

I did what he said.

"Them are perfect. Trim off the branches. Get them nice and close. Don't leave no spurs sticking out."

I did that too. Next my father told me to hack off about twenty feet of rope, which he proceeded to tie between the poles in an intricate crisscross pattern, making a strong travois. I didn't have to ask him who was going to pull this contraption. Here we go, I thought. Here we go again.

I tied my father into the travois, binding his wounded leg to the right pole. Then I got in between the front of the poles like an Indian pony. "Giddap, Wild Bill," he said. "Head due south."

I started walking south over the frozen snow. My father was very light but the terrain was so uneven that the travois jounced terribly. I was afraid his leg would start to bleed again. I kept looking back and asking whether he was all right.

"The best, Wild Bill," he said.

The trees were very thick. Time and again I had to detour out around impenetrable stands. After each detour my father gave new instructions. "Head for the dead tree over on that low knoll, Wild Bill. The one with the three sapsucker holes in the top. We keep working our way south and we'll hit the Yellow Branch of the Upper St. John. Once we get there you can skid the old man right down the ice like nobody's business."

In spots the crust was too thin to hold my weight and I crashed through into snow up to my waist. Once I had to break my way across an old open beaver meadow as long as the village Common, shoving the travois ahead of me over the crust. By the time I was halfway across my shirt, pants and hunting jacket were soaking wet from snow and sweat.

"Take it easy, Bill," my father said. "There ain't no great hurry. Henry's no doubt gotten hay up to the farm by now. We ain't in that much rush. Don't bust a gut."

Sopping wet, panting like a winded hunting dog, I looked up at the sky. "It's going to snow," I said. "We have to get out of here."

"If it snows we'll hole up in the brush like two red foxes and wait for it to stop. I've still got my matches. We'll be snug and warm until she blows over."

I could smell the snow coming. The air smelled slightly acrid, like the faint lingering scent of gunpowder in an old shotgun shell lying in a woods road. I shoved the travois forward several feet, and climbed up on the crust to try to go along on my hands and knees. Immediately I broke through.

A small frozen brook ran along the far edge of the beaver meadow. Its banks were choked with blowdowns, which I had to hack my way through with the hatchet.

"We'll go right on downstream," my father told me. "This runs into the Yellow Branch about a mile south of here."

The bank was high and steep. In order to get my father onto the ice I had to slide the travois down the bank and leave it leaning there like a ladder against the side of a building. I was going to turn it so my father wouldn't be upside down but he told me not to bother. As I jumped from the top of the bank to the ice he told me it was very refreshing to feel the blood running down into his head.

"Some of it seems to be running down your leg," I said as I eased the travois onto the ice. "We've got to do something about that tourniquet."

"Keep going, Bill. We won't jounce so much here on the ice. It'll stop bleeding. Keep going."

My father was looking straight up at the sky. I knew he was thinking about the snow too. It was coming. It could begin at any time. I got back in between the poles and started downstream fast. In places I could hear the water gurgling under my feet.

The swamp was a jungle on both sides. We were committed to the brook. The whole swamp had started to melt during the thaw of the past week. Water had seeped over the ice, then frozen again, creating several translucent layers of ice. In spots, particularly on the downstream side of bends, the ice was only an inch or two thick and I could see the dark water running beneath it.

"Stop," my father called. "Wait a minute, Wild Bill."

I was sure we were going to crash through momentarily, but my father was not concerned with the thickness of the ice. He had made a discovery. For some time he had been twisting his head over the side of the poles and commenting on the patterns and colors of the ice. Now he had found something really unusual that I had walked over without noticing. Trapped a few inches below us was a large brook trout. He was frozen solid into the ice, immobile as a crystalline trout in a glass paperweight.

"Let's cut him free," my father said. "Cut him out of there with your hatchet, Wild Bill. That's a fate I wouldn't wish on man or fish."

"He's dead," I said.

"No he ain't. They'll live for weeks like that."

"I don't trust this ice. I don't want to fool around with it. Even if we do get him out, there's no water to put him back into."

"We'll warm him up and release him down to the open water below the dam. Cut him free, Bill."

I shoved the travois back upstream several yards and began to chop a hole in the ice around the fish. The chips flew every which way. It took me quite a while to get him out without cutting into him or breaking through to the water. He was fourteen or fifteen inches long and still wearing his spawning colors. His stomach was a brilliant orange and the edgings on his fins were much whiter than the ice in which he was still encased. I knew the fish was a male because of the sharp upward hook on his bottom jaw. I presented him to my father, who tucked him inside his jacket against his shirt.

"Good luck," I said as we continued.

"Maybe I'll take him home to show Evangeline, Wild Bill. This would be a fine thing to show Evangeline."

"I'm glad we'll have something to show her," I said.

Ahead of us a big cedar had pulled out of the bank by its roots and toppled laterally across the brook. It took me at least twenty minutes to cut a passage through with the hatchet. I was sweating heavily again. It occurred to me that I was probably going to catch pneumonia but there wasn't anything I could do about it. We had to keep going. I was very worried about my father's leg, and above everything wanted to be out of that swamp when the snow hit. The wind was coming out of the northwest now. That was where all our big storms came from. When I got back into the poles I began to trot.

"Wild Bill's running," my father said. "Wild Bill don't want to get caught out in a Canadian thaw."

"You're right," I said, trotting faster.

When we finally emerged onto the frozen Yellow Branch I didn't dare stop to rest. I knew my father must be in agony from the jolting, but we were still at least ten miles from the big beaver dam where we had put in the canoe three days before.

The Yellow Branch had received its name from the distinctive color of the sand in its bed and banks. It was a deep slow winding tributary of the St. John, cutting through the very heart of the swamp. In places it opened up into backwaters covering many acres. Naked gray cedar stumps, some more than twenty feet tall, stuck up out of the ice like a petrified forest. There were very few live trees here. Even the red alders so prolific elsewhere in the swamp had trouble surviving in this diluvial wilderness.

In spots where the ice had frozen and thawed several times during the past two weeks it was rough as a washboard. I had to be careful to avoid spring holes where the river never froze completely over even in the coldest weather. They were identifiable only as slightly darker patches in the ice, which was uniformly quite dark from partial thawing, then freezing again. Around us the swamp shrieked in long splintering eerie cries, as rapidly freezing water does. The swamp was already illuminated by the peculiar radiance that touches everything just before it snows.

My breath was coming hard. My lungs ached. My arms ached from the weight of the travois. I kept telling myself I couldn't stop until we got down to the trees again. There was no shelter at all in the heart of the swamp, just those smooth naked cedar stumps, mockeries of trees. My head pounded and my vision was blurring. I was no longer sure that we were still on the river, which wound through those labyrinthine dead trees like a rabbit maze in a brush pile.

Some small live cedars began to appear along the banks. I was running in a slow stumble, slower than a fast walk. My arms were heavy as waterlogged limbs and my head throbbed steadily. It occurred to me that my father had not spoken a word since we had started down the Yellow Branch. That might have been an hour or three hours ago. I had no way of knowing.

I laid the poles down and turned to look at him. His eyes were closed. For the first time in four days he was sleeping, breathing quite evenly. Snow was collecting on his face and hair, on his red jacket and on the bad leg, which was stiff and cold and no longer bleeding. Behind us I could see my footprints and the two long wavy grooves left in the new snow by the travois poles. It had been snowing for some time.

"Dad. Wake up. Your leg's freezing."

My father opened his eyes. They were very blue through the snow on his long dark lashes. "Don't worry, Wild Bill, I ain't going to leave you alone here. Go on up ahead another two, three hundred yards. We'll make a camp. You done good, Bill. We're only a couple of miles from the dam. You done very good."

The snow was falling fast. The flakes were small and dry and hard to see. As we started down the river again I tried to guess what time it was. Maybe the middle of the afternoon. Maybe later. It was quite dark, so dark I didn't see the open running water ahead until it was nearly too late. Then I heard it before I saw it. I stopped short, swung around and yanked the travois back upriver toward shore. In the snowy twilight I made out a thick stand of big cedars. Here my father and I would wait out the storm for as long as it lasted.

"Bill," my father said as I started up the bank toward the trees. "Just a minute."

I stopped and looked back.

"Come here."

He handed me something cold. First I thought it was the last bottle of Seagram's. Then I felt a tremor run through it.

"Throw him back in the Christly water, Bill. I told you he'd come to."

I hurled the trout far downriver and waited for the splash, which when it came was muffled by the snow.

"I knowed he wasn't dead, Bill. I knowed we could bring him back to life."

"Well," I said, heading for the cedars, "maybe he'll grant us three wishes. But I doubt it."

My father laughed. "Wild Bill sounds more like his Uncle Henry Coville every day. What do we need to wish for? We've got everything we need right here. Let her blow, we'll be all right. We're still together, ain't we?"

In thinking about my father, I always try not to romanticize him. While he was certainly the most romantic man I have ever known, it would not be fair to him to simplify his personality by eulogizing him as such. He was also in many ways a driven if not exactly haunted man, whose ebullience, while authentic, must have been generated in part by desperation. He was heedless of his own safety and at times of mine. He was both supremely selfish and deeply empathetic, even with fish. A more vainglorious man never lived in Kingdom County, but he was full of awe and delight and humility in the presence of any wonder, and to him, as to me, the world was always a wonderful place. I do not believe that he shared many of the apparently psychic powers that characterize our family, but he had certain instincts that were still more remarkable, instincts most of our race lost thousands of years ago.

Often I have asked myself what I learned from him. To answer this question, I usually begin with the simple things, including many of the things he and I talked about during the twelve hours we spent holed up in the cedars that stormy night in 1932.

I learned how to fish and hunt, in that sequence. From the time I was two, we fished the small brook that flowed out of our maples into the apple orchard. He would hold his fly rod in one hand and my hand in the other and flip a small piece of worm on a number-ten hook into a pocket behind a stone or stump. He would jerk up his wrist to set the hook, then hand the rod to me so I could derrick out a bejeweled five-inch speckled trout. Soon he began handing me the rod to set the hook myself. By the time I was five I was a journeyman trout fisherman.

It is more difficult to shoot a bird on the wing than to catch a trout, and it is a particularly tricky business to shoot a marvelously camouflaged partridge in heavy cover, but by the time I was ten I was doing that too. I got my first deer a year later.

The one accomplishment my father tried without success to teach me was to play the fiddle. I wasn't tone deaf and loved to hear him play. The night he won the New England championship in Montpelier remains one of the most exciting in my life. But for some reason my fingers just wouldn't move the right way, and to his everlasting credit he realized this early on and stopped trying. "Wild Bill would have been one of the great violinists, Evangeline," he said many times with considerable pride. "If he'd ever learned how."

Then there were the things that I didn't know I had learned from him until years later, things that helped me to be a father and husband, lawyer and judge, which I learned laboriously and mastered imperfectly, as I might have learned to play the fiddle if he had forced me to keep trying. These things I believe he knew instinctively, and always had, as he had always known which way north was. The tolerance for variety in people. A sense of one's own worth, and by extension of everyone's. A sense of humor. Of wonder. Of priorities: we're still together, ain't we?

As I remember the closeness my father and I experienced while stormbound in the cedars, the big fire we kept going through the dark while the wind howled, the talk of hunting and fishing, the comfortable silences, the plans, I am also tempted to romanticize our relationship. That is harder not to do, because it was in fact as good as any relationship between any father and son I have ever known. He was somewhat condescending toward me sometimes. Sometimes in my more callow and ironical moments I was condescending toward him. By the time I was fourteen I was filtering most of my perceptions through a layer of irony, like the layer of hardwood charcoal through which good bourbon is filtered. My father was right, I was becoming more like Uncle Henry all the time. My father must have been aware of the irony of that sobriquet Wild Bill, which he used increasingly. Irony helped to solidify our relationship. It became an expression of affection and set the tone

273

of most of our communications. At its source was a strong mutual appreciation.

There are no men like my father in Kingdom County today. They have disappeared as irrevocably as the small family farms and the log drives and the big woods. Such men required room, both physically and spiritually, and even in Kingdom County that room is no longer available. They needed space in which to get away from people and towns and farms and highways, and other people needed space to get away from them since authentic characters are not the easiest persons to live with. To live in a world without them, though, while it is certainly easier, sometimes seems intolerable.

Dawn was still many hours away when my father began to talk about his plans for the future. I had built a lean-to deep in the cedars and cut a big pile of dead cedar for our fire. I wanted to dress his leg with fresh bandages from my long underwear but he told me that it would be better not to tamper with it. It was swollen badly, and he couldn't move it at all. It lay near the fire, steaming like a wet log. The wind screamed, driving snow all around us. It was a Canadian thaw all right, four feet of snow and a hell of a blow, but we were warm and snug, protected by the trees and our lean-to.

My father was making plans to go back into the whiskey business, and in grand style. He and Henry would get Rat drunk enough to repair the government plane, which they would then use to transport whiskey out of Canada to points all over New England. When they weren't smuggling whiskey they would fly the plane for their own recreation. "Wait until I swoop down on Warden when he's out on Memphremagog harassing innocent fishermen and poachers, Wild Bill. I wonder how he's accounting for himself down to the asylum."

"I wonder how he's accounting for us," I said. "What makes you think Mom is going to let you run whiskey again?"

"When she hears how good this trip went off she just won't have no other choice. I never took a sup, Bill. Not a single sup of whiskey passed Quebec Bill's lips. I knowed I could do it. I warn't even tempted."

"You better move your leg back from the fire. It's going to get too hot."

"Bill, do you know what I and Sweet Evangeline are going to do when I begin making money on them runs? I've been thinking about it all day. We're going to take us a trip."

"Another trip?"

"Yes, and not no little piss ant canoe trip to Magog, neither. We're going to outfit that plane and fly back up to Lake Athabasca, where old René went as a boy. That's real country up there. Wild country. From there we'll fly to Washington and Idaho and Montana and I'll show Evangeline where I used to work in the tall timber and on them great cattle ranches. Then we'll slip down along the continental divide and visit Yellow Rose in Texas. She'd like that, Yellow Rose would. She'd like to know how Henry is."

As my father talked on I dozed off. When I opened my eyes he was sleeping and mumbling in his sleep about his cross-country flight. I got up to pile more limbs on the fire. I poked at it with a limb, trying to push a partly burned smoking log further over onto the coals. Something smelled bad.

"Jesus Christ," I said out loud.

I grabbed my father's burning leg and jerked it out of the fire. He yelled and sat up. He yelled again, then passed out. I felt his boot, which had burned through on one side. His ankle and calf had been scorched too, I couldn't tell

275

how badly. I threw snow on the smoking flesh. It sizzled. I lifted my father up by the arms and held him against my chest. His head was dripping wet and very hot. He moaned. I had to do something, anything to alleviate that pain. I thought of the last bottle of Seagram's.

It was right there in his jacket pocket. Holding him close against me, I broke the seal and got off the cap. He moaned again and drew in his breath sharply.

"Dad," I said. "Wake up, Dad. You've got to drink some of this."

"Christ," my father said. "Did I pass out?"

"You went to sleep and burned your leg in the fire. Drink this."

He turned his head aside. "No," he said. "I don't need that. I promised Sweet Evangeline before we left. I can't feel nothing in that leg. I don't need no booze. Jesus, it's hot in here. Bill, put some snow on my head."

"I don't want you to take a chill, Dad."

"I won't take a chill. Put some snow on my head."

I propped my father against the back of the lean-to and went outside again. It had stopped snowing and the wind had died. In under the cedars the snow was not deep, but just outside the tight ring of trees in the tote road running down to the beaver dam the snow lay deep and blue under the clear sky. The moon was out, and quite low in the west. It must have been around five o'clock. At home my mother would be getting up to start chores.

I got some snow and applied it to my father's forehead with his handkerchief. He was burning up. I didn't feel right myself. I was shivering a little. I held my father in my arms with his head cradled on the inside of my shoulder. He slept again, fitfully, mumbling. I tried to keep his head cool with the handkerchief.

From off down the tote road a great horned owl screamed. Not long afterward a long wailing howl broke out. I started,

276

and so did my father. "That sounded like a wolf," he said. "I must have dreamt that. I dreamt I heard a wolf, Wild Bill."

"Dad, it's stopped snowing. I think we've got to try to move again. If we get a good jump we can be over the dam by dawn and home by early morning. We've got to get you to the doctor."

"Yes," my father said. "A dose of salts should be just the thing for that leg. We'll get Dr. Rupp to give me a Christly enema. No, Bill. We'll wait right here till dawn. Then you cut me a good supply of wood and go on out to the dam and up the hill. You couldn't never drag me up that hill through two or three foot of new snow without snowshoes. You get aholt of Henry and Rat and tell them where I be. They'll fetch me out on a toboggan."

"No," I said. "We aren't going to do it that way. You're coming with me."

My father laughed. "Wild Bill," he said, "you get wilder every day. I'm staying here with a warm fire. You go along. Go now if you want to get a jump on the day."

I had never in my life openly defied my father or mother, but there was no way in the world I was going to leave him there to pass out again and die of exposure.

"No," I shouted, pulling him closer to me. "No."

Suddenly there was a high piercing scream from quite nearby.

"Good Christ," my father said. "That sounded just like a painter. There ain't no painters around here no more."

It screamed again.

"That's no painter," my father said quietly. "Put out the fire."

I kicked snow onto the fire. When it was out I stuck the hatchet back in my belt and knelt by my father. "It's him, isn't it?" I said.

"You go back in the trees, Bill. Not too far. Leave the

hatchet with me. When you hear me holler get out on the tote road and start running. Run as fast as ever you run in your life. Don't stop till you're home."

"No," I said.

Loon laughter filled the night. It rose to a mad crescendo. Through some hideous trick of ventriloquism it was joined by a concert of wolf howls, panther screams, hooting, baying, bellowing. I picked my father up in my arms and began to run back through the trees into the swamp.

"LaChance!"

As I came out of the cedar stand into snow over my knees I could hear the crash of brush close behind me.

"LaChance!" Carcajou screamed.

15

FOR many years the next several hours were blank to me. Often I would dream that I was running with my father in my arms through an endless cedar swamp. Just as Carcajou started to bellow I would wake, terrified as a lost child. For months afterwards that is what I felt like, a bereft child alone in a swamp through which I searched with diminishing hope for a river that would lead me out. I ate, slept, went back to school in the fall, went fishing with Uncle Henry and walking with my mother. But I was only going through the motions. I had fallen into a terrible black despair.

Then it was spring again and I felt simultaneously better and guilty to be better. Then the guilt passed, and I could begin to think about my father and the trip again, with the exception of those blank hours. For twenty years my last memory of our flight through the swamp was Carcajou bellowing behind us as I ran through the deep light snow under the cedars with my wounded father in my arms.

Then I recalled lying in a high fever under quilts on the

kitchen woodbox with the starving cows bellowing steadily from the barn.

"They're welcoming us home, Wild Bill," my father said. But I knew he was not really there. I was having a fever dream.

I could hear Aunt Cordelia and my mother talking over that constant loud moaning from the barn, but each time I tried to force myself awake I went under again. I dreamed I was back struggling in the lake under the pulpwood. I heard shots, one after another at measured intervals. Perhaps Carcajou was laying siege to the farmhouse. If so, he would have his hands full with Cordelia.

I did not wake up until late afternoon. I was very weak. Aunt Cordelia was sitting by the woodbox. Except for the crackling stove it was very still. I noticed that some of my mother's seedlings in the windows had grown taller. Outside a snow drift combed up over the windowsill. In the afternoon light the snow was a deep blue. The silence bothered me. Then I remembered the cows. Uncle Henry must have finally gotten up with hay. I assumed that he and Rat and my mother were in the barn doing chores.

Aunt Cordelia put her hand on my forehead. Her fingers felt light and cool, desiccated as slices of dried apple. The woodshed door opened, and Cordelia withdrew her hand quickly.

My mother came into the kitchen. She was wearing her gray sweater and barn shawl. I started to get up to go to her, but she shook her head. I saw that she was crying. It was the first time in my life I had seen her cry. She wept silently, as her Indian grandmother might have, as she must have learned to weep years ago at the convent. She was leaning slightly forward and the tears fell directly from her eyes onto the wide dark planks of the kitchen floor, staining the planks darker where they hit in splotches as large as quarters. Then I noticed that she was holding my father's deer rifle at her side. She shook her head again. "They had suffered enough," she said.

It was twilight. My mother sat by the woodbox holding my hand while Cordelia made supper. The snowdrift over the window was purple. On top of the barn roof the wind had whipped up a strange configuration. Something about it disconcerted me.

"Jesus Christ," I said before I knew I was going to. "It's the snow owl."

Cordelia gave us tea and soup, which tasted delicious to me. Darkness fell. I got quite hot again, and my mother bathed my forehead as I had tried to cool my father's fever the night before. My arms still ached. Intermittently I had more fever dreams. In one of these the snow owl twisted his head around to reveal the shattered face of Carcajou. He swooped down off the barn and beat his huge white wings against the kitchen window, screaming *"LaChance, où êtes-vous, LaChance?"*

Sometime in the middle of the night the fever left for good. The kerosene lamp on the table was flickering low. Cordelia sat in her straight-backed chair by the stove, keeping up the fire. My mother was asleep with her head on the back of her chair.

I could not seem to think about my father, though I had not yet entered the depression that was to last a full year. That would begin a few hours later. I looked at my mother's face. In the lamplight it looked quite wan. I thought about the Jerseys, how she had loved taking care of them. When he first came to the farm my father had started some stone walls to keep them in, but of course he never got further than about ten feet with any of them. Later Rat made some beautiful stake and rider fences from cedar rails he had cut in the swamp. As the herd grew he could not

281

keep up with the need for fencing, and we would never afford barbed wire, so my mother would go to the pasture with the cows on summer days and sit reading or playing with me while they grazed. On those long hot days she taught me many things whose value I did not guess until long afterward.

I have said what I believe my father taught me. The effect of Cordelia's tendentious harangues is obvious. What I learned from my mother was subtler, and perhaps more important. There were the small things that have stayed with me always and that I took great pleasure in teaching Henry, like the English and French names of the common meadow and woods flowers, the birds and the trees, to all of which my mother was gently attuned. There were deeper qualities that I can appreciate without pretending to emulate. The patience to sit for hours on a rock near the brook while the cows wandered through the lower meadow. The endurance year in and year out, not only to put up with the rest of us but to enjoy us and to the extent that it was possible protect us from ourselves—and here I am thinking mainly of my father, whom she loved above anything or anyone in this world or the next, which despite my father's most violent abrogations she continued to believe in and ultimately returned to the convent to prepare for; and where, she believed as implicitly as I have ever believed anything, she would be reunited with her parents and grandparents, her stillborn daughters, and my father.

It was only through Quebec Bill Bonhomme that my mother permitted herself to establish any liaison with this world at all. She was fully her own woman, as strong-minded and independent as any I have ever known, including my wife, but it was toward God and heaven that she was oriented, and except as worldly things and events were important to my father they were not important to her. Even the herd was insignificant compared to the glory of God, and to her Quebec Bill Bonhomme was His chief glory—an opinion with which my father no doubt would have been in full concurrence had he been at all religious. If there has ever been a better example of Emerson's definition of wisdom as the ability to hold two contradictory ideas than my mother's love of God and my father, I haven't encountered it. Yet her faith was intensely private; she did not attempt to inculcate it in me or anyone else. She evidently felt that her belief was enough to guarantee our salvation.

My mother did not look old, but she no longer looked young either. I looked back at Cordelia. In the dim light she appeared incredibly old.

I said softly, "Aunt Cordelia, what happened to your father and brother?"

"Ah," she said. "You would know your birthright at last?"

With no other introduction she said, "In the summer of 1861 my Grandfather René made his grisly prediction on the day before my brother and father left Kingdom County with the First Vermont Militia. At the time I did not quite believe him, though after his disappearance I was less skeptical, and when I learned by telegram of William's death at Bull Run on the day my grandfather had appointed I had no doubt at all that Father also was going to die where and when René had foretold. I knew that there would be nothing I could do to prevent this tragedy, though when the time came I would try.

"You see, William, I was trying to preserve what I then perceived as a sort of civilization by attempting to interfere with fate as it was to realize itself on the village Common later that summer. For me, a girl of nineteen, Father represented all the culture I knew. He had lived for the sake of books and ideas and taught me all I then believed worth knowing. He had also loved both me and my brother as much as any father can love his children. As all Goodman-Bonhomme fathers have loved their children, accepting them as equals almost from the time of their birth. So when William died at Bull Run, Father apparently went mad. He refused to bury his son on what he considered foreign soil. He dressed the corpse in full military regalia, placed it in a flag-draped coffin in a wagon and started north for Kingdom County, driving night and day and changing teams every six or eight hours. He was dressed in uniform himself, a tall gaunt unshaven wild-eyed man who did not slow down for the blue streams of soldiers he met marching south, but stood in the death wagon whipping the horses savagely, laying about with his saber and addressing the soldiers as whores of Mars as he scattered them into the ditches. Orie Royer's father, then a sixteen-year-old private, saw him stop to change horses at a crossroads tavern north of Harrisburg. At first he did not recognize the crazed old colonel who leaped down from the wagon. 'Horses,' Father shouted to the tavern owner as he unharnessed the spent team. 'Rum.'

"By that time the wagon reeked so that no man in his right mind would have denied my father anything he demanded that would hasten him on his way. A captain approached and saluted. Father seized him and dragged him up to the coffin. He threw back the cover to expose the putrefying remains of my brother. 'See your end before you, Jezebel,' he roared, and forced the captain's head close down over the corpse. The captain promptly fainted, and when Granther Royer and several others ran up to revive him, Granther recognized Father. He did not recognize the body of William, which he said was black with flies and seething with worms, so that by the time Granther re-

284

covered from the shock and brought the captain to, Father was already whipping up his fresh team and sweeping the rear of the regiment out of his way, shouting hell-fire and damnation to them in the tradition of his namesake and grandfather, Calvin Matthews.

"No one was about to stop him. On a hot August day a newly formed regiment marched down the main street of a place called Poughkeepsie to the cheers of hundreds of proud citizens. At the south end of town they were met by an overpowering stench. It was followed closely by my father, coming over a hill half a mile away, already rising to his feet in the wagon and brandishing his saber. The troops hesitated. A man shouted that the rebs had broken through. Poughkeepsie's finest turned and raced without order back through the bunting-draped street, followed by the thundering wagon, distinguishable from an apparition out of the Book of Revelations only by the ineffable redolence of death that preceded and lingered behind it. Lingered behind it, William. Lingered behind it for generations.

"There were newspaper accounts of this singular homecoming. One relates how south of Albany my brother's corpse was jounced from the coffin and lay oozing over the road for two hours until Father discovered it was gone and returned to scrape it up. According to the same notice a company of men actually managed to stop the wagon near Troy, secure my father in a madhouse and bury the corpse in a nearby paupers' field. That night he broke out, dug up the coffin and carried it two miles through the woods to the home of a wealthy undertaker of Dutch descent. There he commandeered a team and an ornate rolling hearse with curtained glass windows. By morning he was in Vermont. Two days later, having driven steadily from Virginia except for the two or three hours he spent in the madhouse, he appeared at the south end of the Common, heralded by the scent of my brother's corpse and a hideous flock of soaring raptorial creatures unlike anything that had ever been seen in Kingdom County.

"Now pay close attention, William. You are about to learn some history. At the same time that Father was carrying my brother's body home, a certain Captain Greenwood of the Confederate Army was traveling north on a parallel route some hundreds of miles to the east in a British sailing vessel. It seems that this captain, a very bold young man, had been commissioned along with a scant dozen compatriots to slip through our coastal blockade and journey to Halifax. From Halifax they were to proceed across Nova Scotia and New Brunswick to southern Quebec, where their orders were to mount sudden raids on northern New England border towns. To rob banks, blow up railroad trestles and generally harry the population into believing that a sizable guerrilla force was at work. Their purpose was to divert Union troops back to the north. They had no way of knowing that Father was doing that job adequately himself.

"When he arrived in Quebec, Captain Greenwood picked Kingdom Common as his first target. It was the county seat, and apparently thriving, with eight mills and a railroad, and it was only about ten miles from the border. Memphremagog was closer but that was a larger town and might be more hazardous to attack. The Confederate band could not have known that the Common Bank was empty and that nearly every penny in the county had gone into the state war fund. Nor could they possibly have known on that afternoon in late August when they galloped into town, mistaking Father's library for the bank and riding their horses up the marble steps and straight through the tall carved walnut doors that had been left open for the breeze, that Father would be entering the Common from the opposite end.

"The librarian had been on her way to the door to see what could possibly smell so bad. She got out of the way just in time to avoid being trampled by the woods horses Captain Greenwood had purchased in Sherbrooke. He discovered his mistake as soon as he saw the thousands of books lining the paneled walls. He raised his hat to the terrified librarian, note that, William, whirled on his horse and led his men back through the door, cursing the Frenchman who had assured him that the brick building with the white pillars was too splendid to be anything but a bank. He started across the Common toward the courthouse. Perhaps he planned to burn it. Then he began to curse again, because Father was bearing down on him in the stolen hearse, twirling his saber around his head like a Tartar.

"I am certain it was not the captain's intention to kill or harm anyone. He was no Sherman, but a brave and handsome man performing what he perceived as his duty. But when he saw a bearded and insane old man in a uniform that was still blue enough to identify charging at him on top of that hurtling macabre conveyance for the dead, he had no choice other than to defend himself. 'Stop,' he shouted, raising his pistol. And at exactly the instant Captain Greenwood fired, I, who also had no choice but to defend my father despite my certain knowledge that my efforts would be futile, fired my grandfather's musket from the base of the statue of Ethan Allen, where I had been waiting all afternoon. Captain Greenwood fell from his horse. Father sat down on the seat of the hearse. His team galloped on up the Common and out the county road.

"I stayed on the Common only long enough to ascertain that Captain Greenwood was dead. His men had ridden off down the Memphremagog road, where some of them were captured later that afternoon, at about the same time that I arrived in our reeking dooryard to find my sister-in-law weeping over the coffin and my six-year-old nephew, your grandfather, William, sitting on the roof of the barn his father had built, flanked by a score of vultures and drinking from a bottle of rum he had found under the empty blood-soaked seat of the hearse."

"Empty?" I said. "What about your father? Calvin. Had he fallen out along the way?"

"Yes," Cordelia said, her voice very high now, almost keening. "Calvin. My father. Whom you so much resemble, William. What about him?"

Cordelia began to rock. In her moaning night voice she said, "He had disappeared. Oh yes, disappeared. No one ever saw him again. And that is not all, William. Now you must hear. Because there is more, and herein lies your birthright.

"I dug my brother's grave myself that afternoon as soon as I had fetched his drunken little boy away from his companions on the barn roof and put him to bed with his mother. I dug fast and hard, hurrying because of the stench. When the grave was as deep as I was tall I dragged the coffin to its edge. What I did next was unspeakable work. But I had to do it. I could not commit that body to our ground without making sure it was my brother's. It was dark by then. I got a lantern and a bar, and opened the coffin. Instantly I was sick. That is how bad the smell was. I lay on the ground and was sick in my brother's open grave. But I was strong and young and I must have been brave too because I had just killed a brave and handsome man, so I forced myself to hold up the lantern and look. I looked. I looked into that box that smelled like a charnel house. And when I saw that it was empty, strong and young and brave as I was, I fainted. Do you know now, William? Do you know now the nature of your birthright?"

I did not reply. Cordelia evidently did not expect me to, because almost immediately she fell asleep in her chair, her body still rocking slightly. She was breathing lightly and rapidly, as the very old and the very young do, and already muttering in French, Latin, Greek. Once she said, "Come off that roof instantly, young sir."

My mother had not awakened. It was very quiet. I was slept out. I lay awake thinking about Cordelia's story. Despite all I had heard and seen during the past week, it seemed incredible. I could not believe that it was my birthright to disappear.

My arms ached badly. I tried to remember what had happened after I started running through the swamp with my father. I could still feel his weight in my arms, his arm around my neck. I wanted to remember but couldn't. I felt like crying, but I couldn't do that either.

After a long time it began to get light. Very quietly I got up and went to the window. The snow in the dooryard was blue again. In the sunrise it turned pink, and the long range of the Green Mountains to the west turned from blue to pink in the rays of the rising sun.

Around the corner of the barn a man appeared, large and bulky in his sheep coat. He was bucking his way through snow up to his waist and pulling a pair of huge staggering horses behind him by main force. Hitched behind the horses was a long sledge piled high with hay, and on top of the hay sat a lean man in a blanket coat and slouch hat. His mouth was going fast.

One of the horses went down onto his knees. The big man lifted the horse to his feet. He took off his knitted cap and wiped his dripping forehead. The man on the load was still talking. I rapped on the window. The man in the sheep coat looked up and solemnly raised one big mittened hand, his face inscrutable as a Buddha's.

Cordelia was awake. Once again she had laid the spectres of her ancestors. "Who is it?" she said sharply.

I motioned for her to come and see for herself. I wasn't

crying. I didn't cry for many months. I could only stand at the window and stare out at Uncle Henry and Rat and the hay with the indefinable oppression of the heart that I would wake with and live with and go to sleep with for the next year.

After the big blizzard spring came very quickly. The snow began to melt the morning Uncle Henry and Rat brought up the hay. Under the hot May sun it went fast, dripping from the budded Canada plum by Cordelia's window, sliding off the spruces and firs in great thudding avalanches, cascading down from the barn roof onto Henry and Rat as they lugged the stiff carcasses of our herd out to the sledge in the dooryard. The snow melted into the gullies in the stony fields, into the brooks pouring down to rivers that flowed north to empty into the great lake. The spring birds that hadn't frozen came out of the woods. In a week all the snow was gone, though the snow owl remained on the barn roof.

Cordelia stopped eating and did not return to school. I didn't feel like eating but my mother made me. She seemed sad but not grief-stricken. Rat moped around the barn. Uncle Henry stayed on with us for a while. No one mentioned my father in my presence. It would have helped us to be able to talk about him, but that was simply not the way of our family, or of many hill families.

One morning at breakfast Rat looked up at me and declared that the sins of the fathers would be visited upon the children. He then went out to the barn, and that was the last we ever saw of him.

After a halfhearted search for him, I asked Cordelia whether children always inherited their fathers' sins. She hadn't eaten anything for more than a week but she was still strong and alert. "No, William," she replied, "that is priestcraft. The children, however, are determined to assume them. Yea, even unto the third and fourth generation.''

We were standing in the dooryard. It was another warm blue day, a good day to begin putting in the garden, but for the first time in fifteen years my mother was not going to have one. The farm no longer meant anything to her, or to any of us for that matter.

"Listen carefully, William," Aunt Cordelia said. "They are calling to me. Grampa René. Father. Brother William and his son. Your father is calling. This is not the rambling of an old woman but the truth as I have lived and taught it. They do not seem to be managing their affairs well.''

"Where are they?"

"I have no idea, but I must join them. I saw your son last night. He resembled my grandfather and your father. Rely upon his being troublesome. Your wife will be French. Teach her not to drop her *h*'s. Your mother never dropped an *h* in her life.''

"Where are you going, Aunt?"

"Anywhere. Nowhere. Keep up your Milton. Read *Paradise Lost* at least once a year. It is a metaphor for life, we have all been disinherited. You will read the *Aeneid* in Latin every third year. Prof Corbitt will assist you with any difficult lines. Once a decade is often enough for Homer but do not lose your Greek. If you have an opportunity to learn Hebrew, improve upon it. I should have devoted a summer to mastering that tongue. I do not need to tell you to read some Shakespeare daily.

"In matters of this world consult your Uncle Henry, not your mother. Her attachment to life was through your father. Never regard what is ordinary without perceiving in it the extraordinary. Remember 'Hamatreya.' You can't possess land, any more than you can possess another person. We dispossess ourselves through possessions.

"Your education has been provided for. You will leave Kingdom County for a time and then return, as my father did. The house will be here, waiting for you. I have arranged matters so it cannot be sold."

Cordelia walked across the dooryard to the ledge overlooking the wilderness. I followed her and we stood looking out across the vast green swamp. Cordelia began to quote from the Earthsong in Emerson's poem:

> Mine and yours;
> Mine, not yours.
> Earth endures.

Cordelia bent over and pulled up the rotten planks over the crevasse my father had opened in the ledge.

"I loved a man once, William," she said. "A fine valiant man whom I killed on the Common before I ever saw his face."

She stepped into the hole in the rock and disappeared. A fast shadow passed over the ledge. I looked up to see the snow owl flying rapidly north over the swamp. When I looked down again the opening in the ledge had closed. Once again the dark rock was laved by a trickle of cold spring water.

Later that spring Uncle Henry rented a house for my mother and me in the Common. It had indoor plumbing and electricity and the windows didn't leak. My mother could walk to church and to the store. The Academy was only two blocks away. Uncle Henry bought a Ford and resumed running whiskey. By the time the Eighteenth Amendment was repealed he had saved enough to carry us through until I graduated from high school.

I became intensely involved in sports and in my studies.

It seemed to me that my life had been divided into two distinct epochs: before the spring of 1932, and after it. Sometimes we talked about my father, but never for very long. Later, when I read Proust, I understood why Swann's poor old father could never think for very long at one time about his deceased wife. And for years I had no remembrance at all of the most important event in my own past.

My depression ended as suddenly as it had begun. One morning in May of 1933 I woke up and it was gone, though I still could not remember what had happened back in the swamp after I had started running. My mother continued to act abstracted, as Cordelia had predicted she would.

When I wasn't in school or reading or playing ball I was with Uncle Henry. He came to all my ball games and throughout my high school years we hunted and fished together several times a week, as we would for most of the next forty years. When I graduated from the Academy and my mother returned to the convent in Montreal he kept the house in the Common so that I would have a place to come home to while I was in college.

Somehow Cordelia had established a trust fund that paid for my undergraduate education. There was enough money left in the fund to finance a law degree, which I took partly for that reason, though I've never regretted my profession, except perhaps briefly when I lost my judgeship.

I've never regretted coming home again either. I discovered that it is after all possible to do that in some instances, and if I gravitated back to Kingdom County in 1945 more or less the way I gravitated into law school, coming home was what I was consciously doing when my wife and I moved back up to the farm in 1950.

It was spring once again. My law practice was picking up, and we had been able to afford some basic structural repairs on the farmhouse. We weren't using the barn, which had continued to buckle out in back, but we kept a cow and some hogs in the connecting ell. I intended to cut all our firewood, and my wife was going to raise a big garden in my mother's old plot between the Canada plum tree and the granite outcropping where Cordelia had disappeared nearly twenty years before.

It was a sunny day a week or so after the snow had gone. The plum tree was budding out and Henry, who was just two, was sitting in its low crotch watching us plant peas. Even then he had an intense serious expression, and spent long periods of time apparently just thinking. When we straightened up to stretch and look around, the Green and White Mountains looked close enough to hit with birdshot. I thought that this was the kind of day my father would have spent trout fishing, as Uncle Henry and I had planned to spend the afternoon.

Shortly before noon my wife went inside to get lunch. I planted a last row and stood up, pressing the heels of my hands against the ache in the small of my back. I looked down along the one hundred miles of parallel mountain ranges. When I looked back at the plum tree Henry was gone.

I went into the house and asked my wife if he had come inside with her. She said he had been sitting in the tree when she left the garden. I ran back out to the dooryard and called his name. He didn't answer.

There weren't many places to go on our hilltop. The barn was off limits, but I went through the stables and the hayloft calling for him anyway. He wasn't there. He wasn't in the root cellar. I ran partway down the lane through the stumps of the old maple orchard, growing up to brush now. It was muddy enough so I would have seen his footprints if he'd been there. There weren't any tracks.

Shouting Henry's name, I ran back up to the outcropping overlooking the swamp. My wife was standing beside me and sobbing. I had told her about the disappearances in my family, and now I tried to reassure her that no Bonhomme child had ever disappeared. But she was getting hysterical, and I was close to panicking myself. I hadn't been so frightened since 1932.

I was certain that Henry had wandered down the back side of the hill toward the swamp. I could see Uncle Henry's car coming up the road so I started off down the path toward the river. In traces of old snow under the shade of the firs I could make out his small tracks. I kept shouting his name as I plunged through the trees and brush. I thought I might find him on the new beaver dam across the river but he wasn't there. When I stopped to get my breath the only noise was the water spilling out around the edges of the dam. Then from downriver a loon laughed.

I started across the dam toward the cedar swamp, where I picked up Henry's tracks in the snow almost immediately. I called for him and the loon laughed back. Henry's tracks went straight back away from the river. He was heading due north, up into the heart of the swamp.

The tote road was now completely grown over, but otherwise the swamp was the same as in 1932 or 1796. In open glades between the cedars where the snow had melted I had trouble locating Henry's tracks. I didn't see how a two-year-old could have walked so far in such a short time. Half an hour couldn't have gone by since I had looked up in the plum tree and realized that he was missing.

Near a tangle of red raspberry bushes and windfalls I lost his trail altogether. I backtracked frantically. My own footprints were hopelessly mixed up with Henry's. I returned to the berry patch, which must have covered ten acres. On two sides were deep open backwaters. Repeatedly I called Henry's name. I began running up and down along the edge of the raspberries as though I were the one who was lost. I plunged into the thorns several yards. I fell over a rotten stump and lay gasping and sobbing in the wet moss.

Someone was helping me up. "Take it easy," Uncle Henry said. "We'll find him shortly."

Like my father, Uncle Henry could track anything anywhere. We returned to where I remembered last seeing my son's prints, and Uncle Henry quickly picked up the track again. It headed northeast, toward the spot where my father and I had camped in the snowstorm. We followed it for another quarter of a mile or so, and then what I thought wasn't possible happened. Uncle Henry lost the track. He circled, backtracked, circled again, finding nothing. We went back to the last track. Henry had been crossing a small opening between two thick stands of cedars. There was still about a foot of frozen snow in the clearing, which just revealed the faint heel prints of Henry's small boots. Halfway across the clearing the tracks stopped, as the tracks of old Ned the counterfeiter had stopped in the fresh snow in the swamp two decades before. Uncle Henry got down on his hands and knees. He shook his head.

I had heard or read somewhere that sometimes lost children are frightened by the shouts of searchers; that they huddle up under a tree in a catatonic state and let rescuers pass within a few feet of them, remaining as rigid and unnoticed as a small wild animal. Nevertheless I continued to call for my son. I was close to distraction again. I had never missed my father more than now. He would have been able to walk directly to wherever Henry was wandering.

Uncle Henry was plainly worried, though he never panicked and probably kept me from totally panicking. He told me to make a circuit out to the northeast while he swung northwest. He reminded me to move slowly and watch for Henry under the cedars and blowdowns.

I started out. I was very hoarse, but I kept calling. When I came to the St. John I followed the north bank for a ways, then cut back into the trees along a narrow game trail. Cedar limbs grow very close to the ground. I lifted up the branches of the larger trees to make sure he wasn't sitting back in under them. Where there was snow there were no footprints, only the tracks of wildcats and deer and bear. Once I jumped a moose that crashed back through the brush and into the river. Without realizing it I had gotten turned around and come back to the St. John. I was weeping, panting, bargaining desperately with the God I didn't believe in.

Late in the afternoon I met Uncle Henry back in the clearing where the tracks had stopped. His face was very grave. I knew he hadn't found anything. Henry had disappeared as inexplicably as all the others. I thought of the question Cordelia asked me about my birthright. It was inconceivable to me that my birthright was to witness the disappearance of our son. I thought about my wife, alone on the hilltop and going crazy with uncertainty. I had to get back to her and get up a search party before dark.

Uncle Henry said he would stay and continue to look while I went back to the farm. I started running again. I ran through the trees, jumped muskrat runs, passed the raspberry thicket, the canes blood red in the slant sun, and came out near the beaver dam, where I discovered Henry asleep. He was wrapped in a torn and faded hunting jacket and propped against the dead stump of a tall cedar.

I picked him up and started across the dam. He did not wake up. I held him close to my chest, as I once held my father. The rough wool of the jacket smelled like woodsmoke and tobacco. For the first time in eighteen years I remembered my father's features clearly.

I ran up the hill toward home as our voyageur ancestors had run through the original wilderness, frantically, fleeing time. For some reason I felt that I had to be in the dooryard by sunset. Fleetingly I thought of other, earlier voyagers. Of Odysseus, to whom Cordelia had compared my father, yearning homeward toward his wife and son. Of Aeneas, carrying his old father away from their home on his back. Of Daedalus, watching helplessly as his son soared into the sunlight.

I ran faster, inhaling the redolence of smoke and tobacco, thinking again of my father, no longer sure whether I was carrying my father or my son. I came over the crest of the hill into the freshly planted garden and thrust Henry into my wife's arms just as the sun went behind the mountains. My head was spinning. The garden and hilltop were spinning. Time was spinning backward on its axis, and once again I was fleeing through the swamp with my father in my arms, his jacket pressed close against my face and Carcajou howling close behind us.

16

A S I ran through the deep snow with my father in my
arms Carcajou's laughter seemed to be everywhere.
Wave upon wave of laughter rolled out into the darkness
before the dawn, reverberating on the cold air, filling the
cedar swamp with a palpable terror that seemed emblematic of the wilderness itself.

Anything would be better than letting Carcajou drive
us deeper into that place of deaths and disappearances. I
veered to my left, running with my back to the North Star
in an attempt to strike the tote road. Branches dumped
snow down my neck and lashed my face. I didn't care. I
bulled through a dense stand of cedars, holding my father
to one side to protect him from the whipping branches.

"Put me down," he said. "Put me down. He don't
want you."

As we came out into the raspberry clearing near where
I would lose Henry's tracks eighteen years later my father
passed out again. His head flopped loosely on my shoulder.
In the starlight his long fox's face looked old. Cradling

him against me like a baby, the scent of tobacco and wood-smoke strong in my flaring nostrils, I ran.

I knew that the tote road was some distance south of the far edge of the raspberry clearing. In order to reach the road I would first have to circumvent that immense thicket, through which Carcajou now came crashing, shouting in a strange harsh language. I ran between the thicket and the woods with my heart pounding in my ears.

My father said something I didn't catch. I didn't see how Carcajou could move two feet through those raspberry thorns. He was still shouting guttural deep phrases. "Indian," my father said.

In a different voice Carcajou yelled the words "heathens," "abomination," "hell-fire." "Sinners," he roared, "you are in the hands of an angry god."

Indian words. Then that terrifying illusion of many voices shouting simultaneously: a fusillade of Indian, English, French.

"Put me down, Wild Bill."

I ran faster.

"Close ranks," Carcajou shouted. "Don't let them rebs break through."

We seemed to be outdistancing him. I had my second wind and with it the confidence that I could reach the tote road before he did. Once I was on the road nothing was going to overtake me.

Just as I started into the woods between the raspberries and the road I stumbled to my knees. I held onto my father but my foot was caught in a brush pile under the snow. I struggled to pull it out. Carcajou was bearing down on us and baying like a pack of werewolves.

My father didn't realize what had happened. He thought I couldn't carry him any further, that I was floundering under his weight. "For Christ's sake put me down," he shouted.

Close behind us I could see Carcajou thrashing through the briers. I set my father on the snow and began hacking at the brush around my foot with the hatchet.

"LaChance," Carcajou bellowed, "you are a dead man."

As my foot came loose he burst out of the thicket only a few yards away. His clothes had been torn completely off by the thorns. He was the most horrifying sight I have ever seen. I froze in terror. Then I remembered the hatchet.

Carcajou began to scream as I brought back my arm. It was a long bloodthirsty scream of anger, the scream before the kill, indistinguishable from the roar of agony when the hatchet struck his head. I saw a chunk of his head fly out and land in the snow. He fell back into the thicket, where he continued to thrash after the screaming stopped.

I knelt by my father and put my arm around his shoulders. It was very still again. The thrashing in the brush had subsided. Most of the stars had disappeared. It was beginning to get light.

"You got him," my father said. "This time you really got him, Wild Bill."

I slid my hand under his knees to pick him up. Then I drew it back out again. It was warm and wet. A dark stain was spreading out over the snow under his right leg.

I took off my jacket and began wrapping it around my father's leg. "You got him all right," he said.

He reached inside his jacket pocket and pulled out the last whiskey bottle. He looked at the bottle in the thin early light, and then he tossed it into the raspberry bushes.

I picked him up and headed into the trees. By the time I hit the tote road the jacket wrapped around his leg was wet against my arm and chest. My father was unconscious with his head on my shoulder. I took a deep breath and began running down the trace toward the beaver dam. I tried to avoid the single set of large tracks heading my way, as I later saw children trying not to step on sidewalk cracks in the Common.

I stopped to breathe under the cedar tree where years later I would find Henry. The river was open on both sides of the beaver dam. Upriver over the dark water and white trees the dawn sky was as red as the vivid drops of blood behind me in the tote road. Once my father and Uncle Henry and I had tracked a deer that bled in the snow for miles. A strong animal or a strong man could lose a lot of blood before giving up. Maybe I could still get up the hill to the farm in time.

As I stepped onto the dam and started across, my father stirred. He opened his eyes and looked at the red sky. "Ain't that a wonderful sight, Wild Bill?" he said in his strong, slightly rasping voice.

Laughter burst out from behind us. I whirled around and looked up at Carcajou, standing under the cedar tree and laughing. Large patches of the thick white pelt that covered his body were matted dark with blood. Part of the splintered end of the pike pole still protruded out of his left shoulder. The entire right side of his face was encrusted with blood. There were three holes in his upper chest from the bullets my father had fired into him through the windshield of the Buick. His nose was mashed flat against his face. I could see his skull shining through the missing part of the upper left side of his head. In his left hand he held the hatchet awkwardly. In the other was the whiskey bottle. Without taking his eye off us he poured the last of the whiskey down his throat, then dropped the bottle in the snow at his feet and transferred the hatchet to his good hand.

"*Bonjour, petit LaChance*," he said pleasantly.

"Set me down, Bill."

I was about halfway across the dam, standing in snow up to my waist. My father's leg was bleeding steadily onto the snow. Again I thought of the bleeding deer we had followed. I was transfixed by the dripping blood, the hush of the water seeping out around the edges of the dam, the horror of Carcajou, watching us with his amused keen blue eye.

I tensed my muscles to make one last run for it. Carcajou anticipated what I intended to do. He took a step and raised the hatchet.

"William!"

Carcajou lifted his head. The voice had come from the far side of the dam. I half turned, holding tightly to my father. Standing on snowshoes on a knoll just above the dam, holding René Bonhomme's musket leveled straight across my head at Carcajou, was Aunt Cordelia.

"You ain't changed much," Carcajou said past me to Cordelia.

"No one ever does," she said, her voice harsh and steady. "Put down that tomahawk."

Carcajou began to laugh. He laughed like a loon, bayed like a wolf, roared and crowed and bellowed like a hundred demons. Cordelia held the musket steady. I noticed that the side hammer was cocked back.

Suddenly Carcajou was quiet. Very slowly, he brought the hatchet up behind his great ruined head. "William," Cordelia said sharply. "William Goodman."

Carcajou drew back his arm.

The musket snapped, not loud, and Cordelia was standing in a haze of smoke. Carcajou fell off the bank into the river. His long hair snagged on the dam, and his heavy white body began to twist from side to side in the slow tug of the current. Then before my eyes he vanished.

"William," Cordelia said, her voice harsh on the cold morning air. "We will go home now."

My father's weight seemed to have doubled. I didn't know how I could carry him up the hill. My arms ached as though I were holding generations of my ancestors, but when I looked down I realized that they were empty.

"Come," Cordelia said.

The sun was rising, glinting off René's musket, shining on the snow, illuminating the swamp, Kingdom County, Vermont and Quebec. Downriver a loon hooted. Its long wild call floated over the water and trees and snow as I stood with empty arms on the edge of my youth in a place wheeling sunward, full of terror, full of wonder.

Disappearances

was set on the Linotron 202 in Bembo, a design based on the types used by Venetian scholar-publisher Aldus Manutius in the printing of *De Aetna*, written by Pietro Bembo and published in 1495. The original characters were cut in 1490 by Francesco Griffo who, at Aldus's request, later cut the first italic types. Originally adapted by the English Monotype Company, Bembo is now widely available and highly regarded. It remains one of the most elegant, readable, and widely used of all book faces.

Composed by Crane Typesetting, Barnstable, Massachusetts. Printed and bound by Haddon Craftsmen, Scranton, Pennsylvania. Designed by David Gray.

Nonpareil Books

All *Nonpareils* are printed on acid-free paper that will not yellow or deteriorate with age. All are bound in signatures, usually sewn, that will not fall out or disintegrate. They are permanent softcover books, designed for use and intended to last for as long as they are read.

David R. Godine, Publisher
*300 Massachusetts Avenue
Boston, Massachusetts 02115*